D1291497

NIELSEN'S CHILDREN

by
James Brady

G. P. PUTNAM'S SONS ● NEW YORK

Copyright © 1978 by James Brady

All rights reserved. This book, or parts thereof, must not
be reproduced in any form without permission. Published
simultaneously in Canada by Longman Canada Limited,
Toronto.

SBN: 399-12165-X
Library of Congress Cataloging in Publication Data

Brady, James, 1928–
   Nielsen's children.

   I. Title.
PZ4.B81213Ni   1978   [PS3552.R243]   813.'.5'4   78-7058

PRINTED IN THE UNITED STATES OF AMERICA

For Fiona and Susan

PROLOGUE

"In television," Kate Sinclair was saying, "there are no villains. No heroes either."

"No?" Chester Albany asked.

She shook her head.

"No, there are only the ratings."

BOOK ONE

KATE SINCLAIR

1

On the east side of Manhattan a brief and elegant street called Beekman Place is confronted abruptly at its southern end by the twin towers of a brown-metal, tinted glass apartment building. A decade ago, when the building was being put up, the philanthropist Mary Devereaux waved her delicate hands and warned the neighborhood would surely go down. "To hear Mary talk," said one of her friends, "you'd think they were bringing in addicts and welfare families."

Instead, being resilient, the neighborhood remained much as it was and the new building, which they named UN Plaza, crisply functional and magnificently sited, sold off its cooperative apartments, rented its suites. Truman Capote moved in, Gloria Vanderbilt, Katharine Graham, Gordon Parks, others of influence, of talent, of wealth. Mrs. Devereaux herself, tiring of the endless struggle to maintain her little jewel box of a townhouse and of coping with clubwomen on house tours, fatigued by ancient pipes and wiring , reluctantly abandoned Beekman Place and the servant shortage, smiled gallant tribute to epochs past, and purchased a flat in one of the two towers. Along with the flat came a view of the river, of Long Island City's warehouses and power plants, of four towering smokestacks, of the huge neon Pepsi-Cola sign on the far bank, and even of slight, endangered Beekman Place. Several floors below, with a facsimile view, lived Kate Sinclair.

Kate Sinclair was the "eighth most-admired woman in the world." The *Ladies' Home Journal* had just said so. She had been ranked behind Rose Kennedy and the Queen of England and just ahead of Indira Gandhi and Pat Nixon (both demoted for political reasons). Kate did not take the ranking very seriously but she understood that such exercises did no harm and

11

might even, in her profession, be beneficial. And in her profession one took whatever edge was offered. At this particular moment, however, Kate Sinclair was not thinking about the *Ladies' Home Journal* or competitive advantages.

It was a Friday morning in January and Kate lay spread-eagled on the Aubusson carpet of her bedroom, clad only in a damp sheen too energetic to be described as perspiration. The body that glistened under the sweat of morning calisthenics was taut and well formed, responsive to muscular commands and lithe, well coordinated, the body of a near-athlete. Two television sets were tuned to the "Today" show and "Good Morning America." There was no need for a third set in Kate Sinclair's bedroom: "Captain Kangaroo" held no charms for her. Hard by her outstretched right hand was last evening's *New York Post,* rumpled by reading, a page or a story torn out for later reference. Kate's day had begun, as most days did, an hour earlier with a rap on her bedroom door and the entrance of a large breakfast tray supported by a large woman.

"Missus, it's Friday and it's seven o'clock and the god-damned *New York Times* ain't here again."

"Shit," said Kate Sinclair, pulling herself up into a sitting position to accept the tray.

"You oughtn't swear so much either," the large woman warned, "'cause one day you'll forget and do it on the job and the bosses will have your ass."

"Shit," Kate Sinclair responded.

The rawboned, red-knuckled Irishwoman named Mary Costello paid no attention but went to the windows to pull back the heavy, lined silk draperies. It was a cold morning with ice floes in the river and soot coming from the tall smokestacks of Queens. Kate ignored the view, confident New York could get its act together without her help, concentrating instead on pouring and then taking the first sip of black coffee.

"If the *Times* ain't come yet I'll send the doorman," Mary announced, mumbling as she left the room, "if the son of a bitch is sober."

"Shit," Kate Sinclair said for the third time, more gently after the coffee.

Fifteen minutes later, the *Times* having arrived and been skimmed, a cup of yogurt, a Mackintosh apple and the coffee

12

inside her, Kate Sinclair got out of bed, stripped off her silk nightgown in a single, practiced move, and dropped to the floor for the half-hour's hard labor intended to work off breakfast. As she began with the usual fifty situps, she alternately watched and listened to NBC and ABC, and their accounts of the world's morning.

She was thirty-five years old and looked five years younger except, perhaps, at the corners of the eyes where the years can be counted as accurately as with the concentric rings of certain trees. If Hollywood were casting a movie about Kate Sinclair (the possibility had already been discussed at several studios) they might think in terms of Anne Bancroft or Faye Dunaway or, perhaps, if the English accent could somehow be finessed, Vanessa Redgrave. She had been married once, divorced, and had a fifteen-year-old sister, Shaun, in a very good, and very expensive, boarding school in Vermont. Kate loved her sister very much and the girl was reasonably fond of Kate, but there were the usual communications difficulties and Kate had fallen into the habit of having her secretary write the weekly letter to Shaun which Kate would copyread and then, slightly ashamed, would sign. In her defense, Kate dutifully read Shaun's replies herself and did not shift *that* burden to the secretary.

As she exercised, subconsciously noting with pleasure the flat belly below the lean ribcage and the total absence of cellulite on her thighs and buttocks, Kate permitted herself to think about sex. Women emerge from the chrysalis, spread fragile wings and fly, at different ages. Some, while still in their teens, shed braces and knee socks and instantly are women. With others, growing up occurs during first love, first marriage, first divorce. With an unhappy few, it never happens. And although Kate Sinclair did not realize it, and would have been angered at the suggestion, this miraculous blossoming had not yet been experienced by the "eighth most admired woman in the world." She had been married, had given birth, and had still not achieved her full growth as a woman. This was not because she was retarded or odd or disinterested or lazy. It was because her marriage had failed when she was very young and her baby, the only child she had ever borne, might ever bear, had died. Crib death, they said. How neat a

13

phrase to catalogue tragedy, loss, trauma, guilt. The marriage had been eroding already, not her fault. Then the boy, blue-eyed, pudgy, gurgling, healthy, had died in his sleep. Not her fault, either, she knew. But irrationally she took the blame, carrying it like some great weight, a weight she would never be able to put down. A year later her mother had died, an event of equal stupidity, trying to give birth at the age of forty-two. Kate had taken Shaun, her infant sister, as a surrogate child. Her father was helpless, devastated. Her own child dead, her mother too, her marriage wrecked, all in one year, she could with justification have fallen apart as her father did. Instead, she transferred love to Shaun, wiped away the tears, and set out to rebuild a life from the ruins. No wonder she had not achieved full and balanced growth. What chance had she? So much of her was drained away just in a struggle to survive and then, later, when grief had numbed, in the new struggle to succeed. No, Kate Sinclair was not odd or disinterested or frigid. It was simply that for the past fifteen years she had had other things on her mind.

She enjoyed sex. But for a long time it had been somewhere well down the order of her priorities, below sanity, below happiness, below survival. She understood that sex was important but it was not everything. And in these past few years, especially since the marriage ended and her career had seriously begun, sex was not all that simply attained. Not if you were as recognizable as she was. She shrugged, deliberately halted her musings about sex before becoming aroused, and turned her thoughts instead to that evening's show. Still sweating, she strode into the bathroom.

Mary Costello was shouting something now, but Kate was in the shower, wincing under the tattoo of the heavy, pulsating water, at first shielding her breasts and then letting them be punished, thinking for the thousandth time how fortunate she was that they were small and hadn't sagged, then shielding them again as the nipples stung under the weight of the water. Of course Tom Rees and Ivo Pitanguy were out there, if you needed them, always ready to do a little nip and a tuck. How nice not to need them.

"Missus," Mary was saying, shouting actually, in what for her was a normal tone, "will you be wanting me tonight? Will

14

you want a meal or will someone feed you? I hope so. There's a meeting and I hate to miss a meeting."

She held out a thick, floor-length terry robe and Kate wrapped herself in it. No, no need for dinner. The limousine would take her directly from work to the dinner party.

"That's good," Mary said, "the comrades hate for me to miss a meeting."

Kate nodded. She knew all about Mary's meetings. She left the steamed-up bathroom and then, not ready to dress, she walked through the apartment, acknowledging for the first time the cold gray morning outside. New York! All around her. All below. She stopped at Shaun's room and paused there, looking in. A stranger's room, a child's room, gingham and white furniture and bright prints and dolls and a second teddy bear, not the one she took to school, the one she slept with, not Nubar, but bear number two, never named, intermittently loved, but still, welcome in her room. Fifteen now, my God, sixteen soon. Kate Sinclair breathed deeply, remembering the last time she had seen Shaun, the last visit her sister had made home. When they had fought. Bitterly. It was all so unfair. The girl had started it.

"I know it's a *bore* coming up to school," Shaun had said, a nasty edge to her voice.

"I didn't say it was a bore. I said I simply can't come up that particular weekend."

"It's the only weekend that matters."

Kate ignored the sulky tone. She must be patient, she must understand Shaun was still a child.

"And it happens to be a weekend when I'm working. It's part of my job. I have to be there. There's no one else can do it."

Shaun placed her fists on her blue-jeaned hips.

"Indispensable, that's the word, isn't it? There's no one else can do it except you."

"Shaun," Kate said, striving to avoid confrontation, to make her sister understand, "I didn't mean it that way. But this new job, well, they're paying me all this money and I have responsibilities to them. I just can't take the money and run. You see that, don't you? That I . . ."

Shaun shook her head.

15

"*Money!* Is that all you ever think about? Don't you care that everyone else will have *someone* at school? That I'll be the only one who . . ."

Kate Sinclair's voice went cold.

"The others have husbands or wives. I'm alone. Or they don't have jobs like mine. They have weekends that are free, weekends when they can go to parties or rest or · . . ." she paused . . . "visit their daughters' schools."

The girl, sensing the coldness, did not say anything.

Dammit, Kate thought, it's so unfair. Why should I have to defend myself? Doesn't she understand? Can't she put herself in my place? Doesn't she know it's *my* weekends, *my* work that pays for her school and her jeans and her teddy bear and every other damn thing that . , .

Shaun broke the angry silence.

"It's time for my train," she said. "Don't bother coming to Grand Central. I know the way."

Kate decided to try once more. With a child you didn't give up this easily, you didn't indulge yourself in tantrums or sulky underlips or declarations that you too knew the way to Grand Central. Alone.

"Shaun . . ." she said, dragging out the one-syllable of her sister's name.

"Yes?" Still sulky, still resentful.

"How do you get there?"

The girl's eyes widened. She forgot, for the instant, that she was annoyed at her sister.

"Get *where?*" she asked.

Kate smiled.

"To Grand Central, of course."

They both laughed after that, not a really full-blown laugh, but better than what had gone before.

An hour later the girl had left the apartment and Kate Sinclair was again alone, mingled guilt and frustration etching her heart, knowing she should be closer to Shaun yet aware of her commitments to her career, to a profession as jealously demanding as was her sister. If only Shaun were older, more mature, more charitable. I want to do the right thing, Kate thought. Both to Shaun and to the job.

Angrily, she pushed aside these painful, wounding recol-

16

lections, hurriedly left Shaun's room, and went into her bedroom to dress for the day's work.

"Will it snow?" she asked.

There was no one there to reply but she knew that in another moment NBC would provide the answer. She let the robe, heavier still now with moisture from her body, fall to the floor. Well, if it doesn't rain or snow, I'll wear suede. It was a bitch the way good suede spotted in the rain. And she was damned if she'd wear that cheap ultrasuede Halston was always promoting. He was a dear, Halston was, so good at a dinner party. But that didn't mean she had to wear ultrasuede.

Dressed, she walked through the rooms again, enjoying the sweep of the place, the look of the furniture, the good pictures, the objects, every one of which she knew the cost. To the dollar. Well, why not? She'd worked for it, the view of the river, the neighbors on Beekman Place, the suede skirt and the silk blouse in a Zumsteg print, the Roger Vivier boots, the good Miró and the better Braque, the table that could, and frequently did, seat twenty-four in comfort. She'd earned them all. No father, no husband, no bonded lover to thank. Her hand rested lightly atop a small French table. The texture of the wood, so smooth, almost malleable, gave the impression you could sink fingertips into it as with clay . . . tables like this were not simply bought: they were crafted, rubbed and waxed for 200 years, and then delivered to your door at 670 East 49th Street. Mary interrupted the litany of her possessions, the sensuous delight of her satisfaction.

"I might sleep over in Brooklyn if the meeting runs late," she said, not asking permission but stating a fact.

Kate laughed.

"Just don't bring the anarchists back with you."

Mary shook her head in annoyance and then, grinning broadly, disappeared in the direction of the kitchen. She's good for me, Kate thought, she reminds me who I am.

Who Kate Sinclair was, was the anchorwoman of the evening news for one of the four great television networks. She had been in the job for just four weeks but the first overnight Nielsen ratings, from the key markets of New York and Los Angeles, were more than promising. Nielsen gave her five

17

share points higher than the same show had attracted a year earlier. If the trend were national in scope and continued over a year, five share points would calculate out roughly to five million dollars in additional advertising revenues for the network. Five share points would easily pay for this apartment, for that table, for that Braque. And for the limo that would now be waiting at the door to whisk her across New York to the studio and the morning story conference.

In the car, headed west on 49th Street, sunk deep in the pearl-gray back seat, Kate thought about this first, tumultuous month in her new job, and about the coming weekend, two entire days without a camera or a microphone or a director or autograph hounds or a television critic. Without Bobby Klaus, nervously chewing Kleenex. Without Chester Albany and that bulldog look she just knew would eventually be trouble. A month in the job and she was already tired of Bobby, tired of Chester, tired of publicity and of pressure. She'd never really had a chance to ease into it, gradually developing a style and a pace, building audience loyalty. The advance publicity had promised too much. That first week, marred by flubs and missed cues and awkwardness, by the nervousness of Bobby Klaus and the patronizing of Chester Albany, had been less than adequate television. Normally self-confident, Kate had begun to think before she spoke, begun to lose that wonderful instinctive camera sense and timing polished during the talk show years. The first week was bad, not a disaster. But not good, either.

Then, unexpectedly, still nervous, during her second week on the job, Kate Sinclair had simply exploded. It was Johnny Vander Meer pitching successive no-hitters, Billie Jean King winning back to back Wimbledons, FDR elected to a fourth term. She couldn't miss. Whatever Kate did, worked. Bobby Klaus enthused, Chester Albany growled, and the Nielsens went through the roof. Kate Sinclair was the biggest thing on American television, a Farrah Fawcett-Majors with brains, an Ed Murrow with sex appeal; a Bill Moyers with hair by Kenneth.

It began with an accident, one of those happy flukes of journalism, during a routine split-screen conversation with the

18

President of Egypt, a little Arab hanging on fractionally to power.

"Tell me, Mr. President," Kate had said, "would you ever, under any circumstances, speak directly with the Israelis about the future of the Middle East?"

In the director's booth, they yawned. Out across America men and women got out of their recliners and started for the refrigerator or the bathroom. Kate herself was already searching for a gracious exit line that would neither insult the President nor anesthetize the audience.

"Well, Kate Sinclair," the President of Egypt said, speaking rapidly in clipped, accented English, "I would go into the desert, yes, into the desert, if it were to mean peace. Yes."

Kate Sinclair did not know very much about the Middle East or about international power plays or Israel or the Balfour Declaration. She was not even, as Chester Albany informed anyone who would listen, much of a journalist. But she recognized an opening when she saw one.

"Mr. President," she said, speaking now as quickly as he, "do you mean that you would literally go into the desert to talk, face to face, with the Israelis?"

The Egyptian's dark, faintly Asiatic face filled the screen.

"Yes, Kate Sinclair, that is precisely what I mean. I would go into the desert. Yes."

Kate was thinking quickly now.

"The Israeli desert or your desert?"

Again the camera switched to the Egyptian's face.

"I would go even, Kate Sinclair, into the Israeli desert," he said, "to stand on their sand and to talk peace."

They went to a commercial after that. No one was quite sure later whose idea it was but by the next evening they had arranged for the Prime Minister of Israel to do the same sort of split-screen interview with Kate. The *Times* and the other papers had picked up the story of the Egyptian's pledge, front-paging it. During the afternoon the network beat the drums. Tune in to hear the Israeli response "to Kate Sinclair's unique peace overtures. Watch history being made tonight. At seven Eastern Time."

The Egyptian President was not mentioned. There was only so much you could do with ten-second spots.

It was later estimated that some forty million Americans were watching when the screen focused on the bespectacled, pugnacious face of the old terrorist who was now running Israel.

"Mr. Prime Minister," Kate said respectfully, "last evening over this same program, we heard the President of Egypt . . ."

In the studio even Chester Albany sat motionless as Kate framed the question.

Then the split screen dissolved to a full face of the Israeli. Grimly he said:

"Miss Sinclair, I have today consulted with my cabinet. We have given serious consideration to the Egyptian President's statement. And I can reveal to you now that, yes, given the proper safeguards and providing an agenda can be agreed upon mutually in advance, I would be willing to go into the desert for direct talks on the security of Israel and the future peace of the entire region. Yes, I agree to meet with him."

The New York Times gave it eight columns and three decks of headlines the next morning.

"Jesus," Bobby Klaus complained, "it's *our* story and no mention of the network until the third paragraph!"

"They should have had Sinclair in the headline, I suppose," Chester said sourly.

Bobby nodded vigorously.

"You're goddamn right they should have!" he said.

A week and four thousand miles later, breathless, jet-lagged, more than slightly confused and awed, Kate Sinclair, in a safari jacket by Hunting World, stood under a hot Israeli sun on a sandy waste hard by a jet landing field and watched the two old enemies land, emerge, shake hands, and move to the cleared area where the cameras and the sound equipment and the technicians and diplomatists waited. The Egyptian, as the guest, spoke first.

"Mr. Prime Minister," he said, "I wish to thank you for receiving me today and, incidentally, I wish to thank Miss Kate Sinclair who . . ."

20

Kate did not really hear the rest of it.

But America did.

She came home with her nose sunburned and to a heroine's welcome. From the White House came a telegram, from Bobby Klaus a bouquet, from the Mayor of New York, the largest Jewish city in the world, a reception at the airport. On the 39th floor of Universal Broadcasting executives preened, and in the Atelier bar Chester Albany mumbled, "That bit at the Wailing Wall, doesn't the bitch have any sense of restraint at all?"

Within a week Kate had Marlon Brando do an interview in which he did not mention the Indians, not once; had received, and rejected, an invitation to spend a weekend in California with Warren Beatty; and had seen her picture in *Time, Newsweek, Rolling Stone,* and *The Christian Science Monitor.*

It was wonderful, confidence-building, glorious, and the ratings had been superb. It was also exhausting. Kate Sinclair, her first heady triumph secured, collapsed into bed each night after the show, drained.

It was not just the Middle East adventure or the first month of work that had tired her. It was all the months that had gone before, the negotiations, the publicity. Probably the million dollars a year had been a mistake. As one friend had advised, "Why not take a lousy nine-fifty, Kate, and then no one can object?" But she had taken the million and the press had had its field day and the network's other performers stared as if she were some freak. Thank God the actual work had finally begun. Maybe now she would be judged on her performance and not on all the bullshit. That was why she was looking forward to the weekend. For two whole days she would be away from the studio and the jealousy and the inexorable ratings.

But first, before she rested, there was one more day of work. She was in the studio limo now, being driven west through Manhattan, a lap rug warming her against the January chill. She was alone, the man in chauffeur's livery not considered, and suddenly, for no conscious reason whatever, she recalled a brief item in that morning's *Times.*

Somewhere off the coast of Africa, just east of the Canaries, a woman had fallen from a cruise ship into the Atlantic, wearing only a flimsy nightdress, and the ship had sailed on course for three hours before the woman's husband had wakened and discovered she was gone. The ship had turned back, retraced its route for another three hours, and had, miraculously, found the woman, freezing and nearly exhausted, in the night ocean. What an extraordinary thing, Kate thought, to be able to find a single human being in the infinity of the Atlantic.

Feeling slightly sorry for herself, Kate wondered if she fell from a ship would there be anyone who would turn it around and sail back to find *her?*

2

Robert L. (Bobby) Klaus was the latest in a long and distinguished line of network television "boy wonders." Every few years a Bobby Klaus would explode on the scene at one of the big networks, firing aging stars, unearthing brilliant new talent, demolishing long-running programs, substituting new hopefuls, castigating the television critics, driving aging middle-management to three-martini luncheons or sullen sycophancy, upsetting the delicately balanced relationships of the Nielsen ratings, and eventually in his own turn becoming weary, predictable, raw-nerved, and sullen as the next young genius came on the stage. The Bobby Klauses of contemporary television were small children, some still unborn, when Bill Paley and Lennie Goldenson and David Sarnoff blended the new electronic hardware and the booming American economy of the postwar forties to link a nation with coaxial cables, to create a gigantic new industry based on a hundred million televised homes.

Unlike the television pioneers, who were either great technicians or skilled promoters or financial titans, or a combination of all three, Bobby was a marketing man. At the University of Pennsylvania he had written his master's thesis on the art (even he would deny it scientific status) of scheduling and counter-scheduling programs. The network's chairman, first irritated, then intrigued, hired Bobby directly off the campus as a special assistant at age twenty-four. Now, five years later, Bobby Klaus was the director of television programing. Above him on the corporate ladder were a number of divisional presidents, a score of vice-presidents, and of course the chairman and founder of the parent corporation. But none of this really mattered. The network made money, or lost it, gained in the ratings race, or fell behind, its stock rose, or slumped, in direct proportion to Bobby's scheduling decisions. He would replace a white song and dance man (with a drinking and teen-age girl problem the network had until then chosen to overlook) with a jolly, street-wise black family and its apparently endless succession of nieces, nephews and grouchy or flippant neighbors. The white performer, his contract paid off, had sulked his way to Las Vegas for a series of lucrative nightclub dates, vowing vengeance on "that smart little Jew boy," whenever he tired of fondling his latest protégée, a trim little blonde pompom girl attending junior high school. Other, "creative" Bobby Klaus programing and scheduling decisions boosted the network from a feeble number three in the ratings to a strong two, and in the first eighteen months of his stewardship the stock of the parent corporation had risen from 23 to 31 on the New York Exchange.

Bobby Klaus did not look like a mogul. He was short, balding, and in his 30th year had developed an incipient paunch. He had not taken a day's vacation in nearly three years, neither smoked nor drank, looked blankly when an actress or any attractive woman flirted with him, and had a habit of chewing Kleenex when he was nervous. But Bobby loved his work. If the corporation had told him one morning his salary was to be cut back to two hundred a week or some other patently ridiculous figure, but that his responsibilities and authority would remain absolutely unchanged, Bobby Klaus would have blinked, perhaps shrugged his rounded shoulders into even more of a dowager's hump, and gone back to work relieved that nothing important, *really* important, had changed.

Bobby's formal writ did not run to news. But his entertainment and daytime and prime time programing made money while the news department, as at all the networks, had to be maintained by subsidy. Which irritated Bobby. Being ambitious, wanting to expand his authority, he had decided, more than a year before the hiring of Kate Sinclair, to do something about projecting himself into the news situation.

"It isn't right," he whined to an executive meeting one afternoon in the chairman's boardroom. "We earn and they spend and it just isn't right."

The president of network news, intolerant even when things were going well, slammed a big hand on the tabletop and

24

launched into his usual lecture, about television's responsibility to inform as well as to divert, that the individual stations were trustees of the public interest, that the supremacy of news over all other programing was traditionally sacred ("Haven't we always shit-canned everything else to cover moon shots and Presidential assassinations and Washington scandals on a gavel-to-gavel basis?" he demanded, rather typically mixing his outraged metaphors).

Bobby heard him out, or rather, since he did not listen, permitted him to run on until he was finished, and then said, the chairman later felt "slyly":

"Well, sure, but couldn't the entertainment division sort of lend you one or two of our people to help out? I mean, there's nothing in the FCC rules says you're prohibited from making money on the news."

The president of network news snarled that news personnel weren't jugglers or dog acts or fucking tenors, they were serious folk in serious work, and he'd be damned if he'd have quiz show hosts or soap opera performers reading the evening news or interviewing treasury secretaries. Bobby Klaus worried a dirty fingernail and, as he often did, remained silent so that the news executive's hyperbole hung a moment in the silence of the boardroom, making him look even more foolish than he had.

A month or two later, in a smaller meeting from which the news department had absented itself, Klaus struck again.

"I have an idea," he said.

Since the results of the latest prime ratings period were just in and the network was, at least for the moment, in a virtual deadlock for number one, the chairman and the other senior men leaned forward on the polished tabletop. And listened.

Bobby's proposal was very simple.

"There's no valid reason why an intelligent, attractive performer, with major recognition factors and a good ratings profile can't read the news. Some of our anchormen are, one has to admit, becoming a bit flabby around the collar, a bit worn at the cuff. Look at the BBC: they're realistic. They call their personnel 'news readers . . . news *readers.*' It isn't as if you had Ernest Hemingway out covering the war and then rushing back into the studio in his trenchcoat with the latest from the

25

front. I suggest we can do better with some fresh faces on the evening news. We might," and he paused briefly before letting his voice slide into its most modest, diffident tone, "we might even make a few dollars, win a few rating points."

No one questioned Bobby's programming instincts. He identified with the twelve-year-old mentality at which network entertainment was directed. And he loved television, literally loved it. A legend had grown up around the office about the affiliate meeting in Hawaii where everyone else sported on the beach or on the golf course or toured around the lovely island, while Bobby sat in his suite at the Royal Moana Hotel watching "Hawaii Five-O" on television.

But so long as Bobby's sitcoms and soap operas and game shows got the ratings, intensity, his lack of style, did not matter. If his ratings should slip, of course, the situation would become somewhat different.

There were other men out there waiting, men every bit as ambitious as Bobby Klaus, with their own skills, their own political connections, their own hungers. One of them was George Venables. When Bobby eventually won control of the evening news, serious men laughed. An entertainment specialist running news? Yet, it had happened. Still, the very idea of a sportscaster doing serious news was unthinkable, despite Venables' unarguable success. Not that Venables was your run-of-the-mill sportscaster. His knowledgeable, witty, savagely outspoken play by play commentaries had boosted Universal Broadcasting into first place in the ratings for football, for baseball, for basketball. And George Venables had not rested there. Like Johnny Carson at NBC, he had become a performer who was bigger than the show, more powerful by far than any producer. Soon he was having producers hired and fired, executive producers exiled or promoted. Finally, and logically, he had begun to produce the sports shows on which he performed. His nimble imagination took Universal far beyond what Arledge had done for ABC, to the actual creation of brand-new sports crafted exclusively for television: men versus women in any number of competitions with scientifically weighted handicaps; skiers racing down parallel slopes against one another rather than the clock; weight lifters in a 40-yard dash carrying 400-pound refrigerators strapped to

26

their backs. Now there were plans to pit an expert skin diver with an explosive spear gun against a great white shark, a filmed ascent of the North Face of the Elger in winter, and a created-for-television female rugby league with the girls wearing tearaway jerseys.

If young Bobby Klaus should stumble, a man like Venables might be useful. Venables might have his own weaknesses, of course, drawbacks of his own. One never knew about such things, never bothered to know about them if the ratings held. And George Venables' ratings held just fine. The trouble was, as far as Venables was concerned, so did Bobby Klaus's.

Bobby's ratings rose, the old news executives fumed, a white song and dance man ranted in Nevada. None of it mattered but the ratings. And eventually, after months of quiet debate, Bobby was authorized to begin his search for a new anchorman, a new and credible voice who would become for those millions of Americans who no longer read, their only source of information about the city, the nation, the world, the universe. For them this new oracle would translate the human condition, in simple terms, for 22 minutes each evening.

His new oracle was to be Kate Sinclair, discovered not in Manhattan where she lived and worked, but in the heart of the country. In Kansas.

If you draw two straight lines, one from Key West to Puget Sound, the other from the Baja border to the last rock on the coast of Maine, they will intersect near the town of Centre, Kansas, up near the Nebraska line. The mountains are another half-day's drive west and the scatter of grain elevators, rearing up from the featureless prairie, is for many miles the only thing on the horizon. Centre is not much of a town but it is about as close as you can come to the precise geographic middle of the 48 contiguous states. Which was what brought Harry Flagg there.

Flagg was in the business of motivational research. It was the latest of the contemporary faiths and Flagg, holding the usual degrees in psychology and sociology and having a passing acquaintance with computer technology, was one of its apostles. Comfortable with the Midwest, he settled on Centre as convenient to his clients on both coasts as well as symbolic of his methods which, at least in theory, were to eliminate all bias, geographic and otherwise, and produce only the purest of data.

In the beginning Harry Flagg had specialized in measuring consumer attitudes toward commercial products in the packaged goods field: this brand of cornflakes over that; this detergent; that diet cola; this scouring pad; that line of pantyhose; blind-testing similar but competing products and reporting his findings back to the great corporations that dominated the market place. As his assignments increased in size and complexity, and his fees increased as well, he invested in a computer, hired some bright boys to program and operate it, and took on subtler, more ambitious studies.

He assembled scientifically selected, demographically balanced panels of "typical" Americans to choose between rival station wagons, sanitary pads, touch telephones, premium gasolines, stereo systems, convertible sofas. The programming became more complex and he moved to a second generation computer, demographics gave way to psychographics (not only age and education and income were to be measured; "attitude" became important), more bright boys were hired, larger and more painstakingly selected panels were set up. Flagg roamed farther afield, product-testing throughout the country, yet he always came home. Centre, Kansas was, well, it was the center.

It was Bobby Klaus who had discovered Flagg, given him his instructions, told him his own view of the problem.

"I have these three guidelines," Bobby had said. "You might call them my three commandments. They're terribly simple but I really believe them to be crucial.

"The first commandment, *all* television, even the news, is entertainment.

"Second, never tell people what they need to know. Tell them what they want to hear.

"And third," Bobby Klaus paused dramatically, "the anchorman is far more important than the news."

For the past five years, a time of shrinking ratings, the network had had two anchormen: Chester Albany, once one of Murrow's brightest young men, and Clive Jackson, somewhat older, considerably grayer and rather more dour. Until recent-

28

ly the two had seemed a perfect complement, but now the network, or certain of its executives, had concluded that perhaps what they had here were two gracefully aging savants, two newscasters so much in sync with one another that the casual viewer (and was there any other kind?) occasionally confused them and asked, "Now is that Chester or is that Clive?" Since television works on the principle of immediate recognition ("There's Fonzie . . . There's Johnny . . . There's Farrah . . ."), this was not considered a good thing.

Now after several months' persuasion Bobby had convinced the network to let him pick the anchor replacement and Flagg would have the opportunity to test Bobby's theories, to impose his "three commandments" on the entire nation. He had been assigned to find a new anchorman, perhaps even a new anchor team, for a major network.

Today the testing would begin. Here in Centre. The job would take months. The network was in no hurry. The stakes were too high for snap decisions. But today Flagg had assembled the first of his panels of "average viewers." He would tape electrodes to their temples, to their chests, to the palms of their hands. The electrodes would tell him, far more truthfully and articulately than the panelists themselves could possibly do, their reactions to the various newscasters and television performers they would see on the videotaped telecasts. The wires would monitor brain waves and heart beats and perspiration. They would tell Flagg what he needed to know, tell the network how to climb out of fourth place in a four-horse race.

Harry Flagg stood at the picture window of his office, looking out across the spare brown lawn that fringed the sprawling one-level Flagg Motivations building, looking toward Main Street. It was nine forty-five in the morning and a bank of cloud hung low in the northern sky, threatening. Out on the farms men would be looking at that same sky and wondering about their winter wheat and whether the northers and the snow would come early this year.

A phlegmatic man, Flagg was strangely excited. He would embark this morning on the most challenging assignment of his professional life. He was about to begin the most complicated and subtle series of tests he had ever devised for a new client, for an industry that never before had used motivational

29

research. As he stared out the window, he saw the first member of the day's panel, an enormous woman in pink hair curlers and a matching pantsuit, slide her bulk out of a Dodge automobile and waddle toward the building. Behind her, Flagg knew, would come the others: the overall-ed farmers; a college boy in a monogrammed warmup jacket; a black man of forty; a young mother with a child slung papoose-fashion on her back; two high school girls; an older woman using a walker to inch her way up the flagged path. They would all be there, it would not snow, the project could begin.

He did not really care which anchorman would eventually be selected, which panelists he used so long as they represented a scientifically balanced demographic mix. Flagg knew that except for the sheer size and complexity of the assignment, there was no difference between television and scouring pads. He wished his panelists understood just how important his work was, wished they would put aside their self-consciousness and petty dignity so that he could delve even deeper into their minds and hearts. How ridiculous, he thought, that mere panelists would object, as they had, when he proposed attaching electrodes to their genitals, to women's nipples, to inserting electrodes into their anuses!

Flagg looked at the panelists. "A motley crew," he thought, almost smiling.

Then he turned and headed for the testing room to be certain the television monitors were switched on, the computer hooked up, and the electrodes ready. A literal and dour man in a serious line of work, Flagg could not afford to be amused by the incongruity of his panel. After all, "motley" was his very stock in trade.

Months later Flagg submitted his report to the network. Its key recommendation was that Chester Albany and Kate Sinclair be teamed as the network's anchorpersons on the evening news show.

3

When they first approached her, Kate had laughed and said no. She was the host of a successful morning talk show oriented toward women. Her ratings were strong, her salary sufficient, she enjoyed the work. Why venture into the fierce evening news competition, why leave a stronger network for a weaker, why expose herself to the inevitable critical strafing she could expect as a neophyte in news and, above all, as a woman? But they kept after her, they dangled fame, they promised money, they appealed to pride, to her competitiveness, above all to an ambition even she was not aware burned within her.

Later, when they told Kate they planned to team her with Chester Albany, to "marry them on the air," as they phrased it, uncertainty again racked her. She heard through the trade grapevine that Chester, too, was dubious, that he had instructed his agent to put forward certain conditions, to ask substantially more money, to insure that if he had to suffer this atrocity, they would make it worth his while. Taking a similar stance, Kate reluctantly permitted negotiations to begin on her behalf.

She too had an agent. In this business you had an agent the way you had two feet or ears or a navel. Her agent was Helen Toolan and Helen was a professional. It was Helen who negotiated the million-dollar contract. When Kate, who had a healthy ego but understood there were limits to everything, remonstrated, Helen cut her short.

"Kate," she said, "get the bread. They can screw you six ways from Sunday later on but you get a contract for a million a year, you're gonna *get* your million. Besides," she added shrewdly, "their PR people will go downtown on this. The first million dollar a year television newscaster! I can read the headlines now."

The lawyers got into it, of course, and the bankers, and the accountants. But it was Helen Toolan who had run the show. She had been there before.

"Listen," she told Kate after one exhausting marathon with the network, "I've handled movie stars and heavyweight fighters and rock groups. I've been threatened, I've been offered bribes, I've ridden in limos up front with the chauffeur while thirteen-year-old groupies gave head in the back seat. You think Sue Mengers has seen it all? You think Swifty Lazar has been around? Listen, they're the Little Sisters of the Poor compared to me. Tired? I don't get tired. Just relax, Katie girl, and leave the dealing to me. These network boys better be wearing protective cups when we go back into that room because I'm getting ready to kick balls."

Kate was more than willing to stay out of it. She wanted no part of the negotiation. But in the back of her mind there was this uneasy feeling that insisting on the million, as a symbol more than as a sum of money, was a mistake. It set her up as a target. She was nervous about it. There'd be enough static when she moved behind the anchor desk. Flaunting this much cash made her vulnerable, more than vulnerable. Cronkite didn't get a million. Chancellor didn't. Reasoner, for God's sake, didn't. This took her out of the newscaster category entirely and positioned her with Carson. Who *cared* how much money Johnny made? They took him for what he was, an entertainer. But she, Kate Sinclair, would be a news person. Making more money than any news person had ever made before. She was uneasy. She was more than uneasy. She was goddamned frightened. But Helen Toolan said:

"Listen, kid, you know what Mick Jagger makes? Ahmet Ertegun? Clive Davis? The fucking Osmond kids?"

"I'm not a rock star," Kate said.

Helen Toolan grinned.

"I know," she said, "you don't have any groupies hanging around. Giving you head."

So that was how the million happened. Toolan pushed for it, the network's PR people saw the virtue in it, and Kate suc-

32

cumbed. She knew it was a mistake. But pride and, she admitted to herself, greed, came into it.

They closed the deal.

Her lawyer and the bankers and the tax man worried about the money. An unsheltered million, they warned, would quickly shrink to less than half of that under the new revenue codes. Her new income level called for creative finance, for irrevocable trusts, for deferred remuneration, for tomato futures in Mexico and cattle in New Jersey, for the network to buy her apartment and do a lease-back arrangement.

She had not been paid the first dollar on her new contract when the poor and the worthy came calling. Suddenly she was on mailing lists that ranged from the Sisters of Charity to the Vietnam orphans to a campaign to arrest the elm blight on Martha's Vineyard. Cousins she had never heard of called her, collect, from Oregon. A fisherman in the Louisiana bayous wanted her to back a new frozen creole shrimp dish. A women's slo-pitch softball team in Connecticut asked her to buy uniforms. She was offered a Kentucky Fried Chicken franchise and an ice hockey team in Manitoba. Cranks sent her threatening letters, she had to change her unlisted phone number twice in a month, while a team of writers and reporters and photographers from *Time* magazine buzzed around her like curious gnats.

All this while Kate was working hard.

There was the old job, the talk shows to be taped, the old network understandably hostile. Small problems management had tended to keep from her in the past, cropped up to become tiring, time-wasting annoyances. And each day she would report to the new network. There were conferences on how she and Chester would be billed, on the publicity releases that were going out almost every day, on the layout and the wording of the print ads and the television commercials that would be launched with increasing frequency as December tenth, which she began thinking of as D-Day, approached.

She and Chester Albany were beginning to feel each other out, probing each other's territorial imperatives, learning to dovetail their very different styles.

Theirs had not been a match made in heaven. Still, in the beginning, it sounded a marvelous idea. The mating had been done, tentatively at first and then with the juggernaut momentum of a thing inevitable, over a passage of months in the executive offices of the network, the bar of the "21" Club, in the offices of ICM and William Morris, and, ultimately, in the Nielsen ratings. The simple notion of dropping one of their gray eminence anchormen and pairing the survivor with a woman had been tried before, with Sally Quinn and Hughes Rudd in the morning, with Walters and Reasoner, and on any number of local stations. But those were *other* stations, other networks, another Nielsen season. For *this* network, and in *this* season, my God! what a brilliant stroke, how daring, how logical, how delicious! So, it was done. Clive Jackson was in effect pensioned off and for a million dollars a year, Kate Sinclair, the female talk-show star of another network, was purchased. They would marry her to Chester Albany for thirty minutes every weekday night. "You see," Bobby Klaus had emphasized, "the audience has to think of them as husband and wife. That's the only way it'll work."

Chester didn't like losing Clive, he didn't like the idea of working with a woman, he didn't expect to like Kate Sinclair. But he was a professional, the network had been decent to him, he enjoyed the job, and, when word leaked out in the trade press about the money Kate Sinclair was to be paid, his own salary was doubled. And so he said, yes. He and the woman were mature people, it would be in their own self-interest to work together smoothly. And never before had there been such publicity, such curiosity about him, so much talk about his work, his on-the-air style, his solid news background. The press reports spoke of her quickness, her looks, her uncanny ability to winkle out self-revelatory admissions from powerful people during her interviews. At the same time they spoke of Chester's salty wit, his rugged looks, his unshakability. And so they went to work, months of preparation, of format revisions, of the hiring of new correspondents in Washington and elsewhere to back them up. The publicity people moved in, the lighting experts, the sound engineers so that he would sound masculine and authoritative, she feminine but credible, rehearsals began, and around the globe statesmen and celebrities were urged to make themselves available for on-the-air interviews with Chester Albany and Kate Sinclair.

Nothing was simple. An entirely new set was to be built. Bobby Klaus talked of "a living room, a real American living room, with couches and magazines lying around and a drink on the cocktail table, probably just a cola, we'd have to establish that, and even a TV set somewhere to make it look authentically American." He was talked out of that.

"For Chrissakes," Chester Albany had said, "we're already getting static for turning the news into show biz. If you don't have an anchor desk and some goddamned maps, who the hell is going to know they're watching the news?" He avoided mentioning Kate's lack of news experience so pointedly that she got the point.

Should there be one, somewhat elongated desk or two, separate but equal desks? When that was solved Bobby Klaus asked, quite seriously, "Kate has good legs. Very good legs. Could we have desks with, I don't know what you call them, breakfronts maybe?"

It was Kate's turn to say, "For Chrissakes, Bobby!"

Clothes became a problem. One of the successful local news shows had the anchormen in identical leisure suits, the on-the-air reporters, a lesser caste, in blazers. Perhaps they should consider a his-and-her uniform?

"Oh, hell," said Chester, "I always wear the same pair of baggy pants and slippers because no one sees me below the waist. I have four or five good jackets. Isn't that enough?"

Kate wanted to wear her own clothes ("You can forget uniforms for me, too, Bobby"), but she wanted the network to pay for them.

"After all, I'll have to wear something different just about every night and that's going to run into money."

When Bobby agreed and said he would work out a clothing allowance or maybe Bloomingdale's would do a trade-out, Chester barked, "What about me? Do I get an allowance?"

"Chester," Bobby said patiently, "your old baggy pants. Those comfortable slippers. Remember?"

"Sure," said Chester righteously, "but that was when this was a news show and not the fucking best dressed list!"

Kate's office was marginally larger than Chester's, a pleasant room that would comfortably have graced the pages of *Better Homes & Gardens.* During one of those early scrimmages, they were still good-natured then, this business of offices had come up and Bobby Klaus mentioned that Kate would have a decorator come in and do hers, Parish-Hadley probably, and the bill would be thirty thousand or so, and Chester had exploded.

"Look," he'd said, "she can have any damn thing she wants. Doesn't mean a damn to me. Not personally. But professionally we're supposed to be on a par and I ought to damn well have a few bucks spent on that hole I lurk in down the hall. A gloomy cave is what it is, a goddamned monastic cell."

Even Bobby was impressed.

"Well, Chester, I never knew you felt that way. You've been in there so long I assumed you didn't want it touched. Of course we're willing to spend a little. Just let me know your decorator. I'll make the arrangements."

It was then Chester laughed. It was contagious. Even Kate had laughed.

"Why that's the thing of it, Bobby. You see," Chester said, "I don't *have* a fucking decorator."

Chester Albany's lover was very proud of him and his new status and all this wonderful publicity which she felt, in a way, reflected glory upon her as well. But she was less happy about the reality of the longer working hours, the overtime, the fatigue that sapped Chester. She was happier about how it had been before the Sinclair deal had been announced, when Chester took her to glamorous places where she could see, and might even meet, some of the people she read about in Suzy or Liz Smith or Earl Wilson. But Frances Neale was not a complainer. She had a very keen awareness of her good fortune. She was a working class girl from Liverpool who'd drifted down to London in the wake of a third-rate rock band and had been supporting herself as a mother's helper when Chester discovered her. He was in London for a Presidential summit and had been invited to dine at the great house in Chelsea Square where she was currently employed. He had liked her lively eyes and the livelier way in which her body moved when she toted the baby in for a goodnight kiss, and he had begun by taking her out to a local pub and ended by bedding her in his suite at the Dorchester. When he offered to pay her way to the States, Frances had leaped at the chance. She had tired of being a groupie, was bored by children, and the notion of limping back to Liverpool was a recurrent nightmare. One week she was a slavey in London at twenty pounds a week and the next she was living with a rich and famous man in his big apartment on Park Avenue, which was where working class girls from Liverpool usually did not end up. She was twenty-three years old with good legs and the rest of it and very satisfactory in bed. But her principal contribution was that Frances enabled Chester to relax. Completely. Only rarely did an idea clutter her head and so she existed, and their relationship flourished, on a pleasantly simple and superficial plane. After his marriage ended and before he found Frances, Chester had been attracted to any number of women. They turned out ambitious or jealous or exhausting. There were no such complications with Frances.

Chester'd had enough of bright, brittle women. He wanted Frances because she was comfortable, supportive, never waspish or critical. He worked in a hard trade, a métier constantly subject to criticism written or rated, and it was important to come home to a girl who thought him one of the most influential, well-informed, and important men in America. She never nagged, not even during these last weeks when he was increasingly morose, aware of pressure, occasionally self-pitying, and drinking.

As they moved closer to their first broadcast together the pressures on both Chester and Kate intensified. Little things cropped up and became crises.

Miss Sinclair's hairdresser; Mr. Albany's demand that a certain floor manager be assigned; Miss Sinclair's limo; Mr. Albany's insistence that Clive Jackson do an "essay" a week; Miss Sinclair's dislike of a still photo being released by publicity; Mr. Albany's distaste for the ad agency's first story boards; these things and a thousand others took the time and sapped the energies of both of them and of Bobby Klaus.

Later, Chester and Kate would both recall no time at all was spent on discussing the news.

4

The third greatest prose writer in America shivered as he stood in the dusk on a windy avenue in front of the television studio where Kate Sinclair was beginning her second month of doing the evening news. Harvey Podesta was taking Kate to dinner that evening but he refused to go into the studio. "Your people giggle," he had told Kate. "They giggle and stare. I won't be giggled at." Kate tried to explain that stage hands and electricians giggled at everyone and that they stared at Harvey not to ridicule but simply because he was famous. Kate suspected they giggled and stared because of the spectacle Harvey tended to make of himself on another of the networks where he was a more or less regular guest on a game show where fools capered and the judges clanged loud gongs. She knew Harvey didn't need the money and that these appearances demeaned him, but whenever she brought up the subject, Harvey hushed her. "Life is hard, Kate, hard and cruel. Even an artist deserves a modicum of fun." Since Harvey issued portentous statements like this in a sort of anglicized lisp, Kate Sinclair was tempted to giggle herself. But she was a woman who respected talent and worshipped success and since Harvey represented both, he could stipulate conditions. Besides, Harvey was no threat. She even liked him.

Waiting for Kate to come downstairs Harvey passed the time by surveying great, dribbling piles of uncollected rubbish and rot. How fortunate to have this hard freeze so early in the year, he thought. New York's garbagemen were again on strike and while they customarily chose the stink of summer to dramatize their demands, the union leadership had for complicated reasons decreed January for this latest exercise. Now, granted the streets looked no better nor the heaps of garbage more attractive, but at least the city was spared the stench and those squiggling little things, and worse, that decaying organic matter called up in summer. It was quite dark now and in the wind there was a spit of snow. Harvey shivered but he smiled. He had the poet's love of snow, the deeper the better with drifted cornices and impassable roadways and Eskimos killing the lead dog to get the serum through to Nome. Now, with the Sanitation Department closed down, perhaps the great city would be snowed in! Right into spring. How aesthetically startling for Easter! Harvey thought, and he hugged himself, and that curious notion, with red-furred mittens.

Kate Sinclair came out into the street through the glass doors. The little writer kissed both cheeks.

Kate's car was waiting and they crossed the broad plaza in front of the studio, Harvey's stubby legs taking three strides to two of Kate's. There wasn't much traffic. Either the latest Arab boycott or the threat of snow had taken care of that. Window decorators were at work in the shops they passed, tearing down Santa Claus and dismantling polyester creches. Harvey inclined his head toward them through the car window.

"And I'll bet you thought faggots didn't keep Christmas," he said.

She'd never thought about it, Kate admitted.

"Well, we do, you know," Harvey piped, his voice high and whiny as if he were about to burst into tears even on the funny lines. Kate laughed. Harvey liked that. When he got a laugh he played for more. "Christmas isn't only for Anita Bryant," he giggled.

Harvey Podesta had come to New York twenty years earlier out of Denver, a fact he was careful to suppress both with outright lies and a vaguely English accent. Once, on a talk show, he was asked if he were British. "No," Harvey had boasted, "just affected." He had worked for one of the magazines as a copy boy, helping find taxis for drunken writers, taking messages from their lovers, and eventually graduated to writing some of the most delicate, lightly filigreed prose ever published. He had gone on to writing books, not many but wonderfully wrought, had become something of a personage in New York and Hollywood.

For the moment there was no lover. Harvey had been ill. Oh, he was splendid now, he assured Kate as the car rolled east, just some rectal complications common to people like . . . him. The sort of midlife crisis you had to put up with if you were a pederast. He indulged in a rather clinical analysis of his trouble until Kate, for whom he was the most convenient of escorts, begged a respite.

"Do save it for later, Harvey," she told him. "Connie Heath will be furious if you waste all your good stories on me."

Harvey brightened. "Andy may be coming east," he said. "That relationship at Malibu doesn't seem to be working too smoothly."

Andy was a landscape gardener summoned to Harvey's house in Palm Beach the year before. The boy had mowed the lawn and stayed. And stayed. Until he became fed up with Harvey's bitchy, whining mots, few of which he understood, and until another man, just as rich but with bluer eyes, had beckoned Andy to move on. Harvey's experience with lovers was usually disastrous. He gave them everything, asked nothing but fidelity, and was inevitably abandoned. In one of his bathrooms he had good-humoredly framed the poster of an old foreign film, "Seduced and Abandoned." Kate liked that ruthless honesty. She was glad she'd called him to take her to Constance Heath's. It would do him good to be out, to be among people, especially at this time of year. The most self-reliant of us, Kate thought, automatically assuming her own reliance, should not be alone at Christmas. And Harvey Podesta was hardly the most secure person she knew.

She remembered his reaction four months earlier when he learned she was going to become the network's anchorwoman.

Harvey had clapped his hands so loudly his Yorkshire terrier woke from a nap and growled ferociously at a blameless hassock.

"A cover story in *Time*," Harvey said. "Imagine. Kay Graham will be just ill."

Kate Sinclair shrugged. "Oh, we could have had *Newsweek* too, but the PR people said no, make it exclusive and they'd guarantee *Time* would be upbeat, none of the usual bitchery."

"Oh, Kate," Harvey said. "A *Time* cover. Oh, I knew it would happen. I just knew."

They were lounging in Harvey's living room, that famous living room that had no furniture to speak of, just different levels of flooring, lushly carpeted, with throws and huge pillows and hassocks like medicine balls.

"And not on what's-his-name? You're sure of that?" Harvey said, a cloud of suspicion darkening his round little face.

"Chester Albany," she said patiently. "And no, it'll have some stuff on him, of course, but I'll be alone on the cover and the story will be mainly me."

Harvey clapped his pudgy hands again.

"Kate, I'm so happy. It's like . . . it's like a really good lay and not having to pay for it."

Kate smiled at the blissful look on his face. "Well, now, I don't know about that . . . "

It was extraordinary, really, Harvey's pleasure about *Time*, carrying on as if it were the Nobel Prize, while she, a television host who presumably should be prepared to commit matricide for a *Time* cover, was not reacting at all.

"Let's see," he had said, "a whole *new* 'you' to begin with. We must lunch with Bill Blass and find out where fashion will be in January. Perhaps Bill isn't quite right for you but surely he'll have ideas. Maybe we'll get Calvin or Ralph. Or Halston! Now, there's an inspiration. And your hair. I'd avoid Sassoon. I mean, he does every head on television now. And your flat; I'll call Sister Parish this very moment. We can't have *Time* magazine going in there with cameras until you do something with the color scheme."

And so on. Patiently Kate said no, she had been hired for the way she was now, the hair, the face, the clothes. As for her apartment, she liked it that way.

"The audience knows me, Harvey. They know I'm thirty-five years old and I can extemporize and I can be funny or I can be tough. They like *me*, not some fancy streamlined new image of me. And so does the network, or they wouldn't be paying me all this vulgar money."

Harvey looked shocked.

"Never refer to money as 'vulgar,' Kate. That's the true vulgarity. And never, absolutely never, mention your age. You could be twenty-nine. Twenty-seven, even. And that reminds me, your sister. Keep Shaun away at school. Don't even bring her up in the story. And no jolly photos side by side. There's *nothing* ages a beautiful woman like a younger sister."

"Harvey, Shaun doesn't compete with me."

"Well, then, you have a responsibility to protect her from the glare of publicity."

He looked prim.

"And get rid of that *femme de ménage* you employ, the communist. My God, keep her out of *Time* magazine or they'll crucify you. Joe McCarthy will come out of his bloody *grave!*"

Now it was a snowy January night in Manhattan and Kate's car swung into Sutton Place and pulled up in front of Constance Heath's wonderful house on the river. When they got out Harvey pirouetted once, slowly and rather nicely in the snow, using a canopy pole to sustain him as he spun.

"I do love the snow," he declared.

Kate stood there on the sidewalk staring at him.

"It's so . . . so fluffy," he said.

Kate grunted. New York was falling apart, the garbage wasn't being collected, the police were working to rule, the bonds weren't being underwritten, and Harvey thought snow was *"fluffy."*

Above and beyond them towered the city's skyscrapers. The doorman smiled welcome and they went inside from the cold night.

5

"The former" Spiro Agnew, as Harvey Podesta waggishly referred to him, was mistaken about any number of things, among them the propriety of accepting bribes from road builders while he was serving as Vice-President of the United States. But on one matter, the consolidation of media power in the hands of a few people, Mr. Agnew had been correct. They weren't all Easterners, as he simplistically suggested; some of them weren't snobs, and they certainly weren't all effete. Many of them were, however, clustered now in Connie Heath's apartment and poor Agnew, never very bright, vacant under that sleek head (the nation's barbers had once named him The Best Groomed Man in America), would surely have cried "conspiracy!" The fact was, Connie Heath, whose inherited millions patronized both artists and politicians, gave perfectly wonderful parties and there were people who would do serious injury to themselves rather than to miss one.

Kate and Harvey brushed snow from their clothes and handed coats to a man in livery and then Constance Heath herself was drawing them happily through rooms into the depth of her home, wondering laughingly why she ever came north in winter.

"Because it's chic," Harvey lisped and Constance lifted her hands in that helpless way of hers that was not helpless at all. Parquet gave way to deep Indian rugs and then marble and Kate found herself, not for the first time, surrendering to envy. Beyond Connie she could hear the buzz of voices. There were network chairmen and editors from the *Times*, book publishers, senators, a sitting justice of the Supreme Court, a former candidate for President, newspaper columnists, Broadway producers, authors, Harvard faculty with impressive tenure,

43

delegates from the United Nations with black faces and Ox-bridge degrees, pretty girls, bankers, lawyers from Sullivan and Cromwell, a Kennedy by marriage and a Kennedy by birth, a homosexual poet, the president of the city council, one of the Big Three auto chiefs from Detroit, Mailer and Breslin, horsy women from Oyster Bay, Orsini the restaurateur, and a murderer out on bail from Attica.

A waiter came up and they took drinks and Harvey giggled, "The air is charged with gossip, simply charged."

"If it isn't," Connie Heath assured him, "you'll supply it."

A craggy, elegant old man with a plump and sprightly young wife had ascended the pulpit just behind Connie Heath. The old man didn't converse, he issued statements:

"But there *are* no radicals anymore. They've compromised, joined the establishment."

His wife mentioned the season's latest terrorist.

The old man sneered.

"A milksop, a figure of jest, no more harm in him than there is in a mewling, puking child."

The wife tittered, but someone said somberly, "He plants bombs."

The old man looked scornful.

"Bombs? Bombs? Why if that fellow planted a bomb he'd cache it in a Louis Vuitton bag!"

Harvey was bored. He drifted off. There was a knot of people around him. They were laughing. Harvey was doing what he did so well at parties. He was dismantling a reputation. This time it was an actress. Typically, she was not present. Harvey rarely attacked anybody who might strike back.

"It's not that she's a dog," he was saying, "but she's been asked to do the Alpo commercials." He waited for the laugh. "Mean? Why she'd rearrange the furniture in a blind man's house."

Waiters moved silently through the room over the deep car-pets serving drinks and canapes and bridging conversational gaps. Kate Sinclair wondered how many parties, just like this, she had attended in the past year. Too often with someone like Harvey, seldom with a man. And what was the alternative? Staying at home?

Constance Heath had a young man in tow now, one of several tall young men with ski tans and well-cut clothes, who combined the proper ratio of boredom and lapdog eagerness to please, the sort of young men with whom Connie habitually sprinkled her parties, the way other hostesses might do with pretty girls.

"This is Ronald, Kate, do be tolerant of him."

Kate looked up into the handsome, empty face.

"So I'm to be tolerant," she said.

He smiled.

Connie had moved off, yet another young man in her wake. My God, Kate thought, I wonder if she sleeps with them. This one, Ronald, must be in his twenties. The other, the one trailing after Connie, could be his twin. Connie Heath was at least ten years older than Kate, perhaps more. Kate had forgotten Ronald and when she looked up at him he was still smiling, the white teeth splendid against the tan.

"Oh, get yourself a drink or something," she said, not being at all tolerant, and the young man, simpering just a bit, blinked twice and sidled away from her.

"Sour bitch," he said under his breath.

One of the Harvard professors drew her into conversation and she asked who the old man was, the one so disillusioned with the radicals.

"Oh, dear," the professor said, "such a sad case. Once one of our great men but regressed terribly." He mentioned the old fellow's name.

Kate shook her head. "I still don't . . . "

The professor looked blank. "But I thought everyone knew. He used to be the secretary of the Communist Party," he said.

Harvey skipped by, one of Connie's young men with him. He looked happy. One of the Broadway actors introduced her to an Irish politician, a man who had gone from trolley driver to a big job in city government, in a city blacker and more Hispanic with every year. The politician droned on in a heavy brogue, speaking nonsense eloquently, waving his hands and nodding the great white shock of hair to illustrate empty points.

Jesus, Kate thought, this drink and perhaps one other, I don't remember, and the room is going 'round. It can't be the alcohol, it must be the stupidity of all this. In this wonderful flat, among all these people, loneliness. Kate shook her head angrily, rejecting self-pity, reasserting her personality by force of will, telling herself, not for the first time, that *she* was important, what she did significant, what she thought, meaningful. The hell with these self-indulgent bastards and their empty, echoing . . .

"But then d'ya know what I said?" It was the Irishman, his face close to hers, the yellowed teeth bared, the white stubble crusted with flecks of foam at the corners of his mouth. "Lemme tell ya, I . . . "

He never finished whatever tiresome pronouncement he was about to make.

From behind Kate a loud voice boomed:

"Give it a rest, the lady's bored."

Kate wheeled. A huge man in a tan suit stood there, looking at her and smiling.

"Like all Irish ward-heelers," he said, quietly now, "he's been soap-boxing so long he lies to himself."

The old politician's mouth fell open, the false teeth clacked, and a woman with him, angry but protective, drew him mutely away.

"Blanchflower," the tall man said, sensing her confusion. "Nick Blanchflower."

"Of course," Kate told him, but for a moment she had not recognized him.

"Why should you?" he demanded. "Listening to that old fake would lobotomize anyone. They can't get the garbage picked up in this town and he's telling the Irish how to run Belfast!"

Blanchflower took her arm and led her toward a corner that was quiet and nearly empty.

"I'll buy you a drink," he said. "What is that? Looks like scotch. Good, waiter, a scotch for this lady and another vodka on the rocks for me."

He hadn't really asked, Kate thought, and she didn't really want another. But she was so pleased he simply made the decision that she smiled and decided, yes, she would like another drink.

"The goddamned Irish," Blanchflower said, grinning at her.

"There are a lot of Irish that vote," she cautioned.

46

"Oh, hell, I'm Irish myself," he said. "I can get away with it."

He paused, then grinning more broadly, "I can do that phony brogue too if I have to. And sometimes I have to."

She watched his face. So this was Nick Blanchflower, the notorious, womanizing, dashing, sure-to-be-President Nick Blanchflower.

She thought this but did not say it aloud.

How odd that she had not instantly recognized him from television. Aside from the President's his was perhaps the most famous political face in the country. He was a prodigious vote-getter. Men thought he was a hell of a fellow, women mobbed him at political rallies. There were dark stories about his origins, about the source of his money, about the death of his rich young wife in a plane crash, there were whispers he lived in fear of assassination, that he carried a gun, that bodyguards shielded him twenty-four hours a day, that his mail was a bizarre blend of idolatrous pledges of fidelity and murky death threats. It was said he bought his first election, that he paid blackmail, that a young secretary from his Senate office had killed herself with pills in a Rehoboth Beach love nest during a weekend tryst, that despite all these things he would be the next President of the United States.

"You're not what I expected," Kate said.

"What did you expect?"

"I dunno. But different."

Blanchflower waved his hands expansively.

"Hell," he said, "I'm not strange. Compared to some senators I'm a goddamned paragon. The civics books ought to hold me up as a constitutional example for school children. They ought to erect monuments."

"Oh?"

"Sure," he said, "read the Congressional Record. That's where you learn about senators."

"And not by talking to them like this?"

He grinned. Kate did not like what she knew about him but when she saw the grin she knew why he won elections.

"Nope," he said. "You can't believe anything I say here tonight, with a drink in my hand. But if it's in the Record, well, that's different."

47

"Oh?"

"Absolutely. The Congressional Record. There for any citizen to read. Hell, if everyone read the Record every day you wouldn't need comic books, no one would watch Carson."

Kate grinned now too. For the first time this evening she didn't need a drink to be happy.

"You really *like* being a politician, don't you?"

"Sure," Blanchflower said, "you run for office. You win. Maybe you lose. A big state like this, it's a Heinz state. Fifty-seven varieties. Some neighborhoods you go after the front lawn vote. They've got a front lawn they're worried about the blacks moving in on it. You preach law and order. In the ghetto, where they don't have front lawns and they sleep on fire escapes in the summer and keep the kitchen stove going in winter, you preach jobs, better schools, food stamps. You don't make the same sermon in Vatican City and Mecca."

"Isn't that pretty cynical?"Kate said.

Blanchflower barked his short laugh.

"Of course it's cynical. This isn't the Salvation Army giving out turkeys at Thanksgiving, you know." He drew on the cigar. "What about your trade? What about tonight? What happened, a plane crash in the Azores, two hundred people fried in a jumbo jet. First item on your show. I heard it. Then you come in with a pious little recital. Then some schmuck in the Azores, some stringer who's been waiting ten years for a story like this, and he comes on and gives the grim toll. And you all look solemn and then . . . commercial break . . . back in a minute with a report from Vassar, straight from the Daisy Chain, all smiles and orthodontic teeth and let's not brood about the poor bastards cooking in the fucking airplane. Come on, Kate, where is it so bad I talk to the front lawn people one way and the welfares another?"

She wasn't in an arguing mood. She wanted to know more about Blanchflower, not to engage in polemics.

"What about your children? Do you shelter them? Do you tell them about the cynical business you're in? We're both in?"

Blanchflower looked at her, unsure whether she was continuing the argument from another tack or really asking a question.

He decided to answer as truthfully as he could.

48

"The boys are all I have. All that is important. So, I try to tell them the truth and not shit them. At the same time, they're kids. You don't want to cynic them before they're ready to handle it. You know?"

Kate had never heard "cynic" used as a verb before. But she knew. She knew what he meant.

The cigar had gone out and Blanchflower made a good deal of trimming the ash and relighting it.

"Look," he said, taking Kate seriously, "I think kids like mine ought to go to college, get a degree, then spend six months as a bartender and six as a cabbie. That's education."

She liked that. She laughed.

"You know, you've got a terrible reputation."

"I know it," Blanchflower said, "it's taken years. When I got into politics in the beginning they said I was nuts. Then I won a couple elections. Now I'm not nuts anymore. Now I'm eccentric."

"And you don't mind."

"Why the hell should I mind? Eight million voters in the state, how many of them haven't screwed someone else's wife, haven't gotten drunk, haven't fudged an expense account, cheated on the income tax, found a buck in a cab and shoved it in their pocket? There's no monopoly on virtue. Hell, I work the vice neighborhoods where they understand me. On Sunday mornings in the Bible precincts I tap out. Saturday nights in the gin mills and the bowling leagues and the singles bars, I'm electric."

"So you don't care what people say about you?"

"Of course I care. Nobody likes to be shit on. But I'm ready to take it to get where I'm going." He looked at her, uncertain whether any of this was getting through.

"And where are you going?" she asked.

He shrugged. "Well, where are *you* going? What's *your* upside limit? For me it's the White House. There isn't a politician in the country who doesn't win a city council seat, doesn't start thinking of himself in the Oval Office."

"Politics," Kate said with a certain, practiced distaste.

"All right, it isn't like running for Jesus. It's a game. You win, you've got a year, two years, to enjoy it. You lose, there's another star in the East."

She laughed.

"A politician," she said again.

Blanchflower nodded.

"Sure," he said. "I know people. I know what turns them on, what turns them off."

"And what turns them on?"

Blanchflower knew he was being interviewed and enjoyed it. "You remember Mayor Curley, up in Boston? Spent half his time in jail. Got reelected every time. During the depression Boston went broke. Tap city. Old Curley took himself around to the banks, the way Beame had to do in New York. No play. The banks said no. Curley sent bulldozers to rip up the streets in front of the biggest banks in Boston. Then the water commissioner turned on the hydrants. For two days no one could get in or out without wading through a foot of mud. The banks surrendered. They gave Curley his loans and next day the streets were repaved."

He grinned. "I like that story," Kate told him. "Is it true?"

Blanchflower threw up his big hands.

"Who knows? But it's a good story."

"And Mayor Curley was a good politician," she said.

Blanchflower nodded.

Connie Heath came up to them, yet another young man at her side, and looked up into Blanchflower's face.

"Dinner, Senator, or is Kate staging a filibuster?"

Blanchflower shook his head.

"No," he said, "Kate's fine. I like her. I don't understand why you said she was a stainless steel bitch."

He looked at Kate, innocently. She had trouble not laughing at Connie's reddening face.

"Kate, I . . . " Connie stammered.

Blanchflower grinned wickedly. Then he turned to Kate and stuck out a big hand.

"Kate Sinclair, I'll see you around," he said.

What an arrogant man, she thought. Beyond the fun, underlying the charm, she sensed ambition, self-interest, cruelty even. It was odd they'd not met before. She'd seen him a thousand times on television. Of all the new breed of politician Blanchflower understood best how to use the camera, how to capture and retain an audience. She admired professionalism. She would like to have continued their conversation. Perhaps it was best to have ended as it did. She had an uneasy feeling Nicholas Blanchflower ran over people. And she knew she was not quite the stainless steel automaton Connie Heath made her out to be.

The places were predetermined at dinner and Kate wondered if Blanchflower would find his way back to her table when it was over. He didn't, and Harvey took her home, weeping drunkenly in the car because one of Connie Heath's young men had snubbed him, "after what I did for that boy in Provincetown last summer."

Kate and the driver got Harvey out of the car and into his building. She hoped very much the rumors about his drinking getting out of control again were untrue.

At home she went to bed, thinking first about Harvey, and without meaning to, about Nicholas Blanchflower. Then, unaccountably, and for the first time in a very long while, of Tommy.

6

Tommy. Thomas Hamilton Sinclair Jr. Even now the name summoned visions of white sailboats, the thock of tennis balls, the growl of low-slung cars with wire wheels and straps across their bonnets, of tall, tan young men in understated clothes, of pretty young girls and green lawns, of great houses and the right schools and the right names and the right churches, of Wall Street and a season's subscription to the Met, of carpeted rooms full of splendid things, of girlhood and first sex and happiness. Despite everything, happiness.

She was in her second year at college, Smith, still only eighteen, the youngest girl in her class. She'd sprinted through Dalton in three years, and with honors. She was young, bright, naive and touchable. A tall girl with green eyes and lovely long brown hair, extraordinary legs and good shoulders, and a chest that was perhaps unfashionably small but which promised better things. Eighteen years old, a straight-A student, the second best free-style swimmer on the varsity, and a virgin. In those days she was not Kate Sinclair. She was Kate D'Amico.

Her father was in public relations. There would come a time when Kate, defensively, would laughingly say of her father that, "he was a cheap show business press agent," but that would be later and was, in truth, unfair. Philip D'Amico was an uneducated but intelligent man with a marvelous instinct for a good story, a yarn that would make the columns, occasionally the headlines, and in his best years he represented several of the good Broadway houses and a number of the most talented people on Broadway. He became a partner in, and eventually the head of, a PR firm that earned as much respect as any in that generally abused business. When he was thirty-five he married her mother, a lanky Irish girl who had, briefly, been one of Billy Rose's "long stemmed beauties," a girl with a wonderful laugh and good legs and a fierce loyalty. Her mother was jolly and vague, pretty much leaving the girl to her father, and to Mary Costello, the Irish Trotskyite cleaning woman, to rear.

Dalton, the first of the great progressive schools, full of the children of Manhattan's Upper East Side, quick, spoiled, occasionally neurotic, Jews, enlightened Catholics, avant-garde Protestants, was just right for Kate D'Amico. At thirteen she was hardly aware of her religion or her ethnicity. No one remarked it, her father insisted on none of the rubrics, she prayed before sleeping to a vague God, heeded seriously Mary Costello's verbal manifestos assuring her of the eventual triumph of the proletariat and the final dictatorship of the workers. But Dalton? Dalton was all right, quirky, stimulating, broadening. Permissiveness didn't harm Kate. She minded, as her father liked to say. And so, bright and pretty, and still very much a child, at sixteen she moved on to Smith, a good little girl without a care.

Twenty years ago Smith was not as it is today. Northampton, of course, didn't look much different, the same hills, green half the year, white from November into April, a New England town with its charms and boredom, its civilities and its small-mindedness, its warmth and its town-and-gown frictions. But the college itself was a very different place. Stricter rules (smoking a cigarette, not grass for God's sake, but even a Lucky Strike, merited rustication or worse if performed in certain buildings or at certain times), compulsory chapel, a more structured curriculum, dress codes which legislated (without actually saying so) the wearing of bras, the covering of the knee, the virtually compulsory Shetland sweaters, knee socks, and Brooks Brothers raincoats cut on the men's model. Then, as now, the girls were intelligent (not Radcliffe-bright but close enough), traditional (the rebels and the weirdos went to Bennington), heterosexual (the occasional infamy occurred and was inevitably hushed up), and monied. There were no blacks then, Jews were accepted but not encouraged, Catholics were tolerated, and WASP-dom ruled. Being half-Italian *and* half-Catholic, Kate D'Amico entered Smith with two burdens and was unaware of either.

Her freshman roommate was a plump girl from Connecticut called Alexandra Morley. A veteran of boarding schools from thirteen, Alex had arrived a day or two early and had already staked out her (the preferable) territory in their room, the bed by the window, the right-hand side of the closet, the lower shelf in the bathroom cabinet. Smith was to be Kate's first time away from home and, feeling alien to start, she experienced an uneasy sense of trespass in the room she and Alex were to share. On that first afternoon, having driven up from the city with her father, she found herself asking: "Is it okay if I put a suitcase up on this shelf?"

Alex stared at her and then giggled.

"Hey, it's okay. I don't bite. Last girl I roomed with, at boarding school, she stole things."

Kate's eyes widened.

"You mean, actually *stole* things?"

Alex shrugged. "Sure, sweaters, soap, underwear. Money even."

"Did anything happen?"

"Nah. I couldn't turn her in. I mean, I *could* have, but I would have felt crummy. So don't worry about taking a share of the damn shelf. It's yours. Your parents paid for it."

For all her upbringing in Manhattan and the casual ways of the Dalton school, Kate had never before been exposed to actual crime, and she pursued the matter of the kleptomaniac roommate.

"And you didn't do anything about it?"

"About what?"

"The girl who stole from you."

"Oh, sure," Alex Morley said, "I just stole things back."

Alex Morley was one of those persons superbly equipped to survive, even to prosper, in any ambience. She was healthy, cheerful, and wise, a blunt-spoken girl, hard to hurt, considerate of others without being tentative or over-polite, and if some sort of wondrous computer programmer instead of mere chance had thrown the two girls together, there could not have been a better match for Kate D'Amico. Take the matter of their legs.

Alex had dimpled knees, sturdy ankles, and had played too much field hockey. She loved Kate's legs.

"I mean," Alex would say, "you don't even shave and they're smoother than mine. And God, they just go on and on. I wish I had legs like that. I remember hearing a boy once talk about a girl I was at school with—she had legs like yours—and this boy said, 'She's got legs clear up to her asshole.' If anyone ever said that about my legs I'd die happy."

Kate knew boys talked like that. But girls weren't supposed to quote them. And she didn't shave her legs because, well, she had never been taught how. Did you secretly borrow your father's Gillette and do it, did you use shaving cream, did a depilatory really work or was that just advertising agency copy invented for *Glamour* magazine? Fighting back a blush and swallowing her pride, she said:

"Could you teach me how to shave them?"

Alex could, and would. And she taught her other things.

"You really Italian?" She asked one night when they were both bored with cramming for a French exam, each at her own desk, each in her own quilted robe that was the season's dormitory essential.

Kate frowned thoughtfully. "I guess so. My father is. My mother isn't. I was baptized Catholic but I never practiced it. I don't really know what I am." Then she blurted out, "I wish I were you. Episcopalian. Then there wouldn't be any problems at all."

"Ha!" Alex exploded. "You think we don't have any problems? Well, maybe you're right in some respects. But we don't have legs like yours or your eyes or your skin. I mean, look at these freckles. There's something almost . . . Mediterranean about the way you look. Why, when you're old, in your twenties or so, you'll be, well, I'll bet you're . . . exotic."

·Toward the end of their second year, on one of those pleasant spring weekends when the snow and the mud have gone and the heat and humidity not yet come, Kate D'Amico for the first time began to understand what Alex was trying to say. It was on that weekend that Kate first saw Thomas Hamilton Sinclair Jr.

There had been a swimming meet with Vassar at home. Kate had swum creditably in the 400-yard freestyle and then had anchored the winning medley relay team. That was Friday afternoon. On Saturday Alex, who was allowed to have a car, drove them south into Connecticut, to Cos Cob, where her family lived. Kate had spent weekends there before and liked the Morleys, the father a beefy, successful insurance salesman who now headed one of the mid-sized firms in the field, the mother, slight, neurotic, given to alternating moods of cheer and depression, but parading her party manners and spirit whenever there were houseguests, and a sprawl of younger children swarming noisily over the house and the lawn and down to the battered old dock from which the Morleys swam and fished and sailed their boats.

There was a dance scheduled that evening at the local yacht club and in the late afternoon Morley got out the station wagon and chauffered Kate and Alex to the house of a third girl where they would change into their dresses for the dance. The girl was hospitable but Alex whispered, "She stinks."

The girl, whose name was Elizabeth, was very excited about the dance.

"The Saturday dances are best in the spring. Later on people go away or there are summer people around, outsiders, and it's never the same thing."

"She means you," Alex whispered again. "Outsiders. See what I mean, she really stinks."

Elizabeth, who was quite attractive and had a wonderful bosom, rattled on about the dance and, especially, about her date for the evening. Alex and Kate knew some boys who would be there but weren't actually paired up with anyone and so Elizabeth had the floor.

"He works in New York, for one of the big ad agencies. He went to Yale. He graduated two years ago. He's nearly twenty-five."

"Isn't that pretty old?" Alex asked.

Elizabeth tossed her head. "Last Christmas I went dancing with a man who was thirty."

To Kate, thirty seemed ancient and so, despite her own instincts, and Alex's whispered warnings, she found herself observing Elizabeth with something approaching awe. And when all three girls had changed, her impression of Elizabeth rose another notch.

"Like?" Elizabeth asked and she came into the bedroom Kate and Alex were using. She swirled to show her dress. It

56

was little different from their party dresses except that it was strapless and cut sufficiently low in front to flatter the impressive upper slopes of her breasts. Even Alex stared.

"Hey," she said, "that's fantastic."

Kate's mouth fell open. She glanced down at her own, relatively flat front. What she wouldn't give to have a chest.

"Come on," Elizabeth said, "We're meeting Tommy there. If you behave maybe I'll let you each dance with him."

It was clear from her tone that she felt neither Alex, with her freckles and plump arms, nor this new girl, Kate, boyishly slim, presented a competitive threat.

The yacht club was one of those wonderful old rambling houses on the Sound that had ridden out the 1938 hurricane and a thousand potential disasters since: bridge parties; debutante balls; race-week dinners; cocktail parties; and the depredations of twelve-year-old boys, drunken yachtsmen, jealous wives. The wide-boarded floors were scuffed and scratched, the furniture was typically institutional, the buffet banal, the music routine, the people hale and hearty and relentlessly suburban. And Kate D'Amico, whose father worked with and for some of the most glittering and internationally famous talents in show business, and whose turf was Broadway, thought she had never before in all her eighteen years seen any place as grand. The reason was, of course, Tommy Sinclair.

"This is Tommy," Elizabeth said, hurriedly sloughing off Alex and Kate as casual acquaintances, and sucking in her stomach to accentuate still further the bosom that strained against the bodice of her dress. Tommy smiled, shook hands rather gravely, and went off with Elizabeth for what seemed an endless round of dances.

"Boy," Alex said, gulping dramatically and rolling her eyes. "I've got to admit that for such a mean stinker, she does okay."

Kate could only stare. She was, quite literally, stricken. She was just eighteen years old and except for a few schoolgirl crushes on actors her father represented and who had been to the apartment, she had never been in love. Now she knew, absolutely *knew*, that she was lost.

"I'm a goner," she told herself. "A goner." Beside her Alex chattered on but Kate did not listen and if she made reply it was meaningless noise, polite words that certainly conveyed no message, made no sense. Finally Alex took her by the bare arm.

"Hey," she said, "I just told you I had pleurisy and you said, 'Swell, me too.' Are you listening at all?"

Some undergraduates about their age came by and the dancing began and Kate tried to keep up a reasonable conversation with her partners while looking past their shoulders to where Elizabeth and Tommy Sinclair were in each other's arms. "If only I had real breasts," Kate thought, "maybe I'd have a chance with him."

The dance had begun in the spring dusk but now it was dark with lanterns and bobbing lights on the water and the headlights of cars coming up the graveled drive. The music was slower and more romantic, the boys looked taller and more handsome under the first reddish tans of the season, the girls looked lovelier, their dresses seemed to float, their hair softened and curling in the slightly damp breeze off the water, and a magical mood of love and adventure spread through the tall-ceilinged rooms of the old yacht club and washed out onto the sprawling verandah where Elizabeth and Alex and Kate D'Amico, and a few score other girls and a half a hundred young men, flirted and laughed and whispered and held one another, more or less sedately, in the Connecticut night.

A lanky boy from Dartmouth, abjectly infatuated with her, took Kate to the bar. She had been drinking lemonade. Now, when the boy asked, she said:

"A martini, if I may."

Martinis were things her father and his clients drank. She felt that somehow, if she too were to drink one, it might possibly impart to her some of the sophistication those actors and producers seemed to possess in surplus. Tommy Sinclair, disappeared for the moment with the despicable Elizabeth, might come by, might notice the change, might ask her to dance, perhaps might even want to dance a second time.

The martini tasted awful. She wanted to spit out the first mouthful. But instead she smiled at the Dartmouth boy and said, echoing something she had heard at home, "A bit dry, but quite nice."

Then, as if the script had been written, Elizabeth was there, with Tommy Sinclair beside her.

"Tommy, get me a drink, will you? I'll be right back. You can entertain yourself with Kate for a moment, can't you?"

If Kate were able to talk, she might have said what she was thinking, that the other girl seemed terribly sure of herself, didn't she? but her mouth was dry and her heart pounding and she said nothing. Tommy stood next to her, smiling. He was not very tall but neatly built, compact, his dinner jacket custom cut to his body. He had light blue eyes and blond hair that framed a perfectly shaped head. He looked at Kate, smiling into her eyes.

"So I'm to entertain you," he said.

"You don't have to. It's okay," she said, not sure if he too, as Elizabeth, were mocking her.

"Maybe I'd like to. Maybe I'd like to very much."

"Thank you," she said, quite seriously.

He glanced at her drink. "Is that really a martini?"

"Oh, yes," she said, the words tumbling out now, "I drink them all the time. I mean, I practically have them for breakfast. They're really my favorite. They . . . "

He took the glass from her hand. She stared at his tanned fingers, at the smooth, hairless back of his hand, the slender, sinewy wrist.

"Come on," he said, "teach me whatever dances they're doing at college these days."

He led her onto the floor.

"Thanks," she said.

He seemed surprised. "For asking you to dance?"

"No, for getting rid of that awful martini. I hated it." She laughed, relaxing for the first time.

They danced that dance, and another, and a third. Vaguely Kate could see Elizabeth at the edge of the dance floor, pacing, angry. She didn't care. She could feel Tommy's lean body hard against hers. She was even glad not to have bosoms, not to have anything that would push him away from her. She danced well, she knew that, friends of her father's had always said so. And now that the ice had broken conversation came easily.

59

"You're with an advertising agency," she said.

"Yes, I went through the training program. I'm what's called an account executive now. Or I will be shortly. I still bear the scar of that dreadful word, 'assistant.' "

"I think it's a lovely word."

Tommy grinned. "How old are you, really?"

"Eighteen."

"And you're what, a freshman?"

"Sophomore."

"Bright."

"Well," she said, "I guess so. But being the youngest girl in the class isn't always that much fun. You know, older girls tend to tease you a lot. They . . . "

"Like Elizabeth," he said.

She nodded.

"Elizabeth," he said, "is a bitch."

Kate laughed. She knew she shouldn't. Except in swimming she wasn't terribly competitive. But now, with a prize like this, well, the rules were different, weren't they?

It was past midnight. Elizabeth had recaptured Tommy Sinclair, her eyes spitting hate at Kate D'Amico. Tommy had looked back, his creased brow and his grin begging forgiveness, asking, "Well, what can I do?" as he was led firmly away. Alex found Kate standing alone, by the verandah rail, looking out over the water to where the sailboats rode at their moorings, to the distant Long Island shore.

"Hey," Alex said, "I mean, if it's really a lousy dance we can go." There was no answer. "Kate? You okay?"

Kate D'Amico turned to her.

"I am," she said, "absolutely super."

They danced with a couple of red-headed twins from Greenwich, boys who laughed a lot and tried to get them out in the parking lot to neck, and then it was time to go and across the half-empty porch Kate saw Tommy Sinclair, standing a few feet away from Elizabeth. They seemed to be arguing.

Summer came.

Final exams had never been such a drag. Waves of humid heat came down off the parched hillsides, and girls squirmed in their classroom seats as perspiration dampened their buttoned-down shirts and Villager linen skirts. For the first time in her academic career, Kate found herself struggling. Her once-crisp analysis of Molière, her grasp of the syllogistic method, her instinctive understanding of logarithmic functions, had fallen apart. The problem, of course, was Thomas Hamilton Sinclair Jr. Kate was in love.

She had been seeing him ever since the yacht club dance in Cos Cob. He drove up to Northampton for dances and mixers. She saw him in Manhattan on weekends she was visiting her father. Her swimming suffered and girls defeated her who had no business in the same pool. Once Tommy and Kate had run into the discarded Elizabeth in the backroom at P. J. Clarke's and Elizabeth had snarled at her, "Greasy wop!" and Kate, who had never in her eighteen years been branded one aloud, sat, embarrassed over the scene, puzzled over the girl's hate, and illogically wondering whether Tommy Sinclair would stand up and walk away from her now that her shameful secret was out. Instead, he slid his arm around her shoulders and said:

"What a creep. I don't know why I ever took her out."

Later, when they sat in his car, kissing, her shirt unbuttoned and his hand cupping one small breast and then the other, she said:

"It doesn't matter that I'm Italian?"

He laughed.

"Well, with a name like D'Amico, I didn't think you were Irish or anything."

Now it was her turn to laugh.

"Hey," she said, "I nearly am, you know. Half-Irish."

"Shut up," he said, and lowered his mouth to her nipple.

They did not make love that night. Not really. That was for late summer at the place where they met.

For a young girl who had a sweet, careless mother, a permissive and distracted father, a housekeeper who spouted Marxist cant, and who had attended progressive schools, Kate D'Amico had considerable self-discipline. For two weeks she stopped seeing Tommy, tried, with intermittent success, not to think about him, hushed Alex Morley whenever her roommate daydreamed aloud, kept herself awake nights with black coffee and No-Doze, and succeeded in cramming enough knowledge into her head to finish out her sophomore year with yet another perfect 4.0 average. Her father, vague as usual, patted her on the bottom and said, "Very nice, Katie, very nice," and had she seen his copy of *Variety* anywhere? Mary Costello, deeply impressed by book-learning, told her for perhaps the hundredth time, of those lonely, crucial hours Karl Marx had passed in the British Museum, poring over the dusty tomes that would become the skeleton of his masterwork, *Das Kapital.*

Then, summer and what some of the more sophisticated girls, the ones who'd read Evelyn Waugh, called "the long vac."

Philip D'Amico had expanded his press agentry west, had opened a small office in Hollywood in a building on Sunset. His wife did not like airplanes and he and Kate flew to Los Angeles on the fourth of July. It was her first trip to the coast, they had good adjoining rooms in the Beverly Hills Hotel, young men flirted with her in the Polo Lounge, she tanned mahogany under the California sun, took tennis lessons from Segura, the old champion, and then one memorable afternoon, startled several dozen onlookers by actually going into the Beverly Hills Hotel pool, and swimming twenty laps at speed. When she came out of the pool, a sixty-year-old screenwriter broke into spontaneous applause, and the assorted producers, agents, actors, and mistresses sunning around the pool joined in. Kate blushed, curtsied, ran to the cabana to wrap herself in her father's terrycloth robe. She loved Hollywood. She loved everything about it.

One night they went to Dave Chasen's for dinner and Chasen showed them into "the office," that little room just behind the bar where once he did his ledgers and where now important guests lounged in easy chairs while the bartender passed drinks through a little door behind one of the autographed pictures. Their dinner companion was Pat Weaver, then and later the house intellectual of the television business, a man whose vision stretched beyond the state of the art, and would eventually bring him down. That night he talked business, rather technically, with Phil D'Amico, and then, when the business was done, turned to Kate and asked what she planned to do with her life.

"Why," she said, not having ever thought it through before, "I guess I'll finish college and marry Tommy Sinclair."

Weaver said that sounded like an excellent plan and D'Amico *père*, who would never have thought of asking his own daughter such a question, looked confused (he could not remember *which* young man Tommy Sinclair might be), while Kate, taken by surprise, blushed at what she had said. Weaver, seeing this, quickly changed the subject.

"With your voice," he said, "and your looks, and your obvious brains, my girl, you ought to take a close look at television before you do anything else. That is, if this business of young Mister What's-his-name doesn't work out."

"Oh, but it will," Kate blurted out.

That night, when they got back to the hotel, there was a letter from Tommy in her box, and two days later, leaving a relieved father to finish his work, she flew back to New York. And to the man she had told Pat Weaver she was going to marry.

It was late August. Classes would begin in a few weeks. Her mother absent-mindedly gave Kate permission to stay with Alex Morley in Cos Cob and Tommy Sinclair was on vacation, still an assistant account executive but, he assured her, much closer to the real thing. He could, it seemed, do anything. Growing up in Connecticut, educated at private schools, his family always belonging to this country club or that yacht club, he was an accomplished tennis player, sailor, golfer. Accomplished, impressively so. But not a star. Kate had played some tennis, they taught it at Dalton and she played a little at Smith when not swimming. She knew nothing at all about sailboats or golf. At swimming, of course, she was easily his superior. But at this stage of love even Tommy's failures were endearing. She loved him equally whether he was beating her, respectably at tennis, eliminating the slice in her golf drive, or bringing a Lightning neatly around a racing buoy. Then, one squally day, when Kate had progressed sufficiently to crew in a club regatta, their boat capsized.

They were a long way out in the Sound, the mild chop cresting into whitecaps and the low black clouds tumbling into a thunderstorm. Finding herself in the water, fully clothed, Kate began to do sensible things. She let herself sink, not wasting energy keeping afloat, while smoothly and economically stripping off her oilskin slicker, her sneakers and sweat socks, and finally her jeans. Then she popped to the surface to see Tommy, still dressed, trying to right the boat.

"Hey," she said, "Lemme help."

He shook his head. "S'okay. I've capsized a thousand times. Just take a minute."

She treaded water, holding on to her discarded clothes with one hand, and watching him as he shoved the boat into the wind, swam to the centerboard, mounted it, and heaved on the near rail. It should have risen slowly out of the water, shaken itself, and been righted. Instead, it stayed on its side.

"Hey," she called again, "I can help. Really I can."

She didn't wait for an answer but swam to his side. She tossed her sneakers and her sodden clothes up on the side of the hull and pushed him to the side so her feet could find room on the submerged centerboard next to him. She reached out and grabbed the rail.

Sinclair didn't move.

"Hey, Tommy, come on. Four hands are better than two, y'know."

He nodded, without speaking. They pulled, and with double weight on the keel and both of them tugging, the boat slowly, heavily, came up out of the water and righted itself. When they clambered in, she realized she was wearing only her nylon pants and bra, and that wet they clung translucently. But Tommy didn't look. He was staring out to the west, toward the squall line.

Kate watched him for a while and then, sensing there was something wrong, crawled to him along the bottom of the boat and when she reached him, put an arm around his neck and lowered her mouth to his. It was not precisely a kiss, because Tommy did not respond.

She sat back on her knees, staring into his face.

"Look," she said, "it's okay. You're cold is all. Come on, we lost anyway, let's go in."

He nodded, again without speaking, and after a minute he pushed the tiller and they made the first of a long series of tacks that would get them back into the harbor. By then Kate

64

had pulled on her jeans and shirt and slicker and Tommy had come back to life.

"You musta been hit on the head by the boom or something," she told him. "You were really out of it for a while there. It kind of scared me."

"Scared you?" he said. "Hell, if you didn't stay cool we'd still be out there. I dunno, nothing like that ever happened to me before. I just froze."

"Forget it," she said. "I feel like that before a race. Nerves, that's what it is. Pure nerves."

But she knew it was more than that. And so did Tommy Sinclair. They skipped the usual post-race party that evening and drove along the coast in his car, not talking much, listening to music on the car radio. The thunderstorm had passed and the air was warm and sweet. Near Westport Tommy pulled off the road and parked. They sat there, smoking cigarettes and listening to the radio, and then Kate said:

"I'll be going back to college in a couple of weeks."

"Yeah."

"It's been a wonderful summer. I can't remember when I've been happier."

"That's good," he said. "I'm glad."

"Tommy?" she said.

"Yes?"

"You okay?"

"Sure," he said, trying to smile.

"Okay, then." She leaned over and kissed him on the mouth, as she'd done in the boat, and this time he responded.

Several minutes later she was naked and they were in the back of the car, the radio playing softly, and just west of Westport, Connecticut, Kate D'Amico made love for the first time in her eighteen years, to a frightened boy seven years older than she.

She went back to college in September and a month later, Tommy having become an account executive, she gave up the chance to spend a semester in France, and married him. They moved into his bachelor apartment on East End Avenue and drank wine out of straw-sheathed bottles and read *The New York Times* and discovered cheap Italian restaurants and visited galleries and went to what were then called "art movies" and made love.

A decade later they would have done all this without marrying. But in the fifties and into the early sixties, you got married first. Within a year Kate, still very much in love, knew that the man she married was charming, decent, and terribly weak. And she was pregnant.

Within another year her child was dead, she and Tommy were drifting apart, and her silly, lovable mother was dead in the delivery room trying to give Phil D'Amico another daughter, and Kate, a baby sister.

She remembered all these things, and more, the night she met Blanchflower, and it was nearly three o'clock in the morning before she stopped thinking about them, stopped remembering Tommy, stopped recalling what it was like in those days before she had a million dollars or was made of stainless steel, when she was still only a girl, and in love, and fell asleep.

7

The Atelier, half a block west of Central Park, was Chester Albany's favorite bar. It was convenient to the studio and the lighting was appropriately dim so that a man could go in there wearing television makeup and not frighten the horses or draw the gays. The regulars at the bar were the sort of old shoe technicians and passed-over producers and directors with whom he could relax. Chester liked the lank barman, the stemmed glasses in which they served his martinis straight up, the wood nymphs on the walls, Howard Chandler Christy nudes peeking slyly through the foliage, innocent, lascivious and rather jolly all at the same time. Chester liked the look of the diners in the place, solid, middle-aged men and women like himself, none of the flashy *ye-ye* trade you got at Elaine's or the postgraduate loudmouths at Clarke's. He liked sitting at the bar with his martini and his Pall Mall Golds and his Cricket lighter arrayed neatly in front of him, flanked by his cronies, telling and retelling stories (some of them true) of those splendid times in the newspaper business when it was all so much simpler and although he was not then making half a million dollars a year, so much more fun.

Occasionally when Chester was at the bar before seven o'clock a passerby might doubletake, wondering why the anchorman was not in the studio, not understanding that the network reports are taped and that Chester Albany was hanging around the neighborhood only in case the President were shot or Martin Bormann surfaced in Las Vegas. Such passersby meant nothing to Chester and his pals. They were outside the club. The warm, comfortable ambience of the place, the trade gossip, the shop talk, the corny jokes, the casual girls from Research or Copy or the Sales Department, the easy joshing, the professional freemasonry, these were what counted. These were what drew Chester Albany each weekday night to the bar of the Atelier. These were the creature comforts that made the place a sanctuary, these what made this the best time of day, these the relaxations that enabled him to maintain sanity in a punishing trade, these that enabled him, if only for a few dreamy hours, to postpone tomorrow.

And, oh yes, there was another reason Chester Albany attended the Atelier faithfully every evening after the show. It was here that he could most circumspectly get drunk and forget his broadcast partner, Kate Sinclair.

He and Kate had been broadcasting together for precisely one hundred days. There were full page ads in that morning's *Times* and in the trades. The floor manager at the studio, a longtime crony of Chester's, had arranged a Greenberg's cake with a pink candle between them on the anchor desk and they blew it out, jointly, just as the show went off the air. That evening, in millions of American homes, thousands of wives turned to thousands of husbands and remarked how warm and comfortable they looked together up there on the screen and, yes, how quickly time had sped by. But in Rose's that same night a vice-president who disliked Bobby Klaus handed over ten dollars to an account man from Ogilvy, saying, "And I thought I had a sure thing."

"Want to press? Twenty bucks they don't make it to a year?"

"Hell, yes," the network vice-president said. "There's no way a whole year goes by without Chester murders the bitch."

Now it was an hour and a half after the wrap and Chester Albany and his producer were drinking at the Atelier bar. "A little celebration," the producer had said, "for your anniversary." Chester Albany was drinking a martini and being morose. He did his morose act very well, having practiced it on the air for many years now.

"I thought it was a good show," the producer was saying. "A nice, friendly feel to it."

"You think so?" Chester asked. "You think we're really fooling anybody?"

"Sure," the producer said expansively, "sure you are. Hell, I mean she didn't step on a single line of yours tonight. And once there, you almost smiled. A nice feel, a nice warm feel."

Chester Albany sipped at his drink.

"When she blew out the candle, you didn't see her spit?" he asked.

The producer shrugged. "Hell, you blow out a candle. There's a little spray. It happens."

Chester didn't argue the point.

"The White House call," he said, "whose idea was that?"

"Chester," the producer said, being patient, "it was no one's idea. I didn't even know about it until just before we went on the air. It was the President's idea. Or his press guy. That wasn't a setup, believe me."

Chester was sulky.

"He didn't have to call her," he said. "The call could have come to me. Or to both of us jointly."

The producer, who had been in the business long enough to have a high tolerance for paranoia, shrugged. "I'll bet we're up a couple of points in the overnights. The ad department's getting out another fullpager in the *Times* tomorrow. All about the President calling you."

Chester Albany didn't seem to care about the overnights. Or the ad.

"He called me 'Walter' there once, you caught that, didn't you?"

"Hell, Chester, the President always has problems with names. You know that. I'll bet no one even noticed."

Chester drained his glass.

"The President calls her. David Rockefeller. Warren Beatty. Giscard d'Estaing calls her."

The producer tried to be helpful.

"Colonel Qaddafi, Chester—he called you last week."

Chester Albany beckoned for a refill and after a while the producer gave up trying to be cheerful and went home.

An hour later Herbie Bliss, Chester's agent, came and sat beside him at the bar. Herbie was a partner in his agency, one of their senior people, and he didn't handle just anyone. He handled the heavies like Chester Albany. And he knew enough to sense trouble before it came. Carefully arranging his agent's smile, he clapped Chester on the back.

"What a terrific thing, Chester! The *President* calling to congratulate you."

"Ha," Chester said.

An agent with the experience of Herbie Bliss is sensitive to the moods of his clients. He canceled his smile and ordered a drink and asked where Chester wanted to have dinner. Chester ignored the question.

"If I'd known then what I know now," he said.

Herbie inhaled and pulled his drink closer.

"Look, Chester, so you don't love the dame. So what? It's a job. It's a half million per and a 21 share going on 22 and you got the goddamned President of the United States calling to say he's watching and his goddamned wife and the kids are watching and he can't wait for you to be a whole year together on the air. He can't wait for your *tenth* year together. I wouldn't call that a sharp stick in the eye, y'know . . ."

"Ten years," Chester muttered. "Ten years with her?" His eyes glazed. "Oh, boy."

"Come on, Chester, have another and we'll go over to the Palm, have a steak. We'll go to Grenouille, we'll go up to Elaine's. Have a meal, drink some wine, look at the chicks. You'll feel better about things."

"You noticed he placed the call to her. Not to me. Not to both of us."

"Maybe that was the White House operator's fault," Herbie said helpfully. "Maybe it was just common courtesy, addressing the woman first. I don't see anything sinister in it."

"That's another thing," Chester said. "They want equality. They want to be treated like men, paid like men, and then they still want you to pull back their chairs and open the car door for them and leave the john seat down and have the President to call them first instead of you. You call that fair?"

Herbie nodded. "I'll grant you they want it both ways. That's a valid point you make, Chester."

When his client said nothing Herbie Bliss suddenly slapped a pudgy hand on the table and brightened.

"Hey," he said, "I almost forgot. Someone at the agency told me. Top secret stuff." He leaned closer to Chester and whispered, "She's supposed to have got a little tuck job last summer while she was on vacation. You hear that?" He leaned back again, beaming.

Chester did not react but just continued to stare out across the room. Which surprised Herbie Bliss.

"I thought you'd want to know," Herbie said dejectedly. "It sort of shows she's insecure or something. Age creeping up. Maybe the menopause." He paused. "Doesn't it . . . ?"

He waited for Chester to say something.

"Herbie?" Chester said thoughtfully, "you know my upper lip? The way it never shows my teeth?"

Herbie skewed his buttocks around on the stool.

"Lemme see," he said.

Chester Albany slid into his anchorperson face. Herbie Bliss scrutinized him.

"Say something. So I can see whether your teeth show."

Chester Albany said a few words in that nice, flat western professional voice of his while the agent watched.

"You know," Herbie said, "you're right. Your upper teeth don't show. They don't show at all." Then he said, "Lift up your lip. Lemme see how they look."

Chester used his two forefingers to shove up his upper lip and across the room a woman stared at him curiously. But Herbie Bliss looked only at his client's teeth.

"You know, Chester, those are very nice teeth. Teeth like that could be a real asset. Give you a whole new dimension on camera."

The two men entered into a clinical discussion of Chester Albany's face, specifically his smile, and whether there might be anything the plastic surgeons might do about it. Then, just as Herbie Bliss thought this constructive avenue of possibilities had thoroughly wrenched his client out of self-pity, Chester said:

"Aw, the hell with it. She'd just make cracks about it. She'd have it all over town I had a face job. She'd tell Javits about it, and Mailer, and for God's sake Charlie Bluhdorn."

Herbie Bliss, wanting to go home to his latest wife who would soon be twenty, but nervous about leaving an important client alone in this mood, continued to sit, pleased that since Chester refused to go out to eat he was at least in a place where his drinking would not cause talk. Chester could slur his words and spill drinks and even fall asleep with his face in the ash tray and no one would notice. If he did these things elsewhere a transparently blind item would be in Wilson's column the next afternoon and network executives would be summoned ponderously to the 39th floor to discuss his "problem." But in the Atelier Chester could safely get shit-faced.

Clive Jackson had joined them now and Clive was doing absolutely nothing constructive about Chester. He was, in fact, exacerbating the whole business.

"Come off it, Chester," Clive was saying, "if anyone has a claim on being bitter, it's me. You're still co-host. I got the sack. What the hell do I do anymore except my 90-second Sevareid instant-wisdom sermon on the mount act?"

Chester stared at his old partner through eyes increasingly bleared.

"Easy for you to say, Clive. You went out with dignity. Your departure had style. You tipped your hat and tap-danced nimbly into the wings. I stand out there every night in front of thirty million Americans and have patches of my hide torn off. Public humiliation has never been my favorite form of masochism."

Clive grinned his famous elder statesman grin.

"She *is* a bitch, isn't she?" He sounded almost reverential.

Herbie Bliss, thinking of his bride waiting for him at home, had switched to coffee but Jackson and Albany had shifted to straight scotches with glasses of water on the side that went untouched.

Chester reverted to a familiar theme.

"I've threatened to quit, you know. Told them I was fed up. Scared hell out of them, I can tell you."

Clive Jackson looked startled. "It *did?*"

Chester exhaled and shook his head.

"Nope," he admitted in a defeated voice. "Bobby Klaus said that if I really felt that way of course the network would do whatever they could to make my exit smooth. He made polite noises, naturally, the way Bobby can, but they can read the Nielsens as clearly as I can. They know what she's done to hype the show. Hell, there are a dozen anchormen out there who'd just love to play second banana to her."

Herbie Bliss permitted himself a small eruption. It was bad policy to let a client run himself down this way. Self-doubt got talked around and when contract renewal time came along, an agent could find himself void in trumps.

"There's no one in broadcasting, *no one* could handle your job except you, Chester," he declared. "You're talking non-

72

sense. Cronkite couldn't share a desk with her nearly as competently as you've done. I won't hear such talk. I won't!"

Chester smiled. It was not a convincing smile.

"Herbie," he said, "Walter wouldn't last one show with her. Not thirty minutes. I'm talking about young cats, hungry kids out of Boston, Cleveland. They're out there, you know, just waiting for a shot."

Clive Jackson gave a short, bitter laugh.

"But don't we know it? Haven't we learned?"

Chester waved an arm for the waiter.

"I think I might do a little drinking tonight," he said.

It was an hour later.

"You know something else," Chester was saying, "it isn't fair about the clothing allowances. My Ralph Lauren suits don't cost anything *like* her Halstons. Not anything like."

Herbie Bliss strove for patience.

"Chester, maybe we can renegotiate a point like that. I'm sure Bobby would be reasonable. After all, he went for the Piaget watch."

Clive Jackson did not understand.

"What Piaget watch? What the hell are you talking about?"

"She has this Piaget watch," Chester said. "Terrific watch, jewels, everything. Always flashing it around on camera. You know, when she gesticulated, picked up a script page. Everyone could see it out there. And what did I have, a lousy Benrus or something. She was upstaging me like mad with that goddamned watch."

"Chester," Herbie said, "let's be fair. She didn't start with the Piaget until you began putting the stop-watch out there on the desk to time her segments. Be fair."

Clive Jackson was delighted.

"You did that, Chester? You really did?"

For the first time Chester Albany sounded triumphant.

"Did I not?" He grinned. "Told Bobby Klaus about it. She was averaging four minutes more than me night in and night out. Bobby finally spoke to the control room about it. Raised all sorts of hell."

"*And* he got you a Piaget watch," Herbie reminded his client.

Chester nodded, quite drunkenly.

"Under duress, I might add, under duress."

Clive Jackson began asking Herbie Bliss about the current job market.

"Tight, Clive, tight. Lot of good men on the beach. That's why I'm counseling Chester to have patience. That's how to handle a situation like this. Don't let it get under your skin. Play it cool, be above it all, don't let yourself be maneuvered into a resignation. At least," he added practically, "until you've got something just as good waiting for you out there."

"Such as?" Chester asked dubiously.

"Well," said Herbie, very much the agent now, "let's consider the options. Not, mind you, that I think you should quit."

"Yeah, but if he did . . ." Clive put in eagerly.

"Yeah, *if* I did."

Herbie made a little temple of his hands, the fingertips touching.

"Well, you could always become the spokesman for a great . . . American . . . corporation." Herbie liked the way that sounded.

Chester was indignant. "You mean *commercials?* Do commercials?"

Herbie Bliss was hurt by that. To think that one of his clients would have so little faith.

"Chester," he said patiently, "I'm not sending you out to do floors and windows. Who mentioned commercials? I mean communicating a corporate message through television to the American public."

"Oh," Clive Jackson said sarcastically, "that's different."

"Sure," Herbie said. "Henry Fonda is the spokesman for a great . . . corporation. Gregory Peck. Hugh Downs does Ford. Bob Hope . . ."

"Downs *never* had my ratings," Chester snarled. Herbie ignored him.

". . . Bob Hope does Texaco. Lord-for-Chrissake-Olivier isn't too proud to be a spokesman."

Chester shook his head. "Actors, Herbie. Actors and flimflam men. I'm a news guy. Hard news."

It was midnight and Herbie Bliss was tired and by this time

74

his new wife was probably asleep and most of all he had had enough of nurse-maiding this particular client through this particular bout of depression.

"Sure, Chester," he said sarcastically. "You're a news guy. And maybe if we play our cards right I could get you back on rewrite at the Woonsocket *Call*." He got up from the bar, told Chester he would call him tomorrow and left.

But it was 2:00 A.M. before Chester finally called it a night and went home. He came into the bedroom quietly, moving with great precision the way a man does who knows he's drunk and began to undress in the dark.

"Hi," Frances said, sounding sleepy but cheerful as always, her English accent still apparent despite its exposure to American slang.

"Sorry," Chester said, guilty about having stayed late over drinks, guilty about waking her, guilty because she didn't nag as his wife would have done at this hour.

"It's okay," the girl said. "Hey, that was super, the President calling and all."

Chester grunted and continued to undress. He had still not put on the light but in the gloom he could see Frances moving over to the side of the big bed to make room for him, he could see her lanky young body smooth under the light blanket. In the bathroom he examined himself in the mirror, the eyes bleared, the once-granite face doughy despite the good bones. Well, he thought, at fifty you show the wear.

In bed Frances moved to him. He was wearing pajama bottoms and she was in one of those football T-shirts she wore for nightgowns. Her legs felt good, twining easily into his. He slipped an arm under her shoulders. They were about the same height and their lovemaking usually went very well. Frances, warm with sleep, aroused now in the way middle-of-the-night wakenings can do, put her hand on Chester. She felt fine and he craned his thick neck to kiss her. She had the sweet-tasting mouth of the young that has nothing to do with dentifrice and he was grateful, his own mouth dry, sour. Frances moved again, the football jersey riding higher now, above her flat belly, and under his hand her nipple hardened. They kissed again and then she did various splendid things for a few minutes and finally, thinking he was ready, she guided him toward her. It was then that Chester wrenched himself away.

"Goddammit," he groaned, agony bursting from him, "I can't! I can't!"

The girl recoiled and lay stiffly alongside him for a time, saying nothing, her body rigid, thinking she had done something wrong, that it was her fault. Then Chester said something, wanting to break the tension, something about being tired, about the job. She immediately curled to him and said brightly:

"Hey, I understand. My God, talking to the President like that."

Yeah, Chester Albany said, that was it.

"It's just I'm thoughtless sometimes. I forget how important your work is, how . . . significant."

Chester nodded.

"Well, anyway," Frances said happily, "you were terrific. What you said to the President. That grin you had."

Chester was feeling no better.

"Really super," Frances said.

Chester Albany turned to look at the girl.

"Frances," he said, "shut up."

After a few minutes, as young people will, she slept. Chester Albany got up and went to the bathroom and took a seconal but it was nearly five o'clock in the morning with the eastern sky over Park Avenue beginning to streak with light before he fell asleep.

8

The next morning Chester Albany, who was embarrassed by limousines, had taken a cab to the studio and by ten-thirty was in his office drinking black coffee from an oversized mug that bore the escutcheon of a Greek letter society. Chester could not read Greek, had never belonged to a college fraternity, and had no idea of the mug's provenance. Nor was he at all curious about it. It was enough that it held a lot of coffee, kept it reasonably hot, and had no cracks in the lip that might cut his mouth. Chester Albany was that way, he accepted a thing's utility, a company's role, a job's parameters, a paycheck's benefits, without wondering too deeply whether more subtle truths lay beneath the surface. Oh, he had his momentary cynicisms, you could not be in that business for so long and not, but in general Chester accepted things at their face value. It made for an ordered, and reasonably happy, life. Until now.

The coffee went down well. Chester was slightly hung over. Not badly, but the headache was there. There was mail on his desk, lengths of teletype from the various wire services. Chester pushed at it a bit and then flopped down on his leather couch, swung his legs up, loosened his necktie, and sipped at the coffee. His office, an office he'd had for five, no, nearly six years now, was a warm, masculine room, all deep chairs and the big desk and plenty of bookcases and the smell of tobacco and leather and now, the coffee. Chester's couch dominated. It was positioned so that, with the door ajar as it now was, he could see into the institutionally green hall that led in one direction to the other offices and in the other to the studio. As with the coffee mug Chester had no idea whence the couch had come. It was there when he arrived six years ago, when he and Clive Jackson were first paired on the evening show. A doctor's waiting room might have spawned it, even, he used to grin if anyone asked, a shrink's office. It was that sort of couch, worn smooth, with springs that had seen a better season, a scorch mark or three, and the scuffed places on the far arm where his heels dug in. It was where Chester napped, where he thought, where he read, where he had even, on several occasions, made quick, spontaneous love to girls who worked in the office. Now, under the tension of this new arrangement, Chester's couch had become a solid anchor to the past, to familiar things, to what he now began to think of as "the good old days."

Although Chester Albany took things like his couch, like the coffee mug, like the Underwood on the old typing table, for what they were, he had begun to manifest a new curiosity about people. Kate Sinclair was doing that to him. He had begun to question motives, to explore "good intentions," to look more deeply into people's eyes, to delve, to probe and to wonder. Innocence, whatever innocence remained to a fifty-year-old hard-bitten reporter, had been lost. And Kate Sinclair was to blame.

Down the hall he imagined he could hear the swift click of her electric typewriter with the self-correcting, magically-erasing features which she, apparently, found essential. The tap-tap-tap of her electric, signals the woman was already at work (forget that the work might be insignificant), that too made Chester nervous. Perhaps she was already starting to produce the day's script, a script, he feared, that might turn out devilishly clever and ripe with appeal. Hating to do so, he got up from the couch and reluctantly began to read the morning's wire copy.

Despite popular belief, the people who broadcast the evening news do not stroll into the studio late in the afternoon, skim a script while the makeup is slapped on, wander over to the anchor desk with a few minutes to spare, and begin to read their reports. And since Kate Sinclair had for years worked on a morning show and was accustomed to early rising, Chester found himself coming in even earlier now, not wanting to fall farther behind in what was obviously, to him, becoming a competitive situation. He read for a time, lighted a cigarette, drained the coffee's dregs, and then, once again distracted, restless, looked around the room, seeking familiarity, consola-

78

tion, comfort. On the wall, hung at rakish angles, irregularly spaced, were photographs of Presidents and other great men with their arms around Chester's shoulders, a younger, self-assured Chester, but with the same flat grin that showed no teeth but communicated good feeling. On this morning, Chester was not grinning, he communicated no good feeling.

At noon they came together for the first time. Kate smiled and Chester tried. It was the daily story conference. It would last for an hour. The executive producer, the producer, the director, the news editor, two assistants, a girl who took notes, a youngster to fetch the coffee, were in attendance. The executive producer was enthusiastic. Especially after they screened some tape on the large videotape recorder propped in a corner of the conference room.

"Kate," he said, "I don't know how you do it. I just don't."

Chester looked sour. He hoped sheer joy would not bring the executive producer to hernia. The tape they had viewed was a three-minute and 20-second split-screen transatlantic conversation between Kate Sinclair and another well-known woman: the Queen of England.

"The Queen," the executive producer exhaled, "the goddamn Queen."

"Gotta be a first," the news editor said.

"Gotta be," an assistant assured him.

"Cronkite, by God," the executive producer declared, "Cronkite never had the Queen."

"I should hope not," Kate said drily.

There was a good deal of thigh-slapping over that, you can be sure. Chester Albany restrained his mirth.

"How did we get it?" he asked, a professional asking a professional question and not being nasty, at least not very.

"How? How?" the producer responded. "Why Kate just picked up the phone and called the palace. *That's* how!"

Chester just sat there. The room was silent. The silence seemed to suggest he might pick up a phone himself, dial the occasional palace. The executive producer looked narrowly at Chester. God knows, he liked Chester, liked him a lot. But he didn't need this grousing, these petulant interjections, his self-pity. Chester ought to think of the good of the show and not simply this territorial imperative of his. But, being a patient man, and knowing something about artistic temperament and competitive stress, the executive producer tried once again to cheer his anchorman.

"Chester," he said, "the Queen's fine. Great. But it isn't as if you'll have a no-hitter tonight. You've got a biggie too. Nearly three minutes. Dynamite stuff."

Chester nodded. "Yeah," he said, "dynamite stuff. She gets a face-to-face with the Queen and I get Al Shanker."

Unless there were some new camera angles to rehearse or a promo to tape in advance, they spent their afternoons apart. Chester went off with a couple of pals to The Ginger Man for lunch (no drinks, he never drank before a show), feeling alienated (a word he would never have used). Kate stayed in the office, had salads brought in, submitted to an interview with a bookish sort from *Ms* magazine, made phone calls, read a bit, and waited for the hairdresser to come by.

Kate's phone rang. It was Washington. Idly, as she waited for the call to come through, she wondered if it might be Blanchflower. When it wasn't, she shifted into her professional self and asked and answered questions and got a reasonably firm commitment from the Secretary of State for a broadcast interview about the African business within a few days.

"Just let me clear my head a bit first, Kate," the secretary had asked. "And let this next exchange of notes sink in. I don't want to screw up a chance of agreement by saying too much in public."

"But, Mr. Secretary, you're the soul of tact."

The man laughed. "Not when you're asking the questions, Kate."

Sometimes it seemed to those around her that she was always on the phone. Her range of professional acquaintance was impressive. Even Chester Albany was impressed. Having been a network anchorman for so long he knew a lot of important people. But even he had to admit, she seemed to know more.

She was a hard woman in a hard line of work. For eight years she had worked to get to the top and now that she was there she was not about to permit the petty resentments of a Chester Albany to topple her. So what if Chester was upset about her publicity. When *Time* told her they were planning a cover story, what the hell was she supposed to do? Call Henry Grunwald and talk him out of it?

Chester Albany's concerns were nothing new. For every one of those eight years she had encountered, and coped with, male job insecurity. She knew she was a threat, that she represented danger. With Chester the symptoms had surfaced early, during those first, tentative, exciting, and comically secretive sessions with Bobby Klaus and the network brass. They warned her from the start what Chester was, old line, old time, old school. Okay, she'd said, run his name first in the credits, in the ads, in the voice-overs. Give the bastard a new office, double his salary, lease him a car, a new apartment, let him do six specials a year. Anything. Just so long as she got her million and her story selection and her goddamned interviews with the goddamned President.

One of the assistant directors came down the hall. It was thirty minutes to air and he knocked first at Kate's door, then at Chester's, asking them to go to the studio. They were about to begin another "married" evening together on the air. It was significant, Chester thought, as he got up off the old couch and peered into the mirror to straighten his tie, that even the boy who summoned them onstage would knock at her door first.

As he walked through the hall toward the studio he remembered a fragment of conversation overheard a few days before. It was Kate Sinclair, shouting to her secretary.

"Listen," she had called out, "take this other call. I've got the White House on hold."

9

The painter was third rate, so sluggish in his reaction time that his cribbing of other artists' work was always one fad behind. But the woman who owned the gallery had once done Kate Sinclair a favor, investing considerable time and an admirable ingenuity in procuring, for an exceedingly fair price, a small and quite lovely Fragonard, and Kate felt obliged to come by the vernissage for the ritual glass and the polite murmured nothings in the crowd. The gallery was on Madison in the sixties, the evening was cold and damp. Spring seemed especially reluctant this year and instead of walking across town from the studio after taping the evening's show, cooling out as a race horse does, unwinding as she walked, Kate had the network limo drop her at the gallery.

"I won't be long," she told the driver. "Hello and one drink. Then you can take me home and call it a night."

The gallery was crowded. The East Side of Manhattan is full of people who find the blend of art, however bad, and a free drink irresistible. And there was always a chance Hilton Kramer might be there, or Ashbery, or some slim young model restless and bored, or an actual painter even. Kate Sinclair was a catch, of course, and the owner piloted her around the room, suggesting in her manner and their first-name relationship this was of course the sort of gallery where a woman like Kate Sinclair would come to look at pictures. Kate smiled, sipped a routine champagne, and tried not to look at pictures. Her appointed rounds completed, she was trying to break away from a doctor and his chatty wife who insisted on telling her how they'd once met Jackson Pollock's mistress, when a strong hand took her arm and steered her firmly toward the other side of the room.

"There's one canvas you ought to look at a second time."

She looked up. The man who had her arm was tall, shaggy-haired, bearded, dressed in jeans and a heavy turtleneck under a corduroy jacket. Obviously an artist himself, or on the surface the cliché of an artist. But she didn't care. He'd gotten her away from the doctor and the doctor's wife and their vicarious intimacy with Pollock. They moved through the crowd, the tall man clearing the way, and then they were at the far wall and she was forced, for the first time, to confront one of the paintings being celebrated.

"Well?" he asked.

Not knowing who he was or what his relationship to the artist might be (could he *be* the artist?), she retreated behind, "Interesting."

The man snorted.

"They're dreadful and you know it. You're too intelligent not to know it."

She laughed.

"When I see trash like this being sold I'm tempted to think Tom Wolfe might be right about contemporary art."

She asked if he were a painter. He was. Not *this* sort of thing, of course, something quite different. His name was Haller, he and this evening's painter had been at one or another art school together, they'd once competed for the same girl.

"And you won," Kate thought but didn't say. A man as tall and arrogant and as sure of himself as this would always win.

She was amused that he talked on, about art, about the people around them, cutting and superior, about himself, always about himself, and that he actually didn't seem to know who she was.

"Don't you ever watch television?" she responded when he asked what she did.

"I'd rather look at this crap," he said. "Why, you in television?"

"I'm Kate Sinclair. I work on one of the network news shows."

She wondered why she'd bothered to add that. Her name ought to be sufficient.

He nodded, noting the name but still not seeming to recognize it. They stood there for a moment, the conversation awkwardly halted. She watched his hands as he pulled out a cigarette and lighted it, not offering her one. They were extraordinary hands, large, tanned, powerful, a controlled force suggested by the thick fingers, the large knuckles, the heavy bones of his big wrists. They were hands that might be cruel or they might be tender. Perhaps they could be both. But she had the feeling that either way, a woman who felt those hands would not quickly forget them.

"Well?" he said, breaking the silence.

She looked directly into his face.

"You might have offered me a cigarette as well," she said, trying to reestablish authority.

"Oh, sure," he grinned. No apology, no embarrassment at having committed a gaffe. He was lighting the cigarette for her when the gallery owner approached, towing a prosperous-looking couple in her wake.

"Kate," she called. "Look who's here."

Haller took her arm again in one of his hands, the same pressure, the same authority.

"Look," he said, "let's get out of here. I can't stand all this bullshit."

They went downtown in her car. Neither she nor Haller had eaten and when he said he knew a good place, she sat back against the smooth cushions and relaxed while he gave instructions to the driver, not at all self-conscious about using her car. She liked that. Arguments about stupid things, like whether the man didn't owe it to his manhood to insist on driving his own car, or scouting up a taxi, bored her. The car was there, the chauffeur, it was cold and damp and with a rising wind, and why not travel in comfort.

The restaurant was called WPA and the decor was nineteen-thirties. The headwaiter recognized Kate, greeted her by name, but he was just as deferential to Haller, despite the beard and the old corduroy and jeans. There wasn't a table ready and they sat at the bar. Haller ordered for both of them, again making assumptions without consulting her. The drinks came and he lifted his glass to her in mute toast.

"What is this?"

"Tequila," he said. "Started drinking it a couple of years ago. I was living in Mexico."

"Painting?"

84

"Some," he said. "That and sleeping with American tourists for the bread."

She didn't say anything. Haller was probing, she was certain. She'd sent the car away. There was no reason for the driver to sit out there in a windy SoHo street for a couple of hours. She could easily get a cab home. She was simply being thoughtful. But it wasn't thoughtfulness, it was an unformed but undeniable instinct that this meal, with a man she didn't know, was really only a beginning. And that the evening might become something else and go on. And on. Haller communicated sex, mystery, even danger. She ought to finish the meal and walk away from him. Then, laughing to herself, self-mocking, she remembered the last time she had made love, and recklessly, she decided to stay with Haller. At least, she thought, almost smiling, it would be better than that last time.

It had been more than a month ago. In Detroit, some sort of auto industry anniversary, celebrating the invention of rack-and-pinion steering, something significant like that, and Kate had gone out to make a speech. In her business they frequently made speeches. Especially when one of the "Big Three" car manufacturers asked. There'd been a reception before the dinner and this man had attached himself to her, an engineer, decent and successful, with an impressive title at one of the auto companies, a man just a few years older than she, attractive in a smooth and mindless way. After the dinner and her speech, he'd sought her out again. They'd had the requisite drinks, he'd said very nice things about her speech (which had been written for her by her public relations people), his suite was handy (they were staying in the same hotel in the Renaissance Center), she'd felt the old longing, and they'd found themselves in bed. He had a nice tennis-playing body, it went all right, even well, but then, when she slid out of bed and started to dress, he clutched her arm.

"Wait," he said.

"No, I've really got to go. It's nearly . . ."

"Just another few minutes," he said.

Kate smiled. It was nice to be wanted, sweet of him to want her the second time. She half turned back to the bed, ready to be talked into it.

"Do me this favor. This one thing."

Of course she would, Kate assured him, glad she'd not gotten dressed again.

The man leaped off the bed and strode to the bureau. He picked up a pen and a sheet of hotel stationery. He held them out to her.

"My wife will never believe I really met you," he said. "Would you give me your autograph?"

Haller would have to be better than that. Kate Sinclair sipped her tequila and tried not to stare at him. Instead, she scanned the room which was filled with uptown people like herself, some of them arty, men dressed like Haller, slender girls in ponchos and ankle-length floral skirts. But SoHo was no longer the frontier. It was quite all right to come downtown from the Upper East Side. For the first time since the East Village went bad people were going downtown again. She was glad. She felt very good and wondered how many of the other women in the room had met their dinner companion only an hour earlier. And still didn't know his first name. They got their table and Haller, once again without consultation, ordered for them both. There was wine now and Kate found she was very relaxed, enjoying this temporary abdication of authority, leaving such momentous decisions as the selection of a salad dressing to this formidable, slightly boorish young man with those wonderful, and perhaps awful, hands. He was talking about painting now and he was very good.

"This photo-realism we're all doing now is a shabby confidence trick. Another eighteen months and not even Robert Scull will be falling for it. But there's this to say for it: you've got to have discipline and a steady hand. No tossing-of-the-paint bullshit, no thinning out oil with solvents so surface texture totally disappears, no templates or straight edges or pails of water."

She said she didn't understand. Haller laughed.

"I've got a pal whose last one-man show consisted of eighty or ninety galvanized buckets, you know, the sort of thing you dunk the mop into when you're cleaning the goddamned kitchen floor. And this guy sets the pails all around the gallery, on the floor, a foot, two feet, ten feet apart from one another, and then, just before the vernissage he goes around and fills up the buckets to varying heights with water, just plain tap water, no color, no Ivory soap floating around, no toy boats even. Just goddamned buckets of water. The critics went crazy. Genius! A new and important voice! He was made. People began buying his fucking water buckets."

He paused.

"Then the house of cards came tumbling down. Water evaporates. And kids knocked over the buckets and dogs drank out of them and one goddamned maid poured the whole thing down the drain."

"Couldn't the owners just fill them up again?"

"Why, that's the wonderful part of it," Haller declared. "Everyone was so fucking insecure! No one knew just how high the water should top out at. Jesus, you can't let civilians begin to make artistic decisions like that. Where the hell would it leave the critics?"

They finished dinner and he ordered brandy, again without asking, and Kate realized how atypical the dinner had been, no talk of television, no focus on her, no courteous deference to her opinion on whatever subject. All around her were tables full of people who knew precisely who she was and what she did. Politely furtive glances, half-smiles, lowered voices, all signified a very clear knowledge of her presence. Yet here was this painter (quite possibly a *terrible* painter without a blush of talent) in his ridiculous painter's costume (did he rent his clothes from Brooks Uniform?) showing not the slightest respect for her achievements or curiosity about her work, her fame, herself. My God, Kate thought, nearly giggling, maybe he really and truly *doesn't* know who I am! There was something nice about that possibility, inferring he had picked her up at the gallery simply because she was attractive and desirable. There was also the lurking disquietude: if people began *not* knowing who she was would she herself become muddled as to her identity? An interesting line to explore, she told herself, knowing it was brandy-thought and distorted and therefore not a real danger.

He said he wanted her to see his loft. It was close by.

"I won't insist you look at my work," he assured her, "that's for sunny mornings with good light and sober eyes. But see the place. Loft living has to be seen to be understood."

She knew, without his saying it, what it would mean, and

knew that she wanted it very much. Thinking about it, looking at him, imagining those big hands on her before they had ever really touched her, sent a small but very discernible shudder through her body. Oh, how much I want it, she thought.

Kate thought of other women who were also sexually isolated, successful, attractive women, whose marriages had gone bad, or who had never been married except to their careers: Barbara Howar; Geraldine Stutz; Jackie Onassis. Had it been their fault they were now alone? She remembered what Claude had said when Peter left her. Claude was a comtesse, a beautiful woman, and she and Peter had been together for years and then, suddenly, he was gone, and Claude, still beautiful, still available, was alone. "What happened?" Kate had asked.

"Well, you know," Claude had said, with that ageless wisdom of the French, "Peter found a nineteen-year-old Brazilian girl and, voilà, that was it."

"Oh?" Kate had said, dubiously.

Claude had looked at her with the superiority, the patience of the Europeans, and had said:

"But Kate, she was nineteen and I was thirty-seven. Don't you understand? I do."

Claude had left her husband for Peter. Now Peter had a nineteen-year-old.

A few months later Kate had met her again. Claude had a nineteen-year-old of her own now, a young Italian boy.

Was it always to be young boys or faggots or married men, furtive, guilty, sweating? Wouldn't someone like Haller be better?

As they left the restaurant several people told her hello, using her name, and she felt better about everything, the way a confused traveler does when he finally glimpses a familiar name on a throughway sign.

The loft was enormous. The second floor up in one of those cast iron buildings the real estate people are always trying to demolish and ladies' committees to preserve. Haller walked her through. He had the whole floor. There were stacks of canvases leaning against walls, a sleeping alcove, a modern kitchen agleam with copper, a tiled bath. The floor, a good wood floor, was buffed and polished and gleamed in the overhead light Haller had switched on. Near the bed an old television cabinet, just the big wooden box gutted of its tubes and wiring, hung suspended by a length of insulated flex from the ceiling. It revolved slowly in the draft. Kate asked what on earth that was supposed to mean.

"Simply my disdain for television," Haller said off-handedly, not challenging her really, and she said, "Oh," and then he was explaining the splendid copper kitchen and the good plumbing weren't really to his credit at all, that the place was a sublet from another man who was spending a year abroad. "I have no feel for the decor myself," Haller admitted, "but it's nice to have a decent kitchen and bath. You still get roaches but they're controllable."

He had tossed his corduroy coat over the back of a director's chair and had actually discovered a hanger for Kate's long, mink-lined raincoat, and now he kicked off his shoes and prowled around the place in stockinged feet, restlessly pushing canvases aside and shuffling frames. Sensing he wanted her to ask, Kate said:

"I know it isn't morning and nobody's quite sober, but could I see some of your work?"

He nodded, and without speaking, began to slide out selected canvases, the big wooden-framed toiles moving smoothly across the polished floor. Kate stood there watching.

"Sit down," Haller said, "I'll show them." He waved a hand toward a modular sofa and Kate, again sensing the command, sank down into it. She watched, without saying anything, as Haller pulled out a canvas, propped it against his body, paused, watched her face, and then replaced it with another painting.

The pictures were extraordinary. Photo-realistic paintings of women, life-size and larger than life, erotic, powerful, perverse, strong, sick. Haller slid one canvas after another in front of her. The impact was as shocking as being exposed without warning to an entire gallery of Ensor, the belching and urination, the devil masks and dirty jokes, the shitting and the vomit. These women were doing nothing shocking and yet they seemed infinitely less pleasant. One of the models appeared over and over again, a tall Scandinavian with blonde hair crudely chopped short. Kate could very nearly feel her presence in the room, her purple eyes staring, her large, lovely mouth moist, almost drooling, the sweat on her skin, the lactation of her nipples, the matted, sweaty hair of her body.

Haller slid the last canvas back into its pile. He looked at Kate and was apparently quite satisfied with what he saw in her face.

·"Well?"

He stood there, towering above her, big fists arrogantly planted on his hips.

"They're wonderful pictures. No wonder you hated what we saw at the gallery. You and he aren't even in the same business."

Haller smiled, the flat mouth wide.

"Your technique, whatever it is, is . . . I don't know. It's like photographs set to poetry."

He snarled. "Photographs? Hell, photographers are little men from Rochester with brown fingers. Don't confuse what I do with them."

Kate felt unsure of herself talking technique. She asked, "Who is the model? The girl with the chopped-off hair?"

Haller shrugged. "A neighbor. Lives upstairs. She poses for me once in a while."

Kate said nothing. Haller was still standing over her, powerful, dangerous, magnetic. She wanted to stay. She knew she should not. Then he reached out and her own hands moved toward his. With surprising gentleness he pulled her up out of the deep softness of the sofa.

She stood, facing him, a tall woman but a head shorter. He looked into her face, and then, having read there what apparently he had expected, he said:

"Now we go to bed and make love or whatever your euphemism is."

The gutted television set revolved slowly on its length of insulated wire in the darkened room. The bed was large. Kate, naked, the sweat drying, her damp hair tangled, lay on her back, watching the television set, seeing beyond it the stacked canvases, not the pictures themselves, but the great rectangles

90

of raw wood, of pale toile. Beside her, perhaps asleep, lay Haller. He still wore his heavy turtleneck sweater. The sheet and the down-filled comforter had been tossed aside. She could see, without turning her head, one of his hands, casually thrown across her thigh. Haller had been rough, but not cruel, and now in the exhausted, satisfied tranquility of the rumpled bed, she relaxed, feeling foolish at having feared him, glad she had come with him to the loft, delighted to have been loved by a man who took her as an attractive woman and not for her recognition value. She wondered again if he was really unaware of who she was and then, feeling his hand move imperceptibly on her thigh, she didn't really care.

Kate fell asleep. Conscious of movement now, she woke. Haller was no longer next to her. She pulled her arm free from where it lay under her body. Her watch read two o'clock. There was a light at the far end of the loft. She supposed Haller was in the bathroom. She ought to get up now and dress and go home. It was late and it was a working day and she didn't want Chester or anyone else seeing bed in her eyes. Going home would be sensible. She didn't move. More light streamed into the room and she could see Haller coming back to her, a short terry cloth robe belted around his body. He came to the side of the bed and looked down at her, at her body in the light from the open bathroom door. He smiled his flat smile again.

"I think we should move on now to other things," he said.

"Oh, yes," she said, sliding across the bed to give him room.

He let the robe drop to the floor. Oh, yes, she thought. Oh, yes.

Then there was the noise of a door behind him, across the loft, and Kate, startled, tried to sit up. Haller pushed her back with the flat of his hand.

"Hey," she said, alarmed now.

Someone came across the room on bare feet. Behind Haller she could see it was a woman. It was the girl in the pictures, the Swedish-looking blonde with the short-cropped hair. The girl stopped at the foot of the bed and began to unzip her jeans. She was very tall, she was beautiful, and she was stoned. She skinned off the jeans and started to unbutton her denim shirt.

"No," Kate said, "I don't . . ."

"Shut up," Haller told her. "I said we'd move on to other things."

He reached down and squeezed both her nipples, not hurting her, just applying pressure.

"You'll like Inga," he said. "And she'll like you. She likes everyone."

Moving quickly, more quickly than she thought she could, Kate rolled to the far side of the bed and bounced out onto the floor, landing on her bare feet. Haller cursed and started to come around the bed toward her.

"Don't, you son of a bitch," she snarled, her knees slightly bent and her fingers tensed as if to unsheathe her nails. She had taken the position instinctively. Haller, seeing it, halted.

"Jesus," he said, "I thought you wanted more."

Kate ignored his voice and edged crablike toward the sofa where her dress and shoes and underclothes had been tossed. Both Haller and the girl, now naked as well, watched her move, Haller with a look of surprise, even disappointment on his face, Inga smiling dully, not yet aware of her loss. Kate snatched up the dress and pulled it on over her head, not turning her back as she ordinarily might have done, but trying to keep her eyes on them, especially on Haller. She slipped her feet into her shoes and shoved her bra and pants into her handbag. The pantyhose were gone, she didn't care.

"You're crazy, you know," Haller said. "What the hell are you going for? It was good with the two of us . . . would have been better with three. What the hell are you . . . ?"

Kate glanced toward the door. Haller left his last sentence unfinished. He seemed to be gauging her distance from the door, wondering if he could get to it first, wondering whether it would be worth the effort. It was not that Kate had been sensational in bed, although she had been good enough, and now having Inga there, drugged, voracious, beautiful, imagining how it would be to make love to both of them with the silent canvases as witness appealed to Haller. He was becoming aroused all over again. Even Kate's resistance, part fear, part disgust, excited him. Kate grabbed her coat from the rack and began to back slowly toward the door of the loft. Speaking more calmly now, Haller said:

"It's all the same to her, you know. Inga will do anything I want. Anything you want. We can take turns with her. We can take turns with you. It could be very pleasant. It could be something you've never . . ."

She continued backing toward the door, watching Haller's bare feet for the beginning of movement, watching those large hands that only an hour earlier had given her such pleasure.

Now she was at the door. She felt for the knob. It turned freely and the door swung open. Thank God, she thought, and stepped quickly into the hall, shutting the door firmly but not slamming it, not wanting to anger Haller, and then she heard his voice for the last time, loud, nasty, cruelly triumphant:

"I know who you are, bitch! I knew from the start. I fucked you! I fucked Kate Sinclair! Remember that! I fucked Kate . . ."

She turned and sprinted down the wooden stairs to the street, two and three steps at a time. She threw open the heavy steel fire door and the chill night air hit her face. It felt wonderful.

In the loft Haller had stopped shouting. His face was red and his breath came quickly. Damn it, he thought, he should have locked the door after Inga came in. Then he shrugged. He didn't want to rape her, that was always tricky, but it would have been exciting to debase the bitch, to watch while Inga slavered over her body, to watch Kate Sinclair moaning and writhing and later try to get it all on canvas. *That*, he thought, would make one hell of a vernissage!

Behind him Inga made a small noise, more a moan than a word, and he turned to her.

"All right," he said, "get on the bed. I'll be right there."

The blonde girl moved unsteadily across the floor in her bare feet and got up on the rumpled bed. She was still smiling. And she did not know whether the other woman, the one who seemed frightened, was still there. Not, of course, that it mattered.

10

On the weekend that spring arrived in Washington the President of the United States and the junior senator from New York were preparing to attend a party. The same party. Although they were both Democrats they were not allies. The President knew that if Blanchflower won another senate term in New York in November by a big margin, say a million votes, he would automatically be projected into the next Presidential race. Since the President was determined to name his own successor, someone he could control, he would avoid doing anything that might enhance Blanchflower's prospects. As for Blanchflower, he disliked the President's style: the piety; the cornbread humor; the jerky inflection, the mush-mouth delivery. But Blanchflower recognized genius, knew the man was, by God, a politician, knowing where the votes were and understanding what he had to do or to say or to promise to get them. Blanchflower admired professionalism. And the President was professional. In his own way Blanchflower had learned the lesson, to win you had to appear unique.

The President achieved cultural distinction with a corny southern drawl, and good ole boy yarns. Blanchflower, the child of the city, worked the urban vein in much the same way using instead of jeans and farmers' work shoes well-cut suits and polished English brogues. The President realized early on that despite their surface differences, Blanchflower and he were very much alike. One night sitting late in the Oval Office he told an old and very loyal crony, "Blanchflower is the most dangerous man in Washington." The crony, whose name was Lester and who was old enough and sufficiently loyal to be permitted to disagree, did so. He pointed out there were any number of men senior to Blanchflower, men with broader constituencies, men with greater national reputations. But the President shook his head.

"He can demagogue it with the best of us," he said. "He's smarter than most and as ambitious as they come. He even knows when to tell the truth. And there's one more thing."

Lester leaned forward expectantly, as cronies do, and the President said:

"The really dangerous thing about Blanchflower is this. He understands how to use television."

It was the annual Gridiron Club dinner that would bring the two enemies together. The Gridiron, fifty of the most powerful Washington correspondents, gathering to toast, to tease, to amuse, to lacerate with skits and speeches, the President and his courtiers. Their dinner was as sure a sign of spring as the ice melting on the tidal basin, the blooming of the white, but not the pink, cherry blossoms, the rolling of Georgetown's tennis courts, the point-to-point races in muddy Warrenton to the west, the arrival of hordes of school children at the Capitol, at marbled Mellon. But it was only the Gridiron that concerned the junior senator from New York that Saturday afternoon as he scrutinized himself in the bathroom mirror of his spartan bachelor flat on P Street just off Wisconsin.

Why, Nicholas Blanchflower wondered, was a white tie so much more difficult to engineer than a black tie? The heavy white pique had a mind of its own, lumping and wrinkling no matter how he knotted it. Of course there were pre-tied models that fastened at the back of the collar but he lumped them with such untouchables as doubleknit suits, digital watches, and tennis clothes that were not white. The senator was a man with a distinct sense of his style, his role, himself.

He glanced for a final time into the mirror, accepting reasonable compromise with the tie. Without willing it, he watched a wide grin split his large face and said, aloud to the empty apartment, "Now don't start looking presidential, dammit." He laughed, a short, cheerful bark, and went into the bedroom to stuff wallet and keys and change into his pockets and to put on his vest and tailcoat.

Senator Nicholas Blanchflower did not, even in white tie

and tails, look presidential. For one thing, he was a tall, hulking man who in later life would have to battle weight or become portly. In his forties, he had a full head of ungrayed hair. He looked as if he might have been an athlete and he moved gracefully despite his size. His clothes were tailored and expensive, nothing democratically rumpled about him. He was buoyant and blunt and none of the tactful, careful things politicians are supposed to be, and paradoxically, this seemed one reason why he won. And threatened to keep on winning. Which was why this evening at the Gridiron Club could be important.

Some of the most influential men in the country would attend, meeting at the Capitol Hilton to slosh down cocktails and then sit down to a meal that would last five hours and would feature the Marine Corps band, any number of amateur skits, and various speeches. The President himself would be careful to be late, so as to hear the more significant remarks while avoiding the college humor. His Vice-President would arrive early, playing his Constitutional role of stand-in, exchanging labored banter with the Soviet ambassador, with the Chief Justice of the Supreme Court, with the little newspaperman who was president of that year's Gridiron, perhaps even with a Republican. Blanchflower was excited about being at the dinner. It was not his first Gridiron, of course, any reasonably presentable senator could wangle an invitation, but it was the first time he would sit at the head table with the President, the first time he'd been asked to speak. Only failed candidates, future Presidents, and elder statesmen dying of cancer got to address the Gridiron. Blanchflower had not yet failed, his health was good, and he was to speak.

At eight o'clock in the evening they had progressed through the crabmeat a la Russe and were on the diamondback terrapin Maryland, with corn sticks and a sherry which could have been dryer, to wash it all down.

"That was awful, about the scandal," Blanchflower remarked to the Scandinavian ambassador on his right. The ambassador, being English-speaking, was very stuffy. The ambassador sniffled into his napkin to consider his response. He had no idea what scandal the American meant.

After much consideration he said, "Awful."

"Well, you win some, you lose some. No one goes undefeated," Blanchflower told him.

"Quite," the ambassador said, unsure whether the American was being sympathetic or sarcastic.

Blanchflower turned away from the ambassador to the Secretary of the Treasury, who asked if the senator would be speaking.

"I make the response to the Republican," said Blanchflower.

"Ah," the secretary said, "reputations have been made with Gridiron speeches. And lost."

Blanchflower said he was aware of that. He knew the secretary, being a creature of the President, was hostile, but he was also speaking the truth. A couple of years before John Lindsay had come to the Gridiron very much a man with viable White House aspirations. But John had delivered a stupid speech, and the senior members of the press corps who make up the Gridiron's membership had never taken Lindsay seriously again.

"A Gridiron can destroy a man," the secretary said. "Just ruin him."

"I know," Blanchflower said.

The club's president was on his feet now.

"Before we hear the speeches I must tell you that there are three rules of the Gridiron Club," he said: "reporters are never present, ladies are always present, and the Gridiron may singe but it never burns."

"What a charming phrase," the ambassador said.

"What about this border dispute?" Blanchflower asked suddenly.

"Border dispute?"

Blanchflower nodded. "You and your neighbors. You know."

The ambassador said, "My dear Senator. There's no . . ."

"Always fiddling with currency equivalents," the treasury secretary weighed in. "Bad. Very bad."

"Will it mean war?" Blanchflower asked loudly.

"I say, not at all," the ambassador protested in alarm. "Our common border is . . . "

Blanchflower waved at a publisher friend.

"Hell," he told the flustered ambassador, "I'm sure it will all work itself out."

The waiters came by then to fetch the terrapin plates and to serve the coquille St. Jacques with a very nice Chateau Piron Graves 1972 and Blanchflower sat back comfortably, only half-listening to the ambassador and the secretary argue back and forth across the broad expanse of his starched white shirt. He looked out across the room. "I love being here and being part of it," he thought, "and I love it that in a few minutes the President is going to walk in here and we'll all stand up and then I'm going to speak and he's going to listen, *has* to listen to me."

Some years the President didn't come to the dinner. A feud with the press, the burden of official business, reasons substantive or silly. During his first administration FDR refused to appear in white tie and tails in deference to the depression. More recently, Lyndon Johnson had startled everyone, and dismayed the Gridiron elders, by appearing midway through one dinner in a blue business suit and what witnesses would later swear were yellow shoes. But on this evening the President arrived in proper attire.

It was ten o'clock and the filet of beef and the endive salad had been cleared and the guests were working their way through the strawberries Chantilly a la Chartreuse. The President came onto the dais from the left, followed by his wife, smiling, shaking hands, being touched. The ambassador nearly shoved Blanchflower aside to touch the President's hand. How splendid to be so close to power when you had none. The Secret Service men moved past. Two of them took seats on the floor of the ballroom in front of the dais, commanding both aisles that ran up to the head table. Another agent squatted down on the floor, actually under the cloth of the table at which the President would now sit. The marine band played, the Gridiron was on its feet, and suddenly it was worth the hotel food, the skits, the heavy conversation, to be here.

Now the man who understood television was on his feet in a roomful of 600 of the most important people in America and not a single television camera in operation. The Republican, speaking first, had said nothing significant and without a great

98

deal of charm. Blanchflower's opening sallies, instinctive and unprepared, dispatched the poor fellow without breaking bone. He then moved on to the requisite jests at the Vice-President, a deferential but rather funny line about the President himself, and then a gracious line at the end which struck some as curiously anticlimactic but which the President, who knew a good curtain speech, recognized as effective.

"Good talk, Nick. Enjoyed it. Enjoyed it very much," the President said, grasping his hand.

Blanchflower grinned. "Thank you, Mr. President."

There was a good ovation, not sensational, and Blanchflower sat down. The ambassador leaned over to pat his arm.

"Just splendid, dear fellow," he said.

The secretary turned to him as well.

"Nice bit there at the end, Blanchflower," he said.

Blanchflower nodded. He knew it was a nice bit. The secretary's employer, the President of the United States, had used that same homey line seven years earlier in his first campaign.

The ambassador pointed to an attractive, dark-haired woman with bare shoulders at one of the long tables.

"My wife," he said proudly. "She's very excited about being here. It's her first Gridiron. Mine, too, in point of fact."

"Well," Blanchflower said expansively, "let's meet her later. There are always some good parties upstairs. The newspapers give them. The President drops by. She'll enjoy it."

The ambassador beamed.

"Oh, that's smashing," he said.

The club president rose to his feet and raised his glass.

"The Gridiron Club has but one toast," he said, "to the President of the United States."

Standing, the room echoed the toast. Then the President spoke and when it was over and the lights dimmed except for the bulbs outlining the Gridiron's symbol on the wall behind the President, Blanchflower along with the other men in the great room, slipped his arms through those of his two neighbors. The Marine Corps band played "Auld Lang Syne" and the men, arms linked, swayed with the music, slowly, and sang. Jesus, Blanchflower thought, I never get tired of this. It was corny, he knew, but it was Washington. Linked to the men on either side of him, linked, at several removes, to the President of the United States, a few men distant from where he intended to stand two years from now, Nicholas Blanchflower raised his voice to sing, his pleasure and excitement and satisfaction very close to orgasmic.

Two nights later he was in bed with the ambassador's dark-haired, bare-shouldered wife.

"Did you know this was going to happen when you first saw me?" she asked, wanting to be told yes.

Blanchflower did the gentlemanly thing.

"Of course I did," he said. "From the very first."

She smiled.

"I'm going to love Washington," she said.

He nodded and cradled her closer in his big arm.

"I'm sure you are," he said, and he put his mouth again on hers.

In due course the President of the United States would learn of this romantic little interlude. Blanchflower was not as circumspect as he might be, women talked among themselves of such things, and there were few secrets on the Georgetown cocktail circuit. But given the *mores* of the day, Blanchflower's little flirtation was hardly ammunition sufficient to damage his ambitions. No, the President concluded, and his cronies agreed, Nick Blanchflower would have to blunder in more substantive fashion before they could wreck his future, before they could discourage his yen for higher office, before they could convince a stubborn man the White House was spoken for and that Senator Nicholas Blanchflower was not going to be the next President.

11

Kate Sinclair, rarely seen in the flesh, nightly viewed on the tube, constantly considered, was something of a legend at Miss Horton's School. Part of the legend derived quite naturally from her professional fame. The meatier part sprang full blown from the adolescent imagination of her sister, Shaun. Since Shaun saw Kate infrequently and their correspondence was carried on through an amanuensis, the girl sought to overcome separation and flesh out Kate's two-dimensional video image by invention. Shaun had become, at age fifteen, an accomplished liar.

"My sister doesn't really dislike me so much as feel protective of me," a typical tale would begin for a half-dozen wide-eyed girls in T-shirts or bathrobes sprawled around the floor of Shaun's room.

"It's all those death threats and stuff. She long ago gave herself up for doomed but she kind of worries about me. You know, as the last of the line."

The other girls goggled.

" 'Course, the network does what it can, but as Hitler used to say, 'a really determined assassin can always get through if he's willing to give up his own life.' "

"Ugh," said one of her classmates, "I hate Hitler. All that treaty-breaking stuff and Munich. Hitler's why I flunked European Modern last term."

"Shut up," said another girl, "I want to hear about Kate Sinclair."

Shaun inhaled, assuming a pensive tone.

"Then there's Mary. She's our maid. Kate doesn't really like to have me exposed to Mary too much."

"She a lesbian?" someone asked, sending a tingle of excitement through the bedroom.

"Nah, a Trotskyite. Sort of like being Maoist except a couple of hundred years earlier. Trotsky was Stalin's best friend. And Lenin's. Then they had a falling out, I think it was over who got to marry Anastasia when they bumped off the Tsar, and Trotsky had to flee to Mexico. I think Anastasia went with him for a while but the climate didn't agree with her, or something, and later Stalin sent a secret agent over and he disguised himself as a peasant woman or a priest and he hit Trotsky in the head with an axe and Mary's the last one left of his old ring and she's trying to rehabilitate his reputation."

"That means she's a commie," said a girl with glasses.

Shaun looked patient.

"Carrie, there are commies and commies. You think my sister would harbor just any old commie? My God, there are commies right here on this campus. You know old Selfridge?"

"The organist? In chapel? He's a commie?"

"Sure he is. And maybe lots more. Anyway, being a commie isn't a big deal anymore since Solzhenitsyn escaped and the Red Chinese are selling us vodka."

"How do you know old Selfridge is?" Carrie wanted stubbornly to know.

"I see his mail," Shaun said. "Lots of secret stuff like *Partisan Review*. Mary gets stuff like that so I know what I'm talking about. She holds cell meetings in our apartment and the FBI knows about them but my sister shields her and says that's how she keeps the death threats off and anyway, Mary opens all the mail and she knows what letter bombs look like, so it's really neat having her around even though you could do without some of those smelly guys with beards and long overcoats who come to her meetings."

When Shaun tired of the death threat stories she would play other strings on the theme.

"My sister's always hanging around the White House, too. I'm not sure the First Lady's so happy about the arrangement but what can she say? The President likes having Kate around, and she kind of coaches the cabinet on how to read the prompter without looking goggle-eyed."

"Have you been to the White House, Shaun?"

"Sure, loads of times, always in secret and at night. The FBI and the Secret Service deliver me in a laundry van, just so no one will be able to identify me and we can keep the kidnap plots down."

"You ever kidnapped?"

"Nah, a couple of close calls. Usually in New York I wear disguises, you know, wigs and eyeglasses and sometimes a false nose. Platform shoes, too."

Carrie, ever literal: "Dammit, Shaun, you're already five nine, what the hell were you wearing platforms for?"

"That was last year. I was only five six."

"Shut up, Carrie, we want to hear more about the White House."

"Well," said Shaun, brushing her long straight hair as if trying to recall the best parts, "it's not as big as you might think. Lots of pictures but nothing contemporary. All Presidents in wigs and like that. I mean, it's like Jackson Pollock never existed."

"Who's Jackson What's-his-name?" someone wanted to know.

"He used to come to the house too," Shaun explained. "A famous painter with a bushy red beard and overalls, paint spattered all over them, and his mistresses, and then he got killed in a car crash or something. Harvey Podesta comes too, but he only has some young man along."

"Tell us about the kidnap plots."

"I'd better not. Miss Horton nearly refused to admit me here. She was terrified about them. Didn't want to have FBI men crawling around the grounds all the time getting into the flowers and scaring the caretaker and such. My sister said she'd make me promise to wear a disguise all the time, even in gym and chapel, so the kidnappers wouldn't know who I was, except Miss Horton got worried all over again over that 'cause maybe they'd make a mistake and snatch . . . (she paused dramatically) . . . one . . . of . . . you."

"Are kidnappers always beasts or are some of them handsome?" a girl with pigtails asked.

"My God," said Carrie, "are you oversexed."

The girl in pigtails nodded sorrowfully.

"Yeah, I know, I just can't help it. But I try."

"Shouldn't your sister have bodyguards?" another girl asked.

"She used to," Shaun said, "but they really got in the way of her personal life. I mean, they went into the bathroom with her and everything. She got rid of them, finally. She carries a gun now."

"A gun?"

"Yeah, one of those little derringers gamblers used to keep in their sleeve on Mississippi riverboats. I asked her for one for Christmas but she says not until I'm eighteen."

"Boy, a gun."

"And in case she ever gets captured and held for ransom and they torture her or anything, she's got a hollow tooth with strychnine in it. One bite and you're dead in eight seconds."

The girls stared, happily.

Teen-age confessions of this sort led inevitably to Shaun's favorite theme, her sister's illicit romances. The girl customarily withheld these for a select audience of special chums and for late night, whispered confidences.

"Now, listen, if any of you breathe a word of this, or send a letter to *TV Guide* or anything, and get my sister fired for turpitude, I'll really have your ass. I promise I will."

Circumspection was pledged.

Mollified, Shaun would lower her voice, the circle of girls would grow tighter, and Kate Sinclair's reputation would begin to assume an even brighter burnish.

"Well, you know, at college, she was pretty racy even then. I mean, not just the usual fraternity drags, but like football captains and all-American lacrosse players and the sons of South American generals and such. But it wasn't until she got divorced and then became the anchorwoman she really tore loose. Why, when she had her picture on the cover of *Time* and *Newsweek* the same week, the phone never stopped ringing. Politicians and statesmen and senators and everything, not just rich guys and bankers and movie stars. Even Ralph Nader wanted to meet her."

"Was that when she met the President?"

Shaun looked aggrieved. "You don't listen, do you? It isn't *this* President, it was the last one. But that's over now. And, besides, it wasn't just famous men we'd all recognize. Some of her most passionate involvements were with guys you never heard of, like commies in Mary's cell, and a guy who writes

104

dirty novels under a woman's name, and a Chinese-Portuguese gambler from Macao who's hiding out in New York from Interpol."

"Any black guys?" asked the girl with pigtails.

Shaun stared at her.

"Sure," she said, "you think my sister's prejudiced?"

This promising line drifted off into a personal opinion forum with the girls admitting four to one that, given the proper circumstances, "like if he were really neat, like Clyde Frazier," they too would break the color bar.

"Hey," Shaun said, suddenly no longer the focus, "don't you guys want to hear more about my sister? About her sex life?"

Of course they did. And of course Shaun complied.

Later, after midnight, her audience dispersed, the dormitory silent, Miss Horton herself at rest, Mr. Selfridge presumably curled up with the latest *Partisan Review*, Shaun would remind herself how pleased she was to have a sister like Kate instead of one of those boring Locust Valley mothers in their Bergdorf Goodman linen dresses and without black or famous lovers.

And Shaun, half child, half woman, a future beauty, a present liar, would finally go to sleep herself. But not without, from time to time, wishing that for once, just once, the famous Kate Sinclair would write a letter and not leave the chore to her secretary.

12

Blanchflower was back in New York. Kate had stopped thinking about him after a while, after those first few days following dinner with Connie Heath. What was he, after all, but another ego-oriented political main-chancer, more attractive than most perhaps, but arrogant, ruthless, dangerous even. She was glad he had not called, or that was what she told herself.

Now, still shaken by her night with Haller, she inhaled sharply and grabbed the phone when her secretary told her he was calling. Suddenly her reservations about Blanchflower did not seem all that important. Characteristically he plunged into the middle of the conversation without any apology that more than a month had passed without a word since they met.

"Look," he said, "it's still cold, I know, but they say Saturday's going to be a great day and why don't you get in your car and drive out to Oyster Bay? Come for the afternoon. You can see my house. Meet the little bastards. Stay and we'll have dinner somewhere."

Eagerly, forgetting her legendary control, she said yes.

It was one of those wonderful days of false spring, light and airy and without the cold and the cutting wind. Kate decided against the company limo and the chauffeur and called Hertz. She drove with the sunroof and the windows open, out across the Triborough and then, following Blanchflower's instructions, out on the Expressway to the Oyster Bay turnoff, through the old town and around the bay, past the cheap, cardboard-looking beach houses, to Centre Island. There was a little police booth with no one in it and she drove down the island's single road, passing the estates and the deep lanes down which great houses hid themselves, until she came to the sign at the head of his driveway and turned the car onto the crunching gravel. There was a lawn sloping toward the water, a dock, a white frame sprawl of a house. She parked in front of the big garage and walked across the grass, her heels sinking slightly into the lawn. Down on a bit of shingle Blanchflower and a couple of workmen were wrestling with a small sailboat, trying to get it closer to the water. She stopped just beyond them.

One of the men was huge and red-haired, the other small, and seeming on the verge of apoplexy. While the huge man hauled in one direction, the small man heaved in the opposite. Blanchflower, unseasonal in a white suit, shirt and tie, smoking a large cigar, contented himself with waving a hand and shouting encouragement.

Finally the small man stopped and cried out, "For the love of God and the saints and Mary herself will ya leave off and let me do the fugging thing?"

The red-headed man clenched his fists and kicked at the gravel. Blanchflower puffed at the cigar.

"I wouldn't be surprised if he was right," he said mildly.

The small man, mollified, took hold of the sailboat again, heaved, and it moved smoothly and easily as if propelling itself.

"Ya see?" he snarled.

Blanchflower grinned and then, seeing Kate, turned toward her waving as if in alarm.

"I'd be careful around here, Kate. These men haven't seen a white woman in weeks. I can't vouch for them."

The workmen turned to look at her and the big man laughed.

Blanchflower strode up the shingle to where the lawn began at the high water mark.

"You don't get the class of men you once got in the merchant navy," he said. "I dunno if it's the scurvy or the shortage of breadfruit or what. Maybe it was when they abolished keel-hauling. Anyway, come and have a drink."

He held out his hand and she shook it.

"I haven't the vaguest notion of what you're talking about," she said, "but I'm glad I came. This is lovely."

They walked up the lawn to the house. Before they were at the porch that led to an open door, Blanchflower was shouting:

"Can a man get a drink in this house or are we to perish of the thirst?"

A small boy came to the door.

"Say hello to Miss Sinclair, Marmaduke, and then send the slavey out. You're too young to mix a decent drink."

The boy shook hands, gravely, and then, laughing to himself, ran inside.

"How many do you have?" Kate asked. "I know Marmaduke can't be the only one."

"No," Blanchflower said. "There are four. At least I think it's four. And his name's Charles or something. I call him Marmaduke from the private eye novels."

"Oh," Kate said, not understanding. A black woman came out and took the drinks order. "The slavey," Kate assumed. Blanchflower had a strange way of handling workmen and domestics. The black woman seemed perfectly cheerful.

"Do you always call her a 'slavey'?" she asked quietly when the woman had gone inside.

"Sure," he said. "She knows it's a joke. She hasn't done an honest day's work in years. What it comes down to is the boys and I work for her. And she gets paid."

They sat in old wicker chairs holding drinks. The lawn sloped to the water and across the mile or two miles of the bay were low green hills and here and there a house or a car moving through the trees.

"It's still too cold for boats," Blanchflower said. "In the summer there're sails from one shore to the other. Last weekend there was still some ice floating around. Today's a freak. The bad weather isn't gone yet."

This was his permanent residence. There was an apartment in Georgetown, a *pied-à-terre* in Manhattan.

"That's why you have to be either rich or a goddamn crook to be a senator," he said equably.

"And which are you?" she said.

He laughed.

"A bit of each, probably."

She knew quite a bit about Nicholas Blanchflower by this

108

time. She'd done research in the network's library. He was forty-four, his wife had died in an air crash five years earlier, he had inherited some money, not a great deal, went into the stock market at the beginning of the boom and had gotten out in '72, just before the collapse. He had narrowly won his first race for the Senate, easily won reelection, and was now considered by the authorities as a comer, a future President. He was also said to be a chaser, and notoriously indiscreet about it.

After the drinks they went down to the water's edge, the boy, Charles/Marmaduke, trailing them with an orange frisbee he was learning to toss. His brothers, he informed Kate, were at school. He had had pneumonia and was home to recuperate. This was his last weekend. He went back to school Monday.

"Take off your shoes," Blanchflower said. "Nice smooth stretch along here."

Kate kicked off her shoes and then, rather awkwardly while Blanchflower and his son stared out at the water, pulled off her pantyhose.

"You might have warned me," she said.

"Next time wear pants, Kate. And consider yourself warned."

Very sure of himself, Kate thought, talking about next time. But she knew he was right.

They walked to the end of the island.

"That's Lerner's place up there," Blanchflower said. "Rex Harrison was married up there at the next house. Don't ask me which wife."

He pointed out other historical monuments.

"That's where Adamson's barn used to be. One night last winter the sons of bitches came in with a truck and dismantled the whole damn thing. Barn siding is very large these days in the decorating business, I'm informed."

On the way back to the house the boy's frisbee sailed out over the water. He looked at his father.

"Dad?" he said.

Blanchflower shook his head.

"I ought to let you go out there and get pneumonia all over again," he said, but instead, he rolled up his pants and waded out into the water. Kate flinched. My God, it must be freezing.

Blanchflower strode back up onto the beach and tossed the orange frisbee to the boy.

"Here, kid," he said, "we've all got our troubles."

"It's funny," Kate was saying, "all this time you've been in politics and I've been doing television we've never met."

Blanchflower puffed at his cigar. "I guess you thought I wouldn't do anything for your ratings."

She laughed.

"You're controversial enough to hype anyone's ratings. Don't you ever get tired of having people sniping at you? You do seem to take the most extraordinary positions."

"Sure," he said, "say something outrageous, get their attention. Then slip in one sensible, constructive idea. One sensible thought is about all most people can handle at any one time. I mean politicians, too, I'm not being superior to the great unwashed. We retain only a fraction of what we hear, what we see. That was what Toffler was saying in *Future Shock*, that there's just too damn much data for us to absorb and make any sense out of."

"So you shock people into retaining what you have to say."

He nodded.

"Television's to blame," he said. "An editor, a writer, an inventor, a politician, we're all competing for a small piece of the national consciousness. The goddamn tube is on eight hours a day in the average home. What the hell chance do I have to make any impression at all when I'm mouthing off about oh, the illegal alien problem or some arcane change in the federal banking laws? So I raise hell and people stop and they say, 'Well, now, what's this nut Blanchflower up to now? What's he got on his alleged mind?' And presumably, they pay attention, for a few seconds at least."

"You don't like television, do you?" she said.

"I don't like it or dislike it. I use it. I used television to get elected twelve years ago, and I use it now. I was totally unknown until I bought my first thirty seconds on the tube. But that doesn't mean I go all weak in the knees at the very thought of it."

Kate wondered what Bobby Klaus would think of Blanchflower's assessment.

110

"Look," he said, "you've read *Gulliver's Travels*, haven't you?"

She nodded.

"The third book. I forget the name of it. The satire on the Royal Academy."

"No," she said, "I remember Lilliput and the place where the giants lived. . . . "

"Brobdingnag."

"Yes, and then wasn't there one where the horses were the intelligent beings and people were the beasts of burden?"

"Yahoos," he said. "Well, there was another adventure. Old Lemuel arrived in this kingdom where everyone was a bloody genius. Great thinkers. Postulating new concepts, creating new gadgets, all IQs of a hundred and eighty and not a bit of common sense in the lot. And the funniest part was that all these great brains were so intent on thinking, they'd forgotten how to communicate with one another. No one listened to anyone else. So the people had to carry around sticks with inflated bladders attached to them, and if they wanted you to talk, they rapped you in the mouth with this blown up bladder, and if they wanted you to listen, they gave you a rap on the ear."

Kate laughed.

"As far as I'm concerned," Blanchflower said, "that's the way to use television. Blow up a bladder and rap the audience right between the eyes and they sit up and watch. And listen. If only for a moment."

She looked dubious.

"That's pretty simplistic," she said. "Television's more complicated than that. The Nielsens, for example, you understand about them, how important they are to us?"

He was patient.

"Kate, politicians don't study civics anymore. We major in the Nielsens. There are a thousand homes with Nielsen meters hooked to their sets and connected to a computer. If a goddamn teenager comes down at three o'clock in the morning to make a sandwich and flips on the goddamned set, Nielsen knows about it. That's the frightening thing."

"What?"

"Seventy-two million households with television and they

111

take a sample of a thousand. You ever think about that? The enormity of it?"

She nodded.

"I think about it every day of my life," she said.

Blanchflower was silent for a moment.

"So do I," he said quietly. "And so does the President of the United States, don't kid yourself."

She smiled and said gravely, "In this business you don't kid about A. C. Nielsen. You just pray every night for those thousand families. That a reasonable percentage of them prefer you to Cronkite or Chancellor or whoever."

Blanchflower laughed.

"And I pray they like me instead of Jerry Brown or Teddy Kennedy or Fritz Mondale."

"How could anyone like Fritz Mondale better than you?" she asked flirtatiously.

Now, why did she gush like *that?* she asked herself in irritation.

Later they watched the last clamboat working in the last sun on Oyster Bay. The boy, very proper, served them drinks.

"I think you'll like this, Kate," the boy said. "At least, I hope so."

Blanchflower tried his drink.

"Okay, Marmaduke, not bad. Not at all bad. Considering you can't do this sort of thing legally for years and years. Now beat it while Miss Sinclair tells me what an important person she is."

The boy made a face and then, grinning broadly, pleased by the compliment, left them alone on the great lawn. Kate wished she and Shaun could be this way.

"You're very good with your son," she told Blanchflower.

He nodded.

"Well, maybe. I'm better than I'd be if I were with them all the time. This way, seeing them just every so often, there's a novelty to the arrangement. I don't bore them and they don't bore me."

"Oh, but you could never be boring," she said, indignant.

"Kate Sinclair," he said, "who ever said you were a cold piece of work? You're a marshmallow. A goddamned marshmallow."

"And you?"

"Well, that's a question. I'm pretty good with the kids because I have no choice. When my wife was killed I had to play mother and father both. And since I had to do it, I did it well. When I have options, then I tend to indulge myself."

"And do you consider you have options with me?" she asked, sensing she was going faster than she should, but taking the opening.

"Obviously," he said.

Her face changed, but all she said was, "Oh?"

"Sure," he said, "I can indulge myself with you out here or back in town."

The housekeeper said she and the boy would do dinner for themselves and Blanchflower got out an old car and they drove into Westbury to one of those country inns where the barmen wore little red jackets and there were horse brasses on the walls and pictures of horse show winners yellowing in dusty frames. But the riders were elsewhere that evening, perhaps they had been elsewhere for a decade, and the place was full of solid, middle-class folk to whom a horse was a number at the off-track betting or a potential pot of glue. The captain was very deferential and Blanchflower got a booth in what was called, inevitably, The Tack Room.

"Well," he said, "at least the martinis are good."

After dinner they had brandy. Kate felt the drinks.

"I've never been much of a drinker," she said. "I could never drink with you."

"How wise you are," he said. "I drink, I smoke, I like women. Beyond that I'm a veritable Boy Scout, you know, loyal, honest, courageous, I can build fires without matches and paddle canoes and tie a dozen different kinds of knots."

She laughed. "And all the time I thought you were perfect. A man I could confidently support in the next Presidential election."

"The next," he nodded, "or the one after that."

She looked into his face.

"You're serious, aren't you?"

"Absolutely."

"And you think you have a chance."

"Who the hell knows?" he said. "Teddy's out there, Mondale, Jerry Brown, a half-dozen governors you probably never heard of but who are doing a good job in their states. Maybe some cat even I never heard of is going to come out of the boondocks and promise us salvation. Maybe one of the blacks. And to complicate matters further any one of us could get bumped off by some crazy or the Russians could go nuts or the Concorde could run into the Empire State Building or the god-damned women could get off their asses and organize behind Bella or Friedan or Gloria or somebody and vote the men out."

"But if those things don't happen . . .?"

"Well, if they don't, then why not me? I've got a little money so I don't have to take graft. I'm the right age. I've got brains but no one is put off by my intellectualism. I'm not Adlai. I can make up my mind. The blacks and I communicate about as well as blacks and whites can ever communicate. Wall Street could live with me. I'm not much with the farmers but I could study up on them. I come across pretty well on the tube and when you get down to it, isn't that what winning elections is all about?"

She nodded.

"That's what scares me sometimes about televsion," she said. "The power we have."

"Sure," he said, "nobody reads anymore. You guys have won the war."

Then she said, quite soberly, "I hope we know what to do with it. The idea of people like Bobby Klaus and Chester and me influencing the country is sort of frightening."

"Oh, hell," he said, "compared to some of the old press lords you people are choir boys. You ought to read up on the old newspaper barons, Hearst and old man Pulitzer and James Gordon Bennett. Pulitzer was so nutty he had to live in a rub-berized room set on ball bearings so he couldn't feel the vibra-tions from the streets."

"You're kidding," she said.

Blanchflower looked hurt.

"Literal truth. And I think it was Bennett once traded shots with someone in the city room. Hell, you and Chester are okay."

"Well," she said, "we don't shoot at each other. At least not yet."

114

She told him about the tensions building in the news room between Chester and herself, of some of the criticisms.

"Kate," he said, "they don't snipe at you unless you're worth hitting. They pay you a million bucks, or whatever the hell it is you get. They see your face on the cover of *Time*. You're on the tube every night. You're a damned good looking woman who seems to have everything. Why shouldn't they be critical of you?"

"Yeah, I guess so." She sounded unsure.

"Sure, I'm right," he said.

"But damnit," she said, suddenly irritated, defensive, "I worked for this job. Worked damn hard. I've helped the ratings. And I put up with Chester and his little pouts. Why do I have to be a target? Why can't people accept the fact that a woman can be competent and under fifty and have good legs all at the same time?"

"You a feminist?" he asked.

"No, not in any formal way. I believe in the Equal Rights Amendment, of course. I don't go to meetings or march in picket lines, if that's what you mean."

"That's too bad," he said. "I need some good feminists to back me when I run for the Presidency."

She looked at him.

"You're really serious, aren't you? I mean, about running."

He nodded.

"About running. About winning."

Some young people in the next booth, two pretty girls and their dates, were making noise, laughing. It sounded nice.

"But what happens when a man doesn't win?" Kate asked. "When a politician sets his mind on the White House and then he doesn't get there. Like Humphrey. How pitiful it must be to want it so badly and never to get there."

"Sure," he said, "no one likes to lose. Me, I guess I'd get out of politics completely then, not just hang on around the fringes playing the elder statesman. I'd get a professorship in political science at some nice girls' college up in Massachusetts and give three lectures a week and seduce the students in my book-lined study. Hell of a life."

He was looking at one of the young women as he spoke.

As she drove home that night, the windows open despite

the chill to clear her head, Kate wondered about the way he had looked at that girl, about his reputation. She had no intention of becoming involved with another Tommy Sinclair, another charming man who was all surface with no real strength inside.

Oh, she thought, he's okay. He's *got* to be okay. There's too much confidence there for him to be anything *but* okay.

13

Increasingly, ever since her marriage broke up and she became important in television, Kate Sinclair had been drawn into the world of homosexuals. There was nothing perverse about it. It was simply a function of loneliness. Connie Heath called them "walkers," these young men with their articulate hands and their newly shampooed hair who had all the latest gossip (they called it "dish"), who had seen the new plays, read the new books in galley, who created dress collections, decorated apartments, choreographed musicals, authored naughty books and wrote severe criticisms of each other's works for the *Times*. For women like Kate it was them or married men, or far out players like Haller, brutal, dominating, cruel. Harvey Podesta had drawn her into his set. And, gradually, they became her own.

She and Harvey had gone to La Grenouille for lunch with a boy called Paco, a very talented couturier from Paris who had come to New York to design a dress collection for one or another Seventh Avenue thug, and had just, regrettably, been fired.

"Now, Kate," Harvey said, as the two of them sat on the best banquette, just inside the front room and to the right, "be tolerant of this boy. He badly needs help. He's penniless, totally strapped, and we must encourage him. We must help him find new employment. It's a serious business, *tu sais*."

"I love it when you try to speak French," Kate said, "it's a posthumous insult to de Gaulle."

"I never liked de Gaulle," Harvey said. "Never."

Kate said, "Of course not. He was six feet five."

Harvey simmered.

But only for a moment. The boy, Paco, had arrived.

"Oh, my God," he said, the words gushing out desperately

in a mélange of French, Spanish, and English, "I am disaster. New functions most difficult to employ. Jobs fantastico dificile to found."

Harvey patted him on the back of a lean, tanned hand. He was blond and very beautiful.

"And just why do you think Kate and I are here, dear boy?"

Paco shook his head from side to side as if keening for the dead. He knew that Kate Sinclair was rich and famous and that Harvey had arranged this lunch for the precise purpose of finding him new employment and being aware of just who Kate was, he wanted to make an impression.

"Aiyeee," he moaned.

Kate wondered if she were supposed to take him in her arms. But before she could do this, another young man arrived.

Harvey exuded charm.

"Oh, Kate, you do know Silas, of course."

Kate said hello. Silas was dwarfed and swarthy and talented, an artist. He counted very much, it was quite clear.

"Yes," she said, "oh yes."

The captain smoothly expanded the table and drinks were fetched.

It seemed that Silas had just seen the new Galanos collection.

"You can't know the emotion I felt," he said. "There was one dress, a little cocktail number, slinky, soft, so tasteful, number two hundred eleven. I knew the moment it appeared on the runway, I must have it. There was this cow of a girl showing it, all shoulders and boobs and legs. Quite vulgar, really, and I went right backstage to Jimmy's little woman and I bought it, right on the spot, in size ten. It's in my closet now, a wonderful thing, and even without alterations it's very nearly perfect on me."

Silas looked at Kate when he said this, nodding at her to elicit approval. Kate found herself nodding back.

"I'm sure it's lovely," she said.

Since Silas was bald, bearded and mustached, she found it somewhat difficult to imagine him in the Galanos dress. But she was Harvey's guest and being polite.

Through Harvey, Kate had learned to speak the language of

the gays. Without patronizing them she came to understand them, to see the world through a sexual skew, to appreciate their sensitivity, their creativity, their riotous gaiety and equally profound depressions.

The headwaiter, Marcel, the one who looked like a good welterweight, took orders for a second round of drinks. Paco, the unemployed dressmaker, rolled his eyes. He was drinking Perrier.

"We may discuss my problem, please?" he asked.

"Presently, Paco, just do be patient with us," Harvey chided.

There was a new film. They were all agog about it.

"Nazis," Silas said. "Black uniforms and boots and everything. Frightening."

"Paco would have made a wonderful Nazi," Harvey said. "He's so blond."

Kate wanted to say there *were* other criteria, but Silas broke in.

"It's S-M all the way. Whips and things. But you ought to see the queues along Third Avenue. Every leather boy in town lined up to pay his four dollars."

"I know," Harvey said. "There was this one boy wearing the most darling little dog collar I have *ever* seen."

Now Trappeau joined them. Kate had not met him. But she knew who he was.

"Listen," Trappeau said, "why don't we get a drink, huh?"

Marcel was summoned. Paco again mentioned his search for gainful employment.

"Shut up," Trappeau said.

Harvey beamed.

"Trappeau, I so admire your facility with American slang. I wish I had French argot down as pat."

Trappeau grinned. He was a jewelry designer from Neuilly who'd been imported to New York years before by an American colonel serving with NATO in Paris. His colonel had come from the Bronx and so Trappeau had a curious slangy quality to his English. He also, he informed them, had a new lover.

"A city cop," he said. "Sometimes I put on his uniform and blow his whistle."

That got them started talking about the Nazi movie again.

119

There were now five of them at the table. Paco, semaphoring desperately, caught Marcel's eye.

"Could we perhaps luncheon?" he asked timidly.

The menu came. Trappeau assumed, without having been asked, the role of host.

"And a bottle of Petrus '61," he said. "No, two bottles is better. Let it breathe."

Paco inhaled sharply. The Petrus was the most expensive wine on the card. Kate felt sorry for him.

"You know," she said, "Paco *is* looking for a job. Does anyone have any ideas?"

Harvey looked stern.

"Kate, stop being so materialistic. You'll offend Paco."

"Please?" Paco asked, not understanding.

The smoked salmon came. The room was filled, the thin sunlight slanting in through the windows from above the Cartier building across the street. There were tiny ponies of chilled vodka with the salmon.

"You *can't* eat salmon without vodka," Trappeau declared.

There was a discussion of the age at which each of them had lost his virginity. Kate felt retarded. Trappeau claimed it had happened to him at nine. "Of course not until a year later with my first woman."

The leg of lamb with flageolets came. Two more bottles of Petrus were opened.

"Listen, Paco," Trappeau said enthusiastically, "with so many loyal friends what the hell you got to worry about? Huh?"

"Aiyeee," Paco said.

Silas, becoming confidential with the drinks, confessed how much in love he was.

"You can't know," he said. "Really, you can't."

Harvey smiled and patted his knee.

"But, really," Harvey said, "what is love? An absolute? A relative? Is it one thing for you and another for me?"

Kate laughed. She also felt the drinks.

"Harvey," she said, "I certainly hope so for my sake."

They argued their definitions: total selflessness; passion; possessiveness; craving. Trappeau topped them.

"Listen," he said, "you don't know what love is. One time I

120

meet this boy from Georgia. A farmer. We live together and I say to him, 'Look, in New York you can find a guy like me. What the hell you do down there in Georgia on the farm?' And he says to me, 'Trappeau, on my farm I have a mule.' So, I don't think about it anymore and then, later, when this boy is really in love with me, he looks into my eyes and he says, 'You know, Trappeau, I think my mule would like you too.' That's love."

Paco mentioned his job again.

"I gotta get out of here," Trappeau said. "The cop gets off at four. I pick him up at the station house."

Silas was headed for Bloomingdale's. There was a sale on housewares.

"Come on, Kate," Harvey said. "It's tacky to sit over lunch past three."

Kate looked at Paco.

"But, Harvey," she said.

Harvey got up and pulled the table out for her. "Paco, Kate and I will bend *every* effort to help you. Just you relax and I'm sure something marvelous will turn up. You're too talented a boy to be out of work." He waved for Marcel.

"Do bring Paco the check, will you?" Harvey said. "This is no time for him to be sitting idle."

When they left Paco was still there, trying to add up the bill. Kate imagined she had seen tears in his eyes.

Harvey wanted to shop and Kate went back to her apartment. Mary was out. She roamed through the rooms, restless, feeling the drinks. Sometimes being with Harvey and his friends was wonderful. She would come away amused, exhilarated, replete with witty anecdotes, or new insights into the current rage in the arts. But too often it was like today, black humor which in retrospect embarrassed her, selfishness that left the boy, Paco, to pay for laughter of which he was a target. She remembered something Warhol had said, long ago.

"I get so angry at them sometimes," he'd told her. "They think they're women but they're not. They don't swell up with water or have periods or anything. But they think they're women."

Kate felt the same way. She could be so angry with them. And yet, she knew, they could be so nice. To clear her head

121

she decided to take a shower. How pleasant it would be if everything were as simple as the water beating down, slipping smoothly over her body, pounding her but yet not hurting. When she came out of the shower she felt much better, and the phone was ringing.

"Hello," she said, the towel slipping from her and her free hand scrambling to adjust it so she would not drip. "Hello, Kate Sinclair."

It was Blanchflower. From Washington.

"Look," he said, "I had a subcommittee meeting. It just ended. I can catch the five-o'clock shuttle maybe. Want to have dinner?"

"Of course," she said. And when she had hung up she wondered why the "of course." Their day and evening on Long Island had been pleasant but had not promised all that much. Two weeks had gone by without another call, without a note. And she remembered the way he'd looked at the young woman in the next booth. But she said yes, she said, "of course."

Well, why not? The prospect of Saturday night alone, in front of the television set, or worse, at one or another of the cocktail parties to which she'd been asked was depressing. There was even a vernissage that evening, but she was still shaken by her night with Haller. Better the homosexuals than a night like that. She thought of the SoHo loft and his big hands and that stupid, drugged cow standing naked above her. Blanchflower was an improvement over all those alternatives. Then, suddenly suspicious, she thought again. Blanchflower was a politician. A sympathetic voice at network news was always handy before an election. Still, it was not an unpleasant way to be used and it did not even occur to Kate to despise herself for having such thoughts. In fact, as she dried and began to go through her closet, selecting a dress, she was rather pleased with herself for having discerned a possible motive for his call, pleased that the afternoon's black mood had evaporated and that she was again proving herself a formidable competitor in the male jungle.

14

Blanchflower met Kate for cocktails at the World Trade Center. Joe Baum hustled up, all bonhommie and efficiency, silkily pleased to have yet two more celebrities testifying to his taste. *New York* magazine had called his Windows on the World the most spectacular restaurant ever. This pleased Baum. And it pleased any number of New Yorkers who put aside their usual disdain for tourist attractions to ride the freight elevators 108 stories into the sky and wait in line for a table above the clouds. There was no waiting for Kate Sinclair and Senator Blanchflower.

They sat over drinks, looking down on the great city, watching clouds sail past the stars. Blanchflower was wearing another of those incredible suits, this one pale yellow, vested, brilliant against the muted light of the bar. He was big, bigger even than Haller, she supposed. Thinking of Haller, warmed by the first drink and half through the second, she found herself telling Blanchflower about it when he remarked she seemed distracted.

"Well, I am. I was remembering something. One night I went to dinner with a man. Quite a well-known painter. Later . . . he tried to rape me."

Blanchflower sipped at his vodka.

"Oh?" he said mildly.

Kate put down her glass.

"You ask me if I'm distracted and I say, 'Yes, someone just tried to rape me,' and you sit there and say 'Oh?' You don't find that unusual?"

"Well, since the man isn't here there isn't much point in outrage. You weren't hurt, were you?"

"No."

"That's good," he said.

Kate picked up her glass and shook her head, her hair swinging loose with the movement.

"I like your hair like that," Blanchflower said. "That isn't how you had it the other time, was it?"

"You mean when I went out to your house, or the night I got raped?"

"At my house. I was referring to the impression you make on me. Not on the other chap."

Kate giggled. "The rapist. Now he's 'the other chap.' My God, you're *blasé*."

Blanchflower shook his head. "Not at all. Rape is a terrible act. No argument. It's simply that unless you want to give me this fellow's name, which I don't think you're going to do, there's very little I can do beyond expressing sympathy and nodding and agreeing how good it is that you escaped unscathed. You're an intelligent woman. You've pulled yourself together. I'd assume you won't be seeing the man again or if you do, you'll insure that the circumstances are more . . . seemly."

She was not sure whether Blanchflower was putting her on or if this were his normal reaction to such horrors. She was thinking about that, half-listening to whatever nineteen-thirties tune was coming over the system, when he said:

"The country's obsessed with sex. You're a beautiful woman. The poor bastard probably had a drink too many, you looked good to him, he became aroused and . . . "

Angrily, Kate told him that wasn't how it had been at all. She told him the whole story, even the part about bed, and then Inga's standing there naked in the loft, with Haller orchestrating his little scenario.

"Hell," Blanchflower said, "the whole country's going that way."

"Oh?" she said, suspecting herself of sounding prim.

"Sure. Take today. I've been drafted onto some half-ass special subcommittee on obscenity. Special committees can't write legislation, they just listen to the latest outrage, get a lot of headlines, and then issue a report which nobody reads. Anyway, this subcommittee had one witness this morning, a big New York pornographer, splendid guy, wearing a black hood during his testimony. Said he's quitting the trade. That it's gotten too seamy even for him. Made a hell of an impression. You know, willingness to admit fault. The chairman eulogized him for ten minutes. 'Better that one sinner return than ninety-nine remain pure,' that sort of thing."

"What sort of stuff was he talking about?"

"Well, most of it everyone's heard before. Pimps beating up the girls, teen-age runaways forced into houses, the drug angle, pornographic films, the usual. But this guy was being terribly pious about it all, telling us what dreadful conditions existed out there, and so on and finally I asked him, 'Well, when did this miraculous conversion come about? When the hell did you get religion and decide to come down here and preach us this sermon?'"

"And?" she asked.

Blanchflower reached into his vest pocket and pulled out a very long cigar. "Havana," he said. "Pal on the Foreign Relations committee gets them from Castro." He lighted the cigar, and issuing great clouds of smoke, resumed.

"The pornographer said he'd never been disgusted before, but now they'd gone too far and he wouldn't handle the merchandise anymore."

"I can't *wait* to know what it was turned his stomach," Kate said, somewhat sourly. Blanchflower paused.

"Baby bondage," he said, nodding his head, the cigar dipping up and down. "Baby bondage."

Kate exhaled.

"I think I'm afraid to ask, but okay, what the hell is baby bondage?"

Blanchflower waved an expansive hand. "Oh, you know, middle-aged guys get dressed up in baby bonnets and diapers and stick rattles up their ass and get spanked and such. This guy said he wouldn't handle that trade. Wouldn't stock movies of it."

Weakly, Kate said, "I see."

Blanchflower grinned. "Baby bondage made him see the light, he said. He told us until then it had been all right. Moppet bondage he could handle. But not the baby stuff."

Blanchflower called for the check and when it came he paid it and Kate started to get up. Blanchflower said, "One last thing."

125

"Yes?"

"This painter, the one who tried to rape you."

"Yes?"

"Was he a good painter?"

They had some difficulty getting a cab. Apparently this happened frequently at the World Trade Center. The doorman tried, really he did. It was, "Yes, Senator, no, Senator, right away, Senator." He had greeted Kate ("Evening, Miss Sinclair") but it was Blanchflower to whom he addressed himself. Jesus, Kate thought, how important does a woman have to become just to break even?

They took the FDR Drive uptown. April was warming at last, the dirty crusted snow at the curbs finally gone, the night breezes now out of the south instead of the bone-chilling damp off the Atlantic. The driver had his window cracked slightly to air the cab and Kate could smell the East River. A tanker, as tall as a ten-story apartment building, moved past them in the dark, heading for the ocean, riding high in the water, its holding tanks empty, destined to be filled at some exotic port.

Blanchflower sat in a corner of the cab, his long legs spraddled, the stump of a cigar aglow in the dark, saying nothing but, apparently, at ease. He had a nice profile, she realized, the big nose slightly bent, perhaps broken in some long-forgotten football game. He was big enough. But not gross. She liked that. She wondered why she'd told Blanchflower about Haller and Inga. It wasn't the sort of story she wanted ever to get out. Yet she'd told this man she hardly knew. Was it because instinctively she trusted Blanchflower? Or simply that the experience had shaken her and she'd had, for psychological reasons, to tell someone?

"Paul's okay with you?" Blanchflower asked.

They got one of the good tables, in the back, and Paul sat with them for a while and traded lies with Blanchflower. They had some wine and on the strength of it Kate was tempted to have Blanchflower do his baby bondage number again. She bit her lip and resisted. The man would think she was, in his words, "obsessed with sex." Well, which of us isn't? she thought. And then, answering her own question, responded

126

that she, Kate Sinclair, certainly wasn't. The past eight years proved it, nearly a decade of intermittent celibacy, a decade of serious professional application that had, quite neatly, sublimated any number of other drives under the pounding need to succeed, to be first, to be best, to win.

Over dinner he got her talking again, about herself. She realized he was doing it, admired his cleverness as one good interviewer respects another, and rattled on about things and people and concerns she'd not talked about openly in years.

"You remember, at your house, that evening, when you said you knew all about the Nielsen ratings? That politicians studied them instead of civics?"

He nodded.

"Well," she said, "*we're* obsessed with them. They're *important.* But they worry me in other ways, you know?"

"You mean the sample's so small? Just a couple of households deciding what all the rest of us watch?"

"That. And more than that."

"Oh?"

"Sure. You know, like the audimeter, that's the little black box, it tells when the set's turned on and what channel. But it can't tell when someone leaves the room and the dog's the only one watching. Or if someone falls asleep."

"Or dies," he said.

She laughed.

"Right. That's what I mean. There's nothing qualitative about it." She thought for a moment. "I guess that's why they have a backup system. People keep written logs and send them in to Nielsen."

"Then that solves it."

"Oh, no," Kate said, "that makes it worse. People watch soaps or game shows and claim they were watching channel 13."

Blanchflower's eyes opened histrionically.

"You mean . . . ?" he said.

"Uh huh. Nielsen is convinced the American people lie."

He laughed, loudly, expansively, showing his teeth. It was time for him to talk.

"You're in the wrong business," she told him. "You'd have been a wonderful talk show host on television."

"I might try it," he laughed, "next time they circulate a re-call petition and ride me out of Washington on a rail."

"Oh?" she said, sensing he might, for the first time, say something about himself.

"Sure, some people think that I chase girls too often and shoot off my mouth on the floor of the Senate with unseemly frequency."

"And you do all those things," she said. Blanchflower looked into her face.

"You know," he said, sucking fire into a dying cigar, "people in my line, or yours, we surrender some of the luxuries other people consider to be their due. Privacy, for one. A damned important one. You know how difficult it is to live a private life in the public fishbowl. It's damned near impossi-ble. Take your little 'Perils of Pauline' act the other night, be-ing chased around that loft naked by mobs of ravenous bisexu-als and hairy-handed artists with whips. It was a normal enough thing for an attractive woman to go up there, get laid, go home. But no, because you're Kate Sinclair this son of a bitch had to prove something to you, to himself, maybe even to that Swedish acid-head he dragged into the scene. You were big and you had to be chopped down to size. Fucking you wasn't enough. You had to be . . . reduced . . . brought low . . . minimized."

It was curious, Kate thought, that he could speak about such things, use coarse words, yet not embarrass her. It must be be-cause he was himself not at all self-conscious.

"But what about you?" she said, slipping into her profes-sional questioner's stance that could, she knew, be every bit as frank and disarming as his casual conversation. "What about the things they say about you? Are they true? Or is it simply that your rivals want to minimize you?"

He grinned. A big, boyish grin. Funny, she thought, how young he looked, the blond hair still full and with hardly any gray, falling in unruly waves over his forehead. He scratched his head.

"Anything you hear about me is most likely true. Understat-ed, even. But that isn't my point. My point is that a hell of a lot of men do everything I do, and more, but no one gives a damn. Nobody calls Liz Smith or Evans and Novak or Mary McGrory.

And if they did, no one would listen. Because those other guys don't sit in the Senate and don't run for office and don't go on "Meet the Press" on Sunday mornings when everyone else is reading the funny papers and getting ready for the first beer and an afternoon of pro football." He paused. "But what the hell, no one drafted you into network television, no one held a gun on me and said I had to become a politician. Win some, lose some. We are what we are and we toss away some of the perks of civilian life. Especially the right to make an ass of yourself and to have nobody notice."

They talked about their children, Kate's dead son, the sister she had raised. Blanchflower mentioned the plane crash that had killed his wife and broken his back, but when Kate instinctively began to sympathize, he cut her off. "Oh, hell," he said, "it was a long time ago and we all croak anyway and she was a good woman I probably would have turned sour. Forget it."

Kate told him about Tommy. Why, she wondered as she spoke, did American men use diminutives? She thought of her former husband, she thought even of Bobby Klaus. She liked it that Blanchflower was "Nick" and not "Nicky" or something equally coy.

When he took her home Blanchflower stood with Kate just inside the door of her apartment, held her close, kissed her once. A good kiss, a passionate kiss, but then, unexpectedly, he let his arms drop, stepped back from her a bit, and grinned.

"Good night, Kate," he said. "You're not really stainless steel at all."

While she undressed she wondered why he had not made even a polite attempt to go to bed with her. Jesus, she thought angrily, does it have to be either the Hallers or the faggots?

15

Wall Street's security analysts subdivide, quite naturally, into their various areas of competence. There are analysts who specialize in knowledge of the rubber goods trade, of steel, synthetic fibers, or the advantages and disadvantages of plowing one's life savings into the management of marinas, ski resorts, or health food shops. On this particular day the security analysts who specialized in the broadcast industry sat down in a rather routine private room in one of the lesser Wall Street clubs to listen to, and act on, the words of Bobby Klaus.

The room was full. Bobby was still sufficiently new to the New York scene, and to this particular assemblage, to be a novelty. In years past there had been similarly well-attended turnouts for Jim Aubrey (at the height of his well-publicized troubles at CBS), for Fred Silverman, when he became president of NBC, for Pat Weaver, launching yet again his despairing campaign for pay-TV, for Mr. Paley or the elder Sarnoff. Today, the analysts would decide after listening to Bobby whether to advise their institutional clients to buy or sell the stock of the great broadcasting company he represented.

There never was a chance Bobby would let them sell.

"Look," he said, giving them his "inside" tone as the waiter cleared the roast chicken and parsleyed potatoes and brought on the coffee and the *mousse au chocolat* (a variety of frozen chocolate pudding to be precise), "the corporation did a billion two last year, net—net a hundred eighty million. Of that, broadcast accounted for six hundred and change. This season we're in a sold-up position on network television, spot television is right in there, and both AM and FM are holding their own. As can be said," he admitted disarmingly, "of our competition.

"There is no way," Bobby told them, "reasonably well-run

130

broadcast properties won't simply print money this year. And next year? Well, orders-on-the-books right now are running eight percent ahead of this year, which is, as you all know, the best year we've ever had. I'm not here to hype our stock. You people don't buy hype. I know that. What I'm giving you is a conservative appraisal of where the entire industry stands at this point in time."

He continued for a while, detailing the strengths of his own network. Finally he paused and smiled, and his audience smiled with him.

The luncheon chairman stood up.

"Bobby, if I may call you 'Bobby', you've been more than forthcoming already about broadcast stocks generally, and prospects for your own network. If you would, I'd like to move to questions now."

Bobby Klaus nodded assent. Had the chairman asked him to remove his trousers he would have done so.

There were several technical questions about the stock and the price-earnings ratio and then, from the back of the room, a man said:

"What about all this money you're pouring into network news? Is that wise? Doesn't network news always lose money?"

"Hey," Bobby said, "you sound like my boss."

Laughter flooded the room. These were people accustomed to bosses who asked hard questions.

"In the television business, as anywhere else, you get out what you put in. Frankly, network news never will be a major moneymaker. But we were faced with a continuing last place finish in the news ratings. What did it matter that we were number one in sports, running a close second in prime time? We were being castrated in news. And news, even though it doesn't coin money, pleases the FCC; it lends prestige, status; and it can spin off specials that *do* make money.

"As you know, I'm not a news man. My background is in the entertainment side of broadcasting. But I believe Americans want their news easy to understand and related to their own concerns. They don't want to hear some elder statesman discussing revisions in prime rate or the problems with detente. They want to know what the hell those changes are going to mean at the Safeway next Thursday night. They want real folks, not Harvard professors or State Department specialists telling them what they need to know, and to get the right people you have got to find the best talent available and pay that talent a lot of money." He smiled. "A hell of a lot of money."

"Too much?"

The question came from Bobby's left. He looked in that direction, never really establishing the source. Then he said:

"Well, if you're asking about Kate Sinclair's contract, no, it isn't too much. Maybe it isn't enough."

A million a year not enough? Several of the analysts permitted themselves a chuckle. Bobby did not even smile.

"Let me answer that with a question. In a competitive business like network television, would you rather own stock in the company that owns Kate Sinclair or would you rather be holding someone else's markers?"

There was a hum in the room. Bobby knew he had them. He went on quickly, spouting statistics as he had last year to the board of directors, a man in command of his subject, at the top of his form.

"Kate hasn't done her first special yet and it's already sold out. I'd say, and the figures to date seem to bear me out, that Kate Sinclair, even at a million dollars a year, may turn out to be a bargain."

There was a question then about the techniques that had gone into choosing Kate, choosing Chester Albany, and how they were paired. Bobby said, a bit too smoothly one analyst would later recall, "We employ people who do that sort of thing. They have very sophisticated techniques. It's damned impressive to see."

The chairman, noting it was now two o'clock, "and I promised Mr. Klaus we'd have him on his way back uptown by two," asked for one more, brief question. A man stood at the back of the room.

"Mr. Klaus, this has nothing to do with the future of your company's stock, of course, but I'm curious. Do Kate and Chester really *like* one another?"

There were laughs and Bobby got off a wisecracking line and then people were pressing to the rostrum to shake his hand and he was making his way out of the room toward the street and his waiting limousine. As the car moved north along the FDR Drive he knew what the real answer to that question was, the answer he could not afford to give.

"Nothing to do with the future of our company's stock? Hell, it has *everything* to do with it."

And he lay back against the gray plush of the seat and thought about the two anchorpersons he had introduced, engaged, and finally, married for better or for worse.

At the moment it was for "worse." Chester had catapulted himself into Bobby's office a few days earlier.

"She looks at the ceiling when I talk," Chester said. "I say something and she looks at the goddamned ceiling or raises her eyebrows and I come off like a cretin. Me doing the news and her looking superior and amused."

Bobby Klaus said he was sure that wasn't so.

"It is," Chester insisted. "Clive Jackson told me so and I looked at some tape the other day and he's right. She's always looking at the ceiling when I talk."

"Last month you said she was always biting her hair or tugging her ear lobe when you were talking."

"I suppose it isn't possible to pull your ear lobe and look at the ceiling at the same time? She isn't Jerry Ford!"

Bobby agreed to look at some tape.

"If you find I'm right," Chester said, "then what?"

They discussed whether they could do the show with two anchorpersons but never to have both of them on camera at the same time. "That'd be possible, wouldn't it?" Chester wheedled. Bobby said he didn't know.

"After all, we married you two on television," Bobby said. "Won't it seem a bit, well, strained, for you never to appear together? Sort of like the last days of Tony Armstrong-Jones and Princess Margaret?"

Chester allowed as to that. He thought for a moment.

"Could we cut the desk in half?" he asked.

Bobby went back to his office for Kleenex.

Was this goddamn hack newspaperman going to destroy the entire marvelous operation he, Bobby Klaus, had put across? That Universal Broadcasting had backed so generously? That millions of Americans seemed to want?

Ten years ago Chester Albany had been nothing. Kate Sin-

133

clair was the greatest single discovery Bobby Klaus had ever made. Kate was the one who was going to make their goddamn show number one. It was unthinkable that Chester could ruin it.

Bobby Klaus knew, of course, they did not like one another. How could he not know it? Sooner or later the talk would surface outside the family, beyond the network, then the columns would get hold of it and there would be hell to pay. Bobby decided to have Butch Halvorsen in for a little chat. Butch was the network's press agent. He had a grander title, of course, executive vice-president for corporate relations, but he was a press agent. Philip D'Amico might have known him. Butch was not very bright, but he was shrewd and knowing. He would understand instinctively what to do. He would trot out one of his favorite, homespun anecdotes, a little allegory that might, hopefully, suggest a solution. Like his story about crossing the river.

To clear the dark and sluggish streams of the upper Amazon so their cattle can cross safely, Brazilian cowboys will cut the throat of a sick or injured cow, not deep enough to kill, and drive the poor animal into the water downstream from the fording place the rest of the herd will use. The injured beast, bleeding freely, splashes and lurches its way toward the far shore, wondering what possible mischief it could have committed to be maltreated this way. Then the piranha fish come, the first silvery and small, its tearing bite hardly noticeable above the pain of the knife wound. And then the others come and the cow, by now hopefully dead, drifts downstream, a roiling mass of silver and crimson, while the others of the herd cross at the ford and scramble up the distant shore unharmed. Variations on this clever ploy, substituting people for cattle but every bit as sanguinary, had served Butch Halvorsen well for many years. He had any number of techniques for coping with piranha-infested streams and most of them involved the destruction of somebody else. "For the common weal," Butch was fond of intoning, "individual sacrifice is a noble contribution." It might be noted that Butch himself was never the ritual victim.

Bobby and Butch met outside the office at Rose's. Bobby got

a corner table. Hunched over his Tab, a paper napkin serving for Kleenex, he whispered his tale to Halvorsen.

"Well, Bobby," Butch said, rather too loudly for Bobby, "we ought to be able to handle a little problem like that. Which one of them do you want to shitcan?"

Bobby Klaus explained, patiently, he did not want to "shitcan" either of his stars.

"I want them to love one another," he said plaintively, "and if I can't have that then I want their goddamned feuds kept private, kept out of the papers, kept off the television pages."

Halvorsen nodded. Doggedly, he returned to his original theme.

"But look, Bobby, suppose the worst happens. Suppose the news gets out that she slipped strychnine into his martini or he sent her a live scorpion in a Bergdorf gift box, then what do we do? Seems to me the best tack is to admit they've got their little differences, that the network is sure it will work itself out, but at the same time make damn sure the world knows which one of them is expendable in case, just in case, you can't make peace. You get me? One of them has got to go if they keep battling. Right?"

Miserable, Bobby nodded.

Butch Halvorsen sat back, spread his arms expansively.

"Bobby, don't agonize. If it gets so bad you can't live with the situation the trick is to salvage what you can. Protect yourself, protect the network, protect the more important of the two. Sacrifice the weaker. Right?"

"Yes, I guess so."

Neither of them bothered to say what was obvious to them both. That if one of the anchorpersons had to be "shitcanned" it would be Chester Albany.

BOOK TWO

SENATOR BLANCHFLOWER

16

Kate ignored their office problems. She had her own concerns.

They began on a Saturday that was real spring, hinting of summer, over lunch with Connie Heath.

"Decent health being the given," Constance Heath was saying, "there are only two things that should concern women like us: money and sex."

Considering that Connie was years older and possessed a fortune of perhaps a hundred million dollars, Kate Sinclair was not quite sure whether she should be pleased to be bracketed as "women like us," but Connie seemed so pleased with the aphorism, or with its slightly naughty connotation, Kate simply smiled. And continued to listen.

Orsini's was only half full, Nino kept bringing fresh carafes of chilled wine, and it was pleasant just to sit there, toying with the grilled shrimps and the fried zucchini, listening to Connie's growling monologue, not taking it very seriously and not having to work very hard at the conversation.

"The point to remember, Kate, if it isn't too painful for you to talk about money after all this gruesome publicity, is that a million a year, as straight income, isn't really very much. If it were capital gains, or sheltered in some fashion, well and good. But you've got to be in the very highest tax bracket and there's just no way, without shelter, that you can take home more than $400,000 a year."

She paused long enough to light another cigarette and drain off half a glass of wine. "Which isn't to say a half-million isn't enough to live on, if you're careful, but it certainly isn't the fortune uninformed people believe it to be. That nice little flat you have, why even a place like that could eat it up."

Kate resisted a retort. Connie made her apartment sound

like a *pied-à-terre* in Murray Hill! But the older woman pressed on.

"I think it's plain nasty, simple jealousy, that has people carrying on so about your salary. Why, they ought to be standing up to applaud when you enter a room. Despite everything I've just said about a million not being much money, there's a certain symbolism to the figure, and it does you a great deal of credit for having achieved it as a salaried employee. After all, I've made a great amount of money in my life but I've never gotten a pay check. Not one. It's all in learning how to use capital to make more capital, and if I hadn't inherited a little money to start with, why I don't believe I'd be earning anything like what you get. So there."

Harvey Podesta was at another table with a young man. He waved over, using his pocket handkerchief to get their attention.

"Dear Harvey," Connie Heath said, "a diverting boy. But Kate, listen to me, women like you and me need more than Harvey."

She raised her eyebrows in what Kate assumed was a significant gesture.

"Oh?" she said, delighted money had apparently been dropped as a luncheon topic.

"Of course, which goes back to my earlier remark. About money and sex. We must, we simply must have both. Now you've got your million a year or whatever it is and you've got to lift your gaze beyond, to the very horizon. Tell me," she said, dropping her husky voice, "what about Blanchflower? Anything doing there?"

Kate had long ago resolved not to exchange intimacies with Connie. A whispered confidence had a way of becoming public knowledge within hours, once Connie got onto it. It was not so much she gossiped selectively or to any vicious end. It was just that her mouth worked by reflex action and there was no way to control it. So Kate parried.

"Oh, he's okay. An interesting man. But all politics. You know how those people are."

"Hmmm," Connie said, not sure whether to believe her.

"You were saying about Harvey Podesta . . . ?"

"Well, yes, laugh, laugh, laugh. Good for a chat. Drinks too

140

much but just darling at dinner. But that's where it ends. And, Kate, you and I both know that's where it should just be beginning."

That night, dressing for cocktails, Kate found herself remembering her conversation with Connie Heath. If you could believe half of what she said about her love life, the woman was indefatigable. She was in a young period right now, young men in their twenties, one or two, she admitted, or perhaps boasted, even younger than that. Kate, amazed, had said at one point, "But Connie, what can a nineteen-year-old boy do for a woman like you?" and Connie had smiled smugly and said, "Why, *everything.*"

Oh, she didn't pay them, Connie said, that would be too vulgar to support, but she certainly saw to it that they didn't lose in the transaction.

"Don't underestimate," she'd said, "the coin of experience. Why, some of my young men are frankly astonished at the things I can do. And how often!"

There was more of this and then, perhaps seeing the embarrassment in Kate's face, maybe sensing her own debasement, Connie stopped. There was still some wine and she poured it herself, not waiting for the captain, and she said:

"So now you know my secrets, Kate. Not all of them, just the happy part."

Her voice was higher pitched, tense, not the usual friendly growl, as if she had become suddenly wary.

"And there *are* happy parts, you know," Connie said. "Sometimes, in the night, with one of my young men, I fantasize that he'll stay, that he really does want me, for myself and not for what I can give him, the entree I can provide, the connections he can make. When they sleep I lie there and watch them, all the young bodies, so taut, so hard, so young. And then I get up and go into the bathroom, and I see . . . me."

She made a little deprecatory gesture.

"But you're still lovely," Kate said.

She smiled.

"You know the song, Kate, about the days dwindling down. Well, I guess they are. The days grow shorter. But the nights? Nights can be so long, so empty."

It was six-thirty. Kate was due at a publisher's penthouse.

141

There were to be drinks for a novelist who had a new book out. Kate, half dressed, slumped tiredly in front of her vanity. She looked up at herself in the mirror, saw a handsome woman, still young, still hopeful. But Connie had left her with a tremendous sense of depression. Suppose this thing with Blanchflower didn't work out. Suppose he was in it for variety, for the quick ride, the new experience. Oh, but she was going too fast. She knew that. Native caution told her so. And yet, if not Blanchflower, or someone like Blanchflower, some other intelligent, successful, mature man who could deal with her on her own level, then what future did she have? Was it to be an echo of Constance Heath? A succession of younger and ever younger men so that in the end she was paying them to go to bed with her, to take her out, to be seen on her arm? Young men ever hungrier and more avaricious as she grew older, lonelier, more desperate, driving herself with drugs or drink or just plain sensual hunger to relax her standards more and still more until, in the end, she would simply hand over some money and lie down and hope the boy would fall on top of her and not just pocket the money and sneer and turn away?

Kate did what she rarely did. She poured a stiff drink and emptied the glass, then, guiltily, washed it herself so that Mary would not see it in the kitchen sink. She was not looking forward to that evening's party and certainly not to the next day, Sunday, when she had agreed, reluctantly, to meet with the feminists.

Oh, there had been approaches earlier. The stilted written appeals, cocktail party chat, intimating that Kate was letting down the side, that, really, she owed it to the cause to do . . . something.

One of the women, a friend in the movement, had called ahead, spoken of mutual friends, and it had been impossible to say no.

Kate Sinclair was by this time one of the few women with any sort of reputation in American life who had not spoken out, one way or the other, on feminism, either as a general proposition or on a specific question such as the Equal Rights Amendment. There were reasons she had not spoken. The network's policy was to avoid controversy as the pox. It didn't matter to the network whether an issue was substantive or faddish, whether you took the right side or the wrong. If contro-versy attached itself to the question then whatever side you took was wrong. Women at the network who lobbied for femi-nist causes, who got their names in the papers, who tacked up notices and petitions on network bulletin boards, quickly found themselves in the same situation as Martin Luther at Worms, harried, hustled, decidedly schismatic, and certainly not in good odor with the bishops.

Kate was not a coward. And her position as the only anchor-woman in America provided her job security and freedom of maneuver not enjoyed by a member of the typing pool or a weather girl. Still, she had not spoken out.

She had made her way professionally, had gotten to the top of this most competitive and male-dominated of careers, had won and now earned her million a year, with minimal aid and comfort from the movement. She was, in business, a woman alone. She did not believe she needed the feminists. And now she could not understand why they needed her.

There were feminists she liked. Steinem she knew and en-joyed, Friedan she knew and admired. She had read Simone de Beauvoir and although she found the Camus-Sartre-deBeauvoir relationship a bit strange, she put it down to their Frenchness, and not to Simone's iconoclasm. There were oth-er feminists she considered pushy, dreadful, and quite simply, a pain in the ass. One evening in Liz Smith's apartment there had been a buffet, lots of people, men and women, sitting in couches or on the floor drinking jug wine and eating pasta. Helen Brown was there, the woman who edited *Cosmopoli-tan*, with her husband David. Brown, a courtly mustached man who was making a fortune producing popular films, had finished his pasta and emptied his glass and was sitting there on the rug, talking animatedly with Kate and some others. Helen Brown got up to refill her glass and in a reflex action she reached out to take David's empty plate along with her to the kitchen. She was blocked by a huge black woman who held out her arm in a menacing gesture.

"Let him fetch his own damn plate," the black woman growled.

Helen Brown smiled her little bird's smile, unsure what to say.

"Let him fetch his own. And yours too," the black woman ordered.

David Brown, tactful, sensible, uncurled and got to his feet. He took back his plate.

"We'll both go to the kitchen," he told his wife, "together." They left the room and the black woman glared about her to see if there were anyone else worth attacking on revisionist grounds. Kate did not read *Cosmo* and held no brief for the Browns. But at that moment she had liked them very much.

Now it was Sunday morning and she was herself about to meet the feminists. She thought back across the months to that evening at Liz Smith's house, to Helen and David Brown. Would it be like that this morning, an ugly confrontation? Last night had been spoiled, first Connie Heath's despair, then another empty cocktail party, but most of all by her nervousness about this morning's appointment with the feminists. Although it was Sunday she was up at seven, exercising and reading the *Times* and arousing Mary Costello's suspicions.

"Well, if you don't want them here, why the hell not just tell them so?" Mary demanded.

"Because I promised to see them."

"Oh, for God's sake, you won't let me have the Trotskyites up here once a year for the cell meeting but you allow bull dykes to trample in and out of the place at will."

"Feminists *aren't* lesbians," Kate said, feeling prim as she said it.

Mary raised her eyes and went to make coffee while Kate dressed. As she was buttoning her blouse Mary knocked and came back into the bedroom.

"Well, they're here," she said. "A likely pair. Wait till you see."

"No remarks. Just stay in the kitchen or somewhere. Go shopping."

"And leave you alone with them?"

"Oh, for God's sake . . . "

Mary looked sour.

"They look like agents provacateurs," she said, mangling the French.

"Well, they're not. So bring them in."

One of the women was suntanned, ugly, but with a wide,

144

honest mouth and cheerful eyes under a steel wool hairdo. Kate recognized her, Naomi Curzon, one of the intellectuals of the movement, a woman of very real academic distinction and with a number of serious books to her credit. The other was sleek, blonde and a lawyer. Her name was Marcia Mann-Isaacs and Kate recalled seeing articles in magazines that included photos of her lawyer-husband doing the dishes. They sat down and Mary brought drinks and Naomi said:

"Now, listen, we need you, you know? You've got a pulpit, a hell of a pulpit, and you haven't done a damn thing to get the E.R.A. through."

The lawyer smiled sweetly.

"Naomi always does just plunge in, Ms. Sinclair. Please forgive her. You're awfully good just to give us your time. And to have us into this lovely apartment."

Kate decided she definitely liked Naomi better.

Marcia Mann-Isaacs was talking.

"Ronald says even his life has expanded so, broadened immeasurably, all because of the movement. We've even joined our names, you know. My surname and then his."

Naomi grinned. "With the nicest little hyphen in between, just like a double-ring ceremony."

The lawyer turned less simpering. "I don't think such a significant gesture should be treated sarcastically, Naomi. If more couples would . . . "

"What do they want of me?" Kate asked herself as they talked. "Why must *I* carry banners?"

"Look, Kate," Naomi said, "you know how tough it was for you to make it in television. You know that even today you take your orders from men, that there isn't a woman making policy at your network, at any network."

"I'm not defending the network," Kate said, "or television. But at least you've got to admit they broke the line, they gave me the anchor job, they pay me as much or more than any man in the same role, that they . . . "

Naomi interrupted. "Tokenism. Do you think you'd be making a million dollars a year if a lot of us hadn't started raising hell years ago? Don't you realize that because hundreds of women working in television made damn nuisances of themselves, you got the payoff? Do you think you did it all alone?"

"But Naomi," Marcia said soothingly, "Ms. Sinclair is an extraordinary woman. Unique." Kate had the feeling they deliberately worked this way, like two cops questioning a suspect, one hard, the other sympathetic. "She would have gotten to the top regardless. Which is precisely why we need her now. Why we want her to enlist in the great struggle. Why . . . "

There was more, but Kate knew she could not get involved. In the end she told them the network had very strict rules about endorsing any movement, "no matter how important, how worthy," but that she would probe the situation with her superiors and would think about what they had asked.

She never mentioned Bobby Klaus who had gotten her the anchor job, not as a liberated woman, but as a television housewife.

As they left, Marcia Mann-Isaacs, trying again to be conciliatory, said:

"It isn't as if we simply want you to parrot a polemical message, you know. We have too much respect for you to . . . "

Naomi broke in, exasperated.

"Jesus God! that's exactly what we *do* want. Nobody expects you to be formulating policy. We've got full time people doing that. We'll write the stuff, you read it. Okay?"

Kate said she would think about it. Odd, she thought. The feminists, pushing intellectual liberation, wanted her to do precisely what the network required: to read someone else's "stuff" and neither to think nor extemporize.

Yet some of what they said had struck home. Perhaps it *was* the feminist mood of the past few years that had paved the way. Maybe Bobby *wouldn't* have chosen a woman, maybe Harry Flagg's panelists would not have picked her, were it not for feminist pressure.

Her head ached. It was difficult to know precisely what to do. Well, she would think about it. The network's strict rules about not becoming involved in controversy gave her a simple out. She would permit a reasonable time to pass and then tell Naomi and the hyphenated lawyer how sympathetic she was and how sorry she could not help.

Surely they would understand.

17

But none of this seemed to matter. Blanchflower was in New York. And Kate Sinclair knew she was falling in love with him. She worried that she was going too fast, letting down her defenses too eagerly, fearful her enthusiasm would frighten him away. They were having dinner at Nicola's.

"I like this place because it's across the street from the Ardor Garage," Blanchflower said in one of those non sequiturs that usually drew a laugh. When Kate smiled thinly he reached across the table and took her hand.

"You're in a mood. What the hell's eating at you?"

She shook her head. How much could she tell Blanchflower? Confiding in him would be the same as confessing her need for love, her long, empty nights. Her need for him.

"Oh, nothing," she said. "Office problems, lunch with a sick friend, the usual. Don't worry, I'll cheer up. Let's have another drink and get to that steak you promised."

Blanchflower looked doubtful but he waved and Nick came over and took the order.

Bobby Short was at the Carlyle and Blanchflower said they had to hear him. "It'll be summer soon and he'll disappear for a couple of months and I can't let that happen," he said. "You don't want to let Bobby get off that lightly. Got to make the son of a bitch work a little for us."

Blanchflower's life was a series of imperatives. Kate liked that. It was simpler. She knew she ought to take the initiative herself, originate her own plans for them, insist on her own way. But she didn't. All week at work she made decisions, used her power, gave orders, functioned consciously. With Blanchflower, on a spring evening in New York, she was damned if she were going to insist on anything but the right to

147

have fun, to be organized by him, to luxuriate in passive delight.

"I just don't care," she said happily, determined suddenly that it would be all right.

"Swell," Blanchflower said, without any notion why the change of mood.

Bobby Short came to the table between sets.

"Senator, fill me in on the Washington dish."

Blanchflower told him some improbable gossip.

"You see," Bobby said, raising his eyebrows, "no one tells me anything." He went inside to change his shirt for the next set. A woman came over to their table.

"Miss Sinclair, could you sign this?"

Kate said she did not give autographs.

"Oh," said the woman, quite startled by this information.

"Here," Blanchflower said, taking the bit of paper the woman held, "I'll sign it for you."

"Oh, thank you, Senator."

"Nothing," said Blanchflower, as he signed "Kate Sinclair."

The woman took the paper and her delight turned to confusion.

"But she didn't sign it. This isn't your name."

"It's a swell name," Blanchflower assured her. "A hell of a name. I won't have you run it down."

The woman backed away.

Except for the autograph hound, everyone else in the room seemed quite nice. They were very WASP-y, very clean, no one was really very drunk. The women wore linen dresses and the men had their hair combed. Bobby came back and played some Cole Porter tunes only he could recall and the room went, sedately, wild. People threw kisses to Bobby. He pounded the keyboard. Kate felt wonderful. Blanchflower sat close to her and the waiter brought more drinks.

"We should always meet in places like this," he said. "I hate picking people up at their apartments. There are always those lousy couches and you sit there reading *National Geographic* and remembering doctors' offices and being awkward."

Kate assured him her couches were not "lousy" and she had let her *Geographic* subscription lapse but in the end she found

148

herself doing whatever Blanchflower wanted, agreeing with whatever he said.

"Look around," he ordered. "Every woman in this joint has high cheekbones and straight hair and Jackie Kennedy calves and is named Nancy." He looked at Kate. "Your real name isn't 'Nancy', is it?"

She shook her head. "And I don't have Jackie's legs, either."

"The Carlyle," he said, "is where WASPs go when they die."

She didn't answer. "Do you think I might have a drink?" she said.

Sure, Blanchflower told her, why not, he'd had a few.

"I know."

It was going well. She looked around the room and caught some people watching them. She wondered, not for the first time, whether they were looking at her or the man she was with.

"I like this," Kate said.

"Of course you like this," Blanchflower said, and his big arm pulled her hip tight against his on the banquette.

"You've lost that woman's vote forever," she said.

"What the hell. She's probably from Philadelphia. Or flunked the literacy test. For every vote I lose from autograph hounds I pick up one from a star. Divide and conquer. There is no majority. Just a lot of minorities feuding with one another."

" 'The politics of outrage.' "

Blanchflower nodded.

"Now you get it, Kate. You can't please everyone on every issue, so why try? I stay my nasty, ornery, obnoxious self and there are more than enough nasty, ornery, obnoxious voters out there to defeat the pious every time."

Whether he was talking politics or talking nonsense or just holding her, as he was now, she was happy. The doubts of early evening had dissipated. She knew they would be lovers.

It happened that next weekend.

Kate picked up Blanchflower at LaGuardia on the Saturday morning. Again she drove a rented car.

"I don't want the company driver reporting back on everything I do or everyone I see," she said.

"Come on, Kate, don't let's get all dewy-eyed and bashful."

It was still early in the season and the traffic flowed and by noon they were in East Hampton. All the way out they had talked, talked the way Kate had not done with anyone since Tommy.

She talked too much. Nerves, anticipation, wanting this weekend with him and afraid to show how much she wanted it. She babbled, knowing she was babbling but unable to stop.

"If Tommy had turned out differently I'd probably be a housewife in Darien and not this money-mad czarina everyone thinks I am."

"Is that what everyone thinks?"

"Of course. Didn't you?" She didn't let him answer. "Instead it was simply I married a charming, weak man when I was very young, we had a baby, and when he died *one* of us had to be strong."

Blanchflower watched the road silently.

"People think I'm tough. Steely. All those magazine stories. Castrating Chester. When all I am is a woman and an abandoned wife trying to make her way as . . ."

"Bullshit," Blanchflower said calmly.

Oh God, Kate thought, I *am* screwing this up.

"For one thing, he didn't abandon you. You dropped him. Right?"

She nodded.

"For another however young and innocent you were at twenty you're a hell of a smart, competent, pulled-together woman now."

She did not say anything.

"Which is why that other stuff is bullshit," he said. "You always had the capacity for strength."

This one, she thought, is nothing like Tommy. But he possesses that same ability to hurt me. A man like Haller couldn't hurt her, not really, because not having opened herself to him she had not become vulnerable.

She had opened herself to Blanchflower. She alternated between silly gush and these stupid silences. Then they hit the Hamptons cutoff from the Expressway and he began talking politics. Like Kate, he talked too much. Maybe, she thought with delight, he's as shaky as I am!

Blanchflower drew deeply on the cigar.

"Look," he said, hunched forward, intense now, "men get elected for lots of reasons. It helps to have an image, a clearly defined program or some sort of . . . thing . . . "

"A gimmick."

"Okay, call it that. Look at the President. A psalm-singing farmer. Maybe the Bible's a gimmick. Maybe it's for real. Maybe he never really grew a goddamn crop in his life. Maybe he's in plastics, for God's sake. But it's our perception of him that counts, not the reality. It's what we think a man is, not what he really is."

"Like Plato," she said.

He laughed.

"People in television aren't supposed to know about the cave myth. You better be careful, they'll take your ratings away."

She'd thrown in the reference, unfairly. He'd handled it nicely. She should have let it go at that but, intrigued by the man, she pushed.

"And what's your gimmick, Senator?"

Instead of recoiling, he rubbed his big hand over his chin and said, "I don't know. Maybe 'the politics of the absurd', but that's hackneyed. I dunno, maybe what you said once, 'the politics of outrage'. Anyway, the idea is that I can get reelected, go on to bigger things maybe, on the basis . . . and I admit this sounds catatonic . . . of being totally open and honest about everything, including my own faults."

"Didn't Stevenson try that and Ike just wiped him out?"

"No," Blanchflower said passionately, "Stevenson told everyone how unworthy he was but he wasn't being honest. The fact was Stevenson knew he was a hell of a lot smarter than Eisenhower but he went into this total pose, this horrible bullshit that he wasn't sure he was up to the job. Stevenson was lying through his teeth and the voters, as stupid and unsophisticated and cornball as they are, saw right through it. Jack Kennedy beat Nixon by being outrageous. By saying Nixon was a goddamned trimmer and only an Irish pol from Boston knew enough to beat him."

The blinking light told them they were in East Hampton and Kate slowed the car, nervous again about the weekend yet knowing there was no way she would not have been there.

They checked into their beach-front hotel.

"You know this is going to be talked about," she said.

Blanchflower grinned.

"I know," he said.

Their room was large, the bed acceptable, the windows gave onto the Atlantic and, when the lights were out, they could see the long gray rollers coming in from as far away as the Azores, perhaps even from Africa, or the Portuguese coast, or Land's End in Cornwall, the moon and the stars bouncing off the waves, moving as the surf moved. In the bar below, in the dining room, were all the bearded art directors and advertising agency account men with their girls from the secretarial pool, from Maxwell's Plum, from Peartrees, from P.J. Clarke's, from all the East Side bars and all the empty apartments where girls sat, and waited, and the places where men roved, and sought. Kate felt sorry for the girls, felt sorry for the men, all of them searching and not finding, their false joy echoing off the ceiling.

But while she felt badly about the other girls, she was happy for herself. Nicholas Blanchflower was beautiful. There was no other word for it. She had not seen or touched a man like this since those first delirious days with Tommy Sinclair. His body was nothing like Tommy's, not neat and smooth and compact. It was a large body, curiously pale even in summer, a powerful body that moved with deceptive ease and grace. Blanchflower claimed never to exercise. His body said that was a lie. He had taken his clothes off without either vain flourish or hint of self-consciousness. She watched him, wanting to see him naked. She undressed and then, as if they had been doing this for a long time and had no need of drama, they lay down quietly side by side, their heads against the headboard, talking in low tones, smoking, not touching.

"I could lie here forever," she said.

"No, I don't think so. You'd be bored."

"I'm not bored now."

"No," he said, "I know that."

The waves rolled in, crashed, and swept smoothly up onto the beach, metronomic, reassuring, hushing the laughter and the tinkle of glass and the murmured confidences below them

152

in the bar and outside their windows on the green lawns that ran to the beach. They lay there, the two bodies uncovered by even a sheet. She sensed the pause was deliberate, that their lovemaking, when it came, would be heightened, deepened, prolonged by their having waited. Then there was a momentary uncertainty and Kate wondered, had he decided not to, was there something he saw, or sensed, in her naked that had cooled desire? As for Kate, her entire body acutely aware of him, she was more excited than when they had first come back to the room, when they undressed, more excited than she could remember ever having been. More than with Tommy? Ah, but that was a girl and this was a woman. Blanchflower reached past her to stub out his cigarette in the ash tray and when he brought his hand back he gripped her shoulder, turned her toward him, and his head came down toward her face, his mouth upon hers. She moved toward him, her long legs twining with his. His hand moved from her shoulder to her breast, to her belly, lower then and deeper and she moved more now, more and faster. They were together now, one body instead of two, and the rolling, crashing, smoothly sweeping surf was there with them, in the room, in the bed, pulling her toward Nick, away from him, toward him again.

"You see," she said later, "I wasn't bored."

He nodded.

"I know."

When they had made love again, more slowly this time, she slept. Blanchflower got up and cut a cigar and went to the window. There were only the beach sounds now, the surf endlessly rolling, the conversations and the laughter stilled, the sea birds nesting or whatever it was sea birds did at night. He did not bother to put on a robe. The air was cooler now, but not cold, and he could smell the ocean over the smoke of the cigar. Behind him, sprawled across the bed, Kate Sinclair lay under a sheet he had very carefully pulled up to cover her.

Nicholas Blanchflower was not introspective. He had a very clear sense of who he was and of his relation to the world, to his sons, to the men who were his political life, to the women who comprised his personal life. He was thinking about the women now, about how casual it all was, how pleasant. Pleasure given, pleasure taken. In the beginning, after his wife died, he had counted scalps, remembered names, written down telephone numbers on matchbook covers and jammed them into pockets. In the past few years there had been too many. He ran into women at parties, at his Washington office, at his New York campaign headquarters, and did not remember whether he had made love to them or not. The young ones, most of them were young, would smile conspiratorially, sharing intimate secrets, and he grinned back, not quite sure, but not wanting to appear aloof. Usually it had been their beds. That made it so much simpler when he was through, when the girl slept, to get up and to go home, to wake alone. Rarely did he sleep over. Waking up together connoted domesticity, awkward breakfasts, sharing of bathrooms, suggestions of lunch later on that day. Blanchflower wanted none of that. A tomcat's morality, he recognized it as such, did not necessarily admire himself for it, but neither did he agonize. There was passion, considerable passion, pleasure, also quite considerable. There was nothing beyond that, no commitment, no constancy, no love. He knew the most intimate things about these women, the smell, the taste, the feel of their bodies, of the inside of their bodies, yet he did not know their names, their faces, the color of their eyes. Lately, he realized, he made an effort not to know. It was so much simpler.

Now, Kate Sinclair.

He wondered why. A woman as well known as he, more so even, a powerful woman, intelligent, informed, recognizable. This weekend had probably been a silly idea, this place surely was. For the first time they would awake together in the morning. What would that be like? Did it mean commitment? He had made love to her. No, that was wrong, they had made love to one another, Kate as eager and responsive as he. She had a wonderful body, a matured beauty, a different look and sound and feel. All those younger women with their high, small breasts, their legs, straight hair, the casual joints, the nervous, desperate sniffs of amyl nitrite, the acrobatics, the accepted convention that mouths were simply other vaginas, that tongues must do this and this and this, such girls, rather than imposing their individualities upon him, blurred and blended into one girl, one long-limbed, long-haired, mouth-hungry, pot-dazed, happy and yet frenetic girl. Kate Sinclair he would

154

recognize the next time they met. Kate Sinclair would not blur.

The thought made him uncomfortable and he finished the cigar and got back into bed, moving quietly so she would not awake.

Just before dawn she did wake. Well, she thought, if this isn't the most damnfool thing I've ever done. Blanchflower lay on his back, the lank blond hair tousled, looking, she realized, like an overgrown little boy. She watched him in the half-light, his massive chest rising and falling, slowly, easily. She remembered feeling that chest crushing her breasts flat, remembered his breathing coming in short, violent pants, felt his heart against her chest. Blanchflower had been everything she hoped, more than she hoped, but still, to conduct a love affair in public like this, it was stupid. It was as if they wanted to be caught. Then, happy despite their imprudence, she carefully pulled the sheet off Blanchflower's body, looking down at him as the night sky began to break in the east, watching his body and remembering the feel and intensity and strength of it and then, remembering too well, trying not to touch him, or herself.

Nick had turned out to be a wonderful lover. But there was more to him than that, much more. These things too attracted her, drew her as surely as his big arms had drawn her, as he had opened her, driven into her. Ambition, of course, ambition that gave him a focus and a drive she found exciting. There was a touch of mystery, a feeling that no matter how well you knew him, there were covert layers below, there was that and more, perhaps menace, even. And yet, there was a booming, cheerful, contagious openness about him. Headwaiters recognized him and got him the best table, bartenders in low Irish bars knew him, cab drivers cut across lanes and risked fenders to pick him up in rainstorms, politicians made up to him, newspapermen, his natural antagonists, demonstrated a genuine affection for the man even while assailing his politics. Women, of course, pursued him.

Perhaps, after all, that was what attracted her. What a stupid thing, to think that. No, she knew the first time they met it would be like this, that it had to be. She'd had no choice. Neither, she hoped, without being terribly sure, had he. It was why they were making this ridiculous public display of themselves. Because there was no way in which they would not have come together in love. No, she thought, strike that. Make it, for the moment, "intimacy." It was not yet love, surely not for him. For herself, she was less certain. The first sun came in the window and she lay there, naked, watching the small movements of his body in sleep.

18

The demigods of the network eat lunch in a triplex on the fortieth floor. The architects had cut through three floors to create a series of executive dining rooms where the network's senior men (there were no women at that level) could dine appropriately. On these floors a sort of atrium had been created, around which ran a gallery and into which plunged a circular staircase. The carpets were deep and lush, the piped-in music had been selected by Bernstein at his "serious" best, the china was Wedgwood, the crystal by Waterford, the wines chosen by Alexis Lichine. The menu, which changed every day, was signed by a Frenchman who styled himself "executive chef," and who was represented by an agent at William Morris. The effect was dazzling, straight from "The Hall of the Mountain King," and Bobby Klaus never went there without being deeply moved.

Bobby was still so unused to these exalted latitudes that even a casual lunch there with one of his pals became an experience. To himself he would describe such expeditions as one might Speke's two-year trek to the source of the Nile. Bobby never thought of himself as simply *going* to the fortieth floor; he trudged there, slogged there, dragged himself there. As a factual matter he got there as did everyone else; by swift executive elevator. On this day, a week after yet another of Chester's explosions over Kate, Bobby was to lunch with Dillon, the president of the broadcast division. The waiter padded in silently with drinks.

"Splendid," said Dillon, who had very narrowly missed out on being chosen a Rhodes scholar and had affected upperclass Anglicisms ever since.

"Oh, yes," Bobby said, "very nice."

Actually Bobby hated to drink and the martini, ordered because his boss had ordered one, nearly made him gag.

The two men, alone in a private dining room, sat at opposite ends of a ten-foot-long table. The president looked down the length at Bobby.

"Now, dear boy," he said, "and how is your talent behaving itself these days? Kate and Chester warming up a bit?"

Bobby did not answer right away. He wondered if Dillon had heard something.

"Well," he said, suddenly remembering how pleasant Kate had been when she came in Monday from East Hampton, once even smiling at Chester, "I think we may be coming along. Hard to tell, of course, artistic temperament and all. But I think they're coming along."

Dillon, the broadcast president, sipped his martini.

"Anymore of that static Butch Halvorsen was telling me about last month?"

"Oh, no," Bobby said. He was on more confident ground now since he read, or had read for him, every important television critic every day. "No static from the critics."

The president was more cheerful now. He even forgot to sound English.

"Well, they're all pricks anyway. I don't take it seriously myself. But if we have any dirty linen I want to keep it out of the papers. Butch worries."

Bobby laughed. It was permitted to twit Butch Halvorsen.

"You know Butch," he said.

Dillon sobered.

"But where there's smoke . . . " he said.

Bobby shrugged.

"It's no secret they don't love one another," he said. "I never made a secret of that."

The president looked pained.

"Never said you did, Bobby. You've always leveled. Never equivocated. One of the reasons we've brought you on so fast."

Bobby recognized the lie. He knew he had been "brought on so fast" because his soaps, his game shows, his late night movies had scored well in the ratings, not because he told the truth.

"Well," Bobby said, "I guess it's natural that Chester resents her. He's been around a lot longer. He's a newsman. She's got the million a year. I guess he resents me as well, bringing show biz into the newsroom."

Dillon slammed his hand on the table and the Waterford rang.

"Is he still harping on that? Is he, Bobby? I thought we had that out last summer. I thought I'd heard the last of that when we doubled his wages."

Bobby felt awful. This wasn't going at all well.

Dillon spoke again, calmer now.

"If Chester gives you any trouble, Bobby, I want to hear about it. There are other anchormen out there, good men who'd love that job."

Bobby Klaus nodded. He rapidly made the same decision Butch Halvorsen had made on precisely the same grounds: Chester Albany was expendable; Kate Sinclair wasn't.

"You're right," he said, a new determination in his voice. "It isn't Chester brings in the ratings. It's Sinclair."

"Right," the president. "Right."

Having thrown Chester Albany to the wolves, Bobby felt better. Then the president spoke once more.

"Not that the ratings have been so great in any event."

It comes down to this, Bobby thought, it always comes down to this.

"Well, there was a natural fall off after that first big month. After that show in the desert. The novelty died, and then we cut back a bit on the hype. When the President called her, we went up again. Right now we're five or six points ahead of the same time last year. We've held that much of a gain."

"You're four points ahead," Dillon said, his tone deadly.

"Yes," Bobby said.

The waiter came in with the lunch.

"Wine?" Dillon asked.

Why not? Bobby thought. Could a glass of wine make it worse?

"Yes, please."

The president ate for a while, silent. Then he looked up, looked at Bobby miserable at the other end of the long table.

"Bobby, do you know George Venables?"

Oh my god, Bobby thought. It *did* make it worse, it *did*. He knew about Venables. Who in television did not? Venables who had taken up where Howard Cosell left off in popularizing sports on prime time television. A barrel-chested, stunted figure, a fanatic for physical fitness, a jock with brains, Venables put a comedian and a Hall of Fame quarterback in the booth together and drew better ratings with games between also-ran pro teams than Archie Bunker was drawing on CBS. Venables lived in New Jersey, down by the shore, and he ran five miles every morning with weights on his legs. He didn't smoke or drink, he worked sixteen hours a day. He lived for the network, for his sports coverage, for the ratings. Even his recent marriage to an Olympic swimmer seemed to have been designed to further his career. Venables was a machine, a goddamned machine. He was also, many people were convinced, certifiably mad.

Bobby Klaus remembered stories of how Venables would shout out the names of the stations on the morning commuter train and men would look up from their *Wall Street Journals* or their *Timeses* and then, embarrassed, look down again. Of how Venables once broke a man's nose on Peachtree Street in Atlanta while practicing his tennis backhand as he strode along, swinging his arm and at the end of it an imaginary racquet, but it was the back of his hand, tensed for the stroke, that hit the poor man. Of how Venables ignored taxicabs and, wearing running shoes, would sprint around Manhattan from one business appointment to another. Of how Venables was arrested in the West Berlin airport for having Joseph Goebbels paged over the loudspeaker.

"A good man," the president said, "wonderful ratings."

Bobby Klaus fingered the Kleenex in his pocket.

"I know George. Why?"

The waiter was in the room now, refilling the glasses, clearing plates and serving again. Bobby, ten feet away from his boss, wished he were farther away. At the same time he feared his voice was not carrying. He cleared his throat. And waited.

Dillon smiled.

"I might ask him to take a look at news. You know, bring a fresh mind to this problem between Chester and Kate."

Bobby knew. He knew very well. It meant yet another person looking over his shoulder.

"You mean, officially, or simply as an observer?" he asked.

160

Dillon waved his hand.

"Oh, nothing official. Of course not. It's your department. Your show. You know how I operate. A man runs his department. I don't interfere. Not a bit of it. I simply want Venables to take a look from time to time. He might see something I don't see. You don't see."

Bobby imagined he had stressed the word "you."

He decided he had to take the offensive. The lunch, the confrontation, was getting away from him. If he left the room like this, defeated, Venables would be tearing the meat from his bones within a month.

"There's this to consider," Bobby said, hoping his voice would not crack. "We've had a few difficulties. But by whatever yardstick, the ratings are ahead of last year. Not the ten points we hoped for. But ahead. Chester and Kate can still be a great team. If he gives me problems, then he goes. No argument about it. Chester goes! But I have a feeling, a very real feeling, that Chester is getting on the team, that he's stopped fighting, that he's . . . well, that he's mellowed."

The president of the broadcast division looked at Bobby Klaus.

"I hope so, Bobby, I truly do. For his sake." There was a pause. "For all our sakes."

Bobby sensed that what he really meant was, "for your sake." But he took what solace he could and tried to smile.

"You know," Bobby said, "Venables is, well, he's a sportscaster! Brilliant at it, no argument, but he's sports. Not news."

Dillon looked thoughtful.

"Bobby," he said quietly, "isn't that what they were saying about you a year ago? That *you* were not news? That you were show biz?"

As the executive elevator sped him back to his own floor Bobby Klaus had already begun to conjure up strategies that would keep the dreadful Venables at bay. He wondered whether a new bit of information he had acquired only the night before might be put to use. The knowledge that Kate Sinclair was sleeping with a United States Senator. It worried him to have this sort of information and not to know what to do with it.

* * *

Venables. George Venables. His name echoed through the network corridors, igniting argument, arousing passion. No one was neutral on Venables. The men and women who worked under him in the sports division loved him. In news they despised him. In entertainment they feared his coming. The executives, on the 39th floor, were very fond of George Venables. He had in just six years put the network into first place in sports coverage.

In the beginning it was different. In the beginning no one had taken Venables seriously. He had come out of California, out of a local station's sports operation, a strong, solid-looking but squat little man who conversed knowledgeably of Pac-8 football (he had actually been the team manager), and to the network establishment something of a figure of fun in his button down pink shirts, his crew cut hair. Unlike most new recruits to corporate headquarters, Venables had stubbornly, admirably even, refused to alter his style to suit the New York image of how a broadcasting executive should look. Football had become the national religion and Venables its television evangelist. The other networks, dabblers in football coverage from the start (they thought it was sufficient to show one game every Sunday), snickered when Universal saturated the prime time hours with football three nights and often four a week.

"The women just won't watch," they said, "they'll tune out. Who the hell wants that much goddamn football?"

The answer was, America did. The women did *not* tune out.

The dwarfish Venables encouraged Universal Broadcasting to recruit a supporting cast of ex-jocks totally unlike him, perfectly complementing Venables with their slow minds and their matinee idol profiles. Shrewdly he got the network to choose his broadcast partners for their sexy voices, their thick, wavy hair, their little boy charm radiating out of tall, raw-boned frames. For the male audience there was the game itself, and frequent closeups of chorus girls in hotpants and satin shirts without bras, bouncing up and down and pretending to be cheerleaders. All across America boys determined to grow up and play for the Vikings and teen-aged girls colored their hair blonde and scrubbed their teeth with salt, and wrote letters of application to the Dallas cheerleading squad.

Venables had accomplished all this. And more. Now, for the

first time, there were whispers his realm might be extended beyond sports. Into the production of game shows. Possibly to entertainment. Perhaps even, though the skeptics scoffed, to news. Although neither of these two network divisions was happy about the possibility of Venables, his own people, in sports, rooted for his success as avidly as old grads at homecoming games. Their devotion was a compound of professional pride that he had carried them to the top of the ratings, their own ambition to exercise their talents in a larger, more substantive arena, and sheer, unadulterated loyalty to Venables for the creature comforts he provided. Covering sports, especially football in the damp and snow and cold of late autumn and early winter, lugging heavy hand-held cameras and portable audio-dishes along the sidelines had been the network's Siberia prior to Venables' arrival. Venables could do nothing about the weather, of course, but he made it up to his "troops," as he liked to call them, in other ways. He saw that they flew first class to the games, that questions of overtime payment were always decreed in their favor, that they stayed in the best hotels and ate the thickest steaks and that, back in their rooms, there were quarts of the best scotch and bourbon. Also, he got them laid.

It's never difficult to find a girl around a big football weekend. But Venables did not leave these things to chance. After the game, in whichever city he happened to be that weekend or that night, he would host a little party in his hotel suite. There were canapes, music, drinks, a selection of the more marketable football heroes to rub against. And there were girls. In the college towns the prettiest of the coeds. In the professional league cities airline stewardesses, models, cheerleaders, groupies. The girls did not attend George Venables's parties out of sheer chance. His emissaries had sought them out before or during the game.

"When the camera swings your way, baby, just smile and look pretty, give us a little chest, and you're on network television. And after the game, if you want to meet some players, some of the network brass, just drop by the suite."

A little card bearing Venables' name and the name of the hotel and the suite number would be handed to the girl. Few of them failed to appear at the appointed time or to enter into the spirit of the occasion. George Venables' staff loved it. Understandably, several of their wives did not, and a number of divorces ensued. One of them Venables' own.

"Rub of the green," he shrugged. If a woman didn't understand that the "troops" needed a little R & R after a tough day in the trenches, well, she lacked sensitivity. George's wife had lacked sensitivity. A San Diego girl, she went back to the Coast and, after a seemly period of bachelorhood, Venables married for a second time. Although he had never heard senior men at the network exchange snide remarks about other broadcasters' dumpy wives ("She must be a real dog. Else why hasn't anyone ever seen her?"), he knew instinctively the role his second wife should play to further his career. When he married Bunny Pfeiffer he was sure she could fill the role.

They met at the Olympics. She was an Australian swimmer. One of Venables' keen-eyed scouts had spotted her and all through a long series of hundred-meter heats the cameras focused and refocused on Bunny Pfeiffer. In the broadcast booth Venables squirmed on the specially built-up chair that gave him on-the-air height, and licked his lips as she fussed with the shoulder straps of her sleek, translucent racing suit. After her relay team had been narrowly beaten into fourth place in the finals he ignored the usual salute to the winners (beefy East German girls from Leipzig with underarm hair) and did five minutes live with loser Bunny. Later, in his hotel bed, she had been duly grateful. Two months later, in Paris, they were married.

During the week that his employers on the 39th floor of the network's offices in New York had first begun to talk seriously of Venables as the coming man, beyond sportscasting, even beyond sports, Bunny and George Venables were entertaining. It was Boston, baseball season, and a big Friday night game between the Yankees and the Red Sox. After the game Venables was hosting the usual celebration in his rooms at the Ritz. The suite was a noisy, happy place, filled with television men, a few players from each team, some of the more presentable press (Venables knew their value. And their price.), the usual pretty girls, waiters hustling drinks and trays of smoked salmon, caviar, Maine lobster chunks, shrimp. Bunny Venables, in a clinging silk jersey dress with very little front and less back, smiled her open, Australian smile as she moved through the room, bestowing a kiss here, a smile there, a hug, a throaty whisper, a pat on the buttock. Venables, watching her, beamed pleasure. Already, in their first appearances at network social events, Bunny had made her presence known. How good it was to have a wife who understood the part she had to play, and who played it so well, so thoroughly.

A momentary scowl darkened George Venables' face when an aide informed him Reggie Jackson had not appeared. "Damn," Venables said. "And I invited him personally!" Under the crew cut, his narrow eyes hardened, and the young man who had brought the bad tidings flinched as if he was about to be hit. But Venables, his fists slowly unclenching, regained control and instead of punishment, the young man got a hearty slap on the rear.

"Hell," Venables said, "you can't win 'em all. It's Reggie's loss. Come on, get yourself a glass."

Just then Bunny moved up to him, placed her hands on his shoulder and leaned against his broad back. People tended to notice that even when they were not alone, Bunny was always touching George, curving her exquisite body into his. It did not seem to matter that she was a head taller than her husband.

"He must give her everything she wants. And more," was the whisper of those who did not know them well. Among their closer friends and associates, there were other whispers.

Now it was two o'clock. The party was winding down, the groupies going off with the players, with the television crew, even with newspaper reporters. A big, straw-haired ballplayer, a pitcher for the Yankees, uncoiled his lanky frame from a couch where he'd been nursing a beer and watching Bunny Venables, and stuck out a huge hand to Venables.

"Mr. Venables, George, many thanks. I truly do appreciate all this. Real nice of you to ask me."

Venables grinned and held the pitcher's handshake, patting him on the arm with his other hand.

"Hell, kid, early yet. Hang around."

Across the room Bunny turned back from the door. The last guests had just left. Only the ballplayer was there. She smiled at him.

"You and Mrs. Venables probably want to get to sleep," the pitcher said, not very enthusiastically.

Venables laughed.

"Sleep? Sleep? Boy, you don't know much about television sports. I'm liable to be up all night, looking at the tape, seeing what we did right, what we did wrong."

"Oh?"

Bunny Venables stood in front of the young man, looking into his boyish face, into his eyes.

"It's a terrible responsibility," she said, "and George takes these games so hard."

Venables grinned again and turned toward the door.

"Have another beer, kid, keep Bunny company. I'll be downstairs at the videotape machine if you want anything. 'Night."

The ballplayer watched him go. Bunny picked up a glass and drank from it, watching the young man's face over the rim. He was young, but he had been in the league for two years now. He understood what was happening but he was shy about making a mistake. Bunny Venables put down the glass and ended his uncertainty. She held out a slender hand, pulled him up from the couch and led him into the bedroom.

Three hours later Venables would return to the suite, undress, and lie down next to the naked, still moist body of his wife.

"Tell me what you did," he said hoarsely, his hand on her small, conical breast, "don't skip anything."

Bunny Venables turned her lovely face toward his and smiled.

"Okay, mate," she said, the Australian accent flattening her vowels. And as she told him, in precise detail, Bunny and George Venables began to do those things all over again.

In the visitors' locker room at Fenway Park the next afternoon, a straw-haired young man, eyes bleared, elbows raw, would be grateful his turn to pitch would not come until Monday. He was also grateful to George Venables. What a decent, generous guy George was. The young man determined that if he could ever do anything for Venables or for his network, he would do so. Eagerly.

166

19

Kate Sinclair would not have agreed with the young baseball player in Boston, or any of George Venables' admirers.
She knew he was not decent, not generous. She and Venables
had never worked together. But she knew him. Oh, how she
knew him.

Their mutual distaste began innocently enough a year or
two earlier. Kate's morning talk show guests that particular
day were several of the top women athletes: the skier, Suzy
Chaffee; Billie Jean King and Virginia Wade from the tennis
circuit. Toward the end of the show the question of violent
contact sport for women came up. It seemed that one of the
other networks was considering covering a series of boxing
matches between women. Kate had not heard the report and
her mouth fell open.

"You mean," she said, "women actually punching one
another? On camera?"

She was assured that, yes, this was precisely what was
meant.

Kate threw back her head in annoyance.

"And who's the barbarian behind *that* brilliant idea?" she
asked.

"George Venables."

Kate swiveled to peer directly into the camera. The director
had just flashed the bye-bye signal. They were about to leave
the air. Kate's exit timing had always been impeccable. Now,
as the show ended, she stared into the camera and told ten
million American women:

"Then George Venables is a . . . "

They bleeped the word. But lip-reading was not all that
difficult. The trades had a minor field day with it, prodding
Venables into angry response, citing several medical experts

167

on the possibility of breast damage until finally he exploded.

"Then we ought to have Katie Sinclair on the card 'cause she has no tits."

It might have died there, one of those petty, slightly coarse, internecine network feuds, except for Venables.

Relentlessly, humorlessly, he kept after her, as determined and difficult to discourage as one of those big fullbacks he so admired, the ones who kept coming at you and at you and at you maybe forty times a game so that next morning the defensive linemen and the linebackers could not get out of bed for the pain and the vomiting and the broken blood vessels in their arms and shoulders. Venables was like that.

He and Kate met for the first time at a broadcasters' meeting in Houston. She was still doing the talk show. The anchor job had not yet been proposed. Those attending had been given lists of room numbers so they could reach one another during the three-day session. They were all in the same hotel, the Warwick, out near Rice Institute. Kate's room was on the pool level. It had sliding doors through which she could step in the morning for a quick swim without going down the hallways and getting in and out of elevators. It was a good room. Until the final night of the broadcasters' meeting.

Venables had worked out his scheme in detail. He might not have done it, might not have done anything, had Kate herself made peace. But when they'd met and been introduced by a network vice-president, and he, Venables, had smiled, Kate had turned away.

"I know the gnome, thank you."

She carried it off well, he had to admit, leaving him standing there like a little boy, watching her tall, graceful back recede across the room. The vice-president had laughed. So had one or two people standing close by. George Venables did not like being laughed at. Like most short men, he hated tall women who did not take him seriously. Who laughed, who called him the "gnome." Now, in a corner of the bar, at one in the morning, he had found his means of revenge.

The weapon was Colt Oursler, a former All-American from Wyoming, a whipcord tough cowboy who was now doing color commentary, quite badly, on network football games. Colt was mean, he was drunk, and he liked women. Or to put it more precisely, he liked hitting them.

"Colt," George Venables said, "you've seen her around. Seen her on the tube. You know what she looks like."

Colt nodded.

"Prime," he said, "a prime piece of ass. How old d'you think she is? Thirty?"

"No more. Thirty's about it."

"That's nice," Colt said, "these teen-agers, they're fun, all them little titties and peach fuzz, but a real woman, now, that's another cut of meat entirely."

"Barman," Venables said, "another bourbon for Mr. Oursler and another Perrier for me."

Colt took the drink. Then, thoughtfully, he said:

"You sure about all this? I mean, she really likes the rough stuff?"

Venables looked hurt.

"Would I tell you if it wasn't so, Colt? They tell me she eats it up. You know, back in New York what is it, a lot of fairies and guys can't get it up anymore. They say whenever she's in there with a real man, she just goes crazy, wants to be slapped around. You know who had her?"

Colt shook his head. Venables leaned toward him, confidentially, and whispered the name of a famous running back.

"Jesus," Colt said, sounding impressed, "he's meaner 'n me."

Venables measured his man. Then, slowly, tantalizingly, he said:

"That belt of yours. She's just gonna love that belt."

Colt Oursler looked down. The leather belt was wide, heavy, studded with metal. He licked his lips.

Kate was in bed. The sliding door to the pool opened without being forced. Venables had gotten a master key somewhere. Colt Oursler stepped into the room. He paused for a moment, drunk, but not so drunk that he failed to orient himself. The bed was across the room. He could see Kate's body, blanketed against the Houston air-conditioning. He moved toward her, wondering just how accurate Venables had been in his appraisal of the situation. Suppose she didn't want to play, he thought. I mean, partying with a girl was one thing. Breaking and entering quite another.

Kate woke. She was not sure what woke her but she could see Colt Oursler standing there at the foot of the bed, from her angle immensely tall, powerful, threatening. Oh God, she thought, trying to remain still, trying not to scream.

"Yes?" she said, knowing how incongruous she must sound but not knowing what else to say.

"Ma'am?" Colt said.

"Yes?"

"Howdy, you're Kate Sinclair, aren't you? We met last night at . . . "

Kate pulled herself up in bed against the pillows, trying to keep the blanket high over her chest.

"I'm trying to get some sleep," she said. "Do you know what time it is?"

He looked at his watch.

"Yessum, I do."

"Oh," she said. Oh, how she wished she could think of the right thing to say.

"I'm Colt Oursler. I met you last night at the . . . "

"Mr. Oursler, just how did you get in here? What do you want?"

She was sorry about the phrasing of the last question as soon as she said it.

"Well, Ma'am, we have some mutual friends and they sort of suggested I should drop by and just see if you were lonely or if . . . "

"I'm not lonely," Kate said crisply. "Not lonely at all."

"Well, that's good," he said seriously, "it's hell being lonely."

She agreed with him and then nearly giggled. How silly this all was. A man had broken into her bedroom in the middle of the night and they were philosophizing about loneliness. She felt amused now and not scared. But then Oursler moved, rather abruptly, and she was frightened again.

But he was just looking for a chair.

"I'm kind of drunk," he said, "and the room was sort of going around. Do you mind if I sit for a moment?"

No, she said, that was fine. Please sit. He did.

She looked at his face, clearer now as her eyes became used to the darkness. It was a young face, but a brutal one, the nose broken, the cheekbones high and sharp.

"Look," she said, "Mr. Oursler . . . "

"Colt."

"Colt. I mean, you can't just stay here. I've got to get some sleep. My plane . . . "

He got up, lurching slightly toward her, frightening her again, but it was just the drink.

How pretty she is, he thought. Nearly as pretty as . . . Phyllis George, even. But this was a mistake. A big mistake. Why the hell had Venables told him she'd drag him into bed?

"Well," he said, "I guess I'll be going. Unless you . . . "

"No," she said gently, "it's okay. You can go."

He reached out a lean, hard hand.

"Thanks," he said, "it's been real pleasant."

She smiled and then he was gone, out through the same sliding door.

Later she learned it had been Venables who put him up to it. And when Venables learned that she knew, and that Oursler had not raped her or even laid her, he saw to it that Colt Oursler did not do any more color commentary on the network.

Colt had been a wonderful football player but he was a terrible color man and so no one remarked it when he was fired. That was all a couple of years ago. When last anyone heard from Colt Oursler he was pumping gas up in Casper and was putting on weight.

And that was how Kate knew about George Venables.

Chester had heard all the rumors, but at this point was closing his eyes to the problem. He knew that he should stop fighting Kate, that he should be more politic with Bobby Klaus, or he might end up confronting Venables. He knew he should do this because he was fifty years old and this was, by a hell of a long way, the best job he had ever had and he did not want to lose it. So he tried to cope with the problem by shutting out the present.

Instead of fighting, he spent more and more time lying on his couch remembering happier times. Rather than bicker with Kate or worry about his occasional impotency, he concentrated on the past, recalling men he'd worked with at the network, stories he'd covered, incidents and anecdotes. A chance phrase in the evening's script was all he needed to set him off. He found himself using the phrase, "in the old days," and it frightened him, conjuring visions of garrulous oldtimers he'd known, once vital men with whom no one cared now to have a drink. He caught himself retelling the same story and, shocked, for a time stopped telling stories at all.

He was fifty and afraid for the first time in his life, and since his woman was half his age and his friends might be suffering the same doubts, he had no one to turn to for consolation. He was an old-fashioned man who did not see psychiatrists and so, increasingly silent and alone, he fought out his quiet campaign against the network and his age.

The things that he remembered and which soothed him were diffuse and recurrent, memories of the days when he was a foreign correspondent, taking long train rides into distant cities, or the wars, when he was working for Murrow, or later, for this network. He would recall Korea or Vietnam, the dusty roads, the jeeps with their windshields bolted down and the wind in his face, the distant rumble of artillery, the heavily laden troops moving along the shoulders of the narrow roads.

He remembered train rides from Paris down into Italy, waking up in the sleeping room at night, high in the Alps, when the train would stop at the small Swiss and Italian border towns for the frontier-crossing formalities and he would pull up the shade in his compartment and look out and see the gendarmes and the carabinieri with their lanterns and beyond them the steep-roofed railroad stations and beyond them the mountains looming dark or gray with snow. He remembered once traveling from Paris to London on the night train with his wife, making love in the narrow bed and then, at dawn, waking as the train ferry pulled into Dover. When they had pulled up the shade it was snowing and England looked like one of those engravings in early editions of Dickens.

He remembered Murrow, Cronkite, Huntley, Reasoner, but only the good parts. Remembering the good parts were what kept Chester sane.

20

Shaun interrupted the spring idyll. Kate and Blanchflower had been spending evenings, the long days, weekends together, at her apartment, his flat, a Sunday at Fire Island, a day in Washington. Then came Shaun's letter:

Good news. In fact, super news. I'm playing a role in the school play this month. It's *Oklahoma!* I play a girl. I even have a line.

Kate smiled. Because she was tall Shaun had been doomed to play male roles. Last year, what had it been? *Hello, Dolly,* and she'd been, in turn, a waiter, a railway worker, and a member of the chorus (male). Becoming a girl in *Oklahoma!* was progress. Perhaps Shaun was developing after all. Kate had feared, half-hoped to tell the truth, the girl would be as slow to mature, to ripen, as she herself had been. A girl's role in *Oklahoma!* Well now, attention must be paid! Kate resolved to have her secretary write a letter that very day.

It was the postscript in her letter that was important.

"Could we, please," Shaun wrote, "spend a couple of weeks together? Maybe at the beach? Huh?"

How could Kate not say yes?

She and Blanchflower were at his apartment in Georgetown when she told him. Of course he understood, he had to take his boys to see their grandparents. She relaxed. It was a warm evening, the streets full of kids in shorts with suntans, headed for Martin's to drink beer or to the old movie house where they were always playing *Casablanca* or *Citizen Kane* or *The Magnificent Ambersons.*

They were lying in his bed. Her finger traced patterns on his firm belly. His hand twined gently in her hair.

"You never propose marriage," he said.

"No."

"It puzzles me. I keep expecting it."

"Do you?"

"Yes, I expect it. Always."

"Do you want me to propose marriage?" she asked.

"No."

"Good," she said. She was disappointed but her voice did not indicate this.

"So you don't want to marry again," he said.

"I didn't say that," Kate said.

"But, for the moment, you're satisfied with what you have."

"What *we* have," she corrected, again gently.

"What *we* have," he said, accepting the correction.

There are not many people who have what we have, she thought, and then, correcting herself this time, but of course that's silly. There are many people who have it. It's called love. We have no exclusive on it.

"Yes?" he said, as if he had heard her speak.

"I love you," Kate told him.

"Even though I don't propose marriage."

She nodded, moving her head against his chest.

"I have a commitment," she said, "and that seems quite sufficient for now."

"*We* have a commitment," he said.

She accepted the correction.

Later, after they had made love, they went to dinner at Nicoise where the waiters wear roller skates and the chef comes out and does a corny routine about French television, making fun of a commercial for Dubonnet where, since all the commercials are done live and not taped, the actor in the commercial is stewed at the end of the broadcast day.

"I love you," Kate told him again as they walked down Wisconsin toward his apartment and bed.

"Yes," he said. "And don't worry about Shaun's visit."

Kate rented an old, sprawling, shingled East Hampton house, rose-trellised and charming. These were Shaun's weeks, two weeks away from the job, away from Chester, away from noise and humidity and the nightly thunderstorms and

174

power failures of the city. Blanchflower had taken his sons to visit their mother's parents and then would have them with him in Washington for the hearings that promised to be the only distinguishing event of a slack summer session. A lawyer friend had a realtor friend who knew a lady who wanted to go to Europe and so the house rental was negotiated and Kate and Shaun and Mary were chauffeured east. A guest membership to the Maidstone Club had been arranged.

The summer was hot as even East Hampton can be hot when the breeze is not ocean blown, but comes off the potato fields inland of the golden beaches.

"Isn't it inspiring," Mary declared as they drove up to the club grounds, "isn't it grand to see the rich at play?" Left unsaid, but understood, was Mary's gloating expectation of what awaited the rich after the revolution.

Kate had not seen Shaun for months. The girl had gone west to ski at Easter and to Maine as a junior counselor during the first month of summer vacation, and where she would return for the last two weeks of August. Her sister could not believe how tall she'd grown, how well she carried herself. She never tired of watching Shaun, at the club pool, or on the tennis court, or playing on the beach with battalions of other lean, tall, long-haired, suntanned girls and boys. Shaun lived in a bikini by day. Her gesture to evening formality was to pull on a pair of tattered blue jean cutoffs and a Lacoste shirt. The girl used a rented ten-speed bike as adults used a car, racing from club to house to beach to town.

Now it was the middle weekend of their fortnight and Kate sat on the beach propped up against a backrest, *The New York Times* arrayed about her, watching Shaun spike volleyballs, her long golden limbs gleaming in the sun. And watching the boys and the men who watched Shaun.

Had she herself looked like that when Tommy and she fell in love? Shaun was already an inch taller and, as lean as she was, her breasts promised more than Kate's. A trickle of sweat ran down Kate's nose and fell onto her chest. She watched it run into a little rivulet that disappeared into the valley of her own bikini bra. It was time to get into the surf again, to let the breakers smash over her, to float halfway between surface and bottom, weightless, cool, unconcerned. She ought to run to the jetty, she knew, to work on firming her leg and stomach muscles the way a long run on the beach could do, but it was too hot, she was too lazy, and Shaun's nearly sixteen-year-old body did not encourage competition. She had finished the *Times*, dinner at the Club loomed predictable, she missed Blanchflower, and she was slightly bored with playing mother.

In the beginning, she had been a damn good mother. Damn good! As young as Kate was when she gave birth, her baby had seemed part child, part a gift of the Magi. She had Tommy, and now she had their baby, and the world was a complete and perfectly wonderful place. Then Tommy had begun to be . . . Tommy, still charming, still the passionate lover, but unreliable, impractical, deceitful in small, and then in larger ways, too willing to let his parents do it, uninterested in work, in achievement. It must have been sometime around then, when Kate reluctantly came to her decision to provide the family's sinew, to become the forceful, decisive one, that her son become less a treasured plaything and more a responsibility to be assumed. It was not that Kate's maternal instincts had eroded in the growing friction with Tommy. It was that they had changed their shape and thrust and priority. It was one thing to spend hours brushing the baby's hair and fussing over his clothes. It was quite another to leave such incidentals to Mary and to expend that time in finding ways to keep the family going without a true husband and father at the helm. And when the little boy died, once her grief had numbed and she had taken on the new burden of the motherless Shaun, she had to work even harder to rebuild the shattered family.

She was *not* a bad mother! Maybe she wrote terrible letters, full of the obvious sort of maternal wisdom or dull office chat. Surely her secretary wrote much better letters, letters a girl at boarding school would anticipate and enjoy. Was that a sin? She loved Shaun. She had worked hard for the girl. She had been accused of ambition and worse when all she really wanted was to do a decent job of playing mother and father both. So that Shaun could be as proud, as assured, as confident, as any girl in her class.

The East Hampton sun beat down. A faded belle in a long dress moved past dreamily in the shade of a parasol. A biplane

176

towing an advertisement for a tanning ointment buzzed lazily overhead. The lifeguards sunned themselves and pretended to ignore the pretty girls hanging around the lookout chair, flexing their muscles in secret. Children erected great castles and mothers' helpers, strapping Danish blondes, coped with cartons of Pampers while aging ad agency types with goatees oiled the backs of honeyed young girls they had met the day before. The heat, the pleasant sexual tensions of the beach, the awareness of her own body, sleek, brown, lazy, reminded her that the hotel, the room, the bed where she and Nick had first come together was but a few hundred yards away, just over that dune. Kate felt the stirrings of arousal. It felt good. But right now, damned inconvenient. She got up from her backrest, dropped her towel and her cigarettes, and walked down the steep tidal beach to the water's edge. Even though it was now midsummer, the water was still cold, and her ankles ached as she waded in. A wave came, and another, and then a third, too big to avoid, and Kate Sinclair inhaled, put her hands together in front of her, and dove, without thinking, into the green Atlantic.

It was just before dark. Kate's sister sat in the East Hampton Post Office movie house, watching Gary Cooper make a lovable ass of himself in *Mr. Deeds Goes to Town*. The boy in the next seat, whose name was Willy, slid his hand smoothly around her shoulder and downward, so that it rested on the slope of her breast. Hey, great! He *knew* she wasn't wearing a bra under the pale blue T-shirt. Willy relaxed in his seat and tried to concentrate on Jean Arthur. But he was thinking about Shaun and how she'd looked on the beach that day, leaping to spike a ball over the volleyball net, all five-nine of her afloat in the summer sun above the golden sand.

After the film they drove in Willy's standard pickup out Three Mile Harbor Road to one of the discotheques where it was assumed a teen-ager's I.D. card was phony or borrowed and danced that season's latest dance craze which none of them realized had also been the latest dance craze in 1950 and drank beer and switched partners and gossiped among themselves whenever the music died and giggled at the handful of adults in the place.

* * *

There was dancing too at the Maidstone. At the Maidstone there is a certain reticence, the reserve that comes with old money, but they were dancing to the same music as the kids on the Three Mile Harbor Road. Only here most of the dancers remembered 1950 and glowed in a pleasant nostalgia as they danced. There was no lack of partners for Kate. Even at the Maidstone she was a celebrity, and although it would not do to make a fuss, everyone in the room knew that she was there. The women remarked on it, and the men looked, and people said hello, shyly but pleasant enough, and no one asked for an autograph. Nor did any man, except her host at dinner, dance with her a second time. It was all right for him to do so because his wife, a well-known writer, knew Kate and trusted her. Most of the other women in the room did not. She was, after all, an attractive woman alone. Divorced, wealthy, powerful, and, everyone agreed, ambitious. It would be impolite for one's husband not to dance with Kate Sinclair once. It would be foolhardy to permit him to do it a second time.

Kate did not feel dangerous. She would have laughed had anyone suggested she was a threat. The men were nice enough, but dull. She understood the canons of country club society, so well remembered from her college days, from the early years with Tommy, and she did not resent the defensiveness of the women. The fact was there was not a man in the room she could not have had and there was not a man in the room she wanted. These were the occasions when Harvey Podesta came in so handy, a convenient escort, safe, reliable, and a message-in-clear to the other women that she was not on the prowl.

"Would you like to dance this one, Miss Sinclair?" a gray-haired man asked.

"Oh, yes, I'd love to," she said, smiling, but hating it and wishing it were Blanchflower.

On the way home Willy parked his pickup at Main Beach and he and Shaun walked down to the water's edge, barefoot, the sand cool now, the moon huge coming up out of the eastern sea, spattering the ocean into silvered chips that danced and darkened and shone again in the constant movement of

178

the waves. They had necked in the cab of the truck and Shaun had not objected when he pushed up her shirt and ran his hand over her breast and then feeling her lean body just below. It was then she jumped out of the cab.

"Come on, Willy, let's get our feet wet."

He went along, bashful, ready to do whatever this wonderful girl wanted, but unsure of what she would allow and where she would draw the line.

"Wanna swim?" he asked.

"Hey," Shaun said, laughing, "didn't you see *Jaws?*"

"Oh, yeah," he said. He had hoped she would say yes, not that he wanted to swim but knowing they would have swum naked.

They walked along the water's edge, the foam creaming around their feet. There were other people on the beach, refugees from the sweltering day, older couples strolling before bed, homosexuals cruising, here and there some kids on blankets drinking beer and talking low in the night.

After a bit she and Willy lay back on the side of a small dune, facing the ocean. They necked again and this time Shaun put her shirt under her head, keeping her hair out of the sand. Willy's mouth was at her breast and his hand fumbled at the zipper of her cutoffs. Ah, she felt good, but scared at the same time. He lifted his head and kissed her on the mouth. She could taste the beer on his tongue.

Kate, who had taken her own car to the club, pulled into the gravel driveway of her house at twelve o'clock. A porch light was on and a light upstairs in Mary's room. The moon shone on the gravel and she pulled the car in under one of the great oak trees where there would be shade in the heat of morning. She saw Shaun's bike under the overhang and thought, good, she's home, and then she realized the girl had gone off in that boy's truck.

I ought to be a better parent, she thought. I *ought* to be.

"That you, Missus?" Mary shouted down and Kate answered.

"Shaun's not home yet," Mary shouted.

"Okay," Kate said, "I'll sit up for a while."

She carried a chair down from the porch onto the green

179

lawn. She could not see the ocean but she could hear the surf and above the big box hedge she could see the moon, higher now and smaller. She lighted a cigarette and sat there, very still, watching the smoke rise. Mary's light went out and there was only the dim porch light and the moon.

No one understands, Kate thought. Not even Shaun. I love her so much. I know I don't show it. And I should. Instead to her and to everybody I'm cold, hard, and efficient and so wrapped up in my own success I haven't time for anything else. She leaned back and looked up at the stars, paled by the moon. And I'd give it all up in a moment to have had my son live and Tommy turn out right, to have had a marriage instead of ambition. To have Blanchflower now I'd give up the career, the million dollars.

Then she drew again on the cigarette and knew she was not being honest with herself, knew that what she wanted was both things. Blanchflower *and* the job!

There was the sound of a motor and Willy's pickup truck drove with a crunch onto the driveway and came to a halt a polite distance from the house so he and Shaun could kiss good night.

"Fun?" Kate asked.

Shaun looked less buoyant than usual.

"Yeah, okay," she said. "We went to a neat disco."

"Is he nice?"

"Sure, you know."

"Well, good night."

"Good night, Kate." Shaun kissed Kate on the cheek and bounded up the stairs, two at a time.

As she undressed she thought again about the dune, about Willy. About how she had stopped him at the last moment, not wanting to stop him, and then wanting to, and how when he'd argued, she'd turned nasty and snarled:

"Hey, listen, I'm not my goddamned sister, you know."

Willy had recoiled and she'd put her shirt back on and fastened her shorts and they'd walked back, slowly, to where the truck was parked, holding hands at the end, with Shaun feeling terribly guilty about what she'd said. How unfair she'd been to Kate, how cruel, how unnecessary.

Well, she thought, jumping into bed, serves her right, being

180

so distant and all. How the hell do I know if she's an easy lay or not? She ought to talk to me sometimes so I know *who* she is.

Then the child slept.

At the end of the next week they were at LaGuardia, Mary fussing because Shaun had been able to stuff her entire belongings into one rather proletarian rucksack.

"A person can't tell the difference anymore between the capitalists and the rest of us," she complained.

Above them there was the roar of the jets, curiously noisy and modern after East Hampton, where what might have been the last biplanes still chugged overhead pulling their commercials for Noxzema and Cruzan Rum and for a "happy hour" at one of the local bars, "all drinks fifty cents."

Shaun would fly to Portland and then take a seaplane to the camp.

"Well," Kate said.

"Yeah, thanks. For putting up with me, I mean."

The two stood there, unfulfilled, touching but not close. Kate knew this would in all likelihood be the last summer of childhood for the girl. She wished it had been better, wished they had been able to bridge the gap. As for Shaun, she sensibly took the fortnight for what it had been, a rare and sometimes intimate exposure to someone she loved but knew only from a distance. She had forgotten her guilt, healthily, and her only thought of that night in the dunes with Willy was a certain satisfaction that she had retained control. Willy and his surfboard and his sunpeeled nose and the old pickup truck were yesterday. Ahead, at camp, were other friends, other boys, and one particularly, a tall, curly-haired senior counselor who . . .

They called the flight and they walked toward the gate, the three of them together as they had been, intermittently, for so many years. Mary forgot dialectic and cried, as she always did, and the girl grinned and waved, and then turned and disappeared onto the plane. Some people at the gate recognized Kate and she smiled, absently, and then she and Mary went outside and got into the car to drive back to the apartment. It was Sunday and there would be work in the morning.

21

East Hampton had been an interlude, deceptively placid. Now Kate came back to reality, to the anchor desk, to Chester, and most ominous of all, to a new Nielsen ratings book based on the viewing audiences for the last thirty days. The figures would be issued simultaneously to all three networks on Tuesday. Chester and Kate had now been together for more than half a year. It was time for novelty to have worn off, for habit to have taken over. The figures would be, everyone agreed, "significant," although the network executives would use much stronger adjectives.

Meanwhile, as they waited, Kate and Chester went back to work.

"Good evening, I'm Chester Albany . . . "

" . . . And I'm Kate Sinclair, and this is the evening news."

"In Washington," Chester read, "a series of vital Senate hearings wound up today and for a direct report we take you to Floyd Keller on Capitol Hill."

The red lights on the studio cameras blinked off and Chester slumped back in his chair. Kate fussed with her script, making sure it was in the proper page order, only half-listening to the network's man from Washington when she heard Blanchflower's name.

"Senator Blanchflower of New York is a member of the special committee that late this afternoon finished its public hearings on the crucial question of . . . "

Kate sat up to watch the studio monitor, her script pushed aside.

There was Blanchflower on the screen. How odd to see him like this. Yet how many times had he seen her in exactly this same way, disembodied, two-dimensional. Out of the corner

182

of her eye she could see Chester sneaking a smoke, the floor manager scratching his buttocks, the lighting girl giving her best profile to the third cameraman. Kate listened to Blanchflower.

He was good, very good. He made his points clearly and succinctly. And when Keller once sought clarification of an obscure point, Blanchflower spelled out the details so that both Keller and the audience could understand. He was an impressive performer and toward the end Blanchflower got off a telling, and rather funny, line, that quite neatly capped the interview and left Keller with a gracious exit.

In the studio the red light went back on and Kate said:

"We'll be back with more news after these important messages."

Kate was not yet an experienced newscaster, but she had been in television for eight years and now, for the first time, she saw Blanchflower for the superb professional he was. He understood the medium, used it as it should be used, and she understood despite his iconoclasm, his self-indulgence, his "politics of outrage," why the man won elections. He was a performer, as much one of Nielsen's children as Chester, as Cronkite, as she herself. He appreciated the world in which she worked because it was his world as well. She decided, feeling marvelous for the decision, that nothing could come between them.

Then the commercials were over and Chester Albany was saying something about a typhoon in Bangladesh with ten thousand people dead. A bit of grainy film was shown with a correspondent's voice-over. The bodies stacked like cordwood had no sooner made their impression when Kate was back with a grace note about a member of the First Family and then more "important messages."

Blanchflower phoned her after the show.

"I'll be back soon, Kate. You gonna be around?"

"Yes," she said. "I saw you tonight. With Floyd Keller."

"Oh?" he said.

"It was wonderful to see you. Even on the tube. You were very good."

"Hell," Blanchflower said, "I got off lots better lines with Reasoner."

The following day Kate had lunch with Harvey Podesta at La Grenouille. The regulars were all there. The captain got them a banquette. Harvey had a new book out and everyone wanted to be nice to him.

Their table was in the front room. The back room, approximately limbo, was known as the ketchup room. A newspaperman had once written that La Grenouille would as soon exile Babe Paley to the back room as install ketchup bottles on the tables. The name had stuck. The people in the ketchup room looked as respectable as those up front, the service was just as good, the menu and the kitchen and the prices the same. But the tables up front were for people like Kate Sinclair and Harvey Podesta, for dress designers and visiting grandees, for the better class of gangster, for the Rockefellers, for John Wayne and Billy Baldwin. Kate Sinclair knew people who had turned away, regretfully, and gone down the street to lesser restaurants, simply because they would have had to sit in the back.

"Well," Harvey said, "I hear you're being unfaithful to me. And with a crooked politician."

Kate laughed.

"Well, he's a politician. No more crooked than most, I'd guess."

"But he gets people so mad," Harvey said, turning the word "mad" into a sort of drawn-out whine.

Kate shrugged.

"He must know what he's doing. He keeps getting elected."

"So did Nixon," Harvey said.

"Tell me about the new book," Kate said, changing the subject.

"I might have known you haven't read it yet. And I sent you one, autographed even, with the most delicious dedication."

"I know, Harvey, but you do forgive me, don't you?"

"I always do, Kate. Despite what everyone says about you," he added bitchily.

That afternoon she and Chester were summoned to a meeting with Bobby Klaus. Bobby was jumpy. The coming ratings book haunted him.

"Look," he said, closing the door so that the producer and the others on the staff were excluded and it was only the three of them, "we've been working together five, maybe six months

184

now and you still haven't meshed. There's this friction between you, this tension. People are beginning to notice it. The
critics have been dogging Butch Halvorsen about it. The brass
senses it and they don't like it. They want it stopped."

Chester shrugged. Kate noticed, seeing him without his
makeup, that he was quite tanned. Idly, she wondered where
he had spent his vacation.

"Kate?" Bobby asked.

"Oh, sorry, Bobby, I was thinking of something else."

"Is there anything wrong between you? Anything I ought to
know?"

Kate shook her head.

"No, everything's fine. Maybe Chester . . . "

"No," Chester said. "It's fine."

Bobby Klaus started to look exasperated and then, exercising control, he said mildly, "Well, if there is anything, I want
in on it. Our overnights look awful. The whole concept of the
show was to marry you two successfully on the air. The ratings were great the first few months. Now they've drifted off
again."

"Hell, Bobby," Chester said, "it's summer. The dog days.
Everyone's ratings take a dip in July and August. You had substitutes on for two weeks. It happens."

"Sure, Chester," Bobby said, "that must be it." He did not
sound convinced.

Chester and Kate walked down the hallway together toward
their own offices. There was never any small talk between
them, just office chat and technical business, and the silence
was awkward. Then, thinking one of them should say something, Kate said:

"You have quite a tan."

"Yes," he said, "I was at the beach."

Bobby Klaus's concern, only half expressed, had unnerved
them both. They were, after all, both very new to stardom and
not quite sure they were all that good at it, not sure they really
deserved all that adulation, all that money.

"Oh," Kate said, "where?"

Chester stopped. They were at the door of his office. He
looked longingly at his couch.

"Bermuda."

"Oh," she said, trying to be pleasant, "but that's lovely."

"Is it?" he said sourly. Bermuda had been tense, more problems in bed with Frances, and what had promised to be a tropical paradise had turned out a great deal less.

Kate did not say anything and after a moment Chester Albany turned and went into his office and the last Kate saw of him he seemed to be preparing to lie down.

She paused for only a moment and then walked on down the hall to her own office. Her secretary was there and they exchanged a few words and then Kate sat down behind her desk, wondering why Chester Albany hated her so, when she didn't hate him at all. As far as Kate was concerned, he was a minor irritant in an otherwise quite splendid job.

This, of course, was part of what bothered Chester. The woman did not take him seriously, assumed she was the star and if she had to have a working partner on the air, well, Chester Albany would do as well as the next. And another thing had bothered him from the start, this tacit assumption of hers and Bobby's that news was just another thirty minutes in the evening's entertainment schedule. He should have had that one out at the very beginning with Bobby Klaus, should have goddamn it *known* it was going to be that way when Klaus took over, instead of a news executive. But Chester, honest in most things, knew why he had not had it out with Bobby, or with anyone. Because he was so goddamned pleased to have his name in all the papers, to have had his salary doubled, to be the focus of so much attention. And so, resenting his status as second banana to a woman without news experience, uneasy about working under a programmer whose whole reputation was in entertainment, dubious about the show's philosophy as well as its shape and timing, he had nevertheless permitted himself to be seduced by money, by publicity, and by his superiors. He had, Chester knew, no one to blame but himself.

Kate dismissed Bobby Klaus's remarks as unimportant. Agonizing was a waste of time, she decided. She would leave that to Chester. She was indifferent to Chester, irritable with Harvey, because they were themselves and not Blanchflower, because they were here and he was not.

The new Nielsen ratings book came out. It was a disaster.

Bobby Klaus sat at his desk, staring at the figures. He was too shocked to reach for the Kleenex. The network's evening news show was still in third place. After a year of hype, after six months on the air with his new team, after all the money spent and energy invested, they had made no progress at all. The bright hope of those first weeks, of Kate's Middle East summitry, of *Time* magazine covers and saloon gossip, had been flushed away like dirty rinse water by A. C. Nielsen's remorseless statistics.

Bobby searched the figures for some glimpse of hope. There was none. Chester had scoffed at the overnights. It was summer, he and Kate had been on vacation, substitutes had manned the anchor desk. The fact was, the figures were only marginally better during the fortnight Kate and Chester had worked than during their absence. Bobby should have seen the disaster coming, should have been prepared for the rout. But, like Chester, he had underestimated the threat signaled by the overnights and been sure the national picture would be brighter. It had not turned out that way.

Bobby Klaus was too dazed to call a meeting of his staff. There was nothing he could tell them. He dreaded the ring of the telephone. Up on the 39th floor Dillon had surely seen the figures. It was only a question of time before the summons came. It would be harrowing, the insurance underwriters wondering why the *Titanic*'s watertight doors hadn't worked, a court martial asking who was asleep at Pearl Harbor, the game warden demanding to know just who it was killed Cock Robin. Bobby Klaus had no answers. He knew he must find some.

22

Now when she most needed him, Blanchflower came back to New York. They had not seen one another for nearly a month. He phoned her first at the office, missed her there and got her at the apartment. Mary answered.

"It's the commissar," she told Kate.

"Hello, are you back?"

"Back and in trouble." She didn't understand what he said but it was something about the feminists.

"Oh?"

He came to the apartment. Still a bit self-conscious, she sent Mary Costello to the movies. "And don't hurry back. I'll be just fine."

Mary grunted doubt but left.

"Now what's this about the feminists?" Kate asked Blanchflower.

"I don't know," he said. "I hear things."

"What sort of things? A couple of them came to see me months ago. I told them the network didn't like my becoming involved in issues, in controversy. I suppose they didn't like it very much but there was nothing unpleasant. Why?"

"Vague as hell," he said. "You know, my record on women's rights isn't all that it could be. I mean, I haven't voted a straight Bella Abzug line. But now there's some talk of a feminist campaign against me. Something I've done or haven't done. Your name was mentioned."

"As what?" she demanded.

"That's the damnable part of it," Blanchflower admitted. "I don't know. That's what I'm trying to find out. If there's some way the feminists could use you against me. Something I don't know about. Maybe, even, something you don't know about."

Kate said she was mystified. Blanchflower threw up his hands.

"To hell with it," he said. "I'm not going to rupture myself trying to figure it out. If there's going to be trouble it'll show itself. Then I can decide how to handle it. Now, what about dinner? Or do we go to bed first?"

They went to bed and made quite splendid love and Blanchflower stopped thinking about the feminists, or about anything except about how fortunate he was to have found this strong, intelligent woman and then to find, almost as a dividend, that she was marvelous in bed. The discovery did not mean that, suddenly, Nick Blanchflower had turned monogamous. But it rather startled him and, not coincidentally, his very obvious joy communicated itself to Kate, making her even more tender, more loving, more passionate.

Together with him again Kate forgot her annoyance at Harvey's bitchiness, Bobby Klaus's lecture, the ratings, Chester's sour mood. Even this vague, unformed business about the feminists made no impact. Kate was too happy to worry about anything.

Kate was not stupid. If she didn't know the more colorful details, she was quite clearly aware of Blanchflower's casual affairs. She heard things, she knew people, and Blanchflower himself talked. Without boasting (Kate would have despised him for that) he would mention casually this girl or that as a pleasant interlude, an amusing hour. There was about him the refreshing candor of a naughty child who salvages all by open-faced admission of wickedness and smiles and says, but then, you know how awful I am because you love and understand me.

In her mid-thirties, a vulnerable time for any woman, Kate was waking, opening, expanding. The focus of her passion, her first real commitment since Tommy Sinclair, was this huge, cheerful, notorious rogue. Rather than resenting his adventures, Kate enjoyed them, giving Blanchflower yet another dimension and in a sense reinforcing her own image. This dashing, colorful man, surrounded and pursued by so many, wanted her. She knew she should resent the others, but by this time she wanted him as he was, whatever his defects. Tommy had been furtive. Nick Blanchflower cried his failings from balconies and she stood below and cheered.

Kate Sinclair, like any schoolgirl, had fallen in love with a man she knew to be flawed, yet hoped would turn out perfect. She was thirty-five years old, rich and famous, and was behaving with no more sophistication than she had as an undergraduate at Smith when she first met Tommy and worried that she had no breasts. She failed then, as she was failing now, to discern her real value and made excuses for who she was, for what she had become, for the things she had not achieved. Was it because her child had died young, because she was half Italian, because she had lost Tommy, because she was, at best, an adequate surrogate mother? Blanchflower behaved badly, and she admired him for it. Blanchflower failed her, and she resolved to be better. Blanchflower did not call, and she called him. She did all the wrong things, knew them to be wrong, and did them again.

The senator's contrast to Chester Albany was interesting. Chester was ornery, defensive, and hated her. Blanchflower was buoyant, confident, and loved her. Yet Chester was dependable, reliable, totally honest, while she knew Blanchflower to be unreliable, unpredictable, and acceptably dishonest. But Blanchflower was unique. He was one of a kind. Tommy had been pressed out by the thousands, Chester, probably, by the hundreds At this time in her life, Kate Sinclair preferred the rare vintages This was all, she realized, irrational. But when had love ever been rational?

Three nights later Bobby Klaus phoned her at home. It was nearly midnight.

"Bobby," she said, "what's the matter?"

He had found a way, he thought, to soothe Dillon, to fend off Venables, to hype the ratings. He was going back to what had worked before.

"Kate," he said, his voice excited and once again buoyant, "how'd you like to fly down to Coronado?"

She was too sleepy to understand and she said, "But I just got *back* from vacation."

"No, no," Bobby said impatiently, "not vacation. To do an interview everyone's been after for years. To interview Marcos!"

190

23

Bobby Klaus made phone calls and pulled diplomatic strings and it was arranged for Kate Sinclair to visit Coronado so that the American people, for the first time in years, would see the true face of the tyrant-saint, Marcos. She should take a week ("A whole week," she informed Blanchflower jubilantly, "a week away from the ratings!") and Chester would handle the anchor desk alone ("Seven days without the bitch," he exulted). She would fly to Miami and take the local puddle jumper to the island. It was all very simple. Until Blanchflower decided to come along.

"Why not?" he demanded. "I don't get to see you that often. And besides, next year maybe I'll be on Foreign Relations."

Miami was humid and hot, the shock of the morning sun heavy as they came out of the air-conditioned terminal. The rented car was waiting, a convertible. "You can't drive around Florida in a goddamned sedan," Blanchflower had insisted, and they drove across the great vaulting spans of Biscayne Bay that linked the spits of sand and mangrove and palm dotting the cobalt southern sea. On the ocean at Miami Beach there was a hotel, the rooms frigid, and they went outside to warm themselves in the swimming pool.

That night they drank in a bar where the waitresses wore G-strings and pasties and they ate conch chowder in a Cuban restaurant and key lime pie and crawfish sweet with melted butter and went unrecognized. Later they slept tightly twined under two blankets.

The flight to Coronado was something. An old DC-3 with the pilot taxiing the plane before the co-pilot had pulled the cabin door completely shut. Kate imagined they were still wiping the daiquiris off their mustaches as they took off.

"We fly this low," Blanchflower said, looking out the windows at waves only a hundred feet below, "so if the motors shut down we can just step out without parachutes."

The formalities at Coronado were surprisingly simple.

"Why should there be any red tape?" Blanchflower said. "No one hijacks airplanes *away* from here."

The Coronados had put them up at a hotel where the desk clerk informed them Ernest Hemingway had once stayed and edited or done some damn thing to one of his books. He said he would put them in the room Hemingway occupied.

"I'll bet he says that about every room," Kate whispered in the elevator.

Blanchflower laughed.

"I should have told him I was a Scott Fitzgerald man, myself."

The room faced north and from a little balcony that gave onto a narrow street, shady and full of small shops and motorbikes and tropical noise, they could look over rooftops and see a wonderful old church which, the bellman assured them, had some intimate connection to Columbus but he was not quite sure what. Perhaps he had heard mass there or been buried there or something.

"Sounds like another Hemingway yarn to me," Blanchflower said dubiously.

The bellman, not understanding, smiled and Blanchflower gave him some money and got another smile.

Kate phoned the hotel where the crew was staying and spoke with the unit producer who said the first interview with Marcos was scheduled for the following afternoon. He had spoken to New York and Bobby Klaus had sent his love and said "good hunting."

"Now I wonder what that means," Kate said. "Am I supposed to interview the head of state or go to bed with him?"

Blanchflower looked at her.

"Well," he said, "old Marcos could do worse."

She went to him and put her arms around him.

"So could I," she said.

The sun was low and the room cool and shaded when they got out of bed. They showered and then went down into the lobby. Blanchflower used reasonable Spanish to ask where he could buy some good cigars and they walked through the narrow streets, crowded now after the early afternoon siesta. There were a lot of uniforms, even the girls wore them, and very few cars but lots of trucks and old buses.

"This is where the old Fifth Avenue buses go when they die," Blanchflower said.

They bought the cigars and walked down toward the waterfront. Kate kept looking around, wanting to know whether they were being trailed, but the streets were too crowded to be sure, and except for the passersby, mostly women, who stared at her dress or Blanchflower's blond hair, no one bothered them. They waited for a break in the traffic and crossed the Malecon, a broad boulevard fronting the water, to the sea wall. From out of the north, although there was almost no breeze, long rollers came in to smash against the concrete sea pens that were built into the breakwater. Some little boys swam in the pens, being lifted and then dropped by the waves. Blanchflower shouted down to them, asking how the swimming was.

"Good," one of them said, "why don't you come in?"

Blanchflower shouted back that he was afraid of sharks.

"Tiburons?" the boy asked incredulously. But that was why they swam in the pens and not in the harbor itself.

Off to the right was a centuries-old fortress.

"They used to keep prisoners in there," Blanchflower said. "Chained to the walls in the dungeons, below water level. I wonder if Marcos has any poor bastards in there now. You ought to ask him tomorrow."

"Hey," said Kate, "I want an interview out of this guy. Not an international incident."

A boatman saw them looking at the fortress and he offered to row them across.

"It is permitted to land and walk around the outside," he said.

Blanchflower looked at the boat, which was very small and old, and said no. When they left three men, who looked like Russians, started dickering with the boatman about the price of a tour around the harbor.

They found an open cafe and sat and drank cold beers and Blanchflower smoked one of his cigars while they watched the traffic and the start of the evening *paseo*, the young women walking and the young men watching. Afterwards they had dinner in a seafood restaurant. There was East German beer and when the meal was over Blanchflower said he felt sleepy and they returned to the hotel and he went to bed while Kate sat up, writing notes for the questions she would ask Marcos the next afternoon.

The dictator was very charming.

He was bigger than Kate had expected and his English was quite good. He complimented Blanchflower on his Spanish.

"Two million of my constituents speak Spanish," Blanchflower said. "I had no choice but to learn a little."

"They should have sent you here as ambassador," Marcos told him.

"Senators are more important than ambassadors," Blanchflower said, "but it is nice of you to say so."

They were on a verandah of the Presidential palace and while the crew set up the cameras and the other equipment a woman in an army uniform served them cold lemonade in tall glasses.

Kate was concentrating on her notes and a bit nervous about how the interview would go so Marcos and Blanchflower indulged in small talk while they waited for the crew.

"She is a very attractive woman, Miss Sinclair."

"Yes," Blanchflower said.

"But you two are not married."

"No."

"And yet you share a room at the hotel," Marcos said, smiling slightly.

"We're close friends," Blanchflower said. It amused him that the man had gone to the trouble of learning about their sleeping arrangements. Although, he supposed, it was probably no trouble at all to find out such things when you ran the whole country.

The interview went well. Kate got over her nervousness once it began and Marcos was frank and open, although insisting on the use of an interpreter.

"My English," he said half-apologetically, "it really isn't good enough."

Kate asked the right questions, about this curious blend of old Spanish Catholicism blended with Marxist populism, the whole contradictory structure held together by this man's

194

dominating personality. She drew a blank only once, on the question of just how essential was the Russian presence to the tiny country's internal stability.

When they had finished the filming there were more cold drinks and then Marcos excused himself.

"We will do the second one tomorrow," he told an aide and the American producer. "Perhaps at a school, where you can film the children." Then he turned to Blanchflower. "Afterwards you and I can talk some more."

"You know, Señor," Blanchflower said, "I'm not on the Foreign Relations committee."

Marcos laughed.

"Not politics, I promise. But there is a basketball game I said I would play for a few minutes. You're tall enough. You must play too."

They stayed in the city for two days, sightseeing and swimming and Blanchflower playing basketball with Marcos and coming back to the hotel to complain of shin splints from running up and down the concrete outdoor courts. They saw the Russians and Bulgarians and East Germans hanging around the town and after they'd seen the town Marcos arranged for a helicopter to fly them down the coast for a few days of sun and relaxation before they had to go home.

The beach was the most beautiful Kate had ever seen. They swam with face masks and snorkels, the tropic sun hot on their backs. The water was clear, and at twelve or fourteen feet they could see mackerel and they dove to them, watching as the fish scattered over the smooth golden sand below. They were perhaps two hundred yards off the beach, swimming easily with the masks, not having to keep their heads up to breathe, but relaxed and buoyant in the water. Blanchflower stayed under for a time, and then, as Kate trod water easily, enjoying the sun on her face through the salt, he exploded to the surface.

"For God's sake," he shouted, "there's a shark."

Kate plunged her face into the water, instinctively drawing up her legs. But she saw nothing. Even the mackerel were gone.

"Come on," she said, her head out of the water, "you didn't see anything."

195

Blanchflower's face was red with rage. Or fear.

"I saw a goddamned shark. Eight feet long. Right under us. A gray shark."

Kate sighed and again put her face mask into the water.

"Hey," she said, "don't kid around. It isn't funny to kid about sharks."

"Jesus Christ, I don't kid about sharks. It was there. Swam right past me. Right under you."

"Blanchflower," she started to say, "you . . . "

Blanchflower turned toward shore. "Look," he said, "get out of this fucking water. Don't splash, just swim back in normally. But get out. I'm telling you."

Kate continued to tread water. Blanchflower stared at her for another moment or two and then turned toward the beach, swimming slowly but steadily with that workmanlike crawl of his, opening up surprisingly soon a gap of ten or more yards between them.

Kate watched him go and again searched the water but saw nothing. Blanchflower was now thirty yards away, headed for the beach. Well, she thought, I don't like sharks any more than anyone else, but I'm damned if I'm going to be panicked out of the water.

Fifteen minutes later, feeling very much in control and rather proud of herself, she strode up onto the beach.

Blanchflower, already dried in the sun, his hair matted and bleached by the salt, walked down the slope of the sand to meet her.

"Look," he said, "I wasn't fooling. There was a shark out there. A gray shark. Longer than I was even with the magnification. I wasn't kidding."

Kate looked into his face.

"Then why did you leave me?" she asked in a quiet voice.

They were in bed. Even the sting of the sunburn felt pleasant. Everything physical felt pleasant. He was naked. She was wearing a bit of black mantilla lace they'd bought in town. It did not dignify being called a nightgown. Blanchflower insisted she wear it. "It looks wonderful against the tan," he said. Earlier in the evening they had gone out, not wanting to be alone.

They were surprised to find the casino still operating. The manager explained, "The Russians like it. Of course they despise losing. It's not like the Americans, in the old days. They expected to lose. That was what they were paying for, to lose a few dollars at the wheel. No one came here for profit in those days, only for the sun, to lose at the tables, to make love. It must have been like this at Deauville and Monte during the German occupation."

It was understood Kate and Blanchflower would not permit his remarks to go further. They were all people of the world, disinterested in local politics or transient regimes. The manager bought them excellent daiquiris on the strength of their understanding. When they got upstairs to their rooms Kate was quite drunk and the business of the shark, if not forgotten, was at least on the shelf. When Blanchflower told her to put on the black lace she did what she was told, turning this way and that, cupping her breasts.

"Okay," Blanchflower said. She lay on the large bed, watching as he undressed in the half light coming off the moonstruck sea. She was drunk.

Blanchflower got into bed.

"I wasn't afraid of the shark," she said.

"Fuck the shark."

"Okay," she said, speaking with drunken precision, "but I failed to discern the shark. And therefore could not possibly fuck it."

Blanchflower said "shit" and then lay still. Once or twice she thought he was about to speak, possibly to justify himself, and when he remained silent she asked again, "If there really was a shark, why did you leave me there?"

Blanchflower cursed and then, after some heavy breathing fell asleep without answering. Kate watched him for a time as the moonlight, bouncing off the silver sea, moved across the room, and then, still drunk, she too slept. In the middle of the night one of them woke, neither quite sure which it was, and the lace was torn away and they made love, violently, and without reference to the shark. Just before they slept again, Kate put a hand on his arm and said:

"It's okay. It's Marcos's fault. All that basketball. The shark was just a trick. A lousy commie trick."

Blanchflower half-smiled. But only half. He knew the shark had been there. He knew he had left Kate in the water. But a truce was better than warfare. Guiltily, he slept.

Later, Kate woke again. She went through the open doors to the terrace. The sea, silvered by the dying moon, stretched north before her. Behind her, on the floor, was the tatter of black lace. She looked down at her body, firm from the swim, well-loved, tingling from the sun. Oh, my God, she thought, finally she had found a man, a real man. Now was he to turn out another Tommy, another weakling?

In the morning the commissar arrived to take them back to town for the ritual tour of historical sites.

In Washington the President's men knew only that Nicholas Blanchflower had again preempted the political scene by popping up unexpectedly, dramatically, cleverly in Coronado at the side of Kate Sinclair as she interviewed the charismatic Marcos over network television. "The son of a bitch," someone drawled in reluctant admiration, "he spends a week on that little piss-ant island and he's got the Catholics and the pinkos both salivatin' over him." The President nodded. Blanchflower was becoming a serious annoyance. His cheerful roguishness made it so difficult to pin anything on him. The man *must* have an Achilles' heel. He must.

They knew nothing of the shark, of Kate's doubts.

24

The ratings soared. It was Kate's Middle East summitry all over again. "If only we could have her interview a head of state every night," Bobby Klaus remarked wistfully. The five evenings of filmed conversations with the elusive Marcos pulled an audience. And, Bobby admitted to himself, people got a vicarious thrill out of her now quite public liaison with Blanchflower, clearly a man with the White House as his goal. Not everyone was thrilled, of course. In the sports department George Venables read the ratings as intently as Bobby but found little there to fuel his ambition. Chester Albany's resentment burned. "Why the hell do I get blamed when the ratings go down and she gets the credit when they go up?" he demanded of an old director friend one night as they sat in the bar of the Atelier. The director, one of those survivors cautious with his words, shrugged.

"It bugs me," Chester said, his anger overcoming prudence, "this goddamn trivialization of the news. She's playing movie star. That stuff from Coronado, that wasn't news. It was Hollywood takes. And the little things, the blow dryer they have in the makeup room now, that hairdresser mincing around the studio. I mean, does Cronkite have to put up with that shit?"

"So you don't love her," the director said. "Who says in this business you have to like people you work with?"

"Whoever accused this of being a business?" Chester retorted.

"It is," his friend said stiffly. "It's big business."

"Kid," Chester said tolerantly, "I don't care how much money is involved. This isn't a business. It's chaos in living color. It's a crisis in search of catastrophe. Management doesn't make businesslike decisions. They panic, they yell and scream, they for-God's-sake eat Kleenex! This network puts on a dozen brand new shows every September and before the second week's ratings are in we cancel half of them. By January there are maybe three left. You call that a business? If GM had to plow under nine out of every twelve cars it manufactured, would they give their chairman a half-million dollar salary?"

"Television and the auto industry are not precisely the same thing," the director said defensively.

"This is the highest paid asylum in the country," Chester grumbled. "But the funny thing is that I like television. Not all of it, not the bullshit, but I like the discipline of having to get the news across in so few words. *The New York Times* can afford to take a leisurely ninety-six pages to do what we do with a couple of thousand words, a few minutes of film. Punch Sulzberger can snoot us but it ain't easy."

The director nodded. "You're right, Chester. Hey," he called to the barman, "let's do this again, huh?"

Chester drained his glass.

"The bullshit I could do without," he said. "I don't want to become John Cameron Swayze and attach ballpoint pens to surfboards or any of that stuff."

"No."

"The commercials. Do you ever listen to the damn things? I mean, really *listen?*"

"Not if I can help it."

The drinks were there now. Chester lifted his.

"I mean, who the hell writes that stuff?" he asked. "'The agony of psoriasis . . . the swelling of hemorrhoidal tissues . . . the chafing of jock itch.' Jesus, there *must* be an afterlife to make up to the poor bastards who write that stuff."

"I'm a firm believer in the afterlife myself," the old director said, somewhat drunkenly.

Chester looked into the mirror of the bar.

"I'm not so sure," he said. "I'd like to believe. I'd like to see some of the old gang again."

"Murrow."

"Sure, Murrow. And I'd like to meet Marconi. Talk to him a little."

"Lowell Thomas," the other said.

"Shit, Lowell Thomas is still alive."

"Oh."

"That guy down in New Jersey when the Hindenburg crashed. The guy on the radio who started to cry when he saw the people falling out and they kept the line open and he was crying and getting off one hell of a live remote all at the same time. I'd like to meet him."

"You think he's dead too?"

"Maybe. And Major Bowes. And Benny. And Fred Allen. They were good."

"I'd like to meet Amos and Andy."

"Sure. And see Chet Huntley again. And those BBC guys who used to wear black ties and dinner jackets to read the radio news. Some of them must have stories."

"Yeah," the director said, "what a hell of a thing to wear a monkey suit on the radio. Who the hell could see it but the goddamned engineer?"

"Kaltenborn. I'd like to meet him. And what's-his-name, the guy who invented television."

"What's his name?" said the director.

"I dunno," Chester said. "That's the funny part. I don't know who invented the goddamn thing."

When he left the bar he met Frances for dinner. He was late but she was waiting for him. Damn, but she was loyal, he thought. A good girl. Someone who loved him. An antidote to Kate Sinclair.

In the beginning Frances had feared Kate as a possible rival. She knew Kate was an attractive woman, she understood she was competent, intelligent, a personage. Perhaps Chester would fall for the bitch, perhaps that was part of the contract, perhaps Kate and Chester would have to have an affair, a real affair, in order to render their on-the-air coupling more realistic, more credible. But this had been a false fear, a scare, really, and no actual threat. Almost from the beginning Chester had disliked Kate. Dislike had become irritation. Irritation, aggravation. Aggravation, hate.

Frances had at first been delighted by his distaste for the woman. Kate Sinclair could be disregarded. Chester wanted no part of her. Relieved of competitive pressure, Frances bloomed. Her lovemaking, already highly imaginative, became inspired. To think that she had ever feared Kate. My God, there were things she could do with her legs alone that no woman in her thirties could even have attempted. As for her breasts, her mouth, her goddamned earlobes, why had she ever considered Kate a potential rival? She, Frances, was all Chester Albany had ever wanted, had ever even imagined, fantasized, lusted after. Frances, secure in her sexual domination, relaxed. The only problem was, Chester had not.

He returned to Kate again and again. As he was doing now, after his drinking bout with the old director.

"Look, baby," he said, "I'm sorry to be in such a lousy mood. But that bitch did something tonight, right on camera, that I . . . well, I've been in with some of the best, but I've never seen a scene stolen that way. I mean, Jesus, to bite your goddamn hair on camera just as I'm about to get off a fantastic line about the lynching of a Mexican wetback. Best line I've had all week and she bites her goddamned hair."

"Why did they keep the camera on her if it was your line?" Frances asked.

Chester exploded.

"Because the fucking camermen are mesmerized. Because she pays them off under the table. Because she dammit gives them head after the show. How the hell do I know? I'm not the bloody director. I just read the news."

Frances felt it politic to change the subject. Anyway, she didn't want the evening to be ruined. They were at Tavern on the Green, a huge pavilion in Central Park where you went when you had outgrown Maxwell's Plum. She liked the baroque setting, she liked seeing WarnerLeroy in his coat of many colors, she liked the way diners at the other tables looked over at Chester, recognized him, and then pretended not to have noticed. And, of course, in looking at Chester, they had looked at her and, possibly, wondered just who this pretty girl could be with the famous Chester Albany. She liked all of these feelings and she did not want it spoiled just because Kate Sinclair had chewed her hair on camera while Chester read his lines. I mean, she admitted to herself, Kate Sinclair is absolutely brilliant on television, even if Chester doesn't like her. But, of course, she did not say this. Instead, she moved her leg just ever so under the table and pressed it against Chester's knee.

202

"Chester," she said, stretching out his name to three or four syllables, "I love you."

Chester ground his teeth. He was still focusing on Kate Sinclair.

"She's got them all snowed. Not just the cameramen. The director. And Bobby, of course. She's *his* discovery, his white hope. How could he not be crazy about her? Where the hell does it leave me? Second banana to Clive wasn't so bad. Clive was a pro. Sinclair? Jesus, she's Cher Bono without the sequins."

That night, in bed, he came back again to his theme. Sinclair was an amateur, they were turning television news into show business, Bobby Klaus didn't care about Chester's pride, his sensibilities.

Frances Neale was not an intelligent woman but she had instincts. She understood that to go on like this would hurt Chester, eventually hurt her, destroy their relationship. So, using the limited but very appealing tools that a pretty, healthy, uninhibited twenty-three-year-old had at her disposal, she silenced Chester in the only way she knew how.

Chester Albany had gone mute now, sulking. He neither moved nor spoke. Frances took his hand and placed it, strategically, where she thought it might be useful.

There was no reaction and Frances again whispered, "Chester . . . ?"

There was a moment's silence and then Chester pulled his hand away as if burned.

"Goddammit," he shouted, "what a son of a bitch she is!"

Finally they made love. But Frances had had to work at it, to cajole, to tease, to beg. It wasn't like Chester to be reluctant, not at all. After he fell asleep Frances lay awake, thinking about Kate Sinclair. Despite Chester's hatred, Frances admired Kate, envied her intelligence, her spontaneity, her ability, her presence. She wished she had the brains to be a Kate Sinclair. But she wasn't, never would be, and as truly as she admired Kate she had begun to realize that Chester's antagonism toward her might become an even more disruptive situation than if he had fallen for her, as Frances at first had feared. She would have known how to cope with competition. She had youth, she had sexuality, she had the bed on her side.

If Chester kept on this way about Kate Sinclair, it would destroy him. Frances shivered. If Chester screwed himself with the network over this silly antagonism, if he lost his job, it could ruin the best arrangement she had ever had, a better deal than she had ever hoped. It could send her back to tending mewling babies and chasing after rock musicians and all those other pre-Chester chores which at the time had seemed tolerable, even pleasant, and which now would be quite unacceptable. Even worse, there was the menace of grim Liverpool.

Slowly because her mind was not quick, there was growing in Frances Neale the realization that Kate Sinclair, whom she admired from a distance, might even have liked very much up close, was a threat. And that perhaps she, Frances Neale, should do something about her. Maybe there was someone at the network who hated her as much as Chester did, someone who had real power. Maybe there was something in Kate's private life that would damage her professionally. Perhaps there were enemies out there of whom Frances was totally unaware, who would be more than pleased to help bring Kate down.

As she fell asleep Frances resolved, rather pleased at having worked it out in her own head without any help, to do something about Kate Sinclair. Precisely what, she had as yet no idea. No idea at all. She was not even aware of the existence of George Venables, the network's resident jock, another man who was not fond of Kate Sinclair.

25

Kate was professionally pleased by the ratings improvement. She was aware it might be only temporary, that the crucial fall ratings period would soon begin, on the basis of which the price of commercial time would be set for the new season. Still, there was satisfaction in knowing her week in Coronado, her conversations with Marcos, had been successful. Chester's attitude could be ignored. She knew how he felt about her but, really, was it important? She was too preoccupied with Blanchflower to fret over Chester Albany's jealousy.

Blanchflower was a serious matter. He had put her on a plane in Miami and flown to Washington. Their night of love after that business with the shark had calmed both of them. But it had really solved nothing. He would be off on a swing through upstate New York for the next ten days and she was glad of it. She was confused about Blanchflower. She tried to tell herself she was being silly about the shark, about her doubts. But they were there, would not go away. Being alone like this in New York, only her work to concern her, offered a breathing space, a time to think, to reassess Blanchflower and the depths of her feelings about him. She was in love, she recognized that. But was she for the second time in her life in love with the wrong man? She snapped at Mary Costello, refused to take calls from Harvey Podesta, broke a dinner date with Nelson and Happy Rockefeller, brooded about Nick and questioned her own instincts.

A television critic in Chicago, Mort Gruen, supplied a distraction. He placed a call from his desk in Chicago to Butch Halvorsen in New York. When Butch hung up he knew the piranha fish had begun to swarm. This wasn't just Kate and

Chester at hazard. This was Bobby Klaus and maybe even beyond Bobby. This was the whole network news concept. He pondered how best to handle it, reached a conclusion, and marched into Bobby Klaus's office.

His tactic was to play it down, let Bobby be the one to react.

"Mort Gruen," Butch said condescendingly, "what the hell is he? A provincial critic. So he wants out of Chicago. So he wants to make a name for himself by trashing some big network names. So he wants to be recognized as a major force and get a job in New York."

"Butch," Bobby said, "you start too many sentences with 'so.' You're not Jewish, you're not from New York. Just tell me the problem and don't imitate me."

Butch rolled his eyes and gave Nordic assurances. Bobby did not listen. Butch Halvorsen was good at planting stories in *Broadcast News*, at writing bios, at issuing releases on the new prime time lineup. When it came to crises, well, Bobby wanted better than Butch.

Butch resumed his assault on Gruen. Patiently, Bobby Klaus said, "What does Mort want, Butch? What does he have?"

Butch sobered.

"Chester and Kate are fighting."

Bobby Klaus played with his fingers. He did not chew any Kleenex. He felt it was important to convey confidence.

"Butch," he said, "great talent always fights. Lunt and Fontanne. You think that was sixty years of wedded bliss? You really think Lerner and Loewe sang duets over breakfast?"

"Bobby," Butch said, "Gruen *knows!*"

Bobby Klaus nodded.

"Listen," he said, "this network is pioneering. You don't think there are going to be problems? A little friction here and there? You think great talents like Kate and Chester aren't going to bridle once in a while? Let off a little steam? My God, Butch, don't be naive. Of course some talk has gotten around. You think we don't know that?"

Butch Halvorsen looked thoughtful.

"Did Lunt and Fontanne really fight, Bobby?" he asked.

Bobby was not quite as offhanded about the situation as he intimated to Butch. After the press agent had left his office he phoned Mort Gruen in Chicago. He spent the better part of an hour selling a line. Gruen, dubious, agreed not to run his story.

"But if I find you're lying to me, Bobby . . ." he said, his voice drifting off threateningly.

Bobby decided it was time to see Harry Flagg again. To pin down why the two anchorpeople weren't blending. But when he called Centre, Kansas, Flagg wasn't there.

"He's in New York, actually," Flagg's secretary said at the other end of the line.

"Oh," said Bobby. That was strange, that Harry would come East without telling him.

"Where is he?" Bobby asked.

"Oh," the girl said, "but I thought you knew. He's visiting the network. He and one of your associates were having lunch today. Mr. Venables."

Bobby hung up.

Christ, Venables was moving fast on those stubby legs.

Two days later there was a note delivered by hand from his boss:

"If quite convenient could you drop by this afternoon around four? I'd like to be brought up to date on the evening news situation."

Bobby sat in his office, the clear glass desk void of papers or knickknacks, the walls around him ablaze with first-rate reproductions of Miró and Braque and Picasso. Bobby did not look at the pictures or at the formidable view of New York City beyond the windows. Instead, he chewed Kleenex and felt sorry for himself.

Well, now, he said to himself, let's cut the panic and think positively. An hour later as he entered Dillon's office, he was still thinking.

"Hello, Bobby," the president said, "good of you to drop by."

Bobby Klaus smiled. "Good of you to ask me."

There were nice pictures in Dillon's office too. Except that they were not reproductions. A year ago this office, with its original pictures, had seemed so close. Now it was as distant as Tibet.

They fenced and then Dillon asked for Bobby's thoughts on why the evening news was not doing as well as everyone had hoped, "as well as you indicated to us it would."

"Well," he began, rubbing his hands together, "the original concept was to create a sort of living room set in which this nice, bright husband-wife team would sort of sit around evenings and discuss the news of the day. Naturally we adapted that to include the traditional anchor desks, to provide the team with the appropriate authority. And in the beginning, it worked reasonably well. Share went up four points, the critics took their shots and then stopped carping, it looked as if we had a winner."

Dillon smiled. "A very nice *recherche du temps perdu*, Bobby. But what is the situation now? And why?"

Jesus, Bobby thought, once he starts with the French . . . Exerting his will, Bobby went on.

"Exactly, that's yesterday. As for today, and tomorrow, well, we have a problem."

"We? Bobby, we?"

Bobby Klaus nodded.

"The whole backbone of the show was this relationship between Chester and Kate. Husband and wife. They had to be fond of one another, genuinely fond, to work together as helpmates, to be there when the going got tough, to . . ."

"Yes, Bobby, and what has happened to that relationship, this touching little domestic household you've sketched out for us?"

Bobby Klaus paused, inhaled, and said:

"The sons of bitches hate one another!"

For the next hour and a half Bobby Klaus and the president of the broadcast division examined the situation and considered what might be done. Dillon treated Bobby with respect, recognizing that in other realms Bobby had done quite nicely: late night movies; sitcoms; and game shows. Only the evening news was proving troublesome.

They had reviewed, and rejected, the several options: both anchorpeople could be fired; Chester alone, as the more expendable of the two, could be replaced by a more amenable partner; Chester could be exiled to Washington and Kate run the New York desk as a solo; a third anchorperson could be added, a younger man, perhaps, a surrogate son?

Then Bobby, who deserved his reputation within the network for thinking quickly in a conference situation, slammed his hand on the desk.

"I may have it," he said.

Dillon looked bleak. This was becoming tiresome and next morning he had to report to *his* superior on the situation.

"Yes?" he said.

"Look, when a marriage begins to go bad, you know, when the honeymoon is over and reality sets in, what do couples usually do? They don't separate or divorce, not yet awhile, anyway. And that's what firing one of them would be: divorce! And there are still a lot of Americans out there to whom marriage is a sacred contract, a bond, a . . ."

"Get to the goddamned point."

"So they don't divorce. Not at the first sign of trouble. What they do is . . . they take a trip." Bobby looked triumphant.

"A trip?"

"Sure, get away from one another a bit. Go home to Mother. Or the husband goes fishing. You know. Then, after they've had a chance to get their thoughts together, they get back together, better than ever, more in love, more supportive, more understanding . . ."

"A trip," Dillon repeated, less impatient now.

"Sure," said Bobby, talking faster now, sensing the opening. "Only on television you don't take a trip. You . . . go . . . remote."

An hour later it was decided. For the next month, maybe longer, Chester Albany would work out of Washington, Kate Sinclair out of somewhere else, probably Los Angeles.

"After all," Bobby rationalized, "if the network is going to become number one from coast to coast, shouldn't we be truly national? Shouldn't we be able to brag about being the only evening news show that literally spans the continent?"

The broadcast president, who knew it was George Venables who had leaked to Mort Gruen, gave Bobby Klaus his approval. After all, he thought, the thing might just work. And Venables was the sort of man you wanted to keep anxious, the type you didn't want to give too much leverage too soon. Even when you were president of the whole broadcast division, a George Venables could be dangerous.

Anyway, Dillon thought after Bobby left, if it doesn't work Venables will still be around. And nobody can say I didn't give Bobby all the rope he asked for.

26

Los Angeles, the ultimate road show town, appropriate for the launching of network television's first evening news road show. An entire crew was being transported from New York with Kate and the union technicians traveling first class, the director and the writers in tourist. "A very nice division of labor," one of the more articulate electricians remarked to Kate as the stewardess fetched champagne. Kate knew the New York technicians would do nothing in California. They would lie about, on full salary, playing cards, while the local crews did the work. It was the way the rules were made.

There was, as usual, drought in California, and the tired brown mountains around the city were patched and blackened from burnt-out brush fires. The plane had begun its descent just west of Las Vegas and now, as it came in over the basin you could see the smog and the pilot told them to fasten their seat belts. The stewardess came to reclaim Kate's glass and to give her a hot washcloth.

"Gee, Miss Sinclair," she said. "That's really neat that you're doing your show out here. What a break from New York."

The girl had a western accent and her enthusiasm was understandable. Kate was not nearly so sure.

For all her vaunted stainless steel arrogance, she was frightened. She wanted the show to succeed very much and now she was beginning to sense that it might not. Venables was pushing Bobby, that much was clear from corridor gossip, and Venables, the macho jock, did not like Kate Sinclair. The ratings gave a false impression. They were good, once again at healthy levels. But Kate and everyone else who was informed knew that the ratings were being hyped, that the network was spending extraordinary moneys to promote the show. It was a dictum of television that a show whose ratings you have to buy is a show that will be a memory next season. How long would the network be willing to subsidize Kate and Chester? That was the frightening part. She did not know.

And that was why Kate was now being uncharacteristically flexible. She did not dislike California, but she knew that as an anchor for a network evening news show Los Angeles was a ghost town, Siberia. Still, she had agreed to go. She had surprised even Bobby Klaus.

"Kate," he said, "I appreciate this, I really do. You can't know . . ."

But she knew. She knew that if Bobby were destroyed, she might be as well. Even Chester, dour, negative, grouchy, had agreed to try the Washington anchor.

"As an experiment, Bobby. Just as an experiment. No goddamn permanent exiles now, you understand?"

A year ago, when the job had first been offered, she was emotionally cool. Had the negotiations then not worked out she would have regretted it but could happily have stayed with the morning show, with her two hundred thousand dollars, with her limited fame. She would have laughed at anyone who suggested she would within a year be haunted by failure, willing to essay stupid experiments like this Los Angeles nonsense to save her job. To fail. It was an alien concept. The network just couldn't come out and admit it gave a five million dollar five-year contract to her and then, within a year, announce they had made a slight error.

"Good-bye, Kate, here's your pink slip, your gold watch, your Thanksgiving turkey. Unemployment is right down the block. They'll give you the appropriate forms to fill out. And, oh yes, good luck and let us know how you're doing."

Well, Kate thought, bracing herself as the plane came in low over the Pacific and made its final bank into Los Angeles, that isn't the way it's going to be. I won't let it.

She had become attached to fame, to the job, to the million a year. She thought of the people out there who wanted to see her confident smile fade, to be able to say, "I told you so." Well, she was damned if she'd give them the satisfaction. Which was why she'd agreed to leave New York, to try what might be Bobby Klaus's ultimate ploy.

Besides, it would give her more time to work out how she felt about Nick.

The Beverly Hills Hotel brought back memories of her childhood, of having done laps in the pool while men and women in white sipped drinks and watched, amazed that someone had actually gone into the water. Smitty was still operating the parking concession, still, it was whispered, the richest man in Southern California. They assigned her a bungalow, away off through the jungled gardens, a cool and pleasant little house that delighted her. She wondered if it were Howard Hughes's old bungalow or the one where Gable screwed Lombard or where . . .

Her interview on the first show was with the Governor of California. She found him evasive, obnoxious, vain. It showed. Her questions became more incisive, she put the script aside and drove right at him, fending off his arch circumlocutions, his pedantic syllogisms.

After the show the producer called from New York.

"Kate, if that's a sample of what we're going to get out of you from L.A., it's going to work. It was good. It was very good."

She was pleased. Despite her realization that the producer, like Bobby Klaus, like herself, wanted desperately for the show to succeed and could not be the most objective of critics. The next morning the Los Angeles *Times* gushed. But she knew how chauvinistic the paper was, how it campaigned to make Los Angeles the television capital of the country, how it despised, and envied, New York. Still, the first show was not bad. But how often could they have Jerry Brown as the guest?

Blanchflower phoned.

"Sinclair, just stay away from the goddamn San Andreas Fault," he boomed, "I can't afford to lose any constituents."

"Oh, you," she said. How good he sounded. Her doubts faded.

"And just keep trashing Jerry. Another interview like that and they'll be drawing up petitions to bring back Reagan."

"You watched."

"Of course I watched. I'd watch the Abominable Snowman if it was you up there with him."

Mary wrote.

"If you want me to come out, Missus, just say so. There's a seamen's strike in San Diego and I could go down there on my day off and picket."

Shaun did not write.

Harvey phoned.

"Never, I emphasize, *never*, spend the weekends in Beverly Hills. Borrow a place in Palm Springs. Rent a beach house in the Malibu Colony. But, I implore you, Kate, do not be seen in Beverly Hills during a weekend. It's the pits."

Other than that he had little constructive to offer except that he missed her, that New York was in mourning over her absence, that his new book was dancing, simply dancing out of the typewriter, and that he'd come across the most darling boy just outside P.J. Clarke's the night before.

Kate found she did not miss Harvey, did not need Mary, and had come to reluctant acceptance of Shaun's disinterest. But Blanchflower was another matter entirely. Especially at night as she lay alone in the bungalow, listening to the air-conditioner and occasionally, over it, voices on the garden paths, laughing, murmuring, intimate. More than once she got up and took a pill, not wanting to, but knowing she must sleep. She wanted him there, in bed, and he was three thousand miles away. A single, funny phone call from him and she was hooked all over again. How vulnerable she was. She knew her emotions were running rampant and didn't care.

It being Hollywood and Kate celebrated, they gave parties for her. At first they were pleasant gatherings of old friends, reasons for getting out of the hotel at night, a balm for loneliness. The houses were lovely, deeply shadowed in late afternoon by towering trees such as you see in Rome shading two-thousand-year-old pools, or perched precariously on magnificent cliffs over canyons or hung over the Pacific at Malibu or Laguna where, over the surf, you could hear the seals barking as they came up through the dark-green seaweed hunting for albacore. But those were the first parties with her friends and acquaintances. Later, there were other parties.

Because of the time differential she was broadcasting in mid-afternoon which was already evening in the East and the show, both her segment from the Coast and Chester's from the East, and the regional feeds from Washington and Europe and

Houston, taped, were shown later in Los Angeles. Sometimes she would sit propped up in bed in the hotel smoking cigarettes and having the one drink and watch herself, feeling terribly distant, as if this woman were not she but some smooth and, she would admit, rather clever stranger. Chester, on the other hand, always looked like Chester. He, at least, was authentic. Sometimes she would be at a cocktail or an early dinner in someone's home and the news would be switched on and her host or hostess would assume she would want to see herself on the screen and so, for thirty minutes, the party would languish or the dinner be delayed while Kate, uneasily, smiled at herself and tried to respond to the tinkling, flattering voices around her.

In the mornings she rose early, called New York over the half-grapefruit and the black coffee and the Los Angeles *Times*, which seemed to consist mostly of dozens of sections of classified advertising. When the pool opened at ten she would be there and Sven would arrange a chaise toward the low sun, already hot unless there were smog, and she would drop her long terry cloth robe and dive into the pool at the deep end and do twenty or thirty laps. She wore a maillot, not liking the look of her pale middle in a bikini. The swimming was good, hell on her hair of course and every day at the studio the hairdresser would speak to her about it, sternly, but with the sun and the swimming she felt, physically, quite wonderful. After the first two weeks when she saw herself in the full-length mirrors of the bath she thought she looked slimmer, firmer, younger. Well, she thought, at least there's that to be said for the goddamned place.

She knew she should really get out of the hotel, lease a house somewhere up on the right side of Sunset, a place with a pool and maybe a tennis court, but she could not muster the energy. Again, whether it was Bobby Klaus or the producer or her agent in New York that she spoke with, the fate of this coast-to-coast format still seemed uncertain and she hesitated putting down roots. The hotel palled but it was comfortable and convenient and she liked the big pool and brunch in the garden and that last, late-night drink in the Polo Lounge where tipsy actors and studio executives argued business and the hookers, inevitably more respectable-looking than most of the other women in the place, fiddled with their drinks and played eyes across the small, dark room and caromed glances off the mirrors to try to catch one of the men watching, expectantly.

There was a good trial on in Los Angeles, another "Polanski" case, and there were cocaine arrests in the papers every day and people she met died of overdoses or woke up, damaged, in some intensive care unit or other. Yet none of this seemed to have any impact at all on the parties she attended, the frenzied lifestyle so many of those around her affected to relieve the boredom of the town and their existence.

"Hollywood is different from New York. Just different," a producer told her over lunch.

"But how?" she insisted.

The man struggled for the perfect, one-line explanation.

"Look," he said, "you know, in New York you do business over lunch. You have some wine, you have a couple of martinis. You make a deal. You shake hands and in the afternoon your secretary types it. Here, here it isn't like that."

"No?"

The producer looked around cautiously.

"Do you know out here nobody even *initials* a deal in the afternoon? It's just assumed that by lunchtime we're all stoned on coke."

While Kate digested that information the producer called for another round of drinks and handed her a tiny square of paper, smaller than a postage stamp.

"Just chew that and swallow it," he said. "Sensational."

Kate looked at the paper.

"What is it?"

"Tissue paper," he said, "impregnated with acid. Give you a terrific spectrum of colors for the next twelve hours."

She declined. With thanks.

One night in an incredibly lovely villa high up in the canyons over Westwood, the home of one of the four directors whose name alone meant certain backing for a major film production, Kate attended a buffet. It was a soft night, following a rare early evening rain, and the director, bright and articulate, a transplanted Easterner, had constructed the evening around Kate.

216

"After all," he said, rather self-consciously, "you're our new face, our divertissement. We owe you so much for simply having come here to this arid wasteland, why shouldn't the evening be yours?"

"And besides," said the dress designer who was her "date" that evening, "she brought rain."

Since the director was so powerful a figure, since Kate was the visiting attraction, the house was filled with famous names, familiar faces. Even the dress designer was impressed.

"Not your routine assembly of the great," he said, eyes bulging.

The dress designer was nice, harmless, a homosexual. The same sort of man she'd wasted so much time with in New York, before Blanchflower. Now he was three thousand miles away and once again she was in this velvet rut all over again, a woman without a man. This time, by choice.

There were men around. A glance, a word, a gesture and they knew the dress designer for what he was. The director, a subtle man, had invited several men who might be . . . attractive to Kate. Kate understood.

She was drinking tequila. Dinner was over. Other guests had been asked to come late. The dress designer had disappeared. The talk was of drugs, the smell was marijuana, smoked openly. "I hear all the big tobacco companies have their production lines all set up, once it's legalized," a woman assured her. A man said, "The damn commercials are already on film." Around her people sniffed cocaine. It was offered to Kate. She shook her head. The tequila was enough. Too much. The man with her was quite beautiful. An Olympic champion turned actor. "He's dreadful, of course," the host said, *sotto voce*, "but my God, the body." The young man talked. Kate hardly listened. It was not important. Across the room another man stared at her. He saw that she noticed and he licked his lips. She looked away. Now there was music. Earlier it had been soft, a background to the talk and the sound of ice against glass. Now it was loud. The house had one of those intricate sound systems. Acid rock pulsed everywhere.

"What?" Kate said. She could no longer hear the young man she was not listening to. The house filled up. Kate felt dizzy from the drinking. Dammit, she thought, now don't go all

217

weak-headed and get pissed or something. If only she could handle it the way Blanchflower did, if only the Irish half of her would become dominant.

Over the music someone was arguing the advantages of a Rolls Royce and Kate thought, quite drunkenly, what a shame it was she had not bought a Rolls. Or at least a Bentley, remembering giddily an old *New Yorker* magazine ad about buying the Bentley if you felt "diffident" about a Rolls. What was the point of putting up with all this bullshit from Chester, from Bobby Klaus, from the network, what was the point of working this hard if you couldn't have a Rolls? She turned to ask the young athlete if he didn't think she should buy a Rolls when she noticed he was gone. Across the room, in the haze of smoke, she saw a girl with long blonde hair kneeling on all fours on the floor, swaying slowly so that her hair, heavy and very long, swung back and forth, back and forth.

"What an extraordinary thing," Kate thought. No one else seemed to pay attention to the girl.

Some of the guests were outside, in the cool California evening, watching the distant brush fires on the ridgelines and debating whether to swim. Several people were in the pool already. Women. They'd just stripped and gone in. Kate, a fresh tequila in her hand, felt momentarily superior. Well, she could swim better than any of them. No matter how young they were. Where did the drinks keep coming from? They manifest themselves, miraculously, right here in my hand, she said, answering her own question.

Another man said hello to her. She couldn't hear but she saw the movement of the lips. It was the man who had stared. And wet his lips. Well, so what? She mouthed hello back.

He signaled and a waiter came. Another tequila. She wished Blanchflower were there. Perhaps she could call him. He could catch a late flight and . . .

"Look," the man said. The young girl on the floor continued to sway, her hair swinging. She seemed to be crooning with the music. Kate looked at her face. She was a child, a child, but lovely. No, not lovely, beautiful. The music broke. Briefly.

"Who is she?" Kate asked.

Someone said, perhaps it was the man who'd stared, "Her mother brought her. They're German. Swiss. Austrian, maybe.

The mother was promised a role of some sort in so-and-so's next film. She brings the girl to parties. The girl performs. It's all very amusing. The girl is fifteen."

Kate looked at the girl. Fifteen. Younger than Shaun. And with that face, the long, heavy hair, swinging back and forth. And the body. You got most of it through the black velvet. People looked at her and then looked away. No one seemed terribly interested.

"Which one is the mother?" Kate asked.

Another man, one she had not seen before, said, "There, that one."

The mother was blonde, too, and handsome. About Kate's age. She was smoking a joint and talking, animatedly, with the host and several other people. The host was nodding, smiling, but he was not looking at the woman. He was looking beyond her to where the girl knelt, swaying. At least he was paying attention, Kate thought.

She had another tequila. Two men were with her now. They were all laughing. Kate was laughing. Why had she thought Hollywood dull, superficial, vacuous? It was all quite fun. What nice people these were.

The dress designer returned.

"Kate, can you forgive me? An awful lapse of manners. But this friend I hadn't seen for so long . . ."

Another man, not the one who stared, was standing with her now. A woman joined them.

"I'm Marta," she said. She seemed very nice. Kate drank her tequila. On the hillsides the fires were springing up again. Apparently the rain had not been sufficient.

"The trouble is," a fat man in a white caftan was saying, "is that if it rains there are mudslides and your house falls off the hill. If it doesn't rain there are brush fires and your house burns up."

"If there's a fire," Marta told Kate, "throw everything into the pool. Silverware, oil paintings, furs. They can always be dried out. Nothing burns in the pools."

Marta went away. Kate asked the fat man who she was.

"I don't know," he said.

"Oh," Kate said, "I thought she might be an actress. She's lovely."

The fat man nodded. "I'll find out," he said.

The young blonde had gotten up from the floor. Her body looked even better now that she was on her feet. Two men were with her, talking. She smiled but her eyes were empty, flat.

The fat man came back.

"Marta used to be in films. A stunt woman. Now she runs a house in Brentwood. Very classy."

The fifteen-year-old blonde was taken upstairs now. By two men.

Her mother smiled. Kate stared at her and the woman, thinking she knew Kate, smiled again.

Another tequila. Should she swim? Or would it be in the Los Angeles *Times* that she had taken off her clothes at a party? Better not.

The man who stared was whispering to her. She could not hear him.

"Let's go somewhere," he repeated, shouting.

She shook her head. There was a tequila in her hand. She was uncertain if it were another or the same. The two men who had taken the girl upstairs came down. Two more men went up. With them was Marta.

The German woman was explaining about inflation in Düsseldorf. It sounded shocking.

"What do you think of Los Angeles?" someone asked Kate.

She did not know what to say. Beyond her, in the pool, swimmers splashed. On the ridges the brush fires spread slowly in the still night. And other men and women went upstairs to the fifteen-year-old German girl, while her mother told about inflation in Düsseldorf and how she hoped for a role in a movie, a movie that for all she knew might never be made.

Kate was driven back to the hotel in a Rolls Royce. She was not sure whose it was. She was not even sure it was a Rolls It might have been a Bentley.

27

The ratings went up again. In California Kate interviewed movie stars and Cher Bono and religious crackpots and Sam Yorty and the biggest used car salesman in the world and someone who had just dined at San Clemente and Cesar Chavez and Patty Hearst. In Washington Chester told his drinking companions at Duke Ziebert's and the National Press Club that he felt like a newsman again. But when people asked him about Kate he shrugged and tried not to call her "bitch" or any of his other endearments. Chester had left Frances behind in New York. It was a relief not to have to perform with her every night.

In New York and in Washington Nick Blanchflower fell back into his usual routine, hard work by day, different girls at night. He enjoyed not being with Kate for a time, not having to live with memories of the shark. The girls were all young and anxious to do extraordinary things and although in the end they bored him, and he found himself missing her conversation and her intelligence, Blanchflower concluded that being apart like this, as long as it was temporary, was not entirely a bad thing.

At the network, Bobby Klaus was ecstatic. He phoned Harry Flagg in Kansas.

"Well," Flagg said, "it's what you told me a long time ago, Bobby. Give them what they want to hear, not what they ought to know."

"Right, Harry. And right again."

"But what we have to determine, Bobby," Flagg cautioned, "is whether this is a temporary phenomenon deriving from novelty, you know, Kate on the Coast and Chester in Washington. Or should we shift them around again?"

"Oh, Jesus," Bobby said, "I thought we found the formula."

Flagg said he would do another study.

"You think you have to, huh?"

"I think it's essential, Bobby."

Bobby Klaus groaned.

Kate awoke with the sun coming in through the blinds. She lay in the oversized bed in the bungalow and listened to the sounds outside. She was hung over.

"I'm drinking too much," she told herself.

She got out of bed and saw she was naked. She could not remember having gone to bed. Realizing this frightened her. She had been away from New York for three weeks, away from Blanchflower, she had not slept with a man in that time. She had stopped going to movie colony parties after that business with the young German girl. Now she dined with friends or with people from the network and returned early to the bungalow and turned on television, usually an old movie, and made herself a drink. Several drinks. There were calls from Blanchflower and for a few hours she would feel herself again. But only for a few hours. There were invitations, plenty of them, but she said no unless she knew the people, really knew them. Men called her, men called all the time. But she said no.

She went into the bathroom and looked at herself in the full-length mirror. How many mornings had it been now since she last swam, since she did her calisthenics? Was there a bit extra around her belly, had her breasts dropped, even a fraction, how bad did her eyes look?

Kate stood under the shower. Tomorrow morning, she promised herself, tomorrow morning she would swim. And tonight, well, tonight she would not drink, maybe some wine, and she would take a pill and sleep, really sleep. She thought of Blanchflower then, and felt better. But almost immediately she thought of Haller, and she felt worse. Jesus, Kate Sinclair told herself, if this keeps up I'll be cruising the joints along the Strip picking up guys.

When she was in her robe and felt reasonably better, they delivered the letter with breakfast.

It had a New York postmark and was written in a girlish scrawl.

"Dear Ms. Sinclair," it began, "you may be interested in

222

knowing what Senator Nicholas Blanchflower has been doing to amuse himself while you've been away."

Details followed. Considerable details.

"Shit," Kate said. Of course there was no name at the bottom of the letter. She had not expected any. Nor, to tell the truth, had she expected that Nick would be faithful. She knew the kind of man he was, he'd always been outspoken about his faults, his appetites, his drives. But still, to have it spelled out here, and in such precise detail. Names, addresses, dates. She figured back. Yes, the dates coincided with dates she knew he was in New York, dates on which she'd called him or he'd called her. There were one or two anatomical details about Blanchflower's body, about certain of his sexual preferences. This girl had slept with him herself! Kate realized, amazed. He must have dropped her. He must have slept with her once and then kissed her off and this was the girl's revenge.

Kate had no way of knowing that the girl who wrote the letter and who had, indeed, slept with Nick Blanchflower, was Bunny Venables.

That night, after the show, Kate accepted a dinner invitation from the young anchorman at the network's local station, a man she'd turned down several times before, a young man with razor-cut hair and a perpetual suntan and nice shoulders and straight teeth and perfectly dreadful taste in clothes. At eleven that night she was in his house on Hollywood Boulevard, in his bed, his dreadful clothes strewn about on the floor, her fingers playing with his razor-cut hair, his straight teeth nibbling at her nipples.

In the morning, back at the bungalow, she felt disgusted with herself. But she had slept. Oh, how she had slept.

After that, there were other men. And in the mornings she swam and lay in the sun and did her exercises and felt her body firm again. She was still drinking and the nights were a rather pleasant haze. But the hangovers were less lethal, her eyes clearer, her head no longer ached.

For the first time in many years, for the first time since she had met Tommy Sinclair, and worried about her lack of breasts and squirmed in the night thinking about his spare, disciplined body, Kate Sinclair had become body rather than mind. She stopped worrying about the ratings, gave Bobby

223

Klaus no thought, rarely considered Chester Albany, and for Blanchflower there was only regret he was not here to share this wonderful new awareness of self, this lotus land of sense, these beaches, these poolside lawns, these beds.

Nothing of her new life found its way into the trades. At the local station where she did her network feeds she became circumspect, the poor anchorman with his razor-cut hair a reject. The job was easy, a few hours every day, the work finished by late afternoon. Interviewing was, for Kate, the simplest of tasks. She did her homework, reading the books and the newspapers and the politicians' position papers during the morning as she lay by the pool. As for her lovers, they had nothing to do with her professional life. Every week a check for twenty thousand dollars, minus deductions, was drawn. But her money manager at Marine Midland took care of it, paid her bills, made her investments. Money became unimportant. The work became unimportant, though, almost by reflex, she did it well. She gave value. But she did not agonize over it. There was no longer the great ambition, the drive, the focus. She drifted, drifted pleasantly.

She interviewed Werner Erhard. Erhard's Est movement had launched a new campaign, to end hunger in the world. Erhard was handsome, young, smooth.

"To eradicate hunger we must realize it can be eradicated, that hunger is not inevitable."

"So you want people to send money?"

"Yes."

"And what will you do with the money?"

"Push ahead with the elimination of hunger in the world."

"But how? Is the money to be spent for canned goods or to buy fish lines and seed or what?"

"To eliminate world hunger." Erhard smiled.

Kate stared at him, then looked into the camera.

"Somehow," she said, "I fail to be convinced."

It was a good interview, an effective skewering of an evasive subject, but it did not give her pleasure. Kate had lost her anchor. Work was routine. After work, she drifted. And she made love.

There were beachboys and UCLA students and men she met in bars or in the Polo Lounge. There was a football player from the Rams and a nightclub comedian, a landscape gardener and a bartender. There was even a young man who claimed to be writing a great novel and did not, literally did not, know who she was. There was one nightmare, an evening that began in Santa Monica, at the Oar House, barrels of peanuts on the sawdust floor and pretty girls in ragged cutoff jeans. She drank beer with them, too much beer, and someone had a car, a house on the beach, and at midnight she found herself naked, on a narrow cot, finishing with one boy, and sensing rather than seeing another boy behind him, unbuckling a belt and unzipping jeans and then another boy, and another. The faces became one face. The bodies one body. The penises, thrust into her in various places, one penis. Then a girl came, stoned, and after the girl the boys for a second time. "Haller," she cried out once, or at least she thought she cried out, but no one answered. Perhaps they thought Haller was some antique lover one of them had reminded her of in her frenzy. The stoned girl came to her again. Perhaps there was a second girl, she could not be sure, and then the boys again.

Fortunately, it was a Friday night, and by Monday she was again ready for work.

It was a confused, muddled, perverse slice of life for Kate Sinclair. She had never been profligate. Her night with Haller echoed obscenely in her consciousness. Yet even more obscene postures in this unforgiving California sunshine left her restless, but guiltless. Something had been touched in Kate. Something she did not entirely understand.

On the set in Los Angeles they commented about how well she looked, how relaxed she was, how easy to work with. The local anchorman ran a tanned hand through his razor-cut hair and hinted that, if he chose, he might reveal a great deal about the blooming of Kate Sinclair. In Washington even Chester, out from under the disciplines of New York and the presence of his anchor partner, found himself admitting, silently, of course, as he watched her feed from California, that Kate Sinclair was a hell of a good-looking woman.

But the night in Santa Monica had shaken Kate. It was not that what she had done and had done to her was so terrible. The frightening part was, she had liked it. After work she had rented a car and set out for Laguna Beach, driving across the great stretches of the Irvine Ranch, the road winding through the low coastal hills. She drove fast, her hair blown back. She wore a scarf and glasses and when she was hungry she stopped at a roadside place, ate shrimp cocktail and rare steak.

It was safe and it killed the evening. She began to make a habit out of sometimes going north toward Malibu and Trancas, sometimes south to Newport Beach or Laguna. At dinner at a beach hangout she drank two cocktails or one bottle, only one, of California wine, and smiled away the invitations of men to join them. Then, still alone, she would drive home again to her bungalow at the Beverly Hills, to an empty bed, but tired and able to sleep.

One weekend she had driven farther than ever before, a hundred miles east of Los Angeles, out into the ranch country bordering the Mojave. There was only one place to eat in a scatter of a town. She sat down, alone. The bar was full, the Friday night crowd, cowboys and boys from the farms and the gas stations, girls in pretty dresses and jeans. One or two of the boys asked her to have a drink but she smiled and said no.

In front of the jukebox a cowboy danced alone. He was very drunk. He danced very slowly, feeding the jukebox, always playing the same song, over and over. It was the Beatles' "Hey Jude." Kate watched him, they all watched. No one made fun. The boy was tall and lean in Levis and cowboy boots and a flannel shirt and there was a silly, wonderful look on his face. His lank blond hair, shaggy under the Stetson, swung back and forth as he danced, back and forth. But it was nothing like the young German girl, nothing at all. No one said anything to him, no one asked him to stop, no one tried to play another song. He was a young hand from one of the ranches. He taught skiing in the winter and he was married to a young Mexican girl. He was a Mormon and this was the first time he had ever been drunk. His wife had had their first child that afternoon, a son, and he was celebrating his son, celebrating his wife, celebrating himself.

Kate had checked into a motel but after dinner she went back, repacked her overnight bag, and got back in the car. She sat there in the motel's parking lot, the motor off, the car dark. Above her was the great western sky. Off in the distance she thought she could see the glow of Los Angeles against the sky.

Perhaps it was just the moon shining off the mountains. Then she turned the key and drove slowly out of the lot and onto the highway. Usually she drove with the radio turned on high so she could hear it above the motor and the wind, but now she drove without the radio, hearing instead the shuffle of the cowboy's feet, the strains of "Hey Jude," and remembered how silly he looked. How silly, but how happy. She remembered her own son, not the loss of him but the wonder.

It was nearly dawn when she pulled into the driveway of the Beverly Hills Hotel. The boy took her car and she strode through the lobby and out into the garden to her bungalow. She slept without another drink, without a pill. Without a man.

28

Bunny Venables' anonymous letter, written at her husband's urging, had been only partly true. There were legitimate reasons for Nick Blanchflower to stay in the East, to prevent his flying to Los Angeles weekends to be with Kate. Blanchflower's campaign manager was worried. He worried easily and when he did he would shake his head from side to side and his wattles would sway. His name was Robin and he was very intelligent and a professional and he weighed three hundred pounds. He smoked foot-long cigars and worried mainly about two things: that he might one day be ordered by the doctors to stop smoking cigars; and that one of his candidates might lose. It was not likely Blanchflower was going to lose. The campaign was going well. Blanchflower was a Democrat in a Democratic state and his opponent was a gentle old party to the right of the Pleistocene age.

"Nick, the dicing and gaming I can take. The wenching is going to kill me."

Blanchflower laughed. "No, it won't, Rob, if it kills anyone it'll be me."

"A little more circumspect, Nick, could you try circumspect?"

There had not even been a primary fight in the spring and now it was no longer a question of whether Blanchflower would win, but by what margin. The *Post* and the *News* had both endorsed him early and now the *Times*, ponderous as a glacier, was about to do so. Blanchflower was expected to win big. He expected to win big. To be any sort of factor in the Presidential year after next, he had to carry the state by a million votes. Any more would be largesse, any less a defeat for ambition. No one had yet foreclosed the Presidential nomination and a man who came out of New York with a million-vote majority and the state machinery oiled would be a live possibility on the floor of the convention itself.

But Robin continued to fret.

"Nick, the girls. The campaign workers. All these volunteers. Can't you keep your hands off them, at least?"

"I've got to retain their support."

"Nick, you must be screwing half of them."

"A third, Robin, no more than a third."

The girls came round and Blanchflower could not say no. One school of thought held that he really did not want to become President, that subconsciously he feared the responsibility and his reckless behavior was his way of insuring that he would lose. The other theory, less subtle, insisted he suffered from satyriasis.

"It doesn't sit well with the electorate, Nick. The clergy doesn't like it, the old folks."

On this, Blanchflower knew better.

"The women love the whole idea and most of the men think I'm a hell of a guy and don't they wish they could do it too."

Nicholas Blanchflower sometimes considered how fine it would have been to be a senator, not now in the fag end of the twentieth century but two thousand years earlier. How splendid to wear a toga and strike poses, to hear one's words echoing off Roman marble. To hang around with Cassius and Pompey, with Brutus and Marc Antony, to caucus with Casca and Crassus and Caesar himself, to be written about not by Scotty Reston or Evans and Novak but by Livy and Ovid and Horace.

He was thinking this when one of the volunteer workers came into the office where Robin and he were sitting.

"Senator," she said, "the new mailing's all finished. Is there anything else I can do tonight?"

Robin hated women. For personal reasons. And, for political reasons, he especially hated girls who looked like this. He knew the attractions they held for his client, the attraction and the danger.

Blanchflower looked at the girl. She was tall, with a calf-length suede skirt and good boots and a sweater that moved very nicely as she spoke in her pleasant, funny accent. Grinning at Robin, Blanchflower said he was sure there might be some other chore and why didn't she hang around for a few minutes more until he could get to it.

Robin's wattles shook and Blanchflower concluded, not for the first time, that even without Horace and Ovid, being a senator right now, in New York City, had its compensations.

The girl, the one who would "hang around," was Mrs. George Venables, gathering "local color" for the anonymous letter she would write to Kate Sinclair in Los Angeles.

At the White House they were concerned, although for different reasons than Robin's, about Nick Blanchflower. They knew his reelection campaign was going well. The million-vote majority seemed attainable. A big win in November would set Blanchflower up very nicely for the next Presidential year. The President was not terribly happy about the prospect. If he chose not to run himself in the campaign that would begin in less than eighteen months, the President wanted to be free to name his own successor, probably the Vice-President, a pleasant and malleable young man who made a splendid impression on voters and could, on most matters, be handled. The President knew that Blanchflower could not.

"He's a runaway train," he said in his soft southern drawl. "You got to throw the switch to shunt that boy off somewhere harmless. You can't just signal him to stop. That boy doesn't read signals."

The President's closest adviser, Lester, less pious both in his behavior and in his language, agreed.

"We got to de-ball that son of a bitch. De-ball a rogue bull like that and you got a nice, happy steer. We kin handle steers. And for sure, a steer can't fuck you."

Blanchflower, who characterized the President and his confidantes as "those shitkickers," was too street-wise not to be aware of just how dangerous White House opposition could be to a maverick politician. Gene McCarthy had destroyed Lyndon but in the process had lost the nomination. McGovern had gotten the nomination but had been slaughtered in the general election when a hostile White House launched its campaign of "dirty tricks."

The Israeli Prime Minister had come to Washington and the usual glittering assemblage of guests was whistled up includ-

230

ing Nick Blanchflower. You do not give dinner to an Israeli premier and not invite a senator from New York, even when he calls you "shitkicker." Robin was worried. Puffing away on the ritual cigar he warned his client: "Nick, just don't let them get you off in a corner. Those country boys can get a stone out of a peach without the skin knowing about it."

Blanchflower frowned.

"Who's writing your lines these days, Robin?"

Robin shook his wattles.

"Just you be careful down there," he said. "Just be careful."

Changing into his dinner jacket at the Georgetown apartment, Blanchflower switched on the news. There was Chester in Washington, talking about the Israeli mission and about that night's White House dinner, then there was a European feed, then back to the New York anchor, and finally, Los Angeles and Kate Sinclair. Blanchflower had been listening from the bathroom and now, half-dressed, he went into the living room and flopped into a chair. Kate looked wonderful, very tan, relaxed and smiling. The interview was nothing, trivial. But she handled it smoothly.

"Good girl," Blanchflower said aloud, "good girl."

He sat there for a while after the news had ended, not listening or even watching the commercials and the game show that followed. He was not a man to ponder the what-might-have-beens of life. There was no formal commitment to Kate, none at all, neither asked nor given. Yet, watching her three thousand miles away, doing her job competently and with grace, knowing the pressures she was under, he realized that he missed her very much. And he thought of how often, and with what offhanded pleasure, he had betrayed her during these weeks of separation.

The President preferred small tables for his White House dinners. Tonight there were a dozen of ten each. Blanchflower sat between the wife of the Israeli Ambassador to the UN and a department store owner's wife. It was exceedingly dull. Only an aging czarist nobleman, imported for the occasion as an exotic in the absence of any of the red Russians, relieved the boredom with anecdotes of cavalry duty in 1917. Blanchflower decided to follow Robin's advice, to avoid any cozy little chats with the President's men, but now, as the dinner ran down, he was relieved when a military aide tapped his shoulder.

"Senator, would you accompany me, please."

Blanchflower pushed back his chair and followed the young man into one of the main floor anterooms.

"If you'd please wait for a moment, sir?"

"Yes," Blanchflower said.

He looked around. It was strange. He did not know the name of this room. The chair was comfortable, the portraits on the wall predictable, yet he felt restless, an alien in a stranger's house. Perhaps, he concluded, it was because he hoped one day to make this house his. And the man who now lived there did not fancy the notion. A door opened. Blanchflower stood.

"Mr. President."

"Hello, Nick, nice of you to come by."

The two men shook hands and sat, the President at ease waving Blanchflower to a chair. Nick was much taller, broader, younger, the future before him, but in this room, in this house, the smaller man dominated. Blanchflower understood this and was not diminished by it. He understood how the system worked. There was some small talk about the coming campaign, about Blanchflower's expectations. He was cagey, giving little.

"You'll do very well, I expect, Nick," the President said.

"I hope to."

"You could go into the Presidential year looking good. Very good."

"That's too far ahead even to think about, Mr. President."

"I don't believe that for a minute, Nick. A man starts thinking about the Presidency the first time he wins an alderman's race."

Blanchflower fenced carefully. Then, realizing this, the President cut his losses and got up.

"And how's my favorite television star, Kate Sinclair?" he asked.

"She's fine. Just fine. Out in California for a month or so."

"A good woman," the President said. "Strong woman, too. They *can* be strong, you know, women. Stronger than we are sometimes."

232

"Yes," Blanchflower said, wondering where this was leading.

"Be careful with the women, Nick," the President said.

"I always am, Mr. President."

Jesus Christ, Blanchflower thought, driving away from the White House, what the hell was that all about? An unsubtle hint of scandal over his womanizing? Something nasty about Kate? His nagging, intermittent problems with the feminists? Damn him, Nick thought, damn all southern politicians and their mushmouthed, cornball ways that masked such sly menace. He knew damn well the President was telling him something, that finding himself unable to get Blanchflower to discuss the Presidential year, he'd slipped in that smarmy little preachment about women for a reason. Except that Nick Blanchflower could not fathom the reason.

He was too restless even to call a girl that night and he went to bed early and flew back to New York the next morning on the first shuttle. At that same hour the President was breakfasting with several of his aides. Over the grits he told them that Blanchflower had stonewalled on his plans but that he had seemed bothered by something else the President had said.

"Right there at the end, I said something polite about his girlfriend, Kate Sinclair, and he like to have spit."

"Oh?" said Lester, the fat Georgia boy with galluses and the steel trap memory, "you think maybe brother Blanchflower has a little weakness we don't know about?"

The President shook his head.

"He makes no secret of anything. It's part of what makes him dangerous. He doesn't really care about what people think of his girls or Kate Sinclair or anything. No, there's something else about women that shook him. And I'll be darned if I know what it was."

Lester smiled.

"I'll ask around," he said, and tucked into the rasher of bacon and the grits.

"Do that," the President said. "It'd be handy as all get out to have a little leverage on brother Nick."

By accident, militant feminism gave the President his leverage. Lester was in New York, not even on unofficial business.

He'd been shopping on Fifth Avenue for a gift for his wife and was walking west on 42nd Street when he was drawn by the crowd in Bryant Park. It was what Lester considered a pretty good gate, and being a politician, he hated to pass a crowd by, whatever brought them together. He strolled into the park.

A few cops stood around, looking bored. There was some chanting from inside the crowd, reedy and self-conscious. Lester pushed in, past women carrying signs demanding amendment of the Constitution to include the Equal Rights Amendment. There were a few men in the crowd and the usual bums, sleeping on the benches, their flies opened and stained with urine. People drifted in and out of the park, glancing curiously at the signs, then going on about their lunchtime errands. Only around the speakers' platform was there any real press of people. There it was mostly women except for a few men wearing press cards and a camera crew. On the platform were a dozen women. Several were black. One or two were rather good-looking women. There was a young girl in jeans and a camouflaged bush jacket holding a Viet Cong flag. Well, Lester thought, this all seems rather old-fashioned. The other women looked hard.

The speeches weren't much but the women in the audience whooped it up. They could have read the telephone directory up there and gotten a reaction. Gloria Steinem was the fourth or fifth speaker. She didn't say much but she said it well. The photographers and the television crew shot a lot of pictures while she spoke. She was the best looking thing they had. Toward the end she mentioned the television networks. "Is it really too much to ask," she said, "that the great television networks, all of them headquartered in this city, end their self-imposed silence and speak out on this great issue, the issue of freedom and equality for half the nation? I challenge the networks to stand up and support this most legitimate aspiration on the part of deprived women everywhere."

Somewhere, in the back of the crowd, a man's voice shouted, "Depraved, you mean!"

He was booed by the women and Steinem sat down to applause.

"Good looking stuff," a television cameraman said to another.

234

Lester stood watching for a few minutes and then began to edge his way through the crowd toward Sixth Avenue. A woman shoved a leaflet into his hand.

"Here! Join up. We need men supporting us!"

Lester pushed past her. He could hear the speaker who followed Steinem. The new speaker was taking a biological tack.

Mercifully, her voice faded as Lester left the park. Men were booing and women cheering behind him. It was not until he was in a cab heading north on Sixth Avenue that he scanned the leaflet, and saw there, under a list of "Enemies of Feminism," the name of Nicholas Blanchflower.

29

Kate came back to the hotel to another letter:

Dear Kate:

I'm quite all right and not dead or drugged or become a hooker. I am simply tired of living in your shadow and being Kate Sinclair's baby sister. I intend to make a name for myself. Possibly as a dancer. Popular, not classic. I'll be in New York and when I get established I'll let you know. I have some money. Don't worry.

Love,

SHAUN

Kate read the letter to Mary over the phone.

"She'll go broke," Mary said. "Beautiful she is and smart and healthy. A dancer? With *those* feet?"

That, at least, was a sensible reaction. Kate wished she could call Blanchflower in Washington. Instead, she had to settle for Harvey Podesta.

"She writes a nice letter," he said.

Kate exhaled in irritation.

"Harvey, you're an intelligent man. How do I go about tracking her down and getting her back? Never mind her writing style."

Harvey sobered. Momentarily.

"The police, of course. But then you run the risk of publicity, which I assume you don't want. A private detective. There are some good ones and I could get you the names. The personals column of the *Village Voice*. A sensitively worded appeal that would sound just the right note of love and desperation . . . "

"Harvey . . ." she said, warningly.

"Okay, Kate, I'm being flip. If both of us go all morose and red-eyed that isn't going to help Shaun or anyone. Now, what's this about dancing? Is she a dancer?"

"A volleyball player," Kate said, "She does all the crazy disco dances, of course, but I'd never call her a dancer."

"Okay, then, that eliminates the dancing schools. Or any sort of a job, I guess, except maybe in a topless bar." He sounded thoughtful and Kate bit her lip. Then he went on, "Maybe the discotheques. There are a million of them all over town. Money. How much would she have? How much cash?"

Kate said she had no idea. "She has a small bank account."

"Call the bank, explain things, and see how much has been withdrawn. That'll give you some notion of her staying power, if she has enough for just a couple of days she may be tapping at your chamber door looking for a mess of pottage any time now."

Despite everything, Kate said, "That is the most mixed metaphor I ever . . ."

"Don't split hairs," he said. "Now call the bank and I'll do my private eye number."

Kate phoned Bobby Klaus.

"Of course you've got to come back. Don't worry. I'll fix it."

For the first time in their association she told Bobby she loved him.

"I know, I know," he moaned, "and just when your California ratings were going good."

Kate caught the red eye out of Los Angeles that night after the show. She sat up all night, unable to sleep. Somewhere over the Mississippi valley a talky stewardess stopped by her seat.

"You sure do have a glamorous life, Miss Sinclair."

Kate nodded yes and went back to her book. At eight she was at JFK. Harvey met her.

"Any word?"

He shook his head.

"Listen," he said, "if Shaun's half as calculating as you she owns a disco by this time."

Three days later Harvey found her. In the pages of *Women's Wear Daily.*

There was a photo spread on one of the biggest of the new discos, Studio 54. The copy was all a-gush with social notes and bold-face names and fashion trends but among the photographs, anonymous but unmistakably recognizable, was Shaun, dancing madly, long hair flying. The caption said, "Among the younger dancers, cut-offs and T-shirts are still de rigueur."

Harvey phoned to read her the caption. "I always read *Women's Wear*," he said, "it's important for me to keep up with the trends. Now just call the editor or the publisher or whatever and ask what night the picture was shot, order a print, and then go over there tonight and hang around until she comes in. Take a detective with you. Then, when you find her, well . . ."

"You think she'll go there again?"

"Sure," he said, "those places are fads. If that's the big place to go then everyone'll go there for a month."

"I won't take a detective," Kate said.

"Oh?" Harvey said.

"No, *you're* going with me."

"Kate, you know I can't stand violence."

"I know," she said with determination, "but you'll blend into the scene so much better than a cop."

The dancing madness seemed to have taken hold, straight out of the Middle Ages. Or perhaps it was a dervish resurgence, a religious experience. Or a sexual rite, rife with overtones of Margaret Mead and sunbaked islands. A boy dashed by them on the street as they were going in. He was wearing a yellow track suit. "What time is it?" he asked, desperately, "please?" Ten after ten he was told. "My God, I'm late," he cried and ran toward the entrance. Inside Harvey pointed the boy out to a waiter and was told he came there every night at ten and danced until five, all alone. And when his money was spent he went to work somewhere, until he had earned enough to pass once more his evenings at the dance. He was sometimes late because he had pawned his watch to pay for the dancing. There were plenty like him, the waiter said.

"I'm not quite sure this is at all a healthy thing," Harvey said.

"No," came the solemn response, "it may not be."

Boys with hollow cheeks danced alone or with other boys with similar cheeks. It was not homosexual. It was not anything. Anything but the dance. They wore cut-off khakis and T-shirts, not chic but wet with sweat. They wore track shoes and white socks and they danced. There were multiple turntables and the records switched one to another, without a pause. Kate wondered if they ever urinated, if they ever rested. No one talked, the music was too loud, the dance too furious. They did not smile or flirt or rub one against the other. They simply danced.

There were girls, too, the same dead, sunken faces, the same hollow eyes. Drugged, perhaps, high on something surely. Most were tall and in a haggard way, beautiful. They danced alone, or with one another. Lesbians? There was no passion, no furtive stroke, no lowered gaze. Only the dance and the sweat and the bodies moving. Endlessly, it seemed.

"You think she'll be here?" Harvey shouted.

Kate shrugged. Useless to talk. Useless to guess.

The possessed danced. And continued to dance. The lights revolved, descended, rose, changed hue. A scrim went up. Behind it two beautiful people began to dance. Together. They seemed to be in love. Kate hoped they were a boy and a girl.

The music went on. Without pause.

Sweat, everywhere.

"My God, it's hot," Harvey said.

"Hot," she agreed.

"A sauna."

She nodded, unable to speak above the sound.

Then they saw Shaun.

"Well," the girl said, "I hope there's not going to be a scene."

She was very calm. Kate was calm too, surprising herself. The music crashed around them and the revolving spots flickered across Shaun's face. She looked fine, a bit thin, perhaps, her eyes dark as if from lack of sleep. She was wearing a dress. That, Kate thought, was strange.

"Where are you living?" Kate asked, restraining the one question she really wanted to ask, the "Why?"

"Quite close by," Shaun said. "A small hotel. Not fancy, but it's clean. And," she looked at her sister defiantly, "I'm not living *with* anyone if you're concerned."

"Oh, no," Kate said, trying to be casual. "I wasn't concerned."

"What?" Harvey said.

"I can't hear you," Kate said.

"What?"

"What do you think of my dress?" Shaun asked.

Kate shouted, "Shaun, I can't hear a word. Can't we go somewhere?"

The girl nodded.

"Sure," she said, "come on."

At the door she paused for a moment.

"You and Harvey don't have one of those deprogrammers out there ready to put the snatch on me and lock me up until I renounce Reverend Moon or something, do you?"

Harvey looked shocked.

"Shaun," he said, "your sister and I have demonstrated our good intentions by attending this curious place. Please do have some faith."

They went across the street to a coffee shop frequented by pimps and hookers.

"They have great glazed donuts," Shaun said. "Can we have some?"

The counterman brought the donuts and coffee.

"You like the dress?" Shaun asked again.

Kate looked at her.

"No," she said, "I like you in jeans. The way you've looked for fifteen years . . ."

"Sixteen."

". . . all right, then, sixteen. Anyway, you were born in jeans and it's just alien to see you in a dress. Why, is the dress significant?"

Shaun nodded.

"Sure, represents rejection of school, of childhood, of everything in the past and it's sort of like a change of life."

"Oh, dear," Harvey said.

Shaun made a face.

240

"Not that kind of change, Harvey, for God's sake. It's symbolic, sort of."

This wasn't getting them very far.

"Harvey," Kate said, "would you mind taking a walk around the block so I can talk with Shaun?"

"In this neighborhood?"

Harvey sat and ate another glazed donut.

"They *are* good," he told Shaun.

One of the pimps threw his velour hat down on the counter.

"Damn you, girl," he shouted, "you gonna be on Eighth Avenue the rest of your life less'n you learn some class. How you 'spect to work Lexington Avenue 'less you got class?"

Harvey nodded.

"He's right, you know, the East Side tends to be more critical when it comes to style."

"Shut up, Harvey," Kate said.

Then she saw that Shaun was staring at the girl and her irate protector.

"Lovers' quarrel," Kate said offhandedly.

"Oh?" said Shaun, "I was sure she was a whore and he was the pimp."

Kate said nothing but her eyes widened.

"What'd you say the name of your school was?" Harvey asked.

The pimp and his girl continued their debate while Harvey and Shaun ate donuts. Kate thought about California, a week and a continent away. This fencing was getting them nowhere. She might as well be in the bungalow at the Beverly Hills or down at the beach or listening to the cowboy playing "Hey Jude."

"Shaun," she said, "if you're going to drop out of school and pursue this dance business, why don't you stay at the apartment? There's plenty of room and I promise not to pester you while you work it out."

Shaun looked at her sister.

"But don't you see, that's what I'm getting *away* from. From school and home and like that. It wouldn't be the same thing if I moved in there. It'd just be moving from one dorm to another."

241

"Your sister's apartment is *hardly* a dorm," Harvey said.

"Shut up, Harvey," Kate told him.

"Yeah, but you know what I mean, Harvey," Shaun said. "Besides, I've got a room and it's paid for for a while and it's okay. I mean, not super, but okay."

This wasn't going well, not at all well. Kate tried to think coolly, objectively about the situation. Really, it was grotesque. Here was a sixteen-year-old child dictating terms in a cheap diner to her sister and a famous writer while pimps wrangled with whores and the counterman served up muddy coffee and donuts.

"But you simply can't, at your age, live alone in New York. I mean, you just *can't*," Kate said.

Shaun nodded and then said, quietly and not at all impertinent, "But I am."

In the end she agreed to show them the room. It was two blocks away just off Eighth. The desk clerk looked up from his Racing Form.

"Hi, kid," he said, "you're home early from the dance."

Shaun grinned and waved at him.

"That's Gus. He's nice. We have long talks late at night."

They got into the elevator and went upstairs. It was a typical West Side hotel with the usual smells and noises. The room looked clean enough, spartan, in fact. But it had the necessary furniture and Kate was surprised to see Shaun's clothes hung up or put away neatly in drawers. But it's so, so depressing, she thought. Everything but a neon sign blinking on and off outside the window.

"Isn't it terribly hot without air-conditioning?" she asked.

"Oh, it's not so bad. I don't usually get home till it's cooled off," the girl said. She turned to face them.

"Okay, so now you know where I live. Not great but okay. And I'm not into junk or living with anybody. So, listen, I'll phone you every week and let you know how it's going. Okay? And if I get in trouble, I mean, you know, well, I'll come over to the apartment. Okay?"

They went downstairs together and dropped Shaun back at the discotheque. Harvey seemed relieved they were not going to accompany her inside. Kate said the usual cautionary things and Shaun nodded obediently. Then she reached out and kissed her sister.

"I know I'm a pain in the ass and all," she said, "but I think it's really neat you bothered to try to find me. Smart, too. I bet most mothers in my class couldn't find their kids worth shit in the city."

She ran inside, waving back at them.

Harvey called a cab. He looked at Kate, slumped next to him in the back seat. She was crying.

"Kate," he said gently, "you did the right thing. She'll be back. Don't worry. She's just got to get this out of her system. Don't worry."

"I'm not worried," Kate said. "That's just the first time I can remember that she said anything that loving. About being smarter than most 'mothers.' About how 'neat' it was that I *bothered* looking for her. Did she think I *wouldn't?* Am I *that* far from her?"

Harvey shook his head.

"I'm sure you could be a *wonderful* sister, Kate. When you have time."

They drove across town in silence.

30

Frances Neale was very happy. She and Chester came off the big elevator and walked through the bar and the people waiting for tables and into the private room set aside for the network's guests. Windows on the World! A long way from being a London slavey, she thought with satisfaction. Chester was in a good mood. He looked wonderful, she thought, in a double-breasted suit.

"I hate this suit," he said, spoiling the moment. "You can't sit down in the damn thing without unbuttoning the jacket."

"Oh," Frances said.

Dillon took her by the hand.

"It's good to see you again, Florence," he said.

"Hi, Mr. Dillon," she said, "me too," not bothering to correct him about her name. She had the instincts of the streetwise and did not think it proper to correct the president of the broadcast division.

"Hey, Dillon," Chester said, "are the Drys running this show or do we get a drink?"

Dillon beamed, not really listening to what Chester said. Behind him was Bobby Klaus.

"You know Bobby," Chester said, grabbing at a waiter with a tray of drinks.

Frances said hello. Bobby took her hand. His palm was wet, she noticed.

There were perhaps sixty people in the room. The network executives and talent of course and advertising agency presidents and some of the big advertisers. There were some pretty girls who seemed to fit into no category except that of pretty girls. Frances understood why they were there. You always had pretty girls at a party like this. She had been to enough of

244

them in the pretty girl category both here and in London to understand.

The network was giving this little party ("Just a few of our closest friends," Dillon had told people) to talk about its plans for the upcoming season. Universal Broadcasting was now number one in most of the prime time categories. Tactfully omitted from mention was its continuing grasp on fourth place in evening news.

Frances noticed that whichever group Chester attached himself to, however the party flowed, it was carefully arranged that Chester and Kate Sinclair were always on opposite sides of the big room. She watched Kate, cautiously, so as not to be seen watching. Seeing her like this, up close, made her dislike Kate even more than on television. People clustered around Kate. They seemed genuinely interested in her and yet she held them at a distance as if distracted. No one clustered around Frances. Had she been alone, one of the pretty girls imported for the purpose, some of the ad agency people would surely have come up to her. But she was Chester's property and the men, smiling, or saying hello, did not come after her. They did after Kate. She liked being Chester's property, the implication being that he was also hers, but she would like to have had some of the attention showered on Kate Sinclair.

"I'll be right back," Chester said. He went off to talk with two men close to the window looking out on the night city. Frances had a glass in her hand. She watched the guests, then Dillon handshaking his way through the room. He was saying hello to a very beautiful woman, more beautiful even, and younger, than Kate Sinclair. With the young woman was a man with a crew cut, very fit looking, very strong, but abnormally short. Frances wondered who they were.

"That's Bobby Klaus," George Venables said to his wife, "that little nervous one with five o'clock shadow."

Bunny Venables nodded. She took mental notes as her husband whispered identifications. She did not have to be told who Kate was. She knew. Her husband had told her all about Kate. George Venables had been very clear what was in store for Kate Sinclair, the bitch! if he ever took over the news department. Bunny's poison pen letter was only for starters.

245

Kate saw Venables. How could she not? She remembered Colt Oursler and Houston. She wondered what had become of him. She was as careful to stay a room apart from Venables as Chester was so obviously doing with her. It was fascinating, she thought, we are all paid by the same network, and yet there's all this tension, this dislike. She recognized Bunny Venables from her pictures. My God, she thought, unable to help herself, what an extraordinary looking girl. She knew nothing of how Bunny was so helpful to George Venables in his work, of how eagerly Bunny "assisted" her husband in winning the affection, the gratitude, of strong young men on the New York Yankees or the Oakland Raiders or the New Orleans Jazz, or of Bunny's night with Nick Blanchflower and the subsequent letter.

It was past nine o'clock now and the party was running down. Kate had gone. Dillon was still gladhanding. Several of the pretty girls had disappeared with clients or with the agency people. A few of the guests were tipsy. Frances had stopped drinking when she saw how much Chester had had. Dillon wanted to get a party together to go uptown to the "21" Club. Chester was arguing they should go somewhere else. Frances noticed that George Venables was drinking mineral water. And that his wife was not a drinker. But that she stayed close to Dillon. Dillon did not seem displeased about this. He had an arm around Bunny's small waist and his hand lay lightly atop the swell of her buttock. Frances found it strange that George Venables did not seem to mind. Frances took another drink. What the hell, she thought, why should she be the only one to remain sober.

They went uptown, about a dozen of them in two separate limousines, going neither to "21" nor to Chester's place but to a discotheque. Someone said they should all go to Plato's Retreat later on and watch people screw. Frances thought that would be fun but they never did it. At some stage of the evening she learned that George Venables hated Kate Sinclair. She was not sure who told her. Or whether it was true. Or why he hated her. It was all drunk talk. Bunny Venables was kissing Dillon. They were on the balcony of the discotheque. A girl went by with her shirt open so that you could see her breasts. Venables was talking earnestly with the president of

246

an ad agency. He had his back to where Bunny Venables was with Dillon. Chester and Frances went home in a cab.

In the morning Frances was very hung over and the evening was a kaleidoscope of noise and blurred faces and limousine rides and drinks and smoke and handshaking. She remembered very little of what had been done, what had been said. She did remember seeing Bunny Venables and Dillon lying on a couch on the balcony. She remembered thinking she had never seen breasts as perfect as Bunny's. Oh, yes, she remembered one more thing. That George Venables hated Kate Sinclair.

Frances realized that if she were going to disturb Kate's glacial serenity, truly to damage Kate and to help Chester, she would have to be very clever. Venables had the look of a clever man. She wondered if she should just go to him and say, look, we both think Kate Sinclair's a bitch. Can't we do something about it? Frances decided to explore that promising course of action. Realizing she might have a powerful ally in her campaign, she jumped out of bed and went into the kitchen to drink a glass of milk. Her head felt much better now.

Kate Sinclair was not hung over in the morning and remembered everything. Not that the party was important to her the way it had been for Frances who was not as often on public display. But Kate retained, very clearly, an impression of George Venables. And she realized that despite her unarguable and great beauty, Bunny Venables had a vicious face. Other than that, and the almost laughable efforts of Chester Albany to avoid having to talk with her, the evening had been of no consequence. Unlike Frances Neale, Kate had a life beyond the network and the network people.

She felt an aching void where Blanchflower had been and wondered why she was being so stubborn about not contacting him, even when she was so desperate over Shaun. Anonymous letters were contemptible things. Why should she have been so influenced by it? Blanchflower had never pretended to celibacy, she had been three thousand miles away, there were always attractive women available to him. She should stop worrying about Nick's virtue and concentrate instead on how to handle Shaun. She must stop feeling guilty about the girl,

247

about her own limitations as a parent, and do something, dammit, do *anything* that would heal their breach and bring her home. She feared doing something that would drive the wedge between them any deeper. But doing nothing but wringing her hands was not the answer. In an unexpected way these concerns, and the fact she was trying with intelligence, with maturity to handle them, made her feel better about herself. And it was why superficial episodes like Mr. Dillon's party held no significance for her.

Setting down priorities helped restore her confidence, her sense of being able to cope. She would make peace with Nick, she would reconcile herself with Shaun. Having decided these matters, the call from Bobby Klaus was a jolt.

"Kate, I know how difficult this is. How much you want to be in New York. And I wouldn't ask unless . . ."

"Bobby," she asked wearily, "where?"

Cape Kennedy. Now once more Cape Canaveral, a brief and seemly homage having been paid the martyred President, the spit of sand and swamp and mangrove had resumed its old name. There was to be a shot, a major shot, nothing like it in years, not since the time of poor Von Braun and the moon voyages. All the networks would be covering, of course, the President was expected to attend, and they wanted Kate there to do the honors.

"Bobby," she said, exasperated, "I don't know anything about rockets. Send Chester. He loves that shit."

Bobby smiled.

"Oh, Chester's going too. You and he are going to have a reunion, suitably celebrated with the largest firecracker in history."

The ratings were vacillating again, out in Kansas Harry Flagg had consulted his deities, and a reconciliation was in the cards. Not in New York, not in the studio where love had fled, where the marriage had gone sour, but out in the field, covering a major story.

Kate Sinclair called on her sister in the hotel off Eighth Avenue.

"I got a job, a real job," Shaun enthused.

"Oh?"

"Waitress, in a disco. Not 54 or anything super like that, of course. But it pays. Good tips, really great."

"Shaun," her sister said, "you just turned sixteen. It must be illegal, or something. How did you . . .?"

Shaun grinned.

"Told them I was eighteen. They don't care anyway."

She was back in jeans, at least for the moment. Kate took a certain consolation in that.

They sat over lunch, Kate nervy.

"Shaun," she said, "I may have to go away for a week. The job. We . . ."

The girl patted her sister's hand.

"Sure, I know. The job."

In the end Kate suggested that Shaun go along. She painted vivid word pictures of Florida, of a really big rocket launch (she had never seen one but Bobby Klaus had briefed her thoroughly), of golden beaches and palm trees, of surf and famous people and (this was subtle) young men.

Shaun looked mystified. Her face fell into its serious cast.

"But I have a job too. They're counting on me."

That night Kate thought about their lunch. "The job." It had once again come between them. Her job. Now Shaun's job. A waitress. Word given, word kept. Well, it was admirable, she supposed. Then, defensively, so was *she* admirable, so was her word given, so would her word be kept.

Kate had a final dinner with Shaun ("Let's make it early, I start work at nine."), issued instructions, gave her various telephone numbers, offered her some money ("No, thanks, I've got some."), and told her four times that Mary Costello was at hand if she needed her. The next morning Kate flew to Melbourne, Florida with the crew. Chester got in that afternoon from Washington. He made his own way to the motel. Next morning Kate drove to the airport to meet the NASA plane carrying official Washington to the launch. Towering above the arriving celebrities was Nicholas Blanchflower.

31

"What are you doing here?" she demanded, forgetting in her surprise that she had decided to forgive him.

"You mad, Kate?" Blanchflower roared, "would a politician up for reelection miss a show like this? All that lovely television exposure you're going to give me? Why, I didn't even have to pay my way. NASA flew a whole planeload of us down from Washington." He paused. "And where the hell have you been? I phoned and you never called back."

The chaos surrounding his arrival gave Kate the opportunity to let the question slide.

Admiral Byrd's expeditions to the pole had been more modest. Blanchflower was in a white linen suit and Panama hat and Robin, the campaign manager, somehow stowed aboard, wore, despite the heat, a tweed suit. A small trunk emerged from the bowels of the plane.

"You never know in the tropics," Blanchflower said. "A man likes to be prepared."

Lighting a long cigar with Kate hanging on to his arm, Blanchflower stopped at the souvenir stand in the airport arrivals building. They were peddling Chamber of Commerce material and rocket souvenirs. Blanchflower bought a garish pennant and handed it to Robin.

"Look," Blanchflower whispered hoarsely to the woman behind the counter, "there were some Russians on that plane that just came in. I wouldn't sell them any of this stuff. Classified, you know."

The woman, sobered, nodded. Behind Blanchflower two other senators and a governor came up with their wives. One of the senators asked for a guidebook to the Cape.

"No, no," the woman behind the counter told him, "they're not for sale. We're closed."

Blanchflower grinned.

Kate had a car. "You can get one at the motel," she said, "but I'll drive you there. There's a bottle in my room and I already know where you can drink and where to wear a money-belt. There's a party tonight, I'll see that you're invited, and another tomorrow the contractors are throwing. Better company tonight, more booze tomorrow. You'll probably want to make them both."

Blanchflower stared at her.

"Did I ever tell you what a goddamned admirable woman you are?"

While the other Washington types were still arguing with the wary saleswoman and pulling out credentials, they went out into the midday heat. Blanchflower hesitated for a moment. Fifty yards away, behind a sawhorse, watched casually by a local cop with a Stetson and a pearl-handled six-shooter, were a half-dozen women with picket signs. He tried to read the signs but could not and then someone came out with their luggage, including the trunk, and they were being helped into Kate's car.

They had been billeted in the same sprawling motel. Kate had a room on the ocean but Blanchflower's looked out over the swimming pool. Robin was someplace in one of the wings. Blanchflower unpacked to the smack of bodies into the pool. There was a bottle of Johnny Walker Black in his room. Kate had sent it. An admirable woman, he said again, this time to himself. He changed into a pair of linen trousers and tennis shirt. Looking into the mirror he wished he had a better tan. Kate had a good tan. He called her room. She'd be another thirty minutes. Blanchflower went out onto his balcony. A girl with an excellent ribcage was diving from the low board. He admired the way she sliced into the water.

"Come on," Kate said when they went downstairs, "I'll show you around."

It was all very clubby, very churchy, very reunion-day-on-campus with the old grads come back to see yet another, maybe the last, of the great shots.

Blanchflower had been issued his credentials and a VIP badge in Washington and Kate had her press card and they were waved past the various checkpoints and into the air-conditioned offices. She picked up releases and talked to officials and was handed an updated list of "celebrity guests."

"Jesus," Blanchflower said, "is this a rocket launch or an opening night?"

At four o'clock she left him to tape a two-minute report for that evening's news from the huge network van, packed with electronics and technicians. Chester was there.

"Hello, Sinclair," he said.

"Oh, hi."

They had not been together since her departure for California.

"How was it?" he asked.

"Los Angeles? Oh, you know."

He nodded and she sat down with the director to discuss the two-minute script she had handwritten and Chester went outside to have a NASA PR man show him over the ground. Damn her, Chester thought, of course she shows up with a suntan and here I am straight from Washington, fish-belly white. Thinking of Kate's tan reminded him of Frances. He hoped she was not getting too sunburned on the beach in front of their motel. The English never learned about sunburn.

Blanchflower killed time by driving through the town, a typical beach strip with lots of bars that offered "Saturn Specials" and "Liquid Fueled Rockets." He resolved to stick to straight whiskies or beer. When he got back to the motel the girl with the ribcage was gone but there were other attractive kids using the pool and he sat at a table under a palm tree and drank a beer and understood why remittance men always went south. At six-thirty Kate was back and they went to her room. It was the first time they had slept together since before California. Kate seemed nervous. He did not know about Santa Monica. He did not know about Bunny's letter. But when they had finished Kate lay there, relaxed, watching him smoke, and knew it was okay. She knew Santa Monica was behind her. The letter still rankled but now they were together again. At eight o'clock he kissed her and got up to change.

Their hostess was called Betty Pflug. She worked for one of the wire services and was the senior correspondent at the Cape. She'd been there forever. Her house was on a side street off the coastal highway, overhung with palm trees and as Kate and Blanchflower came up the walk a lizard skipped ahead of them.

"Is that flora or fauna?" Blanchflower asked. "I always get them mixed up."

"Ugh," Kate said, "I really don't care."

A husky young man with surfer's hair opened the door.

"I'm Chet Pflug," he said. There seemed to be six or seven Pflug boys, all of them blond, healthy and handing out drinks. Kate took mental notes to tell Shaun. They didn't ask what you wanted to drink. You were simply handed a glass. The house was very tropical, full of rooms partitioned by wicker and bamboo. Betty Pflug waved to Kate, whom she had met only the day before but who was now an old friend. She came over with a gray-haired gent.

"Meet Dr. Schlosser," she said, "one of the local Nazis."

Schlosser smiled and peered at them through rimless glasses.

"Our Betty," he said, "always the jokes."

"He's one of the Peenemünde alumni, class of '45," Betty said.

"Well, it's true. What the hell. Now I'm a good Yankee."

"Not this far south you aren't," Betty said, and went off to greet someone else.

Kate asked Schlosser if he were with NASA.

"Ja, NASA. We are all with NASA. Betty too she should be with NASA. I think sometimes Betty could make a better rocket than any of us. Better even than poor Von Braun."

"She's been here a long time?" Blanchflower asked.

"Ja, a long time. I remember the first shot we did with Betty here to record the new culture. The shot went up, headed for the moon, and poof, down into the swamp. Oh, how we cried in the blockhouse. What a failure. What an embarrassment. These Americans had kidnapped us all and now we were failing them. A terrible moment. We had to go out and find the rocket, to find out what did not march. It was burned out in the swamp. And under one of the fragments was a big dead snake. Roasted by the fuel. We brought it back, the fragment and the snake as well. And we got drunk that night at Betty's place, not the house but an apartment she had then, and when we were drunk we ate the snake. Rather tasty, you know. Gamey, but not bad."

One of the NASA Americans came by, rare enough to have entertainment value. Introductions were made, Kate Sinclair the attraction. After all, there were always senators at the big shoots.

"Quite a few of your liberated colleagues about," the NASA American said.

"Oh?" said Kate, "my colleagues?"

The American looked blank.

"Of course, feminists. Didn't you know? Raising hell that there isn't a woman going along on this ride."

Blanchflower, who had not been listening, listened now. He remembered the pickets at the Melbourne airport.

The NASA American droned on. "Can't say I blame them, really. Not like a moon shot, there and back in a hundred hours. They'll be gone three years on this jaunt. Having a woman along not all that silly an idea."

Kate asked him some questions. There might be a line in this for next evening's broadcast. After all, how much could she say about payload capacities and celestial navigation? She knew she could say something about the women's movement and its first sortie into space. Blanchflower went from one foot to another. He didn't even seem to notice the small blonde in a halter top who was staring at him, running her tongue over her lips. Kate was all business.

"Kate," he said at last, "I hunger. Come buy me a steak somewhere."

Kate thanked the NASA American and then they looked for Betty to say good-bye but they couldn't see her. The house was full now, noisy, smoky and hot. Outside a deep breeze came off the ocean and they drove with the windows open.

"Do you really want a steak?" Kate asked.

"No," he said.

They went to his room. The lights were on in the pool and some drunks were jumping in and thrashing around. Blanchflower turned off all the lights and left the curtains open. Light from the moon and the stars and from the pool illuminated the room. He sat in a chair, smoking, watching her undress.

She was naked now and she stood there, hands on her hips.

254

"Well?" she said.

He nodded.

"Nice," he said. "Nice to have you back."

"I was back this afternoon," she said, "remember?"

He laughed.

"That was a quickie," he said. "Didn't make up for all that time in L.A."

She started to say something and then didn't. It was as if she should feel guilty about California but that it was fine for him to have tried half the beds in the East while she was gone. Double standard, oh, was there ever a double standard! Now he got up and started to undress and as he shed his shirt and kicked off his shoes she stopped thinking about California and about the letter and felt her stomach sort of flip over and a warm flush move up from her belly toward her breasts. And I used to be the cool one, she thought. Blanchflower tossed his trousers over the back of a chair and walked to her. She stood there, not moving to him. He put his arms around her and lifted her slightly, just off the floor, and she felt him penetrate between her thighs and thought again, good-bye cool, good-bye stainless steel, good-bye everything.

"Now," he said, "we'll make up for L.A."

He picked her up and laid her quite gently on the bed and leaned over her and began to do splendid things.

The next morning, in New York, Kate's first note arrived at the hotel on Eighth Avenue and Shaun ran back to her room and lay on the bed to read it. It was only a postcard, with a color photo of some antique rocket launch, but it was in her sister's own handwriting. It didn't say much but it was from Kate and not from the secretary. Shaun felt wonderful about the card. It was sort of an omen, she thought. The night before, in this same bed, she had given herself to one of the waiters at the discotheque, a nice boy who claimed to be a dropout from Amherst. It had hurt and been pleasurable all at the same time but there was the usual residual guilt.

Now came this communication from her sister, directly from Kate to her, and the final words, "I love you," told Shaun that whatever she had done really made no difference, that Kate loved her.

The fact that Kate had written the card a day or two before

her deflowering did not occur to the girl nor did it seem really to matter. Shaun sat up and put the card carefully on the bed table. She wanted it to be there so it would be the last thing she saw at night. The first thing she saw in the morning. Even before she saw the Amherst boy or whoever else might be there with her.

32

Chester Albany was in an excellent mood. Bobby Klaus had told him last evening, right after the show, that for the next couple of days, leading up to the day of the launch itself, Chester would be the lone anchorman from Cape Canaveral.

"We'll use Kate as we have been doing, short takes, interviews, sidelights. No point in having New York play anchor. All people will want to hear about is the launch anyway. I'll tell everyone. And Kate."

Chester hung up the phone with the air of a man well satisfied with himself and with life itself. Justification! When there was a really big, hard news story, they turned to him. Not to Sinclair. Oh, she was fine with the fluff. None better. Chester wouldn't take that from her. She could handle the software better than anyone he'd ever seen. But when it came to hard news, to an event like this, the network wanted an old pro in the chair. He'd be up against the best, Cronkite, all of them, but he gloried in the challenge. Chester went back to his motel feeling wanted. Frances, sunburned pink, lay naked on the bed with the air-conditioner blowing across her body.

"Jesus," Chester said, "that's painful even to look at, baby."

He hunched his shoulders and screwed up his face. For a moment he even forgot to be angry over her having disregarded his warnings about the tropical sun.

Frances looked up at him.

"Surprise," she said, "it doesn't really hurt that much. I put some stuff on it." She pointed to a spray can on the dresser.

Chester picked up the can and sniffed.

"Really work?"

She nodded.

"Sure." She looked up at him and squirmed a little on the bed. "See, I can move."

He looked down at her. The white parts where the bikini had been were stark against the pink. She stretched her arms over her head.

"Wanna spray me some more, Chester?" she asked.

He said yes and aimed the spray can.

Americans by the tens of thousands descended on Canaveral, arriving by plane, by car, by boat, by bus, in campers and vans, on motorcycles and mopeds. Two engineering students from MIT arrived on skateboards and claimed to have done the entire 1400 miles from Boston on the damn things. The first humans were being aimed at Mars and it seemed everyone wanted to be there to wave farewell.

Among the arrivals were a hyphenated woman lawyer named Marcia Mann-Isaacs from New York and several of her associates, hopeful of attracting attention for their cause where the President, and the cameras, could observe. The local feminists, ignored until now, shunted behind sawhorses and relegated to the handing out of leaflets, rejoiced. Now, perhaps, someone would begin to notice them. Someone who had until now ignored them and their cause, who had hurried by without a glance. Someone whose notice would count. Someone, Marcia Mann-Isaacs suggested, like Kate Sinclair.

Kate had wakened and left Blanchflower's room at dawn. She slept until nine and then woke for a second time. In the shower she felt the sting of the water against the parts of her that were raw, abraded. Her body felt the way it had after that troubled night in Santa Monica but her head felt wonderful. This was different. This was good. This was, after all, the man she loved. In the night, after they had made love and while he caressed her, readying her and himself to love again, she had confessed.

"Nick?"

"Yes?"

"Nick, there's something."

"Yes?"

"In California, Nick . . . "

"Yes," he said again.

"Nick , I fucked everyone out there. Everyone."

258

His hand stopped moving and he looked into her face. Tears were coming down her cheeks.

"Hey, Kate, it's okay. It's okay. Don't cry."

"Why shouldn't I cry?" she blubbered.

"Because I did the same dumb damn thing back here, that's why."

"Really?" she said, knowing it even before he said it, but loving it that he was telling her.

"Yes, really. Now wipe your goddamn face and brush your hair or whatever it is you do when you goddamit weep, and get your ass back here."

Now, in the bright morning, she remembered that he had told her the truth, that she had rid herself of guilt, that the two of them were now closer than they had ever been. She was in a buoyant, jubilant mood. She pulled on a tank suit and went out and did laps in the still empty pool and when she had finished she looked up and Blanchflower was watching from his little balcony, a tentlike terry robe down to his feet, his hair messed from bed, a cigar in his mouth.

"Kate Sinclair," he shouted down to her, "you are the best."

She went off an hour later to do her feature on the feminist protest of the space program. She was very happy, girlishly, giddily happy. Which was the problem. For when she taped the two-minute take that afternoon she committed the unforgivable sin: she did not take the feminists seriously. Instead, she patronizingly put them down as simply another, wonderfully zany facet of the local color surrounding the shoot. Had Kate been less happy, the piece would probably have taken on the properly sober note. And the feminists, having been taken seriously, would have been satisfied. As it turned out, Kate Sinclair's jolly little sidebar to that evening's news affronted and angered them and Marcia Mann-Isaacs vowed that somehow they would pay her back. Kate had patronized them with her little joke.

Robin emerged at noon. He had spent a troubled evening. On alien turf like this it was so difficult to discern where the local homosexuals gathered to frolic. I mean, he grumped, you can't just go into bars shouting for them. He had tried one or two places along the beach, been dismayed by the short haircuts and suntanned machismo of the technicians and engineers, to say nothing of the newsmen, and had retired to his bed, chastely alone, there to worry about whether his client, Blanchflower, was doing something that might lose a vote. Now, at noon, still wearing his tweeds and a pith helmet Blanchflower had insisted on purchasing for him, Robin came forth. Blanchflower was at the pool, chatting up a couple of teen-age girls and signing autographs.

"Oh, dear," Robin said, hurrying across the grass to poolside. He was not sure whether a paternity suit or statutory rape was most ruinous to a candidate's chances. With Blanchflower, he feared, the two menaces seemed to meld into one.

"There you are, Nick, working away at your speech. How energetic of you. This tropic heat renders me immobile. Now, now, young ladies, be off. The senator is here on official business and you are *wicked* to keep him from it. Off!" The youngsters scattered. Robin pulled up a chaise and fell into it. He patted his pockets and came up with one of his "serious" cigars, a foot long and a lethal brown, almost black. Since Kate Sinclair would be working that afternoon, Blanchflower would be free to roam. Robin was intent that he not roam unchaperoned.

As Robin lectured Blanchflower about the necessity, "the absolute essentiality," of discretion, Chester Albany and Kate Sinclair were about their appointed rounds. Chester, who had covered the big Apollo shots of the sixties and early seventies, was right at home with the public relations boys and the military and the contractors and the backup astronauts. He spoke their language, they spoke his, and that evening he would translate the resulting esperanto into four minutes of space talk that would be understood in twenty million living rooms. Kate Sinclair, not nearly the reporter Chester was, and having none of the technical experience or the jargon, did what she did best. She interviewed people on camera.

It was hot now, hot and humid, but Kate, in her white duck pants and a navy blue silk shirt that hinted Lacoste but was Valentino, looked cool. It was a facility she had. In real life, as she thought of it, she perspired, no, dammit, she *sweat*. On camera, under the klieg lights or a Florida sun, she was a veritable deodorant commercial. Kate did not understand why this was. She accepted the phenomenon, and was grateful.

At the airport she interviewed local women on the picket line, at a gracious beach house she talked to the local NOW chapter president, at NASA she asked that day's mouthpiece a few questions, and eventually she even got to talk with a female astronaut who was not going on this mission, nor the next, but (just possibly) the one after that. The female astronaut was brisk and military and did everything but salute Kate and call her "sir." When she wrapped up the two-minute segment, which was to have such damaging impact, the director slapped her on the back and said that no one, not even Cronkite, could have done it better. Kate had the impression that, had she been a man, the director at that moment would have invited her to go out on the town with him and get drunk, he was that elated.

Kate filmed, and did not sweat, and Blanchflower and Robin canvassed the bars.

"You never know," Blanchflower said soothingly, "lots of New Yorkers in Florida at any time. You can't tell how many votes we might pick up with a little selective browsing."

In one of the joints they had posted a list of space-inspired drinks. Blanchflower had no idea of what went into them. "Lunar Module, Eagle Bender, Spider Glider, Mars Lander, Planet Special, Milky Way Hey." He asked a bartender what was in the "Mars Lander."

"Pal, they're all rye and ginger with different kinds of fruit. You want my advice? Stick to beer."

Blanchflower ordered a Heineken's, but Robin, stubborn, asked for a "Milky Way Hey."

A little man in a rumpled seersucker suit stood next to them at the bar.

"I'm not going to bed until the bird goes up," he announced.

"Excited, are you?" Robin asked pleasantly.

"No, I just don't have a bed. After the shot there'll be plenty. Right now they want fifty bucks a night for a motel room and there aren't any. Minimum three nights. I said to hell with it. I'll sleep on the beach if I sleep at all."

It was only two o'clock but the little man in seersucker was drunk. There were a lot of girls in the place. Robin was telling the little man, "What a charming notion, sleeping rough, on the beach." Then, slyly, he asked, "Where does one do that, if one had a mind?"

Behind the bar there was a hand-lettered sign: "You must be 21 and be able to prove it." Looking around, Blanchflower doubted they enforced the code. Some of the girls were still in braces. But suntanned and fine to have on hand. A kid in a body shirt and tight pants came up and asked if she could drag on Robin's cigar.

"I should say not," he said primly, and turned his tweeded back on her.

"Here," Blanchflower said. The kid took a drag on his cigar and handed it back.

"You know what they're calling this place?" she asked.

He said, no, he didn't.

"Cape Carnival."

"Oh?"

"Carnival instead of Canaveral. You get it, don't you?"

Blanchflower liked the girl, he liked the way the cigar tasted after she gave it back, but he couldn't keep up with her repartee. She moved on to someone else. A correspondent Blanchflower knew from the Senate press gallery came by.

"They say there'll be a million people here by Wednesday morning," he said.

"Can't be," Blanchflower said. "Where would they put them?"

"Jesus," the reporter said, "they've got cars parked along the beach for twenty miles in each direction. I believe it. A million fucking people. I believe it."

"Press?"

"Three thousand, maybe more."

"Including television?" Blanchflower asked, thinking of Kate.

"Those bastards. Sure. The big moving vans they've got out near the pad. Like railroad cars. You see them?"

"Well," Blanchflower said, "I guess they need the equipment."

The reporter snorted. "Too bad they never learned to read

and write. They wouldn't need all that shit. Just a pencil and a notebook."

Blanchflower bought the newspaperman a drink, a "Liftoff Special."

"What's in it?" the man asked.

"Don't ask," the bartender said, "just drink. You're better off."

The newspaperman said he heard some blacks were coming in, that they would try to break up the party with a welfare protest.

"They want to bring in mules and set up some tents and generally raise hell," he said. "They think this dough ought to be going to the poverty programs. What d'you think of that, Senator?"

Blanchflower turned wary. One minute he and another fellow were having a drink. Now it was a newspaperman asking questions. On the record.

The bartender provided the out.

"Let 'em in," he said, "let 'em set up camp about fifty yards from the pad. Whoosh. Good-bye mules, good-bye niggers."

The newspaperman ignored him.

"Some talk about women's libbers coming in too. You heard that, Senator?"

Again wary, Blanchflower said, "Nope. Guess they want some more women in the space program. Sounds like a good idea."

The newspaperman, who had taken out his notebook, now put it away. He reverted to civilian life.

The big party was to be that night, paid for by the contractors. Tickets would be scarce. Robin said he had a line on some questionable votes. He thought he ought to pursue them and skip the party. By this Blanchflower understood him to mean he had found a gay bar.

"Sure, Robin, work the hustings. We'll get together in the morning."

Another girl squeezed in between Robin and Blanchflower at the bar. She was really a great looking kid. She asked Blanchflower if he were an astronaut and it gave him the opening but he thought about Kate, and their mutual confessions of the night before, and he mumbled something and shoved the newspaperman in front of him. The girl didn't seem to mind. One or the other, it didn't matter. They were more openminded in the South than Blanchflower had anticipated.

Kate was at the motel when he got back.

"Hey," she said, "you've got to watch tonight's show. I got this really good number with the feminists."

"Oh!"

"Yeah. I went around and talked to them. And to NASA. And to one of the woman astronauts. I think it works. Really works."

Jesus, Blanchflower thought, I spend half my waking hours avoiding the feminists and she goes out and dredges them out of the swamp.

He sat down on the bed. She sat next to him. He put an arm around her shoulder and bent to kiss her.

"Hey," Kate said, "come on. We've got an invitation."

Blanchflower got up and went into the bathroom. The only invitation he wanted was bed. He washed his face and came out. Kate was standing by the bed, looking into the mirror and combing her heavy brown hair. She'd changed into a thin shirt and linen pants. With her arms raised like that you didn't miss much. He did not know about her daily exercises but he could see the muscles working.

"Are you sure you want to go?" he said.

"Absolutely," she said. "You owe me a steak from last night."

They went to the cocktail party first. It was very exclusive, not more than three thousand people had been invited. Then there were the crashers. They got to talk with one of the astronauts. He looked about fifteen years old. He was very small-boned and neat. "They breed them that way," Nick whispered, "like poultry, to save space in the capsule."

He addressed Blanchflower as "sir" and Kate as "ma'am." He had not yet gone up but perhaps the year after next. Their host was an oil man from Colorado. Betty Pflug had told them about him. "A space groupie. He gets his jollies from hanging around astronauts. They think he's flaky but they like him. He spreads it on them pretty lavish."

264

Someone said one of the President's sons was there. An old NASA hand got Kate off in a corner.

"You should have been here in '69," he said. "For the first moon landing. Von Braun and Lindbergh were both right in this room. The two of them. I mean, it was like having cocktails with Orville and Wilbur." He shook his head.

"But this is even more exciting, isn't it?" Kate asked. "Mars is so much farther away than the moon. So much bigger, more mysterious."

The old-timer shook his head again.

"Not like the old days," he said nostalgically.

When he went off Blanchflower said, "To listen to him talk you'd think they went to the moon in a Spad biplane."

Someone said there were Russian subs just over the horizon, watching the whole thing, hoping the bird would come down and they could get a piece of it.

"It must be true," the man said, "I read it in the Orlando paper."

Someone else said the Russians were already there, on Mars, but they hadn't said anything about it yet, so the Americans would spend all this money, all this energy, and then, before the American rocket got there, just before, the Russians would make their big announcement.

"No," said the first man, "I think they'll try to shoot ours down."

Blanchflower suggested they report both theories to the authorities.

Barbra Streisand came in and the mayor of New York and Johnny Carson and Waldheim from the UN and A. J. Foyt and Abe Fortas and Rex Reed and Alex Haley. The Colorado oil man seemed to collect celebrities the way he collected astronauts. There was no way you could fight your way to a bar but waiters carried trays laden with drinks and people reached out to grab them. It didn't seem to matter what the drink was, you just took one. Blanchflower told Kate about the bar that afternoon, about the "Moon Landers" and the "Milky Way Heys." "They're all rye and ginger."

The Vice-President arrived with a phalanx of Secret Service

men and now there was really a crush and Blanchflower grabbed Kate's arm and shouted in her ear and they worked their way out through the crowd and drove up the coast a few miles and had a steak and went back to the motel and made love in Kate's bed. In the morning she wrote another card to Shaun and talked to Bobby Klaus on the phone and that afternoon she taped interviews with the wives of the three men who were going to Mars. Blanchflower hung around, wondering why he was in Florida at all except to be with Kate, and Robin pestered him to stay sober and keep away from the girls and for God's sake to get himself on television a few times before the rocket went up.

"Don't ever forget it, Nick, the tube got you there and the tube is what's going to keep you there."

Blanchflower nodded.

"Robin," he said, "that's one fact of life I know. Oh, do I know it."

Uncharacteristically reticent, he did not mention this to Kate, but called both Reasoner and Cronkite and ended up doing a brief bit about NASA appropriations on CBS, looking very senatorial standing in a reclaimed swamp with the huge rocket gantry rising into the blue Florida sky behind him.

And the countdown continued.

33

Kate Sinclair's brief, witty, and patronizing report on the ineffectiveness of the campaign to include a woman on the Mars trip, had been received by the general public as an amusing sidebar to the far more significant main story of the rocket launch itself. But not by the feminists. They steamed and cursed and vowed revenge. For the next forty-eight hours after her comments, it was all they could talk about. Even on the beach. On a huge blanket, Marcia Mann-Isaacs and two of her militant sisters ignored the ocean and began to formulate their campaign to destroy the woman who had belittled the great cause.

Not everyone was angry with Kate Sinclair. Bobby Klaus, delighted with her offbeat coverage of the Mars adventure during the evening news, scheduled Kate on the network's morning show as well. "Today" and "Good Morning America" both had people on the ground and Bobby asked Kate to do fifteen minutes from the Cape during each of the segments, from seven to eight and then again from eight until nine. Really, he did not have to ask. It was in her contract that, on reasonable notice, Kate was required to appear on other network shows as well. It was the network's way of amortizing their million dollars over the broadest possible base.

"Kate," Blanchflower exploded, "they're working your ass off. Next they'll have you acting in the daytime soaps. Don't you people have a union? Didn't you ever hear of the forty-hour week?"

Kate patiently explained.

"Bobby's under terrific pressure. If he says he needs me on the morning side, then he needs me. Listen, I owe this character a lot. He stuck his neck out for me on my contract and when he yells for help, well, I'm going to be there."

"Sucker."

Kate laughed.

"Oh, come on. It's only for a couple of days. If they abuse the privilege I'll let you make a speech about it in the Senate. Wouldn't that make you happy?"

Blanchflower brightened. He enjoyed making speeches. That evening, when Kate pushed him out the door at nine o'clock so she could go to sleep ("They want me at the van at six tomorrow morning"), he was less enthusiastic. He went back to his room and turned on television but there was nothing worth watching and outside there were still people in the pool, shouting and splashing, and finally he said the hell with it and called a Pentagon undersecretary he knew and fifteen minutes later the two men were in Blanchflower's car driving along the coast highway. They parked in front of one of the bars he had discovered earlier in the week and went inside.

"Looks lively," said the undersecretary, whose name was Nelson.

"Well, at least it's noisy."

The place swarmed with people. Robin was at the bar, still in his tweed suit. But somewhere he had gotten a yachting cap and discarded the pith helmet. When he saw Blanchflower and Nelson, he touched it in salute.

"You look sillier than usual, Robin," Blanchflower informed him cheerfully.

"I thought it gave me a certain dash," he said, narrowing his eyes and thrusting out his chin in what he obviously considered a nautical attitude. "What do you think, Nelson?"

Robin seemed to have attached himself to a group at the bar. They ordered drinks and Blanchflower skinned an eye over his friends. Perhaps it was Robin's obvious homosexuality that made him welcome. He was amusing and no threat. The group pivoted on a blonde with swimmer's shoulders and extraordinary legs. There were two other women, one of them really old, and two men, solid and tough-looking. Except for the old lady they were in yachting clothes. Robin introduced them. The blonde and the men were able to restrain their delight. They continued what seemed a private conversation. The old lady was cordial but vague, more interested in an eggnog she was drinking out of season but with elan. The other woman, whose name was Madge, took Blanchflower's arm.

"I like big men," she said.

"Fine," he told her. "I'll try to find you one."

They were all there for the Mars shot. They had come in on a yacht.

In the audible hiss he adopted when speaking confidentially, Nelson remarked on the girl.

"Isn't she great, the blonde? She's probably worthless trash but I'd give my soul for her."

Blanchflower and Nelson had done any number of carouses together in Washington and he knew Nelson was continually pledging his soul for girls who were no good. He wondered if the Joint Chiefs knew.

One of the bruisers was Madge's husband. He used to be Tarzan in the movies, Robin said. He wasn't sure which one was Tarzan and which was Tarzan's friend. It didn't seem to matter.

"I'm not sure Madge knows either," he said. "The old girl is her mother."

Blanchflower was still getting the business from Madge. He glanced at the Tarzans to see whether they cared, but it was clear they didn't, that to them the blonde was center stage. Nelson kept leering at her. He was a little high. He must have been drinking when Blanchflower called. It was funny to see old Nelson high but Blanchflower hoped the Tarzans would see it that way too. He was bigger than they were but Blanchflower was strictly a pacifist when it came to other people's wars. He did not want to fight for Nelson. Besides, it would upset Robin and be bad for the campaign.

"Are you really a senator?" Madge asked him.

"Sure," he said cheerfully.

"Baltimore isn't that far from Washington. You ever get to Baltimore?" Madge wanted to know.

"I never go anywhere," Blanchflower said, "my doctors won't permit it. They're afraid of another seizure."

"My husband travels a lot," she said. "He's not in the theater anymore. He's a salesman now. They don't appreciate real acting today. It's all this dirty stuff now. No family films at all.

269

No real art. I was convent-educated myself. I don't go for all this filthy stuff."

"Your mother really gets it on with this eggnog, doesn't she?" Blanchflower inquired.

"He's away a lot. It gets awfully empty in that big house in Baltimore. If you think you might get up that way I could give you the address."

"Look," Blanchflower said, "don't mouth it around but I've got mixed blood and I don't like to mess around with white women this far south."

"Do you have a pen? I'll give you the phone number too."

Blanchflower turned to the old lady. "Have another eggnog, Mother, if you don't think it's too fattening."

Madge scribbled on a matchbook as her mother nodded over the eggnog. She might have been mute, while the daughter never drew breath. It must be a handy arrangement around the house, Blanchflower thought. Madge handed him the matchbook who passed it on to Robin.

"Here, Robin, you're the traveling man."

Robin took the matchbook, automatically pulled out a match and relit his cigar. It was the last match and he rolled up the matchbook and put it in an ashtray. That got to Madge.

"I know what's the matter," she said to Blanchflower. "You're a fairy. All three of you are fairies. Else why would you be here alone instead of with a woman? Three men together always means fairies."

"Don't knock it," Blanchflower said. He kidded Robin a lot but now he looked at the fat man to see whether this was bothering him. Robin had a beatific smile on his face and a glass in his hand. It was all right.

"Don't get sore," Madge said. "There's nothing to be ashamed about. Get what you can. I like men but maybe I could like women too. I'd try it. I'd try anything. I admit it. I was convent-educated but I'd try it. Maybe I could dig women."

Blanchflower finished his martini and over Madge's head he spoke to Nelson who was still trying to get into the conversation with the Tarzans and the blonde.

"Nelson, this is classic. Who'd believe they let them run around loose this way?"

The old lady chose that moment to push back an empty egg-nog glass and stand up. She weaved away from the bar. It must have been the last eggnog, or perhaps Madge's girlish revelations.

"Let's get some air," Blanchflower said.

He pushed past Madge, grabbing Nelson as he went. The bar was on an inlet and there was a sort of dock behind it. They went out from the smoke and the noise and the crowd into the cool dark of the waterfront. Nelson was annoyed.

"Listen, Nick, why drag me out here? All the action is inside."

"You'll end up out here anyway if you keep after that blonde," Blanchflower informed him. "You see the size of those guys? They aren't hanging around her for the conversation."

Nelson pulled himself up very straight. His hands moved up as if to adjust his tie. But he wasn't wearing one. He was really very drunk.

"I was only being friendly," he said. "They're all strangers down here, just here for the shot. I was only doing the decent thing. Public servant owes a certain debt to the taxpayer, you know. Can't hold oneself aloof. Was going to tell them all about Mars."

"You're such an old Mars hand yourself," Blanchflower said.

"The Nelson we have come to know and loathe," Robin said drily.

Blanchflower walked down a gently moving gangplank to a float. There were dinghies tied up along the float and farther out in the water the dark loom of larger boats. The water was smoothly black and cold-looking after the heat of the bar. There was no smoke out here, just the waterfront smell of fish and seaweed and red lead and the ocean itself. Blanchflower stretched. He wished Kate were there with him. Instead there was drunken Nelson and fat, homosexual Robin. Where do they come from, he asked himself. He was feeling the drinks himself and now he sat down on the boards and took off his shoes.

"What are you going to do?" Nelson asked.

"I've been advised to take up knitting with my toes. A sort of therapy. My analyst advised it." Blanchflower stood up and stripped. Robin goggled.

"I need a bath," Blanchflower said to no one. He stood there for a moment big and pale and tensed in the darkness before diving heavily into the inlet.

"What the hell," Nelson said. This was quite wonderful. He stripped and went in after Blanchflower. They could hear Robin yelling at them from the float.

"The barracuda! They say they feed at night. They hang around piers."

Nelson ducked under again and came up out of the shock of the cold, a shock he had not felt when he first dove in drunkenly. He couldn't see Blanchflower right away, then could see him farther out, swimming clumsily with a lot of splash. He went after him and they swam to one of the near-in yachts and caught on the anchor chain and hung there resting in the cold and the dark, treading water and breathing hard. Blanchflower was snorting like a walrus with the blond hair streaming down over his big face. It was cold but it felt good in the water. They looked back toward the dock. Outlined against the lights from the bar they could see Robin. They could hardly miss him, the size he was. Robin had not gone into the water, of course, but now in a kind of tribute to their swim he was running up and down in the rowboats that were tied to the dock, lumbering along as an overweight football lineman might in spring practice, giving little shouts. He sounded happy now. Blanchflower whooped back at him. He realized Robin was drunk too. They were all drunk. Then Robin tripped over an oar or something and went down face first. He was out of sight and quiet and then came a string of soft, intense obscenities. Blanchflower poked Nelson.

"Come on," he said, "we'll bear the body home to mother. I'm frozen anyway."

They swam back and pulled themselves from the water, shivering now. Robin was nursing his shins. "Damn, damn, damn," he said. They used their handkerchiefs to dry off, not very successfully. Blanchflower felt as if he were turning blue. Robin limped over to them. "Here," he said, "use this. It's clean," and he handed Blanchflower a crisp white handker-

272

chief. "Do you want my coat, Nelson? It's quite all right if you do."

Blanchflower very carefully refolded the handkerchief and gave it back. He put on his underclothes and then his white suit and smoothed down his hair.

Nelson had dressed now as well. Blanchflower took them each by an arm.

"Come on," he said, "we'll go back to my place for a civilized drink."

From the bar came music and the clatter of glasses. Blanchflower led them up the gangplank and toward where the car was parked. When Robin and Nelson left his room he thought about waking Kate. But it was late and she needed her sleep. He left a call for seven so he could watch her on the morning show.

"Jesus," he thought when he put down the phone. "I never get up to watch *anyone* on television. I wouldn't get up to watch myself."

He realized how much he had missed her tonight.

34

Air Force One landed in Florida the next morning. There had been one stop, at Atlanta, and then the big, converted 707 screeched to a halt on the Melbourne runway. At one that afternoon an invitation had been delivered to Kate Sinclair. A young man with a short haircut handed it to her personally.

"The President requests the pleasure of your company at a small reception in honor of the crew and creators of the first manned flight to Mars."

She phoned Blanchflower.

"No invitation here," he said. "The President isn't very fond of me these days."

"Then you go as my guest," she said. "It says I can take a guest."

"Interesting how the White House establishes priorities. First television, second movie stars, third and last, United States Senators."

"My, we are being stuffy."

"I didn't know it showed."

She laughed.

"Nick, with you it always shows. You're not the most subtle man in America."

"And I thought I was."

The President gave his little party where, at those latitudes, such parties inevitably were held, in a hangarlike banquet room of the local Holiday Inn. As she knew he would, Blanchflower let Kate take him as her "guest." They drove south along the highway, toward the Air Force base where the President would spend the night. They had the top down and Blanchflower could feel the sea breeze on his left cheek, could see Kate Sinclair, her strong hands on the wheel, her legs, under a soft wool skirt, on the pedals. She drove competently, as she did all things.

The right people were there. Kay Graham, David Rockefeller (not Nelson), Ronald Reagan (in Orange County they *loved* outer space), Tom Bradley (defusing the protesting blacks), Cronkite, Jimmy Stewart (John Wayne was poorly), *both* senators from Texas, Ross Perot, the new mayor of Chicago (no one could remember his name), Father Hesburgh, Jane Fonda, Bear Bryant, Walter Wriston, Senator Brooks, Chief Justice Burger, the French Ambassador, the Israeli Ambassador, the Egyptian Ambassador (the Russians were out for security reasons, the British because there was, as usual, a crisis), Tatum O'Neal, Cardinal Cooke, Sally Quinn, two rabbis, eight other senators, sixteen congressmen, four cabinet members, a member of the Chicago Seven, the former head of the FBI, and William Scranton.

The breeze came off the sea, rustling the palms and carrying the rusting damp on the shore, pleasant to the touch, hell to the residents. The troopers waved Kate's car into its allotted space. Inside, surveying them, was the Secret Service, hard-eyed. Blanchflower, who expected one day to be President, resented the whole business. Kate did not.

"Silly," she said, "of all people you ought to know why they make such a fuss."

Unlike Betty Pflug's, where her blond sons passed out the drinks, unlike the contractors' party where you grabbed what you could and reminisced about Lindbergh and Von Braun, the President's party was a model of decorum. Not even when one of the Georgia bankers removed his shirt and waved it leading a rebel yell or when a local real estate speculator passed out business cards or when a senator's wife threw up in the potted palms, did the affair lose focus. The focus, as always, was the President.

"For a farmer, he does it pretty well," Blanchflower whispered into Kate's ear.

"What?" she said.

"I said, for a shitkicker . . . "

"I heard you. I heard you."

There were not supposed to be autograph hounds but, of

275

course, there were. Blanchflower signed a few, Kate signed a few more. Over her shoulder she looked at him.

"Well?" she asked.

Blanchflower scowled.

"Your fan club," he said, "you got them in on Annie Oakleys."

"What are Annie Oakleys?" she shouted across the pressing shoulders and heads.

"Freebies, Kate, and I thought you were in show biz . . . "

"I'm not *in* show biz," she said.

But Blanchflower could not hear her, although he kept looking at her, not wanting to be seen to be looking at the President, not wanting the President's pale blue eyes to meet his.

The President did not so much make his way through the room as the room came to him. There was handshaking, there were smiles, there were truncated conversations. It was impossible really to talk. Kate moved to the President in her turn, towing a reluctant Blanchflower.

" . . . momentous event . . . tremendous courage . . . imagine, three years in space . . . it dazzles me . . . hello, Mr. President . . . Mars . . . wouldn't be in their shoes . . . hello, Kate, hello Nick . . . awesome . . . another drink . . . you know one another, of course . . . how long will it take? . . . Jupiter's next . . . oh, boy . . . the last frontier . . . hello, Mr. President . . . good night, Mr. President."

They were caught up in the eddy and found themselves in a calm backwater of the big room.

"What was that all about?" Kate asked.

Blanchflower looked sulky.

"You know he and I don't like one another."

"But I thought candidates always wanted to be seen with the President."

"Not this candidate," Blanchflower said.

They stood there, sipping their drinks, watching the drift of the crowd through the room toward the President, pausing, ebbing away. Blanchflower had been bubbly, irreverent when they'd arrived. His mood now was entirely different, pugnacious, aggrieved. This man goes deeper than I thought, Kate admitted to herself. Was it a real dislike for the President, some feud between the two politicians, or simply Blanchflower's overwhelming ambition to become the man around whom crowds like this would one day flow and eddy?

In a very real way it frightened her. Which she found ironically amusing, she who was always being accused of ambition, shaken by raw ambition in another. Fragments of Marc Antony's funeral harangue came back to her. She wondered whether Blanchflower knew the lines. "But Brutus is an honorable man . . . " Well, she thought, scanning the room full of sycophants and space profiteers and entertainers and gladhanders and politicians and hustlers, I'm glad someone is.

An hour later they were eating crawfish and drinking white wine and Blanchflower had thrown off his mood.

"A bad chamber, Kate, just a bad chamber. Don't give it a second thought. I go into a bad chamber twice a year and occasionally on a Tuesday or whenever I see the President up close. Don't fret about it. It passes, fortunately. A beautiful woman, a jug of wine, a lobster, and I recuperate pretty fast."

"Crawfish," she said.

"They look like lobsters to me."

They argued over that and over other things and drank coffee and passed up the brandy and went back to the motel and slept together, this once without making love. It seemed to Kate significant. They could share the same bed and not have to copulate. In the night she found his hand and pushed hers into it. They slept that way, together, for an hour and then she slipped quietly from his bed to return to her own room so as to be ready for the morning. It had been, Kate thought just before she fell asleep again, the most intimate night they had known.

35

Blanchflower's alarm clock sounded at four-thirty. He didn't trust room clerks to wake him. He felt seedy but it was better after standing under the shower. He was glad he had eased off on the drinking last night. He turned on the radio and got into his clothes. The radio said it was a perfect day for the launch, broken cloud and hot later. He phoned Kate's room. It rang once and then she was on.

"Shall I order you some hominy grits and candied yams?" he asked.

"You sound pretty cheerful," she said.

"Always cheerful in the morning. Later in the day I go into decline."

She said she would meet him at the car.

Blanchflower checked the identification pass pinned to his jacket, got some cigars, and went out onto the balcony in the early morning. It was chilly, still dark. But there were lights in most of the motel rooms and he could hear radios, television sets. He went down to the car and then he heard a door opening somewhere and Kate came out, running lightly down the gravel to the car.

"Ugh," she said, "I knew I should have gone to bed earlier."

She got into the car and kissed him. She was wearing white pants and a silk shirt. She carried a big soft leather bag and there was a heavy sweater around her shoulders. Blanchflower kissed her again. She looked wonderful, and he could not think of anyone he would rather be with on that morning. Kate felt that way as well. But neither of them said anything about it.

The highway was already bumper to bumper, everyone going north. The troopers, with flashlights, were waving them on. He turned left and pulled into the flow of traffic. In the east

278

the first cracks of light shattered the night sky. Kate lighted two cigarettes and put one in Blanchflower's mouth. His cigar was in the ash tray but he did not object. Kate twisted the radio dial back and forth. No music at all, just the flat tones of news announcers, talking about the launch, about the weather, about the President, about how many people would be there, about "those three brave men." The countdown was going smoothly. The astronauts were already out at the pad. The traffic was very heavy but it moved. Blanchflower dragged on the cigarette and watched Kate's profile. The only cars headed south, against the flow, were police cruisers. They passed some kids with rucksacks, hiking. They'll never get there in time, he thought, they'll miss it all. But he passed them by, not wanting to have anyone else in the car, wanting it to be just himself and Kate beside him, heading for the great adventure.

"Morning still 'ugh'?" he asked.

"Oh, no," she said. "It's perfect."

She slid closer to him on the seat.

Blanchflower knew now he had been wrong about the million people. Along the entire stretch of low, sandy beach from Cocoa Beach to Cape Canaveral there was not an unused foot of viewing space. Out along the highway, where people had slept in their cars all night, the license plates read like a roll call of the states, a catalog of Americans come to see dreams fulfilled. Out across the pool table flatness of the coast the rocket and its gantry rose up on their hind legs. They were floodlit and visible for miles in every direction.

The cars in front slowed and for ten or fifteen minutes they just crept along. Then they saw state troopers and some local cops waving the traffic ahead, hustling it along, their cruisers parked up on the shoulder. Blanchflower craned his neck out the car window and yelled at one of the troopers.

"What's up?"

"Come on, move it."

"What happened?"

"Nothing much. Some Women's Lib ladies tried to block the road. It's cleared now."

"Arrest them?" Blanchflower asked.

"Not today, mister. Couldn't arrest anyone on a day like this."

A hundred yards farther on they passed the women, perhaps

fifty of them, herded up on a dune a few feet back from the road. They still had their signs which they pumped up and down at the passing cars.

"Well," Blanchflower said, "what do you think of that?"

"I don't," Kate said. "I'm thinking about what I'm going to say for my opening lines."

Blanchflower wished he could be as cool about the feminists. But then Kate had not read the signs, seen the one that not only damned NASA and the President but which added, "and sexist Blanchflower!"

As big as he was, as powerful, as outwardly serene and confident, Nick Blanchflower shuddered. He remembered Robin's advice of a few years ago. "Have a few enemies, Nick, always cultivate a few. But if you run against Macy's, make sure Gimbels loves you. Don't feud with too many of the bastards at once."

Blanchflower knew very well that more than half the population of the United States was female.

It was full daylight when they reached the parking lot. Kate kissed him and ran into the big van to have her hair done and to be made up. Blanchflower strolled over to the stand, his hands in his pockets. The white board grandstand was just three miles from ground zero, facing east, toward the sun that was now up out of the sea.

People nodded to him, "Hello, Senator . . . Hello, Nick." There were some news people he knew. He saw the others from the Washington party and one of them waved to him to sit with them. He waved back. "See you later," he called out.

Inside the big white network van the makeup artist, the hairdressers, the lighting and sound technicians, the directors, worked on Kate Sinclair and Chester Albany as painstakingly as the NASA people were doing with the three young men about to leave for Mars. Kate and Chester would not leave the van. But their images would float out over the nation to be seen by millions and in their trade, imagery was everything.

Chester was cheerfully grumpy. When the technicians had finished, he brazenly ran a big hand through his graying hair and grinned to see it muss.

"Well," he said to Kate, "here we are again, Sinclair."

"Hello, Chester."

She had her own hairdresser, of course (they shared a make-

280

up man), and while her hair was being arranged, she jotted notes on a clipboard on her lap.

"I don't know why they can't fire off these things at a decent hour," Chester said.

She did not answer but tried to retain concentration. She knew, as they all did in television, that the best spontaneities are carefully written out in advance.

"Dawn, for chrissakes," Chester said. He had not gotten to sleep until after twelve and then this morning Frances had told him she preferred to stay in the motel to watch the launch.

"It's so much better on the tube," she had said. "You get all those instant replays."

Chester had long ago stopped arguing such points with his young lover. If Frances preferred instant replays to actual events, well, she was not alone. An entire generation felt the same way. Chester was not going to beat his head against the wall over it. As for him, he was glad to be on the actual site. That was, he supposed, terribly old-fashioned of him. But being on the spot and his professional satisfaction at anchoring the shoot were what cheered him even at this awful hour in the morning. So, as Kate doggedly polished her off-the-cuff remarks, Chester wisecracked with the technicians, chatted amiably with Bobby Klaus in New York, tossed a remark or two at Kate. Kate did not listen to him. It was her first space launch and she was nervous. She ran her felt-tipped pen through what she had written and started again. The teleprompter men were waiting to translate her scribbles into type and to feed them into the machine.

Outside the sun climbed and Blanchflower took off his coat and watched the light change in the morning sky. There was tension and excitement and perhaps even a bit of fear in the air. If it was this way at the grandstand, Blanchflower asked himself, what must it be three miles away at the pad? The refreshment stand ran out of coffee early and people breakfasted on chocolate cupcakes and Maryland fried chicken. It was seven o'clock in the morning and the countdown continued.

Inside the big van the red light went on and Chester Albany said good morning and Kate Sinclair delivered her first, carefully-honed ad lib, and in other vans Cronkite and Reasoner and Chancellor and Moyers and Brinkley and Sevareid and

Brokaw all said good morning and in New York Bobby Klaus began worrying about which "good morning" had been the most sincere, the most likely to attract and retain an audience over the next several hours. Bobby did not worry about the launch. Or the three men going to Mars.

Chester gave Kate a line and she segued smoothly to her previously taped interviews with the wives of the astronauts. The red light switched off in the van and both Kate and Chester slumped back, relaxed.

Outside the stands had filled up and behind the stands it was a state fair and the circus midway in one. Boys from *Paris Match* were handling out big white cowboy hats. A former First Lady was wearing one of the hats. In the press bleachers Norman Mailer was talking with William Buckley. The photographers loved it. Norman had a gigantic pair of binoculars. Buckley's wife tottered along on spike heels behind her husband and Mailer. At the ABC van the Vice-President was making a speech. Someone from the network waved at Blanchflower.

"Senator, can we get you next?"

Blanchflower shook his head. It wasn't good strategy to come on after a Vice-President. After the President was okay, barely.

A local seer strode past him, an extraordinary figure with orange hair and a floor-length tent dress, warning anyone who would listen, "Columbus didn't succeed in everything he set out to do."

"Right you are," Blanchflower told her.

Robin arrived, puffing, mopping at his face with a bandanna. In tribute to the now-hot morning sun, his tweed jacket was flapping open.

"Mules," he said.

"Absolutely," Blanchflower responded, knowing he would explain.

"Mules. Mules and poor people, tying up the traffic," Robin panted. "All over route one."

"Oh?"

"They got them cleared finally. Brought them in by bus."

"The mules too?"

"No, just the poor people. They're over there now being interviewed by Johnny Carson."

"Any feminists?" Blanchflower asked.

Robin shook his head.

When Blanchflower didn't say anything his campaign manager groaned piteously, "Nick, don't tell me you've screwed up with the women. Don't tell me that, please."

Blanchflower shrugged. "Okay, Robin, I won't tell you that."

Some little old ladies with parasols mounted the press bleachers. "Women's page," someone said. A Limey photographer came up the steps in starched British Army shorts with high wool knee socks and sunburned knees and a white hunter's hat with the strip of zebra around the crown. There were men in bush jackets and men stripped to the waist. Blanchflower was having a good time. This was more fun than the Gridiron Club. There were girls in leather mini skirts and girls in tight pants. Most of them wore T-shirts with nothing underneath. A lot more fun than the Gridiron Club. It was very hot now and Betty Pflug passed a tube of Sea & Ski to the gentlemen from the *Times*. Someone said Henry Ford's daughters had arrived but Blanchflower couldn't see them. He kept seeing pretty girls with thin shirts stuck to their bodies in the heat. Halfway up the stands a French reporter kept calling into an open line, "Allo, Paree, allo, Paree." Betty went down the steps and came back to report a frog had invaded the ladies' room. That kept them all going for a time. Barry Goldwater, in a fire engine red shirt, came through shaking hands. Blanchflower thought he looked better than in '64 when he did a lot of handshaking but hadn't done much else. Blanchflower sat down, long legs spraddled in front of him. Robin slumped next to him. They squinted into the morning sun and the squawk box filled them in on the details as the countdown continued.

In the van Kate Sinclair was caught up in the electricity. She began to feel what Chester felt. Why, she thought, they shouldn't have to pay us to do this. It's a wonderful job. For the first time, she felt she was a part of it all, not just another of Bobby Klaus's show biz whiz kids. She looked across the van at Chester. There was a beatific look on his face. He feels it too, Kate thought, and smiled instinctively. Chester caught the smile and his mouth fell open.

"What's with you?" he demanded. "You like your own interviews that much?"

Kate felt happy. At least with Chester you knew where you stood. She remembered the old line about Vince Lombardi, "The coach is very fair. He treats us all the same . . . like dogs."

Chester was, well, he was dependable. It gave her a nice feeling.

Outside, at the two grandstands, one for the press, the other for the VIPs, the loudspeaker crackled:

"Launch minus fifteen minutes. Fifteen minutes to launch."

Blanchflower had taken a bench in the press section. "It's okay, Senator," a man from a Miami paper said, "long as we get an exclusive quote if the goddamn thing blows up."

Someone said he'd heard press badges were being scalped in town for fifty dollars.

"They can have mine," a whisky-voiced reporter shouted.

Senator Percy's wife went by with a pink parasol. Chuck Percy kept ducking under it to get out of the sun. Jesus, Blanchflower thought, if I were running against him how I'd love to have a photo of that. Johnny Carson climbed into the VIP stand with his security blanket, McMahon.

Then at 9:32 A.M. there was a flash of flame, the smoke, then a terrifying several seconds before the big rocket began to rise, ever so slowly. Then they could hear the roar and the journalists, who weren't supposed to cheer, gave a little shout and the bird climbed up and away from them, faster and faster into a baby blue bunting sky. More thunder and ground vibration and it was away, bursting through a few wispy white clouds. At that moment someone said Mars was exactly 48 million miles away. Suddenly it didn't seem so far. Blanchflower, the cool politician, shivered. He was thinking about the three men. He was thinking about whether one day he would be the one sending another three men, or a dozen, on an even greater flight.

In the van Kate Sinclair finished her remarks and handed over to Chester and began to cry. She was not the sort who cried easily or often. But she cried now. She had Blanchflower and she had this wonderful job and she was very happy about them both.

She was very happy. Period.

BOOK THREE

CHESTER ALBANY

36

It was fall. The best season. Kate prowled through the empty apartment naked, luxuriating in the deep softness of the rug under her bare feet, enjoying the crisp cool of New York after the tropical heat. As she passed mirrors she glimpsed herself and was pleased. She was no longer a girl, of course, she would not pretend that she was. Kate Sinclair was very aware she was a woman. And she was content. The mindless, stupid lusts of the Coast were behind her, the interlude with Blanchflower had been richer, fuller than anything they had known together before. And at Cape Canaveral she had found a new appreciation of the work she was capable of doing. Kate had come to the network as a star, before she learned her trade. Now she had learned, no, be fair, was learning it. It made being a star easier to accept. Yes, she thought, as she looked out over the city, I am content.

She had seen Shaun that night at dinner. The girl was all right, a bit tight around the eyes, lack of sleep, she supposed, but open, friendly, even close. Shaun was a little less enthusiastic about New York, about making her own living. Her mood hinted of an adolescent, and to Kate a welcome willingness to return at least for a time, to school, to childhood. Nothing had been said. But the suggestion was there. Kate resolved not to hurry the girl, not to push, to let it happen. At the moment she was pleased just to be home.

After the launch the life had gone out of Cape Canaveral like air from a punctured balloon. The space experts had moved on to Houston to track the flight, the tourists had melted away, the networks had dismantled their tents and vans, the politicians had gone back home. The final ecstasy was the arrival, hours after the launch, of a planeload of South

American diplomats from Washington. They had come to see man leave for Mars and had missed it by four hours.

"Well, my God," Betty Pflug had demanded, having apparently served her time with South Americans, "you didn't expect them to get up at dawn, did you?"

So the celebrities and the VIPs drifted off to wherever it was celebrities and VIPs went and Kate had spent one more day lying in the sun before making her way to the Melbourne airport alone. The driver, a local redneck, said the usual things about niggers and nearly killed them both by swerving the cab in an unsuccessful attempt to hit a stray dog trotting across the road.

"I'll go up a tree to get a cat," he informed Kate equably.

Now, at home, she pondered her victories. Behind her were the defeat of marriage, the lonely desperation that had led to Haller, the feuds with Chester, the ratings crises, the degradation of Santa Monica. She had endured, she had survived, she had not cracked up or cried out or surrendered. She had, she told herself with satisfaction, triumphed.

She went into the kitchen and poured herself a tall glass of orange juice. If only Blanchflower were here now, she thought, forgetting that less than an hour earlier she had been glad he was not, and that an entire evening stretched tranquilly before her with no obligation whatever. She quickly forgot that and already she missed Nick Blanchflower.

A great white yacht slipped past her window, cutting through the gray river, heading south. I could buy a boat like that, she thought. I could sail south, out of autumn, out of the city, heading for blue seas, for sunny islands, instead of the gray city. But she knew she would never leave.

In the living room, more an *objet* than utile, stood a great, gleaming brass telescope set on a tripod of polished wood. She rarely looked through it, but now, idly, she swung it toward the river and deftly twisted lenses into focus. There, way off down the river toward the mouth and the ocean, down by the bridges banding Brooklyn and Manhattan, was a freighter, making smoke, preparing for the sea, little tugs bouncing around in the chop, nosing up to the ship like puppies to teats. She stood there, watching the freighter, seeing men move aboard her, then, realizing she was naked, wondered if anyone

288

in Brooklyn with optical aids like this was observing her. Well, she thought, it's more of me than they see on the tube.

The phone rang. She listened, motionless, and then, unable to maintain discipline, she picked it up. It was Harvey. He sounded as if he were drinking.

"A lot you care that I'm dying," the high-pitched voice whined. "That I might be dead."

"Harvey," she said, "I know that before you go you'll send out a release. I don't worry about being taken by surprise."

"Well," Harvey said, "at least a mailgram. I owe it to my nearest and dearest."

He had been beaten up.

"There was this absurdly beautiful boy one night, right after I left P.J. Clarke's, you know, on the corner of Third Avenue where they tend to gather. And this boy was negotiating with a dreadful man in a large car with Jersey plates, right there on the corner, the boy with his head stuck into the car window, talking terms and fringe benefits, I suppose, his tight little ass in white jeans arched just ever so in my direction, I'm sure it wasn't just coincidence! and of course I had to say something. I never learn."

"So the man from Jersey got out and beat you up."

"Hah! If life were only that simple. No, he got out, jealously enraged, and I shoved the boy behind me and said, 'Now, just you stay out of this, *I'll* handle it.' And then, when the man in the car started to hit me, that little bitch, the one I was trying to protect, well, he mugged me from behind."

"Harvey . . ." Kate started to say. He interrupted.

"Now don't go heavy and start lecturing, Kate. I really couldn't take a lecture. It would be too cruel. You know I am painfully aware of my folly and don't need homilies. Besides, I didn't really mind the mugging. It was sort of kinky."

There was more, Harvey was so amusing, so outraged, so vulnerable. But Kate had had enough of it, once more impatient with the shadow world of homosexuals. For God's sake, she told Harvey, the guy from Jersey thought he was going to get laid. You got in the way. Did you think he was going to award you the croix de guerre? While Harvey blustered she remembered the lunch when they had gathered to help Paco get

289

a new job and had succeeded only in drinking his wine and eating his food and had not helped the poor boy at all, and she felt justified in her anger. She found it difficult to empathize with Harvey. He found her attitude unfathomable.

"I mean," he said, "you've been off in Florida watching rockets and sleeping with senators and I've been slaving away here in New York. And being pummeled by parties unknown. Don't I deserve any sympathy? Have you become that hard? That important?"

Oh, Harvey, she wanted to say. If only you knew how vulnerable I am myself, how easily bruised. Instead she said bright and brittle things and eventually he laughed, and blew kisses into the telephone, and hung up, promising that, if he survived, which was indeed doubtful, to take her to dinner at some chic new establishment that was reputed to be even more expensive, more exclusive, more surly, than the last such place he had unearthed.

On the late news that night, there was Blanchflower. Kate, sleepy, sat up rigid in bed and reached for her glasses. He was in Albany, campaigning, a big arm thrown casually around the shoulders of Mayor Erastus Corning. *Erastus*, Kate thought, how marvelous! She wondered if they knew in Albany how Blanchflower referred to them, to anyone who didn't live in the great cities. Shitkickers! What do you think of that, Erastus, she said to herself. Long after his image had faded and the late ball scores and the Puerto Rican weather man had come on, she could still see Blanchflower etched into the glass screen as if with acid. This was how she had known him for years, a flat, two-dimensional politico, with the usual smile and the usual words and the usual lies, just as he had first seen her, a two-dimensional anchorwoman reading someone else's news script. How wrong she had been about Nick. He about her. Why, they were nothing like their images. They were rounded, breathing, feeling human beings with private emotions all their own. And how glad I am that we are not Sony-perfect, Kate thought, exulting.

Kate went to sleep happy, ignoring the fact that fall was also the cruelest season in television, the time of "the November sweeps," the new Nielsen rating period when the networks tossed budgetary restraint, and taste, to the winds, and flooded prime time with the most extravagant specials, of memorable movies, of Harry Flagg-least-common-denominator programming. The thing in November was to have "the numbers." Nothing else, *nothing* else mattered.

Kate did not think of these autumnal concerns as she fell asleep. After all, wasn't that what Bobby Klaus was for?

37

Bobby felt like a clubfighter, overmatched, in the late rounds. Venables, he feared, was inevitable. Furtive, self-pitying, Kleenex-chewing, neurotic Bobby, now seemingly doomed, demonstrated an unexpected gallantry.

"I just don't care," he told the broadcast division president who had just given him the latest bad news from A.C. Nielsen.

"Oh?"

"No, Kate and Chester did a hell of a job. So did the crews. If we didn't increase share, well, there were other factors."

"No one cares about 'other factors', Bobby."

How well Bobby knew. The network's ratings had risen substantially during the week of the Mars launch. The trouble was, so had those of the competition, and by a larger percentage. So that, despite higher ratings, the network's share of the actual viewers had declined. In this most pragmatic of businesses where results, or lack of results, were available the very next morning, Bobby Klaus knew their relative failure at Cape Canaveral brought Venables one sinister step closer to power.

His secretary pulled a computer printout of the comparative ratings of the major networks for the entire year. What were the high spots? What the low? The interviews in Coronado with Marcos, unarguably a plus in the ratings. So too Kate's California series and the Middle East. Now, despite the share problem, the Mars launch was another ratings winner. In each case Kate had been in the field, away from the anchor desk. That was the single constant. Chester had once been in New York, once in Washington, once in Florida. No pattern there. The answer had to be, Bobby concluded with a sudden small hope, to get Kate permanently out of New York and into the field. That night, tossing and twisting so violently he nearly tumbled from bed, it came to him: Kate could go to war!

The best days of evening news had been the time of the Vietnam war and of Watergate. It was too much to hope for another Watergate, Bobby concluded sadly, but somewhere there *must* be a war. He switched on his bedroom lights and clawed the phone toward him. He rang a friend in Washington, in the State Department.

"Jess," he said, "this is Bobby Klaus. Yes, I know it's after midnight but listen. What wars have you right now?"

At ten the next morning he summoned his key people.

"As a nation," he said portentously, "we have a tremendous stake in the maintenance of peace. Peace not only in our time but for all time. Never again must generations of young Americans shoulder arms and . . ."

"Jesus," Chester thought, "now he's Woodrow Wilson."

Bobby got up and pulled down a rollout map. He even had a billiard cue pointer.

"There are no major wars at the moment," Bobby admitted sadly, "anywhere on the globe."

"Gee," said the director, "that's tough."

Bobby looked sternly at him.

"That is not to say there aren't several interesting possibilities," he went on, using the pointer.

"For example, we have the Somalis and the Ethiopians. The really exciting part about that affair is that the Russians are supporting both sides. The disadvantage is, of course, that we support neither and so our potential for leverage, for getting cameras and crews in there, is virtually nil."

The pointer moved a few inches on the map of Africa.

"Big Daddy Amin is, of course, always fascinating. His war has two aspects. There is the border unpleasantness with Kenya and the internal suppression of certain of the tribes by his own version of the tonton macoute."

Kate asked who or what they were. Bobby nodded to Chester.

"Sort of an elite bodyguard and secret police Papa Doc used to employ in Haiti," Chester said. "They wore dark suits and dark glasses and pulled out your fingernails if you didn't genuflect to Papa Doc."

Kate shuddered.

Bobby continued. "The Uganda situation holds promise,"

293

he said. "But the problem is Amin has been known to eat people who displease him. Journalists included."

Chester held up his hand.

"Bobby, can you tell us just what in the hell you are talking about? Are you telling us we're going over there to cover some goddamn African war? Is that what you're saying?"

Bobby disdained the simple reply. He smiled, knowingly. All in due course, Chester, he said without saying. How confident he felt now. These props, the map, the pointer, the telephoned briefing last night by his friend at State, these were the security blankets that enabled him to feel superior, calm, capable, to discourse glibly on a world scale. What could Venables possibly know of the Ugandan situation, of Rhodesian chrome, of Mr. Vorster's latest opening to the blacks and their sullen rejection of it?

"If I may continue?" he said. And the pointer moved north and east. Egypt, Israel, Lebanon. What possibilities there were! On then again east, and ever east, southeast Asia, dependably unstable, Taiwan, and those two splendid little specks that had contributed so much to the militarists' cause a generation before. Quemoy and Matsu. Again the pointer moved, piercing the borders of great China, then northeast toward, yes, toward Russia itself.

Bobby stepped back from the map, and asked in a voice husky and tremulous:

"Well, what do you think? Marvelous, isn't it?"

Chester Albany cleared his throat.

"Bobby," he said, "you're fucking nuts."

Bobby maintained a dignified silence.

Surprisingly, Kate came to his support.

"You know, Chester, he's right. I mean, isn't war one of the most basic human conditions? It isn't as if Bobby wants to start one. He isn't proposing we play William Randolph Hearst."

She had suspended skepticism, understanding that it was Venables looming close which had sent Bobby round the bend. Chester did not understand either of them. He was still functioning on a rational plane.

"I don't know if this is one of your elaborate jokes, Bobby,

294

but you can count me out. I signed on as anchorman. I've covered my war."

Bobby Klaus looked at him, puzzled.

"But I wasn't suggesting you go, Chester. It's Kate."

Chester stared at Bobby. Then at Kate.

"Sinclair," he said, "for chrissakes it doesn't mean anything to *me*. But are you really going along with this guy? Do you *understand* what he's telling us?"

The director and the other staffers shifted their eyes from face to face as if watching a three-sided court game.

"Of course I understand," she said. "It isn't that I'm enthusiastic about it. It's simply that maybe Bobby's right. Maybe we can pull the show together. Maybe the ratings will . . ."

"Fuck the ratings," Chester said quietly, angrily.

There was a shocked silence.

"Chester," Bobby Klaus said with dignity, "you know you don't mean that."

The others moved nervously in their chairs. One might think such things but they were not said aloud. Not at the network. Not in front of others who might report such madness.

Chester shrugged, recognizing he had gone too far.

"Hell, what do I care. You want to go to war, Sinclair? Okay, go. Blessings."

She smiled. Bobby Klaus exhaled.

"That's better, Chester. That's the spirit I knew I could count on."

Nothing was decided, only the principle. Bobby would have to go back to the broadcast president for specific authority to send a team. The most promising theater of war would have to be selected. The meeting broke and Kate left for lunch. Chester hung back. When they were alone he walked down the hall with Bobby.

"Look," he said, "I don't want to make a big deal of this. But if you're serious, really serious . . ."

Bobby stopped and looked up into Chester's craggy, somber face.

"Oh, but I am. If it can be worked out."

"All right, then," Chester said, "send me instead."

Bobby shook his head.

"I've studied the ratings. For the whole year. When Kate's on location somewhere, doing remotes, we do better. When you leave the studio it doesn't do a damn thing to the Nielsens. I've checked."

"Bobby, we're not talking about sending her to interview Marcos. Or do the Los Angeles gig. We're talking about war. You know, where people get shot."

"She goes," Bobby said stubbornly.

"For God's sake I have no great yen to cover another war but I've *been* there. I know the ropes. A woman? And it isn't as if Sinclair were Marguerite Higgins or something. She's never covered that kind of story in her life. She belongs in a studio. With hairdressers and makeup guys and air-conditioning. What the hell does she know about running a crew, getting footage, living in the field?"

"Chester, we pay Kate a lot of money. She's smart. She'll learn. She'll have to learn."

Chester went into his office and threw himself down on the old couch. Bobby stood in the doorway.

"Besides," Bobby said, "she wants to go."

Chester muttered, "Doesn't make it right."

"Chester, I don't get it. You hate her. Why this touching concern?"

Chester didn't say anything.

Bobby stood there for a moment.

"Well," he said, "I'll tell Kate what you said. She ought to appreciate . . ."

Chester shook his head.

"No," he said, "don't tell her. This is between you and me."

"I don't get you at all, Chester."

"Just don't tell her," Chester said pugnaciously.

Chester's odd gallantry, Kate's unexpected enthusiasm puzzled Bobby Klaus. He was a pragmatic man who expected pragmatic reactions. Chester and Kate disturbed him with their unpredictability but he did not dwell on it. Instead, that afternoon after the show, he pored over maps, made telephone calls to Washington, called for the network's file on Vietnam. Not a bad idea to learn how they did it then. Bobby Klaus had never read Admiral Mahan, he could not spell Clausewitz. But he had become a student of military science. If wars were what hyped television ratings, then he would produce a war.

Just before he slept that night another inspiration came to him. If the war (whichever war it was he settled on) could continue through the autumn, then Kate Sinclair could be with the troops at Christmas, by god, at *Christmas!* just like Ed Murrow. Hugging that splendid notion he fell asleep, vaguely wondering whether it should be Halston or Bill Blass who should design Kate Sinclair's war correspondent's wardrobe.

38

"I love you," Kate Sinclair said.

She lay next to Blanchflower in her bed. It was night. The curtains were drawn back and across the river the neon of Long Island City shimmered on the water. Blanchflower's arm was around her bare shoulders. Her hair, usually brushed and gleaming, sprawled about her on the pillow. Blanchflower's body curled warmly into her own. She turned her head slightly to look at him.

"Hello, Kate."

"Hello," she said.

He had come in directly from the airport. She had not expected him. Mary Costello answered the door.

"It's himself," she said, and, disapprovingly, disappeared into the depths of the kitchen and her own rooms beyond.

Kate was wearing jeans and a silk shirt. She was barefoot and the glasses she wore for reading were stuck atop her head. He took her in his arms just inside the door and kissed her. It was an awkward kiss. He was holding a soft leather club bag and she had a book still in her hand. They laughed, simultaneously, a nice laugh, unprogrammed, natural, and she led him into the living room. He looked tired, which was unlike Blanchflower. She never thought of him as subject to fatigue. Yet all that animal energy now seemed gone.

"Bad trip?" she said, going to the bar to make him a drink.

Blanchflower opened his tie and collar and flopped into a deep couch.

"Listen," he said, "don't ever run for office if it means three speeches in three cities the same day. Better to get a nice appointive no-show job on the Thruway Commission or rob gas stations."

298

She brought him the drink and as she handed it to him leaned over. He looked up appreciatively.

"Good," he said, "a woman who doesn't need a bra."

"You've got a dirty mind," she said.

Blanchflower nodded.

"Only reason you keep me around," he said.

She poured white wine for herself and sat at the other end of the couch, curled up with her legs under her so she could watch him in profile.

"Goddamn women," he said, half to himself.

"What?"

"Hecklers. In the audience. Two out of the three speeches. Demanding that I vote the feminist party line, get out and stump for ERA. The hell with them."

"Was it that bad?" she asked.

He nodded.

"You know how I am. I mean, 'politics of outrage', all that stuff. I make enemies. Irritate people. That gets me on television where I grin boyishly and show my teeth and get off a few good lines and I get most of the votes back again and more. But this stuff, with the women, it kind of scares me."

He was serious.

"Why? Why should it? I mean, feminists heckle most male politicians, don't they?"

"Sure. This, I dunno, it's different. I can't really spell it out. It's more a sense of menace than anything real. But I don't like it."

He'd finished the martini and Kate uncoiled and took his glass. He watched her move across the room.

"I'm glad I came," he said.

They talked about the women. Blanchflower was jumpy. She'd never seen him like this before. She put it down to the anxieties of the campaign. The election was but a month away and he'd driven himself without respite. Wasn't that it? she asked. No, he said, it was more than that. He thought for a few moments. Kate could feel the tension.

"Ever since I got into it, into politics, there was one rule. Feud with this one, get sore at that one, always have a couple of people, a couple of groups after my ass. Otherwise a pol is flat, gray, boring as hell. If he doesn't have a fight on his hands, he lacks a cutting edge. You've got to fight."

He looked glum, rather than determined. Kate sat next to him on the couch. She was out of her depth. She assumed he had made his point. But he had not. He sat up, the glass cupped in his large, strong hands.

"But you never want to start a fight with too many people at once. If you've got trouble with the blacks, woo the Puerto Ricans. Don't get everyone down on your ass at once." He paused. "That's what scares me about the women."

She shook her head.

"I don't understand."

He laughed, a short, bitter laugh.

"Don't let it worry you, Kate. Maybe I don't understand it myself. Only I have this terrible feeling I've got half the electorate down on me. And I'll be damned if I know why."

"Half?" She still did not comprehend.

He drained his glass and looked at her.

"Half," he said. "The female half."

It was then, without really understanding, knowing nothing she could say would shake him from this uncharacteristic depression, only sure that she loved him and wanted him to be the strong, confident man she loved so well, she stood up, took his hand, and led him into the bedroom. It was not the time to tell him about Bobby Klaus sending her to cover a war. He was troubled and Kate would not make things worse.

Now they lay together in the big bed. He reached out and ran a hand through her hair, then took a cigarette from the night table. He drew in the smoke, passed the cigarette to her. She inhaled and lay there, thinking. How good it felt, being with him. How good it was that, at least for now, he needed her. She had been able to relax him, comfort him, distract him. Knowing she was wanted was fine. Knowing she was needed was finer still. It didn't matter that he was wrong about the women. He would see that himself in the morning, after a good night's sleep. How he had made too much of nothing. He would realize how mistaken he had been.

Only he had not been mistaken at all.

In the morning, after she had gone to the studio, he phoned Robin. The campaign manager spouted statistics.

"What about the feminists, Robin? Am I in trouble there?"

Robin double-talked for a while.

"Rob, the truth."

"Well, you might be, if they could get a handle on you, Nick. All they have right now is a sort of vague sense about it, that maybe you're not too fond of them, that you haven't voted a straight party line. But you know how it is. All my polls indicate you're okay. More than okay. No one's ever coalesced a female vote in the country yet, for or against anybody. Christ, they can't even get their goddamned ERA ratified. You think a bunch of out-of-sorts females are going to be able to unite just because you play the chauvinist pig? Forget it, Nick. There's only four weeks to go and unless you do some damn fool thing, you haven't a worry. We'll get our million majority. Just stay cool and stick to the game plan."

Blanchflower knew he should feel better after having talked with Robin. But he didn't. The sense of unease remained. That afternoon he flew to Washington and when he called Kate that night she asked him how he was.

"Wonderful. Perfect. Forget that stuff I spouted last night. I must have been out on my feet."

"You were," she said.

"Well, you set me right. You were damn good last night."

"I know I was," she said, smiling into the phone. "You weren't bad yourself."

"When am I ever?"

She liked the way he sounded, cocky, full of himself, strong.

But the next morning, when she went to the studio, a line of pickets ringed the building. They were all women. There were perhaps a hundred of them. They were carrying signs with her name on them. They were chanting her name. A sudden chill, tangible, heavy, seized at her belly.

One of the women grabbed her arm, turned and shouted, still holding on, "Hey, it's her, it's Kate Sinclair."

Kate nodded, not knowing whether confirmation would bring a blow or an autograph request.

"Well," the woman said, "we're with you. All the way."

"Why, thank you," Kate said, "that's very nice."

Four or five women gathered around her now. She started to edge toward the revolving door.

"They can't shit on you anymore," another said. "You're not alone."

"Not anymore," someone shouted.

"Well . . ." Kate said, and moved closer to the door.

"The hell with them," yet another woman shouted, "you've paid your dues. They can't treat you like this. They can't dictate what you do outside the studio."

Kate turned to her. This was ridiculous.

"But they don't," she began to say, "you've got this all wrong. I . . ."

"Right on," the first woman said, not listening, brandishing a big, red fist. "We're with you all the way."

Kate was at the door now. She slipped into the revolving space as it slid past.

"Thank you," she yelled back, "thank you all."

Behind her the women waved and gave a little cheer. And resumed their chant.

"Jesus, Kate," said Bobby Klaus, "how could you do this to me? Just when I had everything worked out, about the war."

"It isn't precisely my idea, Bobby," she said coldly. "They didn't get my permission, you know. They didn't consult with me."

Chester Albany came in, straightening his collar and tie.

"Christ, I wouldn't want to tackle a few of those dames," he said cheerfully. "You see the size of them? And the mouths on them! There must be a couple hundred out there. We ought to send out a film crew. Great spot on tonight's show."

Bobby Klaus looked stricken.

"They're picketing our show, and you want *film* footage?"

Chester was hurt.

"It's news, isn't it?"

Bobby ignored him.

Kate threw herself into a chair. "Will somebody get me some coffee and tell me what the hell's going on? All those signs with my name on them. What is it they're after?"

Bobby looked stunned.

"Kate," he said, "you mean this isn't your stunt? They aren't yours?"

"*My* fan club usually gathers after the show," Chester said sarcastically.

"Shut up, Chester, just shut up. Now, Kate, don't you know?"

"Bobby, I swear, I barely read the signs," Kate said. "A bunch of them got around me and started telling me they were on my side, that no one could push me around anymore. I haven't the foggiest."

Bobby Klaus thought for a moment. Then he called over one of the directors.

"Go on out and ask them," Bobby said. "See what they want."

The director grinned. "Not me, Bobby."

"Chester?" Bobby said.

Chester shook his head.

"Send a woman, Bobby."

Kate stood up.

"Listen, I'll go out myself. After all, it's my name they . . ."

Bobby held out a hand as if to restrain her.

"Kate, you don't go out there. Not until we find out what's up. This may be a plot."

Chester laughed.

"Chester, it isn't amusing. Not amusing at all."

"All right, Bobby, but Jesus, a plot? A plot to do what?"

Outside they could hear the women chanting. The chant came through clearly now.

"Free . . . Kate . . . Sinclair . . . free . . . Kate . . . Sinclair . . . free . . . Kate . . ."

There were more women now, several hundred perhaps, and more coming up the street toward the building. Chester looked out the door for a moment and then he turned back.

"I never took you for an indentured servant, Sinclair," he said, smiling.

By mid-morning Bobby Klaus was in the president's office on the 39th floor. Mirós, Klees, and Dillon looked down at him. It seemed to be his fault the women were picketing.

"You must have done something to Kate," Dillon said. "There wouldn't be all this protest if you hadn't."

"Nothing, I did nothing. Not even Chester has done anything nasty. Not for days, maybe a week. No one did anything."

Dillon was skeptical.

"No one? Nothing?" He inclined his head toward the window. The chanting of the women was faint at this height above the street but it was there.

Bobby threw up his hands.

"In fact I was working on an exciting new project for Kate. Something she was really looking forward to. My entire thrust has been to stroke her, shield her, comfort her in her hour of need. You don't know how much I . . ."

"Bobby," the president said, "then why are they picketing? Why are we 'unfair' to Kate Sinclair? *How* are we 'unfair'?"

Bobby absent-mindedly tugged a sheet of Kleenex from his pocket.

"And stop that disgusting habit," Dillon said.

Bobby ignored him.

"Kate is mad for this new assignment. Delirious. I never saw such emotion."

"Oh?" said the president, curious. "What is it?"

Excitedly, Bobby told him about the war.

Dillon looked stricken.

"No wonder they're picketing. You're sending Kate off to be killed and you tell me you're *shielding* her, *comforting* her?"

Bobby's tone was almost haughty.

"It'll give us sensational ratings," he said.

"I don't want Kate hurt, Bobby. She's too . . . you think the ratings will be good?"

Bobby Klaus nodded.

"More than good," he said. "Great."

Dillon paused.

"But that isn't what they're picketing about?"

"Absolutely not. We just discussed this idea a few days ago. No final decisions have been made. No one's had a chance to talk it up outside."

The president stood up.

"Okay, Bobby, go ahead with the war. But I want to be kept informed. Every step of the way. No international incidents, now. I don't want heads of states writing letters." Then, after a few beats, "And I don't want Kate getting killed. Or any of the

304

crew. The unions are hell on that sort of thing. All sorts of lawsuits and damages. Just be careful."

Bobby said they would be careful, very careful.

"And find out what this picketing is all about. Probably one of our weathermen said something chauvinistic. Let me know."

"Yes, sir," Bobby Klaus said.

The broadcasting president sat thinking for several minutes after Klaus had left. Then he picked up the phone and buzzed.

"Get me George Venables," he said.

The thing about Bobby was you had to watch him. He was young, he developed enthusiasms. Better to have Venables in the wings. Just in case.

39

That evening the other networks carried the story. Big. Cronkite himself handled it on CBS.

"A feminist group here in New York today picketed the studios where the Kate Sinclair-Chester Albany evening news is produced claiming that Ms. Sinclair had been pressured by her network not to speak out on women's rights or, in their words, 'to protest injustice and unfair hiring and promotion practices within the network.'"

Kate's own show ignored the demonstration. The local station carried a brief item on the late news coupled with statements from both Kate and the network saying there was no truth to the allegations.

Kate had long before committed herself to a literary dinner that evening. The dinner was fine. Louis Auchincloss told how it was possible to write twenty-seven books and practice law at the same time and Jessica Mitford got off some good lines about having been a communist. But no one seemed to want to hear from anyone but Kate.

"I don't know anything about it. I really don't. I don't know what they're talking about. I can't imagine . . ."

No one listened. Women patted her on the hand and told her, "I'm with you, my dear." Men, depending on their levels of consciousness, smiled or snarled. One man came up to her and said, "A million a year and you're complaining?"

Finally Kate got out of the hotel and slipped into the chauffeured limo. The driver, a black man, turned to her.

"The working people are with you, Miss Sinclair," he said.

"Good," she said, "that makes it all wonderful."

At home Mary Costello was indignant.

"In the name o' God if you're going to take up for a cause

why in hell couldn't it be something worthwhile like Cesar Chavez and them poor spicks of his in California?"

Shaun had called. The message was, "I'm proud of you. Love."

Harvey phoned. He was drinking. But it didn't dilute his malign sarcasm.

"Really, Kate, it's so tacky to turn militant right now. I mean, in the sixties when it was more or less expected of the better sort to demonstrate and boo the police, you were little goody two-shoes. Why turn into a bomb-thrower now, of all times?"

Blanchflower, calling from Washington, was jubilant.

"Well, you've done it. Anyone now who says I'm anti-feminist is certifiable. I think I'll get a speech into the Record tomorrow saying how strongly I support your gallant stand. How your fight has touched my . . ."

"Nick," she said, "there *is* no fight. This is all crazy. The network never gagged me. I never tried to speak out for women's rights. Maybe I should have, but I didn't. This whole business is perverse. It's as if someone wants to screw me up with the network. You know how they are about getting involved in anything controversial. Jesus, this could cost me my job, don't you see that?"

He didn't.

"Look," she said finally, "just come up here as soon as you can. I need any allies I can get."

"Okay," he said, more soberly, "it ought to be before the end of the week."

"I love you," Kate said.

In the morning Kate did not go to the office for the story conference. It was the first time she had missed. Bobby phoned, distraught.

"She's playing squash or whatever it is she calls that hitting the ball," Mary Costello explained.

"Squash?"

"Uh-huh. Said she didn't want to face them pickets any earlier than she had to."

Bobby hung up. He felt the same way. The day before there had been a hundred, perhaps two hundred women ringing the

307

building. This morning, even before he came in at eight, the first demonstrators were on the sidewalk. Now there might be a thousand, he reckoned. It was frightening. So far, fortunately, none of the crew was observing the picket line. The cameramen and the lighting men and the electricians simply bulled through as if they enjoyed the confrontation. God knew what would happen if some of the female employees decided to join their sisters. Who would type the letters, make luncheon reservations, brew coffee? It was all so unsettling. So unnecessary. So unfair. Just when he had pulled off this sensational coup of sending Kate to war.

Kate called from the club.

"Is there some way I can sneak in without going through it?" she asked.

"I've been thinking about it," he said, "because Chester asked the same thing."

"Chester? Yesterday he was practically orgasmic about it. What happened?"

Bobby giggled.

"I think he ran into a picket who was bigger and meaner than he is. It sort of clarified his thinking."

There was an underground entrance with ramp access for trucks. Bobby was setting up a shuttle service of panel trucks ("with one way glass") to get the talent in and out of the studio. "The crew will just have to tough it out with the pickets," he said. He told Kate where the panel truck would be and she hung up.

The rival networks would give the story even more expanded coverage on their evening news shows that night, causing the broadcast division president to call his counterparts at the other television companies.

"Hey, this could happen to you too," Dillon wailed. "Shouldn't we hang together on this?"

There were chortles at the other ends of the line. One told him, "That's what you get for hiring an anchorwoman in the first place." Another said, snidely, he thought, "But Al, you're in show biz, remember?"

It was indulgent, she realized, but Kate stood under the shower of the Racquet Club for fully fifteen minutes after her lesson with Gus. She had not played squash for months and her shoulders, her arms, her legs (and by tomorrow, surely, the long stringy muscles in her buttocks) communicated strain, pleasant, but strain nonetheless. How nice it would be never to leave the shower, to feel the hard, driving water pounding against her, then running off in sheets to the cool tile beneath her feet. How good it would be if she could shower away the feminists and this strange demonstration. Why was she the target? For there was absolutely no doubt in her mind that she was a target and that, far from manifesting on her behalf ("free . . . Kate . . . Sinclair") the feminists had embarked, for reasons unfathomable, on a campaign to destroy her.

She wrapped herself in her robe and strode on her long legs down the corridor to the masseur.

When she went out into the street, instead of being relaxed, refreshed from squash and the massage, she was tight with coiled-spring tension. The network panel truck was to pick her up at Park and 57th. When she got there the truck was waiting. The driver waved.

"No, thanks," she said, and stepped into the Avenue to hail a cab.

She was damned if she were going to let them scare her. She slumped back against the seat, not quite sure what she would do when she got there, not at all sure what the women's reaction might be.

"Hey," the cabbie said, "what they doin' to ya over there, Kate? They don't let you do what ya want? Huh?"

She said something vague and the driver continued to talk. She did not listen.

The picket line plodded methodically around the building. There were more than a thousand women now. It seemed more. Kate got out of the cab and when the first pickets saw a woman coming toward them, they began to boo. Then someone recognized her.

"Kate. It's Kate Sinclair!"

They swarmed to her. Three or four women were closest to her and Kate tried to talk to them. There was one gray-haired woman with a pleasant face.

"Why are you doing this?" Kate asked her, shouting to make herself heard.

The gray-haired woman smiled.

"We're with you, Kate," she shouted back. A hand reached to touch her face. She recoiled.

"But why? Why are you . . . ?"

She was in the crush now, bodies pressing in on her, and she began to panic. A foot tangled in hers and she almost fell. There were hands all over her now.

"Why?" she cried. "Why?" A handbag swung through the air and glanced off her ear.

Then a half-dozen network guards reached her and bulling their way through, they rushed her toward the door. Women's hands tore at them as they moved.

She was crying. The collar of her coat was torn. Why? she was saying to herself, won't someone tell me why?

Chester Albany was furious. He grabbed her by the arms and shook her.

"What the hell do you think you're doing? You want to get yourself killed out there?"

Kate sobbed and shook her head.

Now Chester turned on Bobby Klaus.

"I thought you had a system. I thought you had a panel truck."

He was shouting at Bobby. Bobby held up his hands.

"There *was* a truck. I told Kate. I told her."

Chester was not mollified. He left Kate and stalked away, then turned back again.

"Was there a truck? *Was* there?"

Bobby tried to calm him.

"Chester, I'm telling you. The truck was sent. It . . . "

"Shut up, Bobby, I'm warning you. I want to hear it from her."

Kate inhaled deeply and wiped her eyes. She was trying to regain control.

"Well, Sinclair?" Chester asked. "Was there?"

She nodded.

Chester whirled, his arm flying in the air.

"Then why the hell didn't you get in the goddamn truck?"

By an act of will Kate had stopped her tears, had taken control of herself again. She reached for a handkerchief and could not find one. Chester turned to Bobby.

"Give her a Kleenex, if you can do without one."

Bobby looked hurt.

"I've *never* hoarded my Kleenex," he said. "Here, Kate."

She sniffled a bit.

"Well," she said, "it just didn't feel right. Sneaking in like that. After all, why should we? We work here. And they're supposed to be demonstrating *for* me, aren't they?"

"I knew it," Bobby said, "you *are* part of it, aren't you?"

Chester stared at him. Bobby backed away.

"Now, Sinclair," Chester said quietly, "that was very brave of you. It was also very stupid. Right? You see that, don't you?"

She nodded, subdued.

"I thought I could talk to them. Find out why they're picketing. After all, no one seems really to know, do they?"

Chester shook his head.

"No, we don't know why the hell they're picketing. But what we do know, at least I hope you know it now, Sinclair, is that you can't talk to a mob. You can't have a dialogue with a thousand shouting women *or* men, for that matter. You can't carry on a rational converstation with . . . " he waved a hand, "with that out there."

In her office the hairdresser and the makeup man examined her.

"I'm all right," she said, "I'm not hurt."

"That's right," the hairdresser said, "you were just scared. That's all. Scared."

Kate sat up and threw off the towel they had draped around her.

"Get out of here," she said. "Get out now."

She tried to think. There was some explanation for all this, something she had done or said, or Bobby had, or Chester. Someone had gotten everything terribly wrong. Perhaps Blanchflower had said something in one of his speeches, about feminism, about her, about the network. She picked up the phone. His office said he was on the Senate floor. Should they send in a message?

"No," she said. She had another idea. She began to look through the telephone directory.

Bobby Klaus and Chester were in Chester's office.

"Don't snarl at me like that, Chester," Bobby said. "I told you it wasn't my fault. The panel trucks were all laid on. But she . . . "

Chester lighted a pipe.

"I know, Bobby. I apologize. That damned Sinclair. Why she'd pull a fool stunt like that . . . "

Glad to be shorn of blame, Bobby Klaus said, "You're right, Chester. She could have been hurt. Badly hurt."

Chester looked at him.

"So much safer sending her to war, isn't it, Bobby?" he said sarcastically.

Bobby shrugged.

"Well, under controlled conditions, yes." He paused. "Anyway, what's with you? Why all this touching concern for Sinclair all of a sudden?"

Chester ignored him. "I just wish somebody would explain to me why they're demonstrating."

"You believe Kate? That she had nothing to do with it?"

"Yes, Bobby," Chester said. "It may sound strange to you but I believe her. I don't think she knows *what* the hell is going on."

Bobby did not know. He was bored by the subject. Just when everything was going so well, a disruption like this. It was, well, it was inconvenient. His friend at the State Department had phoned him at home last evening. Northern Ireland was festering again. And Tibet. Some tribesmen in the Himalayas were ambushing Chinese supply convoys. "Tibet!" Bobby breathed into the phone. He remembered how it was in *Lost Horizon*, the original, of course, with Ronald Colman and H. B. Warner and Margo, with all those wrinkles.

"Do you think we could get a crew in?" he asked.

His friend thought it would be difficult. But he would ask around.

"Tibet!" Bobby said as he hung up. "Shangri-la and Lamas." Then he stopped. Were Lamas the monks or those funny-looking animals that spit at you?

Kate had found the number she wanted. It was that of Marcia Mann-Isaacs, the one who'd come to her apartment to push the cause so many months earlier. Marcia was no help. No, she knew nothing about the demonstration. She'd simply assumed Kate had asked one group of feminists or another for their support in her fight for freedom at the network.

"But there is no fight," Kate said exasperatedly.

"Then why is anyone demonstrating?" Marcia asked sweetly.

That night in Washington the President's man, Lester, listened to the news reports and smiled. The demonstration was, after all, only the first step in his campaign to take some of the shine off "ol' Nick Blanchflower."

40

By week's end there were feminists circling not only the New York studio but other Universal Broadcasting facilities around the city. Kate issued another statement. The network issued its own statement. A press conference was held. It was all ineffectual. The feminists would have their martyr, it seemed, no matter how willing the martyr was to abandon the faith and espouse heresy. At last, Nick Blanchflower flew into New York from Washington.

"Nick, tell me what to do. This is crazy. They're indicting the network for something it didn't do. How can I stop it? How can I get through to them?"

They were in his apartment. Even the UN Plaza had its pickets now, shouting their support for Kate Sinclair, clogging the sidewalks and jostling the tenants. A committee was being gotten up among the other tenants to force Kate to move. Mary Costello, who had never crossed a picket line in her life, waded into the line of marchers that afternoon swinging a punishing umbrella and Kate had to send her own lawyer to bail her out. Blanchflower was still not taking the whole thing seriously. Now he sat in his living room and rubbed his big hands together.

"You're a genius, Kate, a goddamned genius. Here I was plucking at the coverlet over the feminists and what they were going to do to me at the polls and you've lined up a million of them in your corner. Why, you and I ought to go right back down to Washington and chain ourselves to the White House railings. Susan B. Anthony lives! Betty Friedan for President!"

Kate looked at him sourly.

"I don't think that's funny, Nick."

She wanted support from Blanchflower. There'd been enough jokes. The night before she'd dined with Harvey Podesta. At his apartment. Again, the need to escape, to be anonymous. I just can't face a restaurant, she'd told him, all those faces, those unwanted vows of support, those unleashed hates. Harvey, feeling much better, thank you, had been delighted. He loved to cook. With the cooking, unfortunately, came the hectoring. Finally, she'd shouted:

"For God's sake, Harvey, stop telling me what I should do, what I've done wrong. I don't need that, I need understanding, sympathy, love."

"Kate," he said primly, "I'm giving you love. I'm preparing an exquisitely loving meal. I cook (he paused dramatically) . . . with . . . love."

She grumbled.

"Then stop all this criticism, this hostility."

Harvey was standing in the doorway of his kitchen with a casserole dish in two gloved hands.

"Kate," he said, "I want you to know I have never, *never* cooked a hostile meal in my life."

Now she flopped down on the couch next to Blanchflower. He'd opened a bottle of Frascati, very chilled. She could feel it down to her toes. She curled up against him, marveling in the warmth and security of his pressure, even when he didn't take her seriously, didn't say the right thing.

"Nick?" she said.

"Yes?"

"Nick, do you think the feminists are doing this simply because I ignored them last spring? When they came to see me and wanted me to become active? Do you think that's possible?"

He shook his head.

"That's paranoia time, Kate. Forget it. Come on, do we have to talk about it?"

"No, I guess we don't. Actually, I'd rather not. I live with it all day at the studio." She brightened. "No, we won't talk about it. Not a word."

And they didn't. They drank, they ate whatever it was she found in his refrigerator, they made love. It never occurred to Kate to contrast Blanchflower's casual, cheerful indifference to Chester Albany's angry concern.

The next morning Frances Neale sent her letter. The postal

service being what it was, the letter would not arrive at the network for two days. And the network bureaucracy being what it was, the letter would wander from desk to desk for a third day before it reached the president of the broadcast division to whom it had been addressed. Meanwhile, as Frances's letter meandered its fateful way across New York, the demonstrations diminished and Kate, in blissful ignorance, put the affair down as one of those inexplicable phenomena that occurred without apparent reason and, again without reason, faded away.

It was the weekend. Blanchflower returned to town. Kate had spent Sunday afternoon with her young sister. They had brunch at P. J. Clarke's and had gone to a movie. Shaun tried to talk about the feminists. Kate cut her off. She wanted to talk about what the girl was doing, whether she was happy, whether she might give yet another hint about returning to school.

"I'm thinking about it," Shaun said.

"Oh?"

Shaun lifted her shoulders.

"Well, you know. I mean, it's fun being on your own. But, well, Eighth Avenue isn't exactly all that great. I mean, everyone thinks it's the pits, but it isn't that bad either. It's just, well, it's kind of predictable. Like school. The same assortment of characters, the same good guys and the same creeps. Some laughs and some boring days. I dunno, let me think about it."

"Okay," Kate said, treading cautiously.

Shaun pushed her hamburger plate around the table.

"You know, I really appreciate your attitude," she said. "Most parents would have gone ape over a dropout. You just, well, you sort of understood."

She didn't say more but Kate understood she meant more, at least she thought she did. And that was sufficient. They left Clarke's and went to the movies. Shaun did not tell her about the boy she'd been sleeping with, about the girl at the disco who'd overdosed, about the exhibitionist who waited for her in the corridors of the hotel, about the pimp who kept asking her to join his stable.

That night there was a party. The network's publishing division, after considerable market research, had decided the time

316

was propitious to put another magazine in the racks of the nation's supermarkets, another spinoff of *People,* itself a spinoff of something else. A million had already been spent in research, two million in development, and a million and a half in advertising (these figures were smilingly available as constructive and significant; the minuscule monies being spent on the actual editorial product were held too small to be disclosed lest the company be embarrassed). Reasoning that another few thousand would have little negative impact on the bottom line, a party was given. A "launching" party. And to emphasize that the magazine was a "serious" popular magazine, with real literary content, the party was given at Elaine's.

Inside the front door of Elaine's is a broadsheet that quotes Dr. Johnson on the appeal of a good tavern, where, unlike a private home, the more you drink, the greater your demands, the louder your shouts and the more boisterous your behavior, the more welcome you are. Of course not every celebrity is welcomed at Elaine's. And the occasional innocent, arguing with a waiter or questioning the arithmetic of his bill, did not usually return after having been informed by Elaine: "The waiters I have to get along with; you I don't need."

It was the place to launch a new magazine because it was a hangout for writers. While David Halberstam was writing *The Best and the Brightest,* he dined there several evenings a week. No bill was ever presented. When Halberstam had finished his great work and made his fortune, he called for his tab. Elaine would not have thought of presenting it earlier. Willie Morris used to negotiate with writers over its tables when he was at *Harper's;* Bruce Jay Friedman and Jack Richardson and Anthony Haden-Guest are regulars; Irwin Shaw and Bill Styron and Sterling Hayden and Frances Fitzgerald and Paddy Chayefsky and Tom Wolfe and James T. Farrell and so many others. There are movie people, attracted, perhaps, by the literati. There are fashion designers and athletes and models and politicians: John Lindsay used to come in late each Sunday night with his cronies and sit in the back. Onassis liked the place and would come in with Jackie. Now her children attend instead. Woody Allen is always there and so too Chevy Chase, and in their wake press agents and groupies and

Mick Jagger and Alice Cooper and the President's son and daughter-in-law.

On the night the network "launched" its new magazine, a press agent had been retained to organize the evening and since the food and drink were free, there was no difficulty in gathering a crowd. Kate Sinclair and Chester Albany were there since the network considered the launching of a magazine worth their appearance. They did not arrive together, of course. Chester was there early, alone. Kate came with Blanchflower.

"It'll be a bore," she warned.

"No gathering of voters is ever a bore," he assured her.

The press agent had assigned pretty girls, and two bouncers, to the door and in the background lurked Elaine herself. Crashers tried the door and were rebuffed, some of them waving bogus invitations or press cards issued by trade journals or claiming intimate relationship with this celebrity or that glimpsed through the front window. Alan Jay Lerner, Lee Radziwill, and a rock group swept in past the guardians. Chester Albany refused several places at table and wedged his backside against the bar, intending to have a drink or three, enjoy the circus, and escape early. Chester was a veteran of this sort of event and understood the dodges. He chatted briefly with a girl he thought might be Bianca Jagger and then, more easily, with the barman who had once been a narcotics detective and had been writing a book about it for several years.

"How's the book going?" Chester asked.

"Great," the barman said. "I'm up to the part where they framed me."

A pretty girl came up.

"Hey," she said, "is Walter Cronkite coming?"

Chester shook his head, "No wheelchair access," he said happily.

Elaine had been in the hospital for the past week, some problem with her knees.

"I checked myself out tonight for the party," Elaine said. "I'll go back in when it's over. See," and she held up her plump wrist to show the hospital's plastic patient identity bracelet.

The inaugural issue of the new magazine had a photo of

Paul Newman on the cover and a huge cake had been baked with a full-color reproduction of the Newman picture in icing.

Bella Abzug refused to cut the cake. "I'm not going down in history as the woman who plunged a knife into Paul Newman."

Rex Reed offered to do it. "They always accuse me of being a hatchet man, anyway," he announced.

Newman, who was apparently unhappy about the cover story, was not there. Someone told Kate his wife, Joanne Woodward, was expected. "But that's not confirmed," the press agent interjected.

John and Mary Lindsay came in and Blanchflower got up to talk with Lindsay for a moment and Kate sat, alone, watching the door where a TV crew was interviewing guests. Geraldo Rivera was holding a microphone under Walter Cronkite's mustache. She noticed Chester Albany standing at the bar, talking with the barman. He looked over and she smiled. Chester nodded and went on talking.

There was a commotion at the door. Another crasher, a short, stocky man in a dark suit, mild, bespectacled, was arguing with the gatekeepers.

"Not unless you have an invitation," she heard a girl's voice say.

The little man said something else and then, with a shrug of resignation, backed out into the street. Kate noticed that he went to the window and peered in.

After dinner a few of the invited began to drift out into the night and Kate and Blanchflower had gotten up and were standing at the bar, watching Mick Jagger and listening to the talk and having a last glass.

"Well," she said, "I guess we've done our duty. Want to go?"

He nodded.

"Just let me finish this," he said.

Kate looked around the room once more. It was funny, she thought, the small man with glasses who had been turned away earlier in the evening was in the restaurant now. He was smiling, as if to some secret joke only he had heard, and he walked toward them. An autograph hound, Kate guessed. I wonder how he . . .

The man was in front of them now, perhaps six feet away, just standing there, looking at Blanchflower and herself, still smiling his little smile.

Blanchflower had seen the little man now too. Shy, he thought, wanting to say hello and not knowing how. Then the man opened the jacket of his neat, dark suit and suddenly, without any great show, there was a gun in his hand.

"Nick!" Kate said.

The man raised his gun hand, still smiling. The gun looked huge to Kate. It seemed to be pointing directly at her chest. Why me? she thought.

"Jesus!" Blanchflower said. Somewhere, off to the right, a woman screamed. People moved, one of them very quickly, and the gun went off. The echo of the shot was still bouncing around the crowded room when the little man was submerged in bodies.

"The son of a bitch," someone shouted.

"Why don't they get the police?" a woman asked.

No one asked if anyone were hurt.

Kate stood there, frozen. My God, she thought, he could have killed me. He was just that far away.

The bodies were unscrambling now. Chester Albany got up, holding the little man by one arm. The gun was now stuck into Chester's trouser top. His face was red but he looked calm.

"Will somebody call the cops and get this character out of here?" he asked.

The shot had gone through a photograph of George Plimpton on the wall behind the cash register.

"I thought he was a friend of yours," a man said.

"Not mine," another man said indignantly. "I don't have friends like that."

"Who is he?"

Elaine bustled through the crowd.

"Okay," she said, "nobody's hurt. Now maybe we can have a little action at the bar?" She glared at the barmen who began busily pouring drinks again. The normal hum of conversation resumed.

After the police had taken statements and led the man away, Kate told Blanchflower she wanted to go home.

"Sure," he said.

320

They said good night to Elaine and to the others they knew and went out into the street. Blanchflower called a cab. They drove to her building in silence.

For once there were no pickets. The doorman tipped his cap. They went inside but at the elevator Kate turned to Blanchflower.

"Look," she said, "I just want to get to bed. This has all been a bit much."

"I know," he said, "I feel the same way."

She pushed the elevator button.

"Well," he said, "try to get some sleep. Don't let it bother you. These things happen. There are a lot of nuts."

"Of course," she said.

She noticed he still looked pale. The elevator came and she got into it and he turned and walked away. The door slid closed.

Upstairs Kate undressed and washed. Mary Costello came out looking sleepy and Kate told her good night. She turned off the lights in her bedroom and pulled the curtains open so she could see the river and the city. She had pulled a nightgown over her head and now, in the chill of an October night, she shivered against the cool flimsy fabric. She stood there at the window, thinking.

What a strange thing for Blanchflower to have told the police, she thought. That the little man had tried to shoot him.

When Kate *knew* the gun had been aimed at her.

She got into bed but was unable to sleep. Maybe she should have had him come up, to talk it out, to settle it between them. They could have made love. Perhaps that would have cleared the air. Then, without knowing why, she remembered Coronado, and the shark.

Finally she got up and took a pill and then she slept, a series of unrelated and silly dreams shunting back and forth through her consciousness.

41

The weekly magazines came out on Monday morning and, once again, Kate Sinclair was in them. A year before it had been such fun. To have one's name always in the papers, in *Time*, in *Newsweek*, in *New York* magazine. It confirmed what one had always suspected: one's own greatness.

How complicated it had all become. For long stretches of her life Kate Sinclair had considered herself a simple person, her life if not preordained at least focused, reasonably predictable. Even recently her days had order, wound tightly around the magnet of work, of regularly spaced contact with Shaun, of mildly amusing but unimportant friendships and affairs. Then, suddenly, there was Blanchflower, who had turned out to be not at all casual. But it had been Chester, not Blanchflower, who had saved her, and Blanchflower who stubbornly insisted the bullet was for him. She got up and moved to the phone.

Chester Albany was lying on his couch in his office daydreaming. He was in Korea. At Panmunjom, in fact, where just a few days earlier the bastards had butchered another UN truce official and compounded the felony by issuing statements full of nationalistic jargon about imperialism and freedom when all the poor fellow had done was mow the lawn under the gaze of the wrong commissar. Chester did not really care. His Korea was decades earlier. His Panmunjom then just a scatter of huts and dun tents and the truce teams going out through the narrow corridor each day while the fighting, and it was real fighting then, went on all night. Chester was one of the correspondents who went along, jouncing over the rutted trail in an old jeep, wondering if this would be the day someone had planted a mine or the day the marines would have to come barreling in to fetch them out, or as many of them as were still alive. The marines were bored with the truce zones, they made no secret of it, and to the correspondents, like Chester, they confided their hopes the communists one day would try to scoop up the whole negotiating team (the correspondents, of course, included) and make off with them to those terrible mountains to the north. Then the troops could go in, shooting up the place, sacking and pillaging as they went. To the marines it was a cheerful fantasy, to Chester a nightmare. But now, as it came back to him, he recognized how simple, how black-and-white it had all been. How long ago. He tried to recall who else rode with him in the jeep. There was . . .

"Hello," Kate Sinclair said.

He opened his eyes. They were very blue and Kate realized it was curious that after nearly a year at the same desk, on the same screen, she had never realized this.

"Hello," Chester said, neither defensively nor with antagonism.

"I'm sorry. Were you asleep?"

He pulled himself to a more upright position on the old couch.

"No, just daydreaming. Can I do anything?"

"Oh, no, I just wanted to thank you."

He sat up straighter.

"For what?"

"Well, for grabbing that man last night for one thing. And for getting mad last week when I was so silly with the pickets."

"Don't be stupid. The gun thing was reflex action. I just happened to be standing there. And last week, well, you know I enjoy yelling at Bobby." He paused. "And at you."

She smiled.

"I know. You do it very well. Yell, I mean."

He laughed.

"I've had a lot of practice."

"Well," Kate said, feeling awkward, uncertain quite how to continue this abnormally cordial exchange, "I just wanted to . . ."

"Listen," Chester said, "you already thanked me. Forget it. Remember, I'm the guy you feud with."

"I know," she said, "I think I'd sort of miss if it we ever stopped."

At the story conference thirty minutes later it was the old familiar Chester.

"For chrissakes, Bobby, she has two out of the top three stories and then the one long interview. Do I get to do the station break or what?"

Bobby Klaus was having lunch at Rose's. Just before two o'clock the headwaiter called him to the phone. It was the broadcast division president.

"You better get back here. More trouble with Sinclair."

"Not the goddamned feminists?"

"No," Dillon said, "maybe worse. I don't know. Come right up to my office."

When Klaus got there Dillon handed him Frances Neale's letter.

"What do you make of that?"

Bobby had read it slowly, carefully. Now he put it down on his boss's desk.

"I don't make anything of it," Bobby said. "It's scurrilous. I'm surprised that it's signed. This sort of garbage usually isn't."

"Then you think there's nothing to it?"

Bobby shook his head.

"Absolutely not. I'd stake my . . . "

Suddenly Bobby felt like a man leaning over a bottomless abyss. This was all too pat. A silly, trumped-up letter full of wild accusations against Kate. Yet the president was taking it seriously. And Bobby, that most cautious man, was laying his own career on the line in declaring something he did not really know, no matter how strongly he suspected it, that the letter was bogus. Yet . . .

"You were saying," Dillon said, "something about staking your reputation . . . ?"

Bobby sat up straight.

"These are serious charges," he said, a different note in his voice. "We'd better look into them."

The president nodded.

"Considering who wrote it we've begun to do just that," he said. "George Venables is on it."

"Oh," Bobby said.

It was a small and lonely sound in the large office.

It was an hour later when Blanchflower phoned Kate.

"Look, I've got to see you. It's important."

She said she was free that evening, after the show.

"No, I'm flying back to Washington. Got to be this afternoon. Now."

He gave her the address of a bar on Second Avenue.

Blanchflower was waiting for her in a booth of the bar. It was dark inside and coming out of the glare of the late October sun she did not see him at first. Then she saw the movement of a hand waving. She slid into the seat opposite. There were three or four men drinking at the bar. The other booths were unoccupied. Blanchflower gestured toward the drinkers.

"Salesmen. Filling in their call reports. Claiming they're making a big sales pitch to J.C. Penney right now. Over the Jack Daniels. You want a drink?"

"I go on the air in two hours. You have one."

"I've had one. I think I'll have another."

There was no waiter and he got up and went to the bar. The drinkers didn't pay any attention to him. He came back with something on ice.

"Well," he said.

"Nick, what is it? What's the matter?"

"I've got trouble. Big trouble. With your feminist pals."

"You've got trouble? You? I'm the one they picketed. You've been telling me for weeks it was great publicity, that it was just splendid for your campaign. Now suddenly it's trouble."

He nodded.

"Up till now they've been attacking the network, claiming the TV boys gagged you, wouldn't let you speak out."

"I'm sick and tired of telling you and everyone else that's a lie."

"I know," he said. "But now the tactics are changing. They've got a new target."

325

"What?"

"Me," he said.

"You?" she asked. "Why you? What did you have to do with it?"

"They have it that I'm exercising an unhealthy control over you, that I tell you what to say, that I've got you taped and programmed."

She laughed.

"You're right to laugh," Blanchflower said. "Tough cold stainless steel bitch like you. How the hell could anyone program you?"

"So it's nonsense."

"Sure," he said, "sure it is. But people, some people, are going to believe it. And Election Day is, what? ten days from now?"

"Nick, how do you know all this? From what I can see the pickets are still trashing the network, not you. How can you be sure that . . . ?"

"I've got my sources," he said mysteriously. "They say there's going to be a press conference tomorrow. All the big guns of the movement. Big, dramatic announcements: 'Senator Nicholas Blanchflower Revealed as Svengali.'" He grinned then, and Kate felt something move inside her. "Or is it Trilby?"

"Trilby's a hat," she said.

He finished his drink.

"That's what I like about you, Kate, you're well read."

"But you can't be taking it so seriously," she said. "Women don't vote as a bloc. You taught me that. And certainly we aren't all feminists. You're going to win easily. Even Robin says so. It isn't like you to get nervous like this."

"Election fever. And I know what I said. And what Rob said. Still, I don't like it. Look what this goddamn silly campaign by a couple of hundred crazy broads has done to you, to the network. Just before an election anything that happens is bad. When you're ahead the way I am what you want is total calm. Don't stir anyone up. Keep your mouth shut and don't make mistakes. Now these dames are going to hold their press conference and raise a lot of hell and I don't need it. Believe me, Kate, I don't need it."

326

She thought for a moment.

"Then what are you going to do about it?"

"Deny it, of course. You'll have to deny it as well." He looked at her. "You will, won't you?"

"Nick, you don't have to ask. Besides, it isn't true."

He looked somber.

"But it wasn't true about the network and that didn't stop them."

"That's life," he said. "Unfair."

"Unfair," she repeated dully. "And when is this infamous press conference to take place? When is someone going to stand up and tell more lies about me?"

"Tomorrow," he said, "that's what my sources say."

Blanchflower was wrong. Or his sources were wrong. When she got back to the studio from the bar one of the assistant directors handed Kate an AP tape.

"Feminists in New York today accused Democratic Senator Nicholas Blanchflower of anti-feminist activities including the muzzling of television anchorwoman Kate Sinclair when she attempted to speak out in favor of the controversial Equal Rights Amendment."

The assistant director looked embarrassed.

"Sorry, Kate, but I knew you'd want to see it."

"Sure, Bernie, sure. Thanks."

She walked down the corridor to her office. She was not sure her legs were really shaky or if it just seemed that they were. She buzzed her secretary.

"Try to get Senator Blanchflower. He's in New York, somewhere. Or he was an hour ago. Try his Washington office too."

Bobby Klaus did not wait.

"Kate, this is great," he said, bouncing into her office. "They're finally off the network's ass."

She looked at him, frowning.

"Bobby, I want you to know how pleased I am for the network."

"Well," he said, "you don't look it. Blanchflower is a big boy. He can certainly take care of himself."

She stood up.

"And what about me, Bobby? What about Kate?"

Exasperated, Klaus walked out of the room. When a woman

was in a mood like this, well, there was just no reasoning with her. You'd think she'd be happy for him, for the network.

Kate expected to hear from upstairs, from the 39th floor. Bobby Klaus did not. He knew about Venables's investigation, about Frances's letter, about how the network had begun to peel away the layers of Kate Sinclair's life, picking among them as one might an artichoke, looking for imperfections, for sediment, for worms. This latest eruption might destroy Kate, it might damage Blanchflower, might delight the White House. It did not affect the network and therefore could be ignored. The letter could *not*.

Others did not ignore the feminist screech. A boy tugged at Bobby's arm.

"Jesus, Bobby, you won't believe this, but a CBS camera crew is outside. They want in."

Bobby stared at the production assistant.

"CBS? Here?" he demanded, incredulous.

"They say they want to film Miss Sinclair. Her comments on this women's lib bullshit."

"The aspirations of American women are not 'bullshit,'" Bobby declared. "They are a reasonable and understandable striving for equal treatment under the law by a segment of society which has for too long been the target of discrimination and unfair treatment."

The boy shrugged.

"Okay, Bobby, but the CBS guys, they still want in."

It was agreed that Kate would go out onto the plaza surrounding the studio to be filmed. There were still pickets out there but they were calmer now, veterans, and they crowded around, not in a hostile manner, but simply hoping to hear what was being said or to get their faces on television.

"This charge that Senator Blanchflower influenced me in any way is totally untrue," Kate said. "He is a personal friend. I can never recall his pressuring me on any substantive matter and we have in fact rarely if ever discussed the feminist movement. Whoever is promulgating these stories, that either the network or Nick Blanchflower or anyone else makes up my mind for me, is, to put it bluntly, out of touch with reality."

The reporter, who like most reporters did not listen to her

reply but was thinking about what his next question would be, then said:

"Are you, Ms. Sinclair, sympathetic to the feminist cause?"

Worn down, irritated, frustrated and angry, Kate Sinclair permitted herself to be drawn. She lost her famous cool:

"After all the crap I've heard in the past couple of weeks, no. Not at all. . . . NO!"

The reporter, who had heard that at least, goggled at his good fortune.

"Do you mean to say that . . . ?"

"Yes," Kate said, knowing she had just committed a terrible blunder, "that's precisely what I mean. Good day."

"Well," Chester said when she came back upstairs, "so the shit has really hit the fan."

She nodded.

"Boy, do I know it. What do I do now, Chester, say it was all a big mistake or what?"

He grinned.

"Do a Ziegler. Your statement is 'inoperative.' Do a Nixon. You never said it in the first place. Media bastards, always inventing quotes."

"Chester, I'm on tape."

"I know," he said, "let's not forget to watch Cronkite tonight."

42

The founder of Universal Broadcasting and chairman of its executive committee, a committee that never met, was now a very old man. He lived in a penthouse on the East River, spending his days and the frequent sleepless nights in an old Atlantic City boardwalk wicker chair which a manservant pushed around the apartment or onto various terraces as his employer commanded. The manservant had other duties, one of which was to smoke the occasional cigar, so that the founder of the network, himself no longer permitted to smoke, could sniff the air and at second hand, savor the cigar. Although the network was now but a division of a much larger conglomerate, the deal by which the network was sold resulted in the founder's receiving a great number of shares of stock so that, despite his age and intermittent senility, he was still consulted on those rare occasions when the active executives floundered. This seemed to be one of those occasions.

Bobby Klaus had never been to the founder's apartment. He had seen him once, and then only briefly, emerging from a board meeting at the network. He remembered him as very old then and he wondered how he would look now. Possibly he would resemble that grizzled monk of Shangri-la who imprudently climbed out through the mountain pass into the modern world. Bobby had a pocket full of Kleenex and he chewed them industriously in the taxi that took him across town. He would be the junior man at the meeting. The others were all his superiors, the president of the network, and the chairman of the network, and his own boss, Dillon. It was the chairman who opened the meeting with what apparently was a ritual tribute, redolent of the courts of certain Middle Eastern despots.

"Well, now, Chief, don't you look splendid," he said, addressing the founder. "We'd all better be on our toes down at the shop or you'll come bouncing in there one of these days to give us what-for."

The chairman turned to his companions, beaming. As if on an applause cue the others, Bobby Klaus included, grinned and nodded and said, oh, yes, how fine the chief looked. Bobby did not think the chief looked well at all, but he did not mention this.

The founder was sunk deep in the wicker chair whose back and sides, higher than his head, seemed to wrap him within them. A heavy scotch wool blanket, bundled about his knees and up to his middle, added to the womblike effect. No sound came from within the chair and Bobby wondered whether the old man had perhaps passed away. No such doubt seemed to curb the enthusiasm of the chairman, who plowed ahead.

"Chief, you're a sly dog, I'll bet you know exactly why we've come, why I requested an audience. I'll just bet the old spy network's still functioning and you know what we're up to down at the shop before I know myself." He turned to embrace his companions with his glance. "Why, the chief has the most amazing setup. Prettiest girls in the shop. All reporting straightaway to him whenever anything goes even the slightest bit wrong."

There was again an appreciative chuckle but the mummy in the wicker chair remained motionless, silent.

The chairman pressed on.

"Well, now, Chief, I know how busy you are and so I'll get to the point. There's a little problem we have at the shop, Chief. With some of the talent. You know talent, Chief, they get carried away by the ratings and how much we pay them and they start to think they count, start to believe their notices and think they're important. Well, that's what's happened with one of the new talents. She . . . "

There was a growl from inside the wicker chair.

"What was that, Chief?" the chairman asked, very alert.

The growl was more distinct now.

". . . give . . . woman . . . big job . . . you're . . . damn fool."

The chairman nodded vigorously.

"Exactly, Chief. Just like always, you put your finger on it. A woman. Trouble. Never fails. Anyway, this woman, Kate Sinclair . . . "

" . . . . . . " the chief growled.

"I didn't get that, Chief," the chairman said.

The voice came stronger now, clearer, from inside the chair. "My man. Is he here?"

Three of the four men in the room turned to find the servant. Only Bobby Klaus stood motionless, petrified. The manservant sidled up to the boardwalk chair and asked what the founder wanted.

"Light a goddamned cigar," the founder barked.

"Wonderful idea, Chief," the chairman said. "Nothing like the smell of a good cigar to brighten up a room."

The founder growled.

"So this talent, Kate Sinclair," the chairman resumed, "has become something of an embarrassment to the network and she . . . "

"Fire the bitch," the founder advised.

"Well, now, Chief, exactly what I said. 'Fire the bitch.' Solve the problem right there. Only . . . "

"Only what?" came the growl.

"Well, there's this new thing, Chief, a sort of feminist movement, militant, *very* militant, and they buy a hell of a lot of merchandise our advertisers market, and there's this big pressure group that's gotten behind her. They think the network pressured Kate, that we won't let her speak out for feminism. They're talking boycott and we thought we'd better come by and see you and . . . "

"She strong with the advertisers?"

"Yes, Chief. Strong."

"I wouldn't fire her out of hand, then."

"No, Chief, exactly the way I felt. Just what I said. Not out of hand, I said."

The founder, gaining strength, asked precisely what *was* the problem, what else had this woman done? Or was it just this feminist nonsense?

No, the chairman said, as if reluctantly. There was another aspect to the Kate Sinclair problem. One that could prove "embarrassing" for the network, that could be terribly damaging if it came to public knowledge.

332

The chairman snapped his fingers and Dillon pulled out a photocopy of Frances's letter.

He handed it to the founder.

"Goddammit," the old man said, "read it to me."

Dillon cleared his throat and read. When he was finished the founder sat silently for a moment.

"You actually employ a woman like that?" he asked. "You pay her a wage?"

The men nodded. Bobby Klaus sensed heads turning toward him.

He wadded up the Kleenex in his pocket. How foolish he had been to think that a woman, any woman, could hold down an anchor chair. Even more foolish to have chosen this particular woman, this Kate Sinclair, who had turned out to be a viper in the nest.

Frances's letter was devastating:

Kate Sinclair employed a known communist subversive in her home; consorted habitually with homosexuals; had a younger sister living in an Eighth Avenue house of prostitution; was committing adultery with a United States Senator; had whipped the feminist sisterhood into a frenzy of hatred for the network; and who, while in California on assignment, had indulged in shocking orgies of drugs and sex with any number of young men. And even, it was hinted, a few women.

It was Venables who had carried out the corroborative investigation. His detectives had provided documentary evidence. Bobby Klaus's bright discovery, his nominee for the network's most influential news job, the woman to whom they were paying a million a year, had turned into a frightening, terrible, destructive nightmare.

And it was also Venables who had done the research and supplied it to Frances to reproduce on her own stationery, after his earlier project, the anonymous letter from Bunny, had apparently failed.

Had Bobby been a Catholic he would have fallen to his knees and begged forgiveness. Instead, he stood, mute and trembling.

The founder sighed.

"What does she look like, this paragon we pay to represent our little company on the air?"

"You've never seen her?" Bobby asked, without thinking. Heads turned again.

The chairman stared at him coldly.

"The chief does *not*," he said, "watch television."

"Oh," Bobby said. Of course not. How could he have been so naive. He felt an urge to giggle. This was Alice's line of country, not his, these hardfaced men who lived by the bottom line, not executives at all but Tweedledee and Tweedledum.

"So you'll fire her," the founder said.

The chairman squirmed.

"Well, Chief, that's an option, of course. Fire her. Just like that. But . . . well, there's the feminist movement and the threat of secondary boycott, and, well, frankly, I'm not sure we should."

The founder nodded.

"Boycotts are bad stuff. Bad."

The men, Bobby included, nodded solemnly. Bad. Bad stuff.

"We were rather thinking exile," the chairman said.

The founder sneered.

"You have this anarchist . . . this leper . . . in your midst and you think exile? Ha!"

The chairman was out of his depth.

"Just precisely what do you suggest, Chief?"

The founder grinned, a humorless grin, his eyes narrowed and his upper body shook with slight mirth.

"Two things," he said, quietly. "First you get her to make peace with the women. Get the feminists off your back. I don't care how, some gesture, some statement, but make it clear she's not their enemy, that the network is sympathetic to their damn cause."

He paused and Bobby wondered for an awful moment whether the old man had forgotten what he was about to say, forgotten what the second piece of advice was that he wanted to give them. But he had not. The founder stirred a bit in the wicker chair and his eyes blinked.

Now, in an even quieter voice, more terrible than before, he continued:

"And second, get the network out from under this ridiculous five-year contract. Force her to take on jobs that she'll hate, give her assignments she'll resent. Demean her, abuse her, force her to quit."

He stopped again and the four men leaned forward, waiting.

The founder's nose was running. A silver drop of water hung like a pendant in the groove of his wrinkled upper lip. Bobby watched it, mesmerized, waiting for it to fall, expecting a cymbaled crash when it did, but the valet moved in noiselessly and smartly whisked a handkerchief under the old man's nose. The drop disappeared and then, just as the room had begun to relax, he spoke again.

"Destroy the bitch," he said. "Be hard, be clever, be cruel."

The room was quiet and Bobby Klaus, a creature of the network system, shivered. The other men nodded, solemnly, meditating perhaps on what "cruelty" they might conjure up that would ruin Kate Sinclair, cause her to resign, rid themselves both of her and the threat of boycott. The founder watched them, closely. Then, like a petulant child, he twisted his thin torso to the right and barked at the valet.

"You smoking that thing or masturbating with it?"

The valet resumed puffing at the cigar and the network executives said their good-byes.

43

They met in Dillon's office, Bobby Klaus and Dillon and Kate. Venables was there too, triumph and hatred mingled in his face. He said nothing. He knew he had won the war. He did not want to spoil his chances of winning the peace by speaking prematurely. He just sat there, lethal, listening.

"You've got to make peace with the feminists," Dillon said. "There's no longer any room to maneuver. Our options are down to this: Get the bitches off the network's back."

"All you think about is the network," Kate said stubbornly, angrily, "what about Nick Blanchflower? They're out to get him too. What am I supposed to do? Cheer them on? Wave the flag? Sign petitions?"

"I want you to do any damn thing you have to do. Just end the picketing, stop the boycotts before they destroy us!"

Dillon glared at her. He was painfully aware of the founder and the chairman and the network president counting on him to bring Kate to heel, to end the feminist attacks, to protect the network. He was also aware, as Bobby Klaus was not, that Venables had won, that he would take over the evening news. It had also occurred to Dillon that if he failed to solve the Sinclair situation and solve it quickly, Bobby Klaus would not be the only victim. He himself, president of the broadcast division, could go under. He shivered. Bobby was talking now, persuasively.

"Let's not bog down in recrimination, Kate," Bobby was saying. "Maybe there's common ground somewhere."

He had never functioned as a diplomat before but, desperate, realizing the stakes, he was willing to try anything. Now, slyly, he sought to insinuate himself, having spent hours on the telephone, trying to make his arrangements. If only he could pull it off, he thought, if only Kate would go along, there

336

was still a slim chance he could outflank Venables and retain control of the news.

"Look," Bobby said, "I've talked with several of the feminists."

"You?" Kate said scornfully.

Bobby nodded, controlling himself, remaining cool.

"And I got the impression that if Kate would make some gesture, if she'd . . . "

"I won't," she said, "I won't apologize."

Bobby waited until she stopped.

"Some *symbolic* gesture," he said, "very clearly not an apology. Just an appearance. You won't even have to speak."

Dillon leaned forward expectantly. Bobby Klaus had surprised him. He noticed that Venables, for the first time, shifted uneasily on the leather couch. Kate still had a stubborn, bulldog look on her face. But she was listening.

Bobby spoke more quickly now, sensing he had caught their interest.

"There's a big rally at the Garden, tomorrow night. In support of the Equal Rights Amendment. Every feminist in the country will be there. We're carrying it live. So are the other networks."

"And?" Kate said, suspicious, but attentive.

Bobby rubbed a Kleenex between damp palms.

"And I've gotten them to agree that if you'll sit on the rostrum, stand up and be introduced, say hello, perhaps a few conciliatory words, not really do anything at all, that will satisfy them. They'll call off the pickets. They'll forgive you."

Kate withered him with a look.

"I was not aware I had to be forgiven," she said icily.

Bobby cringed.

"I put it badly," he said. "Look, we can make peace. You don't have to back down. You don't have to do a goddamn thing. Just go up there on the platform and be introduced and wave a hand and sit down. Is that asking too much? Is it?"

Kate sat there, silent. Dillon picked up on Bobby's thread.

"Kate," he said, "that's not bad. Not a bad thing Bobby is asking. It could be very important for the network. Important for you."

Kate still said nothing. She looked at Venables. He sat there, mute, a scorpion on a stucco wall. Waiting, watching, silent.

If Venables had spoken then, added his voice to Bobby's and Dillon's, she would have refused. Instead, since he made no recommendations, she said, after a sulky pause, "Okay, if all I have to do is sit there and wave a hand."

Bobby smiled. "That's all," he said encouragingly.

Kate smiled now too. But it was not an encouraging smile. "Do any of you *really* give a damn about the feminist movement? About the amendment?"

There was an uneasy silence.

She nodded. "I *do*, you know. I really do. And now *I'm* the one who has to go up there and say I'm sorry . . . "

"Just hello," Bobby broke in, "a gesture, is all."

"That's all it better be," she said, her voice trailing off ominously.

The women had taken over Madison Square Garden, really taken it over, and it was perhaps, make that *surely*, the first time they opened the Garden to a sellout crowd and there was no cigar smoke hanging blue in the air. Kate was very nervous. The committee, specifically Marcia Mann-Isaacs, had promised she would have to do nothing but sit with them on the platform and, at the appropriate time, when her name was called, to stand and wave and, if she felt like it, gesture with the Vee sign in the air. And then she could sit down again.

"It's your presence we want," Marcia Mann-Isaacs said. "Just being there with us. That's solidarity right there. You don't have to say anything that might get you into difficulty at the network. You don't have to say a thing."

Still, Kate was nervous.

Jane Fonda was very good as the chairperson, steely-eyed, enthusiastic, the short hair and the intensity and the obvious belief all very Jeanne d'Arc. Kate tried to watch her, to listen to her, anything rather than watch or listen to the crowd, quiet, crouching, a vaguely menacing animal presence. She thought, how silly this is for me to have stage fright before 17,000 women when every night I speak to millions. But the millions were safely at the other end of the coaxial cable or the ether or whatever damn thing it was that carried her face, her voice. Here, there was no insulating distance. Here the great animal crowd was all around her.

Just then another speaker took the stand. It was Marcia Mann-Isaacs, her sponsor, Kate supposed. She heard her own name being spoken. Not spoken, shouted.

Kate tensed. And leaned forward to listen.

"Kate Sinclair," Marcia repeated, "Kate Sinclair knows what ERA is all about. She's fought for it, for its principles, all her working life."

There was an appreciative roar from the crowd. Kate smiled, not knowing if they could see it, but knowing a smile had come up on the cue card.

"And it hasn't been easy for Kate Sinclair to stand up for the cause. Not easy at all," the woman lawyer went on. "Do you think it was easy for a woman in her position to take unpopular stands?"

There was a chorus of "no's," not quite a roar, but clearly shouted.

Kate smiled again. Well, she thought, so it's to be a love fest. She still did not relax but she began to feel better.

Marcia Mann-Isaacs continued.

"Do you think it was easy for Kate Sinclair to withstand the powerful forces aligned against her?"

"No!" This time it was very nearly a roar.

"Do you think," the woman lawyer went on, knowing she had them now, confident the chorus of shouted "no's" would be there on cue.

Kate shifted in her chair, a bit uneasy. I must look inscrutable, she told herself, serene. I must not react. She smiled the implacable smile. The speaker continued.

."Do you think her television network encouraged Kate to speak out on the great question of women's liberation?"

"No," they roared, and the Garden trembled.

Marcia half-turned now and gestured, urgently, for Kate to rise, to join her, to stand with her at the microphone.

Kate hesitated but the applause had begun and now it built and she was on her feet, waving tentatively to the crowd, the crowd she feared even as it was cheering her.

Marcia asked another question which Kate did not even hear, and again the crowd shouted, "No!"

Then came the crescendo.

"Kate Sinclair, who is one of us, isn't afraid of the sexist toads! Is she?" shouted Marcia Mann-Isaacs.

"No!"

Kate's stomach leaped inside her.

"And she won't be influenced by the chauvinist pigs, not even by Senator . . . Nicholas . . . Blanchflower! Will she?"

"Nooooo!" the animal crowd responded.

Kate was alone now at the microphone. The women were all standing. The speaker had drifted off behind her. Kate's eyes watered. She could not see anyone clearly now, just the massed faces. She could hear the cheering and the applause and she stood there, not even listening to it anymore, thinking how rottenly she had been set up, how they had lied, how she had been maneuvered into this appalling, impossible, destructive position. Whatever she said now would do damage. However she played it, she would lose.

She inhaled deeply, sniffled to clear her nose and eyes, using professional techniques to regain control, to enable her to think, to say something that made sense, yet to strike back at the nasty, cold-blooded viciousness with which they had set her up.

She could discern individual faces now. As the crowd slowly, gradually returned to its seats, as the noise faded and died, she waited, knowing that what she was about to say, to these thousands and to the millions watching on television, would either damage her career in television as surrogate for all those women out there or it would surely destroy Nick Blanchflower's ambitions and, more meaningful to her, his love.

She now was very calm. Her choice was made. She held up her arms, palms downward, so that the last stirring of the great crowd was stilled, and in her trained, professional, so familiar microphone voice, she began to speak.

"I believe in the feminist movement. I voted for the amendment. I support its ratification. I hope the final two states will act shortly to approve it."

There was applause, but not frenetic as it had been a moment earlier. There was something in Kate's voice, her pos-

340

ture, her face, intimating that what she was saying now was just a preamble, that there was something more, perhaps something quite significant, to come. Kate paused and did not smile. And went on.

"The name of Senator Nicholas Blanchflower (a few catcalls and boos) has been mentioned on this platform. It was said I was influenced by him to withhold support for ERA, for the movement."

"Screw him!" a lone voice called out. Kate ignored the interruption.

"I did not come here tonight to make a speech. I was told (she glanced toward Marcia Mann-Isaacs) that if I sat up here, said hello, joined all of you in supporting the amendment, the boycott of my network would end. I was willing to do that. Now, instead, I am asked to turn away from a friend. From more than a friend."

There was a nervous, silly, vulgar laugh. But only one. The Garden was hushed, waiting. Kate's voice was still strong, still polished, but tense, taut.

"Nick Blanchflower has never tried to turn me against the movement. I do not agree with his position on many issues. Nor he with me. But . . ." and her voice slowed, steadied, and went on more slowly and with dramatic emphasis . . . "I'll be *damned* if I join this woman (she turned toward Marcia and stared for a full second) or any of you in a public attack on a man I love."

For an instant there was no reaction. There was silence, the audience frozen. Kate stepped back from the microphone, looked to right and to left, and began walking, in control, across the rostrum toward the exit ramp.

As she went the silence shattered. A woman ran up the center aisle toward the platform, screaming obscenities. A few hundred others took it up, standing in their places, shouting, brandishing fists, and the throwing of things began.

Most of the 17,000 sat silently. A few applauded. But Kat did not hear the silence, the applause. She heard only the hatred and the curses of the few.

Outside the Garden there were long ranks of yellow cabs but she ran past them, not stumbling but running blindly, not seeing them. She slowed at the revolving door of the Statler Hilton Hotel. In the lobby she paused. There must be a telephone, she could phone for her car. The thought of having to negotiate with a cabbie was beyond her. She went through a doorway to get away from the lobby crowded with salesmen and suburban women and conventioneers from the bottling industry. The door she had chosen did not lead to phones. It was the bar. She stood there, quietly, but confused and helpless. Around her men and women sat at booths and drank. A young man with a nice smile and crooked teeth grinned at her.

"You look lonely," he said.

He was so silly she had to smile. Her panic ended. She breathed deeply, looked around and went outside. There was a line of cabs at the curb. She wondered why she had not seen them before.

44

Kate tried to recall when she had *not* been alone, when she had not been subject to betrayal, harassment, ridicule. She ached for support, friendship, for love. In the apartment, her door locked and bolted behind her, the horror of Madison Square Garden shut out, she remembered how it had been two days earlier, when Cronkite and all the others had picked up on her, had reported, smirking, her gaffe, when the magazines and the newspapers had joined the awful Greek chorus denouncing her, she remembered that in the darkest time, Nick Blanchflower had phoned.

"Listen," he had said, his voice hard and rasping and familiar, "don't let the bastards get you down. *Illigitimi non carborundum.* You make a million a year and they don't. So they're out to get you. You make a little slip and they're at you. Kate, don't fold. Don't cry. Don't beg. You fold now and they'll tear you to shreds. Everyone says you're a tough, hard bitch. Well, now's the time to prove it."

Two days earlier he had said all that, and more, and he had bucked her up.

Where was he now, now when she needed him more than ever, when she had thrown a career, a life away for him? Where was he?

She imagined again the tough, gangster talk, the slangy, easy obscenities, the rough texture of his voice. She could picture him, in the little Georgetown flat, a can of beer in the big hand, the familiar furniture and tossed necktie and thrown shoe, the pictures on the walls, the cigar clenched in his teeth or reeking in the big pewter ash tray. Tell me more, she wanted to say, talk to me, comfort me, strengthen me. And as he spoke to her in imagination she put aside, surely for the final time, the uneasy memory of the little man with the gun, of the shark at Coronado. Now, now that she really needed him, Blanchflower would be there. Oh, so much there. He would tell her everything she wanted to hear, needed to be told, and when he finished she would say, aloud, "I love you, Nick Blanchflower, I love you."

Remembering how wonderful he had been two days before, the things he had said, the support he gave, now helped Kate put behind her the anger of the Garden and confirmed that her gallant, stubborn refusal to jettison him, even at the cost of her career, had been the right course. What she did not know was that very afternoon, hours before she entered the Garden, Robin had handed Blanchflower a new poll. It showed a substantial slippage in his lead in the Senate race. Especially ominous was his shrinking share of the female vote.

Robin did not have to spell it out for his candidate. Nick Blanchflower knew what the poll was saying. Irritated, frustrated, he dismissed the loyal Robin. He knew he must do something to reestablish himself with the women voters. And he knew that whatever he did must be done publicly, where everyone could see it. He must do it on television.

Kate would learn of Blanchflower's about-face on the eleven o'clock news.

The anchorman came back from a commercial break to announce they would go to Washington with an important sidebar to the Kate Sinclair story: Senator Nick Blanchflower was issuing a statement. Kate, sunk deep in a couch, straightened. The picture flipped once, twice, and then there he was, big, strong, a consolation even at this distance. A couple of TV reporters with hand mikes were with him. It seemed to be a corridor in one of the Senate office buildings, she wasn't sure, but everything was marble, glistening. Later, as she remembered everything, she would remember that.

The reporter mumbled something. Then, Blanchflower, the customary grin absent, nodded.

"Yes, I do want to say something."

Kate leaned forward. He knew precisely how to use the camera. She had no idea what he was about to say. She knew only that it would be effective, credible. And that it would help.

"During the past several days I have been the target of the most vicious sort of criticism, of innuendo, of rumor. All of it

344

associated with my friendship for Kate Sinclair, the television personality, who tonight broke with the national feminist movement and declared herself disinterested in its eventual goals."

Kate tensed. She hadn't broken with anyone. She felt a sudden chill.

Blanchflower continued to speak, so familiar to her, every line and plane of his face, every bone, every muscle of his big, powerful, graceful body.

"It's clear now that Ms. Sinclair was less than candid with me about her opposition to the Equal Rights Amendment and the legitimate aspirations of American feminists, a lack of candor that seemed to suggest that I shared her attitudes. Which I most clearly do not."

"No!" she said. "No!" The words were torn from her in agony.

"Don't say it, Nick! Don't!"

She wanted to stop him before he did this terrible thing that would destroy her. He could *not* betray her. "No," she said again, and reached out instinctively to touch his face. But he was not there. He continued to speak, ignoring her, betraying her.

The beloved face she touched was only glass.

45

Politics, dialectics, feminism and anti-feminism. Causes. She knew they were important but she didn't care. Why must they mess up her life? Why, once she found the man, did he have to betray her to satisfy a philosophy, to win an election, to win by so and so many votes?

"Oh," she cried aloud, and then, silently, "Why not say to hell with the election and hurray for Kate Sinclair?"

He could have said that. But he did not.

She thought she had found in Blanchflower strength. She had not. She had thought him a man who knew who he was and who was at peace with himself. Instead, she knew now, he was just another man.

She was battered, numb, but the numbness quickly gave way to pain. She got up and went into the bathroom. She soaked a hand towel and rinsed her face. In the mirror she saw her eyes. Funny, she thought, I'm not crying. They're not even red. In the living room the phone rang. Before she could think she had picked it up. It was a reporter from the *Times*. No, Kate said, she hadn't heard what Senator Blanchflower had said. The girl started to paraphrase his statement.

"No," Kate said, "I'm sorry."

She hung up as the girl talked. Another light blinking on the phone. She let it run out this time without picking up. The television set was still on and John Wayne and his horse ambled across the screen. She flipped the switch. It went dark. She turned off the other lights in the room and stared out the window at the river. Behind her the phone rang again. She turned quickly, went into the bedroom, and pulled on a Burberry trenchcoat over her sweater and pants.

It was cold, damp, hinting at rain. The doorman saluted and

asked if she wanted a cab. Kate shook her head and walked west on 48th Street.

Eighth Avenue at midnight. The girls huddled in the doorways against the wind and at the curb the pimps sat in their cars and listened to the Knicks game on the radio. The hotel lobby was empty. The desk clerk looked up. "I know my way," Kate told him. He nodded and went back to his paperback. There was a light bulb out in the corridor and Shaun's door was in shadow. She knocked. There was no response and then, sleepily, the girl's voice.

"It's me," Kate said.

Behind Shaun she could see the boy sitting up in bed. Well, she thought, it can get worse, can't it? The boy did not seem embarrassed. At least it's a boy, Kate thought, and not some dirty old man.

"This is Philip," Shaun said. "This is my sister."

Shaun was naked. Nervously, she grabbed at a robe on the back of the door.

"Hello, Philip," Kate said, "and now would you mind getting the hell out of here so I can talk with my sister?"

He got up and scrambled into his clothes. He has a nice body, Kate thought, surprised at how cool she was.

"Hey," Shaun said, "I mean, you come up here without letting me know and . . ."

Kate turned to her.

"Shaun," she said, "just shut up."

The girl sat down.

"I'll call you," the boy said at the door. Neither of the women said anything.

"Good night, Miss Sinclair."

Shaun looked at Kate. Embarrassment gave way to defiance.

"So you've even got *him* in awe. 'Good night, Miss Sinclair,' " she mimicked.

Kate shrugged.

"At least he has manners. Which is more than I can say for you."

Shaun stared at the wall, sulking.

Kate stood up. "Get your clothes. We're going home."

"The hell we are," Shaun said.

Kate walked over to her, stood over the girl.

"Shaun, we can do this with a certain amount of dignity or you can go out of this dump kicking and screaming. But you are going home with me."

Shaun stood up, facing her sister, fists on her hips.

"She's taller than I am," Kate thought. For a moment she weakened, then she said:

"This is a non-negotiable demand, Shaun. Get dressed."

"I . . ."

"Non-negotiable," Kate repeated firmly. "I am in a rotten mood and have no intention of debating the issue."

Shaun's shoulders slumped and she picked up her jeans from the back of a chair and slowly began to put them on.

"You walk in on me like this and shame me in front of my friend and then say you're in a lousy mood. Ha!"

Kate's face responded and the girl pulled on the jeans and grabbed for a sweater.

Now they were downstairs. As they went through the lobby Kate stopped at the desk.

"Does Miss . . . does my sister owe you anything?"

The clerk looked befuddled.

"You pay in advance in places like this," Shaun said.

The wind was up and on it the first rain. Kate looked down the avenue for a cruising cab. A black pimp stared at them from his parked Cadillac.

"Hey, look at this," someone said. Kate turned. Two men, businessmen on the town, had turned into the avenue and now they stopped. One of them tipped his hat.

"Good evening, girls. Listen, my friend and I would just love to buy you two ladies a drinkie. Or two. We . . ."

"Beat it," Kate said crisply.

The other man said, "Come on, baby. I just love tall girls."

Kate ignored him and stepped into the street, trying to see a cab.

"Hey," the first man said to Shaun, "if your pal doesn't want to play, how about you?"

Kate whirled and moved to him. She was not carrying a bag, she realized, as her hand and arm tensed, ready to swing.

348

"I'm a police officer with the morals squad taking this runaway in," she said. "You want to come along too?"

The two men backed off.

"Hell, no. Sorry," they muttered.

When the cab came and turned east Shaun said, "That was neat. The morals squad."

Kate turned to look at her. Passing under the street lights alternately lit and darkened her face. It was still sulky. But the morals squad had been "neat."

"I'm glad you think so," Kate said. "Anyhow, it worked."

Shaun nodded.

"That's pragmatism," she said, and lapsed back into silence. The doorman took the bag and when they were upstairs Shaun stood in the center of the living room and looked around, defiantly.

"You locking me in?" she asked.

Kate understood she was being tested.

"I might," she said, "I just might."

Shaun flopped down into a deep chair. "Why?" she said. "Don't you trust me?"

Kate did not answer. What she wanted to say, what was the truth was that she did not know her sister. If I don't know her, how can I know whether I trust her? And then, recognizing she was now indicting herself, that not knowing Shaun was not Shaun's fault, but hers, she said:

"All I know, Shaun, is that I love you."

Her sister remained motionless, slumped in the chair, her face iron, determined, and then, as Kate waited, tensed, not breathing, Shaun's square jaw softened and she jumped up.

"Hey," the girl said, her arms opening to her, her eyes suddenly moist, "I love you too. Really, I do. I love you."

Kate hugged her tall young body, trembling in her arms. She was crying now too.

"Oh, Shaun," she said, "I missed you."

The girl nodded, hiccupping. "Me too," she said.

Kate pushed her away to hold her at arm's length and to gaze into her face, the face of a child-woman, beautiful and vulnerable, wise and innocent.

Still crying, Kate said, "Your nose is running."

349

Shaun rubbed her sleeve across her nose.

"Hey," she said again, "the morals squad. That was neat, that was really neat."

Mary Costello made them tea and cooked eggs for Shaun. When she'd gone to bed Kate and Shaun sat up talking. Until nearly four. It was as if a dam had collapsed between them and their emotions, their pain, their love had all rushed together.

"I didn't go there to spy," Kate said. "I was lonely, I'd been hurt, and I just wanted to talk to you. You were the only one I really *could* talk to. I wanted to see you. So badly."

Shaun's arm was around her sister's shoulder.

"And I didn't mean to be so snotty. It was just, well, being caught like that, with Philip, well . . ."

"I know," Kate said. Then, "Philip, is he . . . important?"

The girl shrugged.

"No, I guess not. Except in one way. He was the first. And I guess that's always important."

Kate told her about Blanchflower, about what he'd said on television.

"That son of a bitch!" Shaun said.

Kate smiled. Despite her pain she could not resist it.

"I mean," Shaun said, "what a shitty thing to do. What a gutless creep. Boy, he sure won't get my vote."

"You don't have a vote," Kate reminded her.

"Well, next time then. We'll get that bastard."

Kate liked the sound of that "we." Then, wanting the girl to understand nothing was that simple, that black and white, she said:

"You know, Shaun, Nick is still the same man I was in love with yesterday. He didn't mean to hurt me. People aren't cruel because they enjoy it, not unless they're really sick. Nick is ambitious, I was hurting his chances, I suppose, and he caved in."

"It still isn't fair," Shaun said angrily. "Everyone says you're so goddamned ambitious. That's all anyone ever says. In the magazines, in the papers, in all those filthy stories. Yet this creep can dump you overboard just for a few lousy votes. I mean, it stinks."

Kate nodded. She thought of Jack Kennedy's line, life *is* unfair. Shaun was speaking the bitterness, the anger, she herself wanted to shout. Yet, having just reclaimed her sister, perhaps in a way having claimed her for the first time, she resisted the temptation to agree. Having just established a relationship, she was not about to abdicate.

"Shaun, of course I'm angry. I'm hurt. But to permit what Nick did to make me hate him would be destructive. Not to him. To me. It's going to be hell but I'm going to be better than he is. Maybe not in every sense, but in this, I'll be damned if I'll descend to his level. It may be idealistic, maybe I'm just storing up anger that will come out later. But that's the way it's going to be. I lost him tonight. I found you again. And I'm going to be a goddamned grownup woman and accept the deal. Besides," she said, looking at the girl, "with you here, with us together, it doesn't seem a bad deal at all. Not at all."

But strips of flesh had been gouged from her that night and she knew it. Oh, how she knew it.

46

Bobby Klaus was not Chester Albany's favorite drinking companion. Vicissitude had brought them together. They were at the bar of the Atelier, later that same week. The lank barman poured Chester's Stolichnaya on the rocks.

"A Tab," Bobby said.

"Jesus," Chester said, "you ought to start drinking, Bobby. Be a great consolation in your hour of need. Like now."

Bobby nodded. A new Nielsen ratings book had just come out.

"I know," he said. "I've often wished I could get drunk with the boys. I've tried, actually, but all I do is become ill, make a total ass of myself. I do envy your ability to drink."

Chester started to say something but then, recognizing truth, he shut up. The vodka tasted fine. It tasted like just the first of many.

Bobby looked around as he sipped his Tab.

"So this is where you come," he said. "Nice place."

"They don't water the drinks."

"Oh, do they do that other places?" Seeing the scorn on Chester's face, he added, "I'm sorry. I don't mean to be naive. It's just this sort of thing isn't really my line."

Chester forgave him.

"Don't worry about it, Bobby. What the hell, we're screwed, both of us. Might as well hang together instead of separately. You tell Kate about the new ratings?" he asked, making conversation.

Bobby shook his head.

"No. I haven't spoken with her at all today."

Chester heard something in his voice.

"Oh?" he said.

It was then Bobby Klaus told him about the conference at the founder's apartment, about the founder's instructions.

"Of course," he added, "it was the letter that forced us to do something. If that letter got out . . ."

"What letter?" Chester asked in irritation. He hated missing pieces in puzzles, he didn't like guessing games.

Bobby stared at him.

"Why, *your* letter. I mean, your *girl's* letter. Where she says Kate . . ."

Chester's hands gripped the bar.

"My letter? Frances's letter? What the hell . . .?"

Bobby Klaus told him.

"I'm sorry, Chester, I just assumed you knew. We all did. That was why we took the letter seriously, that it came from someone, well, *inside* the network, not just another crank."

Later, after Klaus had left, Chester sat quietly at the bar, observing himself in the old mirror, slowly drinking his vodka. He was surprised that he could still drink, that he had been able to maintain his stolidity with Bobby, that he was not now in the men's room, retching out his guts. But there was no joy in the booze, no release, no abandon. Finally, recognizing the inevitability of what he had to do, he went home.

Frances was there. She jumped up and kissed him.

"Listen," she said, "you don't want to eat, do you?"

No, he shook his head.

"Me neither. I figured you were out drinking with the boys. I decided to get high myself. I'm really flying."

Chester looked narrowly at the girl. It was true. This was more than her usual buoyancy. Her eyes were brighter than normal.

"What are you on?" he asked.

She giggled.

"Come on into the bedroom," she said, "and I'll show you."

Wearily, confused, he did not argue but followed her. In the bedroom she snatched a nasal inhaler from the dressing table.

"Amyl nitrite," she said cheerfully. "It's super."

She put the cylinder to her nose and sniffed.

"Oh, boy," she said, her face turning up toward the ceiling. She was wearing a silk shirt and the uniform jeans. Her breasts moved under the silk and the jeans were sleek on her long legs, cradling her small, high buttocks and the lean hips. It was warm in the bedroom, his face flushed and he could feel the booze. The girl smiled at him.

"Come on," she said, starting to unbutton her blouse.

Wanting her, and not wanting the confrontation that was now inevitable, he looked at her for a long moment and then, sadly, shook his head.

"No," Chester said quietly. "We've got to talk. Now. About the letter. Bobby Klaus told me."

Her fingers froze on the buttons of the blouse.

"I was afraid of that," she said.

She sat up against the headboard of the bed. He felt awkward standing there, towering above her, so he sat down in a soft chair across the room.

"Look," he said, "I'm not even sure how to say this."

"Then don't," she said, not feeling nearly as flip as she sounded.

Chester shook his head.

"I'm afraid I have to. And I'm afraid you're going to have to talk about it too. Are you okay?"

"Sure," she said, "I'm okay. I'm not high now."

He knew she was telling the truth. He inhaled deeply and began, his hands kneading one another between his knees.

"What you've done is unforgivable. I know your motives were good, that you were trying to help me. But, Frances, such things simply aren't done by civilized people. If I condoned that letter, I could never work with people I respect. I couldn't for God's sake look at myself in the mirror of a morning. You thought you were helping me by destroying the career of another person? No, Frances, that's the sort of help I can't accept."

Frances, who had been listening docilely, sat up rigidly.

"But she's a bitch. You said it yourself. A bitch. How many times did you . . .?"

"All right, I said it. I suppose I meant it. But I kept my jealousy in acceptable bounds. What you did was destructive, mean, sneaky. And in destroying Kate you destroy me."

"Damn you, Chester, you just going to roll over and die and

354

let her shovel the dirt on top of you? I never figured you for a quitter. Not ever."

"You don't understand," he said. "I'm not quitting. But I'm not going to ruin another career just to advance my own."

"You said it's a tough business, didn't you?"

"Oh, yes," he said, "I don't know a tougher. But as hard as we fight for advantage, for an edge, for the goddamn Nielsens, there has to be a code. There have to be rules of behavior. Otherwise we aren't anything but animals, clawing and snarling and snapping at one another."

"The others do it," she said sulkily, "the bosses. They destroy people."

"Okay, suppose they do. It's a hard, cruel business and there are hard, cruel people in it. But when I compete with Cronkite or Reasoner or Sinclair, I compete on ability. You think I don't hate it, when Walter is voted newscaster of the year? You don't think that gets to me? Jesus, it hurts like hell. But I don't try to destroy the son of a bitch. I don't write letters or lie about him."

Frances stood up.

"I didn't lie. I told the truth. Everything I said about her was the truth. She . . . "

"Frances, shut up. You said she was a communist. She isn't. You said . . . "

"I said she was fucking Nick Blanchflower and she is."

"*Was.*"

"Okay."

"And I fuck you. But Kate Sinclair doesn't write letters to my boss about it. You ever think of that?"

"I'm not a senator," she said, head down and stubborn.

"No," Chester said gently, "you're not."

Frances mistook his gentleness. She thought he was relenting.

"Chester . . . "

"Yes?"

"Can't we just forget her?"

He looked at the girl. She still had no sense of having done wrong.

"No," he said, "I'm afraid we can't."

She was quiet for a moment.

"Those things you wrote about her sister. About her not being a good guardian. That stuff's awful. You can't . . ."

She was angry now, angrier than he had ever seen her, angry and dangerous.

"Okay, Chester, it was a terrible thing that I did. But do you know *why* I tried to ruin her?" She got off the bed and walked to him and stood in front of his chair.

"Because she ruined you, Chester. She ruined you and you're too nice or too American to realize it."

"Come on, Frances, this is the best job I've ever had."

Frances paused, and then she said it:

"Kate castrated you, Chester. She cut off your balls. That's why you can't screw anymore. That's why you . . ."

He stood up, his fists clenched.

"Frances," he said, "I'm leaving you. Stay here as long as you want, until you make some arrangements. I'll get a bag together and get out."

He went into the bedroom. Well, he thought, she finally said it. And maybe she's right. But he could not live with a woman who said or did such things. He pulled a soft leather weekend bag out of the closet and began to stuff socks and shirts and underwear into it. He went into the bathroom for his toothbrush and razor. My God, he said to himself, catching sight of himself in the mirror, you look awful. He did not say what he really felt, that he looked old. He washed his face, letting the water run until it was cold, then soaking the washcloth and plastering it against his face.

"Chester?"

He turned and went back into the bedroom. She was standing in the doorway, in the shirt and the jeans that obscured none of the lines of her body.

"Chester," she said, "I'm sorry. About what I said."

"Are you, Frances?"

She nodded.

"Come on," she said, "come to bed. You'll be able to, I know you will. I'll help. I'll . . . "

He picked up the bag and walked past her into the hallway.

"The studio will know where I am," he said. "I'll leave some money on the table, as much as I can. I'll write you a check to-morrow."

He walked through the apartment, stopping to put some bills on the table. Behind him he expected to hear Frances saying something, yelling something.

The apartment, as he closed the door behind him, was silent.

He was out in the street before he realized it. The doorman had said something as he went by but Chester had not heard him, had not answered. His eyes glistened with tears, but he did not know this. The image of her body, of a girl he would never have again, called up memories of the hotel rooms and the endless empty nights of separation when his marriage had first gone bad. He was too upset to arrange a hotel room now, too lonely to face a strange room. Instead he took a cab across town and let himself into the silent studio and walked through the echoing hallways to his office and lay down on the battered old couch.

He fell asleep by remembering the Gare de Lyon and a train ride to Geneva through the snowy Alps. But before the train ride and sleep cleansed his mind, he thought of Frances, of the last few wonderful years, of present loneliness, and he wept.

47

Kate Sinclair still did not know about Frances's letter. Chester had been as brusque as usual, for different reasons, but she did not know this. Bobby Klaus seemed to have disappeared. She did not know he was fighting his own despairing battle for survival. Shaun was with her again, she had lost Blanchflower. These were her concerns. She went to work each morning, going through the motions, professionalism carrying her. Then, one morning, there was a letter from Blanchflower.

"I'm sorry," it said, "but I had no choice."

She looked at the Senate stationery, crisply white with blue printing, with his signature reproduced on the envelope. The letter did not touch her. She read about him in the papers, saw him on the news, on the paid political broadcasts. The election was a few days away. It was November, gray and cold in New York. The littering and posting laws were ignored. Every candidate had his name, his face, his slogan, pasted to lampposts, to telephone poles, to board fences and brick walls. She could not escape Blanchflower. She did not try. He came at her on the tube, in the papers, on the sides of buses, came at her blown by the wind in a leaflet scudding across sidewalks to wrap around her ankle.

On Election Day she voted, in the YMCA. She gave her name, of course. No aliases at the polls. No privacy. Someone in the line asked for an autograph and she shook her head. In the booth she grimly pulled the levers, not really concentrating except on the one race. Outside someone asked if she had voted for him and she froze the questioner with a look.

Of course she had voted for him. He was a good senator. Was there another criterion?

She worked late that night. It was exciting, stimulating, rewarding. Chester was wonderfully loud and obscene during the commercials.

"Look at those shitkickers upstate," he'd cry when some aberrational return flashed on the computerized board. "Shitkicker," she thought, that was what Nick had called them. Bobby Klaus was there, strangely buoyant after his recent absences and depression. Late in the evening, when most of the major races had been decided, someone passed scotch around in the coffee mugs. Kate drank hers eagerly. It tasted wonderful. No one was drunk. They were all happy, high on work and tension. It was the best session she had known since Cape Canaveral. Once when the cameras went to Blanchflower's headquarters in the Hotel Roosevelt, she caught a glimpse of women demonstrators marching, chanting. So that was where they'd gone from the network. His betrayal of her hadn't worked. Oddly, the knowledge neither cheered nor depressed her.

Blanchflower's opponent conceded just after one in the morning, claiming a moral victory. Blanchflower had won by a resounding half-million votes. A tremendous performance, overwhelming, people said. But Kate knew what Blanchflower had told her privately weeks ago.

"Kate, I win by less than a million and it's a loss. I'm dead. Bye-bye, White House."

She'd laughed at him then, telling him there was no way he would not win by a million, no way he would not be President. Now, when the pundits assessed his performance, and the returns came in, she knew, better than they.

Kate had never been paranoid. But now, looking back at the feminist pickets who, seemingly without reason, had so damaged her and through her, Blanchflower, she wondered. The President had been against him, the feminists, there were rumors around the studio of mysterious letters about her and about him. Had the enemies set out, knowingly, to destroy them both? Or had it all just happened, accidentally? She instinctively rejected conspiracy theories, but elsewhere there were knowing smiles, satisfaction at a demolition job well done.

At the White House they were, publicly, noncommittal on

Blanchflower's Pyrrhic victory. The President, his press secretary said in reply to a question, was "delighted" that the party had held its important New York seat.

Later the President and Lester had coffee together in a room not far from the Oval Office.

"Well," Lester said in a voice dripping with southern honey, "that fixes ol' Blanchflower. Shee-it, only half a million vote margin in a no-contest race! That does it for him. No White House for ol' Nick."

The President grinned.

"What really tickles me, Lester, is after all the conniving, all the strategy sessions, we weren't the ones who did him in."

Lester sobered a bit on that.

"Yeah," he said glumly, "I tried like hell, though, you got to admit that."

The President nodded.

"You tried, Lester. I tried too. But I think that ol' boy just destroyed himself."

"Don't agree," Lester said stubbornly. "Once I learned the libbers were out to burn his ass I had our people pushin' them, kept feedin' them anti-feminist stuff about him."

The President thought for a moment. "Maybe so," he said, "and maybe it was just he had the bad luck to fall in love with Kate Sinclair and got caught in the middle between Kate and the libbers."

Lester shrugged. As intimate as he was with the President, he recognized there was a moment when you stopped arguing a point, when you admitted the boss was right.

"I guess so," he said. Then he added, "Damn shame ol' Kate got dragged into it. But I guess you don't make omelets without breakin' eggs."

"Funny," said the President, "I never thought of Kate Sinclair as an egg."

Kate avoided discussion of Blanchflower. Connie Heath had called and she was chilly to the probing questions. Harvey Podesta laid siege. She did not want to talk about it, she told him. He wheedled. She agreed to see him, on condition he made no mention of Blanchflower. Of course, Harvey bubbled, did she think he was *totally* lacking in tact, in sensitivity, in devotion?

"It had occurred to me," she said tartly.

Harvey took her to dinner. It was his equivalent of donating blood or making contributions to the United Way.

"I am devastated," he announced, "devastated."

"Bullshit," Kate told him.

"Well," he conceded, "I never liked him but I dislike seeing you hurt."

They were at the River Cafe, a small barge moored just south of the Brooklyn Bridge, on the East River. It was a clear night, clear and cold, with the western sky black against the blazing towers of the World Trade Center. They had a table against the windows and the tugs and the coastal freighters loomed very close, close enough it seemed that you could touch them, their wakes rocking the barge gently. Kate asked Harvey to unscrew the lightbulb in the table lamp so she could see the river without the glare.

Harvey was uncharacteristically sympathetic which made her suspicious. "Harvey," she said, "you're being nice. I fret when you're being nice."

"Kate," he said, "I'm shocked, deeply shocked. I simply wanted your side of the whole sordid story. You know, as a friend, so I can defend you in the *salons* of the metropolis."

His phony English accent extended the word *"salon"* several syllables beyond the French.

"I don't need a defense, Harvey. I can take care of myself. And I don't want to talk about what happened. I told you that on the phone."

He wheedled.

Finally Kate exploded, "You're just nosy. You want some more dish to peddle around town. You're a goddamned parasite, Harvey. A parasite."

He looked hurt.

"You're right, I suppose. But do you seriously believe you're the only one to have suffered? Do you?"

"Of course not," Kate said coldly. "I know how you suffered when those boys beat you up."

Harvey looked sour.

"I didn't mean that. That particular incident is a closed book."

"Oh?"

"I was referring to my recent loss." He lowered his eyes. Kate never knew when to take Harvey seriously. She waited, her face a mask. He looked up, curious to see her reaction. When there was none he related the lugubrious story of a cat that had choked itself on a flea collar.

"My attorneys advise against suing," he said, "but I think I have a prima facie case against the manufacturer."

Kate laughed. Despite herself.

Harvey looked around the room. He pointed out an actress, a famous newspaperman, and a very pretty brunette. "That's Margaret Trudeau," he said. "They're all here, Kate, and you know what?"

"No."

Harvey paused. He was very good at pauses. Then he said, "And you're the biggest star of all, Kate. The biggest. Don't ever forget it." He gulped down another drink.

"I thought Margaret Trudeau was taller," she said, passing over the "star" remark.

The waiter came and they ordered. Harvey rather liked the waiter.

"I must get his name," he said, "such a pleasant boy."

Jesus, Kate thought, and I used to find it amusing. Harvey wandered off into his familiar homosexual almanach de gotha, the latest chic spots, the newest divertissements, who was still in the closet and who had come out. He mentioned a party someone had given for a magazine editor in a West Side duplex with extraordinarily high ceilings.

"The ceiling had to be high," he said, "they were all flying."

Six months ago she would have laughed. Now she smiled crisply and sipped her wine. He knew she was not reacting, that his feats of verbal tumbling and legerdemain, unfailingly successful in the past, had gone flat, his nimble wit had grown stale. He thought for a moment and then brightened:

"I'm sure you could write a book," Harvey said. "Or get someone to write for you," he added, rather too innocently.

Kate examined his face for malice.

"A book about what?" she asked, suspiciously.

"Your struggle," he said, "you know, 'Mein Kampf on the Tube.'"

"I don't think that's amusing."

He ignored her.

"Swifty Lazar could get you a million for it," he said, slurring the words.

Kate Sinclair had the glass halfway to her lips. Her hand froze. My God, she thought, "a million." The phrase reverberated through her head, a million . . . a million . . . a million.

She put down the glass and got up.

"Harvey," she said, "I'm not feeling terribly bright. Don't get up. Please, finish your dinner. I'll get a cab."

He had drunkenly started to rise but she ran from the table, vaguely seeing heads turn, hearing, quite clearly, her name repeated, repeated, repeated.

In the cab, high over the river, the tires whirring on the steel grid of the Brooklyn Bridge, the two refrains blended:

". . . Kate Sinclair . . . a million dollars . . . Kate Sinclair . . . a million dollars . . . Kate Sinclair . . . a million . . ."

What a fool she had been, how vulnerable she had made herself, how exposed a position had she taken. A million dollars. A million blows. She had been warned, she had been wary herself, but ambition, pride, her greedy agent and a smart PR man had created the million-dollar monster, the million-dollar trap.

As the cab turned north on the FDR Drive, the spell broke. She laughed.

"If I'd settled for nine-fifty, no one would have been jealous."

The arc lights of the Drive illuminated her face. It was smiling.

48

George Venables moved swiftly. If Bobby Klaus, last year's boy wonder, had been a rapier, Venables, the new hero, was a broadsword.

"I want to save you if I can, Bobby," he said. "The brass wants you out. I think you're too bright a boy for that. Your contributions have been substantial. I want you to stay."

Bobby chewed a bit of Kleenex. His mind raced. Venables didn't give a shit for Bobby's "contributions."

"Oh, yes?" he said warily.

Venables nodded.

"I think you ought to stay on. Continue to work with Kate. You and she are a team. It was only bad luck that the goddamn ratings didn't reflect it. Rotten luck and Chester, that was what screwed you."

Bobby Klaus said, yes, there was something to that. What the hell was this jockstrap killer getting at?

"So you'll be keeping Kate, too?" Bobby asked.

Venables shrugged.

"A million a year and four more to go on the contract? What do you think?"

Bobby said that made sense.

"Sure," Venables said, expansive now, "and dumping a name talent like Kate is a public admission of error. We don't want the network to look bad, do we? Plays hell with the stock. Plays hell with our image. No, you don't fire Kate Sinclair."

"Then what do you do with her?" Bobby asked, wanting to add, wanting to end the uncertainty, "What do you do with me?"

"We're going to play to Kate's strength. Interviews. She's superb at that. No one does it better. Kate Sinclair has been misused. Remember that Marcos interview? Remember the

Secretary of State? The President? Man, she does it. She really does it."

Bobby Klaus smiled agreement. What *was* all this bullshit? He knew Venables hated Kate. Why this ecstasy, this buildup?

"Of course," Venables said, less enthusiam in his voice now, "as a newscaster she's a used tampon."

Bobby squirmed. Oh, you bastard, he thought, you stunted, little bastard. But he was hanging on the cliff with less than ten fingers and he knew he had to grin, had to throw what remained of Kate Sinclair to the vultures.

"Well," Bobby said, "in fairness to Kate, she tried. She did try."

Venables laughed. It was not a joyous laugh.

"So did Rudolf Hess."

Even in his agony Bobby had to admit it was a good line. He was surprised Venables knew who Rudolf Hess was. Maybe he had heard the line from someone else.

"And? . . . " Bobby said.

"She's damaged goods," Venables said coldly. "Shopworn, mildewed, and raveled around the edges. Me? I'd dump her. But I can't. The board won't let me. So I'll get what I can for her, trade her in, swap her for a new model, work her ass, get whatever reasonable return I can, force her to quit!"

"Which means?" Bobby asked.

Venables shrugged.

"Use her on specials, of course. What the hell else do you do with television flops?"

Bobby Klaus nodded. He knew. How many times had he done the same thing himself?

"Specials," he echoed. The salt mines of the trade. The Siberias to which rebels were exiled. Specials were where you sent Dick Cavett when his talk show failed, where Jack Paar went when he finished and everybody but Jack knew it, where Howard K. Smith was sent, where poor Dave Garroway ended up, where Bill Moyers droned and nobody listened. Now it was Kate's turn. And his.

"And me?" Bobby asked.

Venables smiled again. Bobby preferred it when he didn't.

"Why, you'll produce the specials, Bobby. You'll be her producer."

Later, Bobby Klaus would think of all the things he might

have said, the clever, incisive insult that would have skewered Venables, the cold, crushing gesture with which Bobby might have exited. With dignity. Instead, being a survivor, recognizing that in this business a man might be on top today and on a skateboard tomorrow, knowing that a man as eccentric, as narrowly based, as abrasive as Venables might be a demigod now but in the same shape as himself next year, Bobby decided to hang on, to go along. Crazies like Venables were splendid to have around when the ratings were good. But when they sagged, eccentricity became an embarrassment and a man like George Venables a burden.

"George," Bobby said, "make it executive producer and you've got your boy."

Venables, less subtle, smiled back.

"Okay, Bobby, it's a deal. Now," he said, the smile fading, "let's have the bitch in."

They had to wait a day. Kate was out of town. There was a dinner for an FCC commissioner in Washington and she had agreed to attend. She decided to take the Metroliner and as the Jersey landscape slid by, first the industrial parks and the refineries and then the dairy farms and the small towns, she thought about how she would act, the tone she should take, the pose she could convincingly adopt. In this business there were few secrets. She did not know the specifics, of course, but she was aware of Venables' move, of the unsettling uncertainty that nightly pervaded the set, that hung shroudlike over the daily story conferences.

At the FCC dinner everyone would know. The questions might not be asked openly. But they would be there. The temptation had been to plead illness, to remain in New York and send regrets. Doggedly, Kate did not take the easy out. If she were to go down she would go with pride. Then, in Washington, she was, cruelly, dealt yet another blow.

Both public figures, it was inevitable that sooner or later they would again meet.

As Kate walked through the lobby of the Madison Hotel there was Blanchflower. A thrill went through her body, part desire, part revulsion.

"Hello," he said, "I guess it's all right to say hello."

She nodded.

"Of course. How are you?"

He looked fine, but then he always did. More subdued than usual but that might be shame or embarrassment or whatever it was, if anything, that men like Blanchflower felt when they encountered their victims. And even as she thought it, Kate told herself to stop, told herself that as tempting as it was, she was not going to adopt the loser's psychology.

It was three in the afternoon and the hotel was quiet, with only a bellman and an elderly woman watching them.

"Look," Blanchflower said, "can we go someplace? This is awkward standing here trying to talk."

She did not make it easy.

"I'm not trying to talk, Nick, I simply said hello."

His face darkened. Then he took her arm.

"Come here," he said, and she let herself be steered into a dining room off the lobby. It was empty. Large windows gave on the lovely city, bright under a thin winter sun.

They stood there, facing one another in the quiet room, surrounded by white linened tables with nothing on them.

"I wrote you," he said, "to say I'm sorry. Did you get it?"

"Yes," Kate said. "You didn't really expect an answer, did you?"

He shook his head.

"Well," she said, trying to smile, "it didn't work, did it? Maybe it wasn't meant to work."

"I never pretended to be anything but what I was," he said.

"No," she said, "I've got to admit that. You always told me you were a son of a bitch."

"Prime."

"That's right, prime."

"Okay," Blanchflower said, "let's not run it into the ground."

"I want you to know I'm not vindictive. I asked for everything I got."

He looked unhappy.

"No," he said, "you didn't ask to be screwed the way I did it on television."

"I'd prefer not to think about that," she said. "We weren't children, either of us. We were old enough to know what we were doing."

"Old," he said, not looking at her, "I *hate* getting old."

"We all do."

He turned to face her. "I know. But I play the fool, play the child. All this 'politics of outrage.' Kid stuff."

"Nick, you can't fool time."

"Oh, hell, you've got to try," he said.

"And I thought women worried about growing old. But here you are."

"I know," he said, "and if I became President, it wouldn't have mattered. A President under sixty is young. But if you lose, ah, if you lose . . . "

He was feeling sorry for himself so she said, "Lots of good men lose. Stevenson lost, McGovern."

"You don't understand. When you lose young, what the hell does a politician have left to hope for? Who wants to be Rockefeller? Who wants to be Harold Stassen?"

She was losing patience with him. She knew how deeply hurt he had been by the vote, she recognized his despair. But she was damned if she'd help him to indulge himself.

"Nixon lost young and then he won, remember?" she said.

Blanchflower looked at her.

"But does anyone want to be Nixon?" he asked quietly.

They stood, awkwardly, without speaking, and when he said, "I suppose there's no point in trying to . . . you know . . . "

She shook her head and smiled.

"No point at all, Nick."

They shook hands again and after he left she stared from the window of the empty dining room amid the empty tables with their white linen shrouds. Her eyes burned with tears. Then she saw Blanchflower leave the hotel, walking with those familiar long strides, and a low sports car pulled out and rolled slowly toward him. When it stopped a girl got out and ran to Blanchflower and threw her arms around him and kissed him on the mouth. Kate could not see the girl's face clearly but she had long hair and a kilted skirt and red wool knee socks. The girl stayed in Blanchflower's arms for a moment, and then ran around to the other side of the car and got into the passenger's seat, showing her long legs as she did. Blanchflower paused for a moment to look back at the hotel and then he squeezed into the driver's seat and the car pulled away slowly into the street.

It was all so casual, so contemporary, so controlled. He had smashed their love on a television program. Now, seeing her again for the first time, they had shaken hands and he had gone out of the hotel to get into a car, with another woman.

It had puzzled Kate that Blanchflower should be so obsessed with age. Now, seeing him with this girl, this child, she understood. He had had his fling with an older woman, with her. "An older woman," she thought ironically, ten years younger than he was. Just then a bus boy came into the dining room carrying a tray of silverware and he stared at her and said good afternoon in Spanish. Kate smiled and left. The bus boy, because he did not speak English, had never seen her on television. But he thought she was a very pretty woman and he wondered why she had been standing alone in an empty dining room in the afternoon.

The next day she went with Bobby Klaus to answer Venables's summons. She understood what he was telling her. She sensed his hatred, his pleasure at having leveled her. And although she did not contemplate revenge, as Bobby was already doing, she, like Bobby, cooled the impulse to throw the job in Venables's face. Aware of her own strengths, she saw in the proposal to do specials the opportunity to return to what she knew, what she did best. Self-knowledge told her the anchor job had been a mistake from the start. She understood the million a year had been a psychological blunder, that she had unnecessarily aligned the demons of jealousy, of envy against her. There were those who wanted Kate to fail simply because she had reached too far. Kate knew this instinctively and although she recognized in the assignment to do specials a cruel punishment, she also saw in it the potential for professional rehabilitation. Doing interviews again would tap her proved resources, would parade her abilities, would demonstrate she was the best they had.

"Okay," she told Venables grimly, "who's my first victim?"

Then she sat back and watched Bobby Klaus fidget and Venables expound. There was talk of Streisand but, no, Barbara Walters had done her. Of the First Family, of Bette Midler ("Too special," Venables snarled, "middle America doesn't know who the hell she is."), of Ethel Kennedy ("She won't play," Bobby said flatly).

Venables leaned forward.

"Bobby mentioned something that intrigued me. This idea of yours about going overseas, covering a war."

My idea? she thought.

Venables grinned. A slight grin.

"Beirut," he said, "a lovely city. And the Lebanese are killing one another again. Perhaps you could . . . "

"Beirut," Bobby said lingeringly, lovingly; as he slid smoothly into his new role as sycophant.

Kate ignored him. Looking at Venables she asked:

"But is there a special in it? Wouldn't I just be getting standard combat footage?"

George Venables smiled again. More broadly this time.

"But you're Kate Sinclair. Surely you'll come up with memorable stuff."

"Memorable," Bobby echoed.

She knew then the treatment had begun.

They would make the announcements in the usual way. Butch Halvorsen would handle it. Television is like a great army: the communiques never contain anything that might provide aid and comfort to the enemy. Small triumphs become historic victories, minor setbacks become meaningless standoffs, debacles are not reported. In television the exile of a major talent was inevitably trumpeted as a bonus for the viewer, a promotion for the performer involved. Kate's departure from the evening news would not be a retreat but a handsome advance. Her "long-awaited" series of specials would now go into production. Neither Butch nor anyone else said who it was had "long-awaited" them. Some of "America's greatest names" would be interviewed. Kate was described as ecstatic. "This series of specials is something toward which I've worked for years," she would gush. It was not explained that Butch choreographed the "gush."

Shaun had returned to school. Kate phoned her there.

"I didn't want you to read about it or hear it on television," she said.

"Oh," Shaun said, "does it mean you got fired?"

"No, darling, you don't get fired in television. You go on to better things."

Shaun nodded, solemnly, forgetting that her sister could not see her.

"Hey," Shaun said, "when my friends ask me about it, is it okay if I level, if I tell them you got canned but they're being diplomatic about it?"

"Why on earth would you want to do that?"

"Well," Shaun said, "you know what a liar I am, how I always exaggerate. Maybe this time I'll tell the truth and then none of the kids'll believe me anyway. I mean, I won't do it if you don't want, but just this once I'd kind of like to tell the truth, you know, to protect your reputation."

Kate smiled.

"Yes, Shaun," she said, "I think it would be quite all right, just this one time, to tell the truth."

She wished she had someone else to talk to. Mary was helpless, of course. Telling Mary would mean picket lines, worker rallies, boycotts, and cell meetings. No, she could not seek consolation from Mary. Harvey was out. Even when he was sober his troubles had become obsession. Harvey was so self-oriented that if she told him she had terminal cancer he would say, well, yes, that's terrible, and have I told you about my hangnail? Connie Heath was out. To Connie Kate's defeat would become, instantly, a tidbit of gossip to be shared over dinner tables and on the banquettes of the good restaurants.

It was then that Kate missed Blanchflower. Only he could have boomed out simultaneous outrage and encouragement, telling her the news job was a slough of despond and she was well out of it, and blackguarding her employers for their failure to recognize true genius when confronted with it. But she could not tell Blanchflower.

Really, Kate knew, there was no one to tell.

49

The network shakeup made the front page of the *Times*.

MAJOR TV NETWORK OUSTS TOP EXECUTIVE:
TEAMS UP NEWS AND SPORTS UNDER ONE MAN

As was customary, wrote Les Brown, no one had actually been fired. The ousted executive had been "assigned to important new responsibilities."

The irresistibly gabby Gallagher Report would crack, a few days later: "This means he has three months to prepare résumés and clean out his desk."

Kay Gardella wondered in print just how long Kate Sinclair would remain with the network, whether negotiations had already begun to settle the remaining four years of her contract. In Chicago, Mort Gruen gleefully suggested Chester Albany would be sent on the road, another Charles Kuralt doing pleasant little essays on motels and Grange meetings and Boy Scout troops in middle America. Chester would, he remarked, "be ideally suited for the assignment." *Variety* headlined the shakeup: WEB BOOSTS JOCK'S STOCK and Hank Grant in *The Hollywood Reporter* whispered that Kate Sinclair was talking with an "indy producer" about doing a version of the Dinah Shore show "for stay-at-homes who don't watch the soaps." A week later *TV Guide* would run Venables's face on its cover. And in the Sunday *Times* John J. O'Connor fretted ponderously about the desirability of having a sportscaster producing the evening news. To read O'Connor one would have thought that Bobby Klaus, contemptuously dismissed twelve months earlier, had miraculously metamorphosed into a blend of Ed Murrow and Arthur Krock.

More than a thousand letters came into the network's mail

room, saluting Kate Sinclair and urging that her role remain unchanged. Four hundred letters hailed Chester Albany. Three thousand letters said they should both be sacked. Another fifteen hundred recommended that one or the other be retained. Twelve letter writers threatened boycotts of the products marketed by the various commercial sponsors and these, at least, were carefully read and circumspectly answered. All the other letters were tabulated and shredded.

In Centre, Kansas, Harry Flagg assumed a protective coloration.

The data he supplied had been correct, he told Bob Williams of the *New York Post*. His data was *always* correct. His system was foolproof, the computer never lied. It was clear to Flagg that "someone" at the network, tactfully he did not mention Bobby's name, had "misinterpreted" the data. It was depressing, Flagg mused, when supposedly competent executives misused the tools of modern, sophisticated research. He regretted very much what had happened at the network but, to a man who dealt in the pure realm of market analysis, such corporate upheavals were beneath notice.

Kate and Chester went about their chores as if nothing had happened. What else were they to do? They had been told that the "revised format" would be implemented gradually. What they heard whispered was that the changes would occur at year's end. Bobby Klaus flew off to a half-dozen major cities to meet with local station chiefs to soothe the nervous. Venables closeted himself with a small task force of bright young men he was bringing in from sports. November became December, an early snow snarled the city, and then, finally, the week before Christmas, Bobby Klaus returned.

"Bobby," Kate told him over the phone, "I've got to see you. It's important."

"Better see George," he said cautiously. "George is making the decisions, Kate."

"I don't want to see George," she snapped. "I want to see you."

Reluctantly, he gave her an appointment.

His office was a shambles.

"What's all this?" she asked, looking at the bare walls where the faded outlines of pictures remained.

"George wants me closer to him," Bobby said. "I'm moving."

"Upstairs or down?" she asked, a nasty edge to her voice.

"Upstairs, of course," Bobby said. "Really, Kate, I'm quite hurt that you'd even suggest otherwise."

He *was* moving up, but to a smaller office, something he did not want to admit to Kate.

"That's good, Bobby," she said sarcastically, "I'd hate to think you weren't coming out of all this smelling just wonderfully."

He looked sour. "Kate, you didn't come up here to start a fight. What can I do for you? If anything."

"I like that, Bobby. 'If anything.'"

He set his jaw and did not say anything.

Kate sat down. "All right, Bobby. I won't beat up on you for what happened. I simply want to know *why*. Was it the ratings? Or what?"

He relaxed. He hated confrontations. Now absentmindedly he pulled a Kleenex from the dispenser in the top drawer of his desk.

"Of course it was the ratings," he said. "Up and down, up and down. No overall patterns of improvement to hold out promise. And then, you and Chester, well, the team concept just wasn't there, was it?"

She shrugged.

"We learned to work together," she said. "Not at first. But certainly these past few months."

"And that crazy letter his girl friend sent. That didn't score any points for you."

Kate sat up, her back straight.

"What letter?" she asked. "Whose girl friend?"

Bobby Klaus shoved the Kleenex into his mouth.

"Why, Chester's girl friend. Frances what's-her-name. You mean, nobody told you?"

Kate stood up.

"Jesus Christ, Bobby, nobody tells me anything. What did this Frances write? To whom? Why was it important?"

Klaus told her.

Kate exploded.

"But that's such bullshit. I mean, how can serious people take a letter like that seriously?"

374

She paced the room.

"Kate," Bobby said unhappily, "please, sit down. Calm yourself."

She glared at him. Oh, my God, he thought, I've never seen her like this. But everyone said she had an awful temper. Bobby felt terribly sorry for himself. Why must he be the victim? He hadn't done anything.

"Kate, they believed it. George had detectives check it out. They . . . "

"Don't mention Venables to me, you little worm!"

Bobby Klaus's eyes darted. He sought the door, wondering if he should make a dash.

"Detectives! Anonymous letters!" she raged.

Bobby pointed out the letter had been signed, that it wasn't anonymous.

"Spare me the technicalities," she said coldly. "Spying on my personal life. Slandering my sister. Libeling me." Her voice dripped contempt. "I wonder what my lawyers are going to have to say about all this," she shouted.

"Oh, my God," Bobby moaned. If there were anything the network feared more than boycotts it was lawyers. They'd blame everything on him. He knew they would. Venables would make sure of it.

Kate started out, head high, neck arched. At the door she whirled.

"And did Mr. Albany think his girl friend would salvage his job by hurting me?" she asked chillingly.

Bobby gulped at the Kleenex.

"Chester didn't know anything about it. He was furious with the girl."

"I'll bet he was," she sneered.

"Well, for your information, he was," Bobby said, delighted to be off the defensive.

"Oh?" she said, frozen at the door.

"Yes," Bobby nodded. "He threw her out of the apartment or something. I thought everyone knew about it."

Kate turned slowly and opened the door. Bobby watched her vanish down the hall.

He put his head down on the desk and wondered what could possibly happen next.

In an odd way Kate was relieved. It hadn't been simply *her* failure, neither the exorbitant salary nor her stupid blunder with the feminists, not even her inability to mesh with Chester, that had brought the show crashing down. It had been something outside of her, something uncontrollable, that had been the final straw. The knowledge made her feel better, neither tragic nor defeated nor to be pitied. She felt instead a sort of controlled joy, a sense of having stood up to adversity and having lost through plain bad luck. The flaw had not been hers. As she had survived the loss of Blanchflower, she would survive this. Feeling this way, experiencing a new, a more mature self-confidence, she found herself able to respond when Harvey Podesta cried out wretchedly for help.

Harvey was drinking heavily again. The long telephone conversations became longer, weepier, more bathetic.

"I don't really feel like getting out of the tub," he would whine. Yet his nights, at Studio 54 or in the leather bars of the Lower West Side or the Upper East Side pubs, went on until the sun came up. Some mornings he didn't get home at all.

"Harvey," Kate said firmly, "you're killing yourself. If you can't say no, if you can't stop, don't you think it would be worth trying Silver Hill again? Or Smithers?"

There was an exhausted attempt at gaiety.

"But dearest Kate," he giggled, "if I don't drink, how will I be able to know when I'm happy?"

Then, a day after Bobby had told her about the letter, Harvey told her he had pulled himself together long enough to accept a speaking engagement. "God knows what it cost him," Kate said to Mary Costello, "where he found the strength."

"The wee scalpeen," Mary said, shaking her head. For dialectic reasons she had grown to like Harvey. He was a writer, and all writers, *a priori*, were revolutionaries, whether they knew it or not, whatever their sexual preferences.

The lecture was to an audience of earnest young people, college and university students. They filled the auditorium of the Central Synagogue. Harvey sat quietly on a straight chair before the burgundy velvet curtain. A dean of studies or letters or something embarked on a long-winded and flowery introduction. Kate Sinclair, who with one of his gay friends, Ronald, had gotten Harvey to the hall, sat in the last row, slumped down, nervous. She did not want to be there. But Harvey had cried out and she had answered.

Harvey Podesta was standing now and there was a stir in the audience.

"Please let him be good," Kate said to no one.

He riffled nervously through a sheaf of notes. Perhaps they weren't notes, Kate thought. Perhaps they were laundry lists and library cards and canceled checks. Several bits of paper fluttered to the stage. When Harvey attempted to pick them up he staggered. The audience laughed, nervously.

But he hadn't been drunk when they drove over with him, Kate was sure. Agonized, she searched for Harvey's young companion. Ronald looked at her and shook his head. On stage, Harvey announced he was not going to make a formal speech, but that, if the audience behaved, he *might* read to them. From the body of his work. There was no book on stage, no manuscript, no body of his work. Harvey began to recite.

He could not remember the words.

Kate cringed. She looked around again and saw that Ronald was gone. Some of the students started to get up. The dean, so proud of his literary catch a few moments earlier, fidgeted.

Harvey was repeating himself.

"You're drunk," a boy shouted. They all took it up then. "Drunk! He's stoned! Let's get our money back!"

Harvey swayed onstage, looking out at them, defiantly now. He held up his hands. The audience, half on its feet now, stilled.

"If you don't want to hear readings from my body of work," Harvey said, quite reasonably, "then let's hear from yours."

He smiled out at them, beatifically. Someone threw a rolled-up paper. It landed near Harvey's foot. He looked down at it.

"Well," he said, softly so that only the dean and those in the first rows could hear, "if I *knew* I was going to live this long I would have taken better care of myself."

Kate heard the line. She was mounting the stage now. She could not remember standing up or leaving her seat or striding down the aisle. Now she was on the stage, standing next to Harvey, her arm around his wispy shoulders. She stared out at the crowd.

"Kate Sinclair . . . it's Kate Sinclair."

They froze. The sound of protest died. Kate looked out at them.

"You are," she said quietly, "in the presence of talent. For perhaps the *first* time in your young lives. Mr. Podesta will be leaving now."

She led him off stage. Behind her there was silence. Then, low at first and scattered, the applause. It was still building as she led Harvey onto the elevator and the doors slid shut behind them.

In the cab he lay back against the seat. Where had Ronald gone? he wanted to know. He was absolutely sure Ronald was back there now, calming the crowd, lecturing them on manners.

"That's Ronald," Harvey said, "he is loyal. Faithful unto death."

Kate did not say anything. She knew Ronald had fled when the jeering started.

The doorman and the cabbie helped her get him into the elevator. She was big enough, strong enough, to handle the apartment. She undressed him and put him to bed. He grinned up at her, and she was shocked to see the wasted face, the stringy neck. He had always been plump. Booze had always swollen him. Now, he was eroding before her eyes.

"Harvey," she said, "will you be all right? Is there someone I can call? A doctor?"

Harvey smiled.

"Ronald will be here shortly," he said. "Ronald will do the necessary."

Kate did not say that she doubted it. Was there someone else? she asked.

Harvey shook his old, wizened munchkin's head.

"No," he said, "nobody." He waited for a moment, moistening his lips. Then he said:

"Kate, don't ever be alone, Kate."

No, she said, she would follow his advice. She would never be alone.

50

It was Christmas week, after the show, and Chester Albany was sitting on the empty set, shirt collar unbuttoned, Ralph Lauren jacket slung over the back of a chair, the familiar carpet slippers on his feet. He had been out the night before with one of the girls from the office, a pretty, vivacious, stupid girl. In the end he had put her in a cab and gone home alone, to the furnished apartment. Better loneliness than stupidity. Now he had stopped thinking about the girl and the minor hangover blessedly was fading. He had fallen into one of his pleasant daydreams, shutting out the present with nostalgic memories of youth. Only this time he was slouched in the anchor chair instead of stretched out on the worn leather couch in his office. The couch had been moved out that morning and stowed. His office was being redecorated for his successor. But Chester did not brood about it. He was remembering another Christmas week, in Korea.

It was midnight and as Christmas day began the artillery had sent up red and green flares over the line and the Chinese, understandably confused, thought it was an attack and they fired off all their primary concentrations until one of the marines sharing the tent with Chester waved a grimy handkerchief out the flap. Later, when the *sake* and Johnny Walker had been passed around, two marines had stolen Chester's jeep and driven south through the snowy hills in search of whores, gleefully pointing at the "War Correspondent" sign on the windshield as they roared past the MPs. Chester Albany lay back in the chair, his eyes closed, and remembered the war. It helped keep him from thinking about Clive Jackson.

Clive was dead. Dead a week but they had gotten the word only that morning. He had died in the Himalayas.

"What the hell was he doing in the Himalayas?" Chester Albany screamed in anguish when they made the announcement during the morning news conference.

What Clive was doing, it would come out, was filming a television commercial for a new, but inexpensive, brand of digital watch, worn by a team of highly trained Swiss alpinists and Sherpa guides. At the 21,000-foot level of a great peak, at Camp IV, the digital watch was still clicking methodically along. But Clive Jackson's sixty-year-old heart had stopped.

The advertising agency which dreamed up the commercial would swallow its disappointment and pay Clive's estate the $50,000 fee despite his failure to fulfill the contract. The consideration that would swing the vote was an insurance policy which would repay the agency all but $2,500 of its investment.

Dozing behind his desk, trying to forget the pain of Clive's death, Chester remembered something John Chancellor had said when he said he wanted to leave the anchor job at NBC, pressured by the ratings and by younger men. "I decided that I don't want to measure out my life in thirty-second introductions to other people who do the reporting."

Maybe it was all for the best, Chester thought, borrowing Chancellor's words for himself.

He had fallen asleep when Kate wandered into the big, dimly lit studio. She had been cleaning out files, dictating letters into a machine for her secretary to type in the morning and now, not wanting to be alone, not really wanting to go home, she roamed restlessly through the hallways and into the studio. The three huge cameras, dark, untended, stood there like Gog and Magog, powerful tools when the red lights were on but now only large chunks of expensive, lifeless metal and wire and glass. The anchor desk mocked her. On camera it looked so rich, so tasteful, so . . . so important, but now it was simply cheap molded plywood. How many battles she and Chester had fought across that desk, over the shape and the position of the desk itself, over what seemed at the time important issues, and which she knew now to have been trivial. Above her the klieg lights in their serried rows, under her feet the smooth linoleum on which the cameras rolled silently on oiled wheels, behind the desk the network's logo, the evening news symbol, the map of the world.

How dared we? she asked herself, how *dared* we try to translate the world for so many millions on so many nights?

She did not answer.

Behind her there was a stirring. She turned to see Chester Albany sitting in his chair, blinking sleepily. He stood up and started to do up his collar and and put on his nice jacket. Below the jacket were the old, baggy gray flannels, wandering vaguely about his ankles, and exhibiting, proudly it seemed, the old carpet slippers.

"Well," he said, "not many more times."

She shook her head.

"It was kind of fun," he said. "I'd sort of gotten used to you. Instead of being out here every night with poor old Clive."

She smiled, gently. "I'm sorry I never really knew Clive," she said.

He walked to the anchor desk and sat down, not on the chair, but atop the desk. His strong hand rubbed the wood, feeling the grain, as if for a last time.

"I'm going to miss it," he said. "Someone has to tell the fucking people what's happening. I may not be brilliant at it. But who the hell is better?"

"I don't know. Who *is* better?"

"Rhetorical question, Sinclair. Not meant to be answered."

There was an awkwardly silent moment. Then Kate, feeling she should say something, said:

"Bobby told me about the letter. About your . . . friend. The letter she wrote."

"That son of a bitch."

"No, don't blame Bobby. He thought I knew."

"He shouldn't have said anything," Chester said.

God, you're stubborn, Kate thought. But she did not say this. What she said was, "Look, she did it. I'm sorry it caused, well, a problem between you. I mean, I understand that your friend should resent me. I *understand*."

He was silent for a time, then, his face strong, set, he said:

"I'm sorry for what she did. It wasn't called for."

Kate smiled.

"If it hadn't been that it would have been something else. This whole thing, you and me, it just wasn't fated to work."

"Still," he said, "I'm sorry."

"Okay," Kate said lightly, "hey, you said you're sorry. I get the picture. I'm sorry it broke you two up."

Chester laughed. It was a short, bitter laugh.

"This may sound silly," he said, "but that girl meant a lot to me. A lot. My marriage went bust and there she was. Three years we were together. A good three years. She was, well, she was a wonderful lay. Her whole world revolved around me. I was never a great man, not even a very good man, I suppose, except to her." He paused. "She was twenty-three and I was fifty. What future did we have? I knew that at the start. But it didn't make it any easier losing her."

Kate thought of Nick, the last time she had seen him, with the young Washington girl in knee socks. Chester Albany had grown up. Blanchflower was still playing with the toys of a youth he was reluctant to, could not, surrender. Chester was talking again.

"Frances had this idiot idea you were my problem. That if she could eliminate you it would all be swell again. Maybe the letter wasn't her idea. Maybe Venables suggested it, I don't know. But she was the one who loused you up with the brass."

"I don't know," Kate said. "I did a pretty good job of fouling myself up, making fun of the feminists at the Cape, getting involved with Nick. Then my little Barbara Frietchie speech at the Garden."

Kate threw herself into a chair.

"Oh, Jesus," she said, "no one's to blame. It's the system. It's the business we're in. I don't blame you. I don't blame Bobby. I don't blame myself." She waited a moment and then she said, "I don't even blame that prick Venables."

Chester laughed.

"Venables," he repeated. "You know, pro football used to play exhibition games. Venables changed that. Now they're 'pre-season' games. In the old days you used to talk about an overtime game as 'sudden death,' except now it's 'sudden victory.' That's what Venables did to sports. Can't you imagine what he'll do to news?"

"No," she said, "I really can't."

"Well," Chester said, sounding happier now, "brinksmanship and crisis and nuclear threats will all become part of the lexicon. It'll be an extraordinarily diverting time. The next Cuban missile crisis should be marvelous for the ratings. Everyone will want to watch."

She picked up on his line of thought.

"How about the end of the world?" she asked. "How do you think Venables will handle that?"

"Oh, Christ," Chester, said, rubbing his hands together, "George should be so lucky. Listen, first of all, the rating card is completely revised. Fifty thousand dollars for a ten-second spot in that last hour. He won't just give it away, you know. And the remotes! Oh, boy, they'll cover the White House and the Vatican and Red Square and the fucking Dalai Lama. I mean, they'll really want the eyewitness stuff. And when the mountains start to crash down and the sea starts to come up out of its banks and the goddamn comets begin to collide, that fucking Venables is just going to go crazy. He'll be up in a command helicopter shooting down the opposition and getting the great camera angles . . . " His voice trailed off.

Kate did not say anything. She was still enjoying Chester's apocalyptic script. He had lighted a cigarette and now, through the smoke, he said, subdued:

"Still, I'm sorry. I was a bastard myself in the beginning. That makes me at least the partial villain."

"You? A villain?" Kate said. "No, Chester, we don't have villains in this business. No heroes, either."

"Oh?" he said.

"No," Kate Sinclair said, "there are only the ratings."

They sat there for a time, the two anchorpersons, in the big studio, without talking. Then Kate got up from her chair and walked to one of the cameras. She leaned on it, her arm and hand cradling the lens, the machinery that brought them both to life.

The door to the studio opened and one of the young assistant directors looked in.

"Oh, hi, Kate, Chester. Didn't know anyone was in here."

He started to back out, then he paused.

"Hey, it's snowing. Just started."

He left. Kate and Chester were again alone. She looked down at his feet. At the old slippers. "He said it's snowing," she said. "You don't wear those slippers out in the snow, do you?"

Chester frowned. What the hell business was it of hers if he wore his goddamned slippers?

"Well?" he said pugnaciously.

She shrugged. He liked it when she moved her shoulders like that, the way her hair tossed, her breasts moved.

"Oh, hell," Chester said, "if it's really bad I'll put on some proper shoes."

She smiled.

He grinned back at her.

"Chester," she said, "where is it you go drinking? After the show, I mean?"

"The Atelier usually, why?"

"Is that where you do all your bitching about me?"

He looked embarrassed.

"Well, that was a long time ago, Sinclair. I haven't done that in . . . "

She shook her head.

"I know, I know. That isn't what I meant. I mean . . . " she hesitated, looking into his strong, battered, open face, "I mean tonight, would you buy me a drink there?"

He was silent for a moment and then he grinned. "Why not, Kate? Why not?"

It was the first time he had called her "Kate."